Tri Quarterly 102

Editor
Susan Firestone Hahn

Associate Editor
Ian Morris

Production Manager | Design | Production Editor
Bruce Frausto | **Gini Kondziolka** | **Hans Holsen**

TriQuarterly Fellow | Bennington College Intern
Ben Pauley | **Elizabeth Williamson**

Assistant Editors | Editorial Assistants
Francine Arenson, Rachel Webster | **Russell Geary, Jacob Harrell**
| **Dylan Rice, Karen Sheets**

Contributing Editors
John Barth, Rita Dove, Richard Ford, Sandra M. Gilbert, Robert Hass, Edward Hirsch, Lee Huebner, Li-Young Lee, Lorrie Moore, Alicia Ostriker, Carl Phillips, Robert Pinsky, Alan Shapiro, Mark Strand, Alan Williamson

TRIQUARTERLY IS AN INTERNATIONAL JOURNAL OF WRITING, ART AND CULTURAL INQUIRY PUBLISHED AT **NORTHWESTERN UNIVERSITY.**

Subscription rates (three issues a year) — Individuals: one year $24; two years $44; life $600. Institutions: one year $36; two years $68. Foreign subscriptions $5 per year additional. Price of back issues varies. Sample copies $5. Correspondence and subscriptions should be addressed to *TriQuarterly*, **Northwestern University**, 2020 Ridge Avenue, Evanston, IL 60208-4302. Phone: (847) 491-7614.

The editors invite submissions of fiction, poetry and literary essays, which must be postmarked between October 1 and March 31; manuscripts postmarked between April 1 and September 30 will not be read. No manuscripts will be returned unless accompanied by a stamped, self-addressed envelope. All manuscripts accepted for publication become the property of *TriQuarterly*, unless otherwise indicated.

National distributors to retail trade: Ingram Periodicals (La Vergne, TN); B. DeBoer (Nutley, NJ); Ubiquity (Brooklyn, NY); Armadillo (Los Angeles, CA).

Reprints of issues #1–15 of *TriQuarterly* are available in full format from Kraus Reprint Company, Route 100, Millwood, NY 10546, and all issues in microfilm from University Microfilms International, 300 North Zeeb Road, Ann Arbor, MI 48106. *TriQuarterly* is indexed in the *Humanities Index* (H.W. Wilson Co.), the *American Humanities Index* (Whitson Publishing Co.), Historical Abstracts, MLA, EBSCO Publishing (Peabody, MA) and Information Access Co. (Foster City, CA).

Photograph taken by V. G. Tchertkoff, at Kochety, May 1910.

Contents

Cover: Photograph of Leo Tolstoy taken by Sofiya Tolstoy at Yasnaya Polyana, 1909, courtesy of the State Tolstoy Museum of Moscow

Back cover: Photograph of Isabel Hapgood, courtesy of the Isabel Florence Hapgood Papers, Manuscripts and Archives Division, The New York Public Library

Cover design by Gini Kondziolka

Tolstoy's American Translator: Letters to Isabel Hapgood, 1888–1903

Robert Whittaker

Isabel Hapgood (1851–1928) was more than just Tolstoy's translator. First of all, she translated more than just his works, and, second, she did more than just translate for him. None of Tolstoy's other translators had her scope: she translated the full range of Russian literature—Gogol, Leskov, Turgenev, Bunin, Gorky, the poets Tiutchev and Nikitin—as well as from the French (Victor Hugo, Ernest Renan) and Italian (DeAmicis). She translated not only Russian fiction and poetry, but memoirs (Veretschagin, Kovalevskaya), biographies (Sergeyenko), folk

This is the third in a series of articles presenting Tolstoy's correspondence with Americans, based on material from the joint U.S.–Russian project "Tolstoy and His U.S. Correspondents" ("Tolstoy's American Mailbag: Selected Exchanges with His Occasional Correspondents" and "Tolstoy's American Disciple: Letters to Ernest Howard Crosby, 1894–1906" appeared in *TriQuarterly* 95 and *TriQuarterly* 98). Begun in 1986 under the auspices of the International Research and Exchanges Board, the Association of Learned Societies, and the Academy of Sciences of the USSR, since 1991 this project has been sponsored by the Gorky Institute of World Literature of the Russian Academy of Sciences in Moscow. The project has received major and essential institutional support from the Tolstoy State Museum in Moscow, especially the staff of its Manuscript Division. Activities of the project in the United States have greatly benefited from the support of the staff of the Slavonic and Baltic Division of the Research Libraries of the New York Public Library. The director of the project for the Russian side is Dr. L. D. Gromova, the chief editor is N. P. Velikanova; the activities of the American side are coordinated by the author of this publication, who expresses his gratitude to the staff of the Tolstoy State Museum and its Manuscript Division and to the Gorky Institute for assistance in this research.

epics (*byliny*), and the Russian Orthodox liturgy. She also wrote literary criticism, travel commentary, and general features on Russia for newspapers and magazines. Of all Tolstoy's American translators, only Hapgood knew him personally. She became close to the Tolstoy family (120 letters were exchanged between the Tolstoys and Hapgood),[1] advised Tolstoy's wife and elder daughters on a variety of literary and general subjects, and served as self-designated guardian of the quality of translations and of Tolstoy's public image. Furthermore, Hapgood assisted Tolstoy in alleviating the suffering of Russian peasants during the famine of 1892 by gathering and sending contributions from America. Of all these activities, the most significant remain her translations of his fiction and her memoirs of meetings with him and his family in Moscow and at the family estate in Yasñaya Polyana.

Tolstoy's principal British translators, the husband and wife team of Aylmer and Louise Maude, also enjoyed a personal relationship with the Tolstoys. However, unlike Hapgood, the Maudes shared his philosophical beliefs. They easily accommodated Tolstoy's shift away from prose fiction to philosophy, essays, and didactic, moralistic works after 1878. Not so Isabel Hapgood, who came into sharp conflict with the later Tolstoy and ceased translating his works out of moral and religious scruples. A popularizer and interpreter of Russian culture for Americans, she found herself supporting Tolstoy's wife and the interests of the family but not the philosophical and ethical principles of Tolstoy himself.

Isabel Hapgood first wrote to Tolstoy in 1886 to send him a copy of her translation of his trilogy, *Childhood, Boyhood, Youth*, together with her collection, *The Epic Songs of Russia*.[2] In this same year Hapgood also published her translations of Gogol's major novel, *Dead Souls*, his historical novel of Cossack life, *Taras Bulba*, and a collection of his best short stories.[3] This output was remarkable, given the difficulty of the originals, the uniqueness of the task (there were only a few translators from Russian), and its sheer size (over fifteen hundred printed pages).

The few known details of Isabel Hapgood's early life help to explain how she achieved such a prodigious and unusual output by the age of thirty-five.[4] Born in Boston in 1851 to Asa Hapgood, an inventor and manufacturer, and his wife Lydia, in 1860 she moved with the family (she had two brothers) to the industrial town of Worcester in western Massachusetts, where she spent the next twenty years. The Oread Collegiate Institute, a private school for young ladies in Worcester which she attended from 1863 to 1865, enjoyed a reputation for excellence in the teaching of language and literature. From 1866 to 1868 she studied at Miss Porter's School in Farmington, Connecticut, where she followed

Tolstoy with guests at Yasnaya Polyana, July 1899 (Alexandra at left; Leo third from left; Maria, Leo's sister, fifth from left; Sofiya fifth from right; Tatyana second from right).

the fashionable curricula of French, Latin, mathematics, and the usual English subjects.[5] Her considerable linguistic talents manifested themselves early: a classmate at Miss Porter's recalled, "Words were to her fairy messengers of thought flying at her bidding, clad in any costume: French, Italian, German, Spanish, or English," and added that "her most brilliant achievements were attained through the Russian tongue."[6]

Hapgood apparently began studying Russian after she returned to Worcester to live with her mother upon her father's death in 1868. It remains unclear what led her to study Russian and how she acquired this language, rare in a well-to-do lady of non-Slavic origins. According to one account, "She had labored for two years at Russian with dictionary and grammar before she chanced to meet a Russian lady who taught her the pronunciation."[7] However she acquired this facility, less than fifteen years later she had published her excellent translations of Gogol and Tolstoy, as well as translations of folk ballads that displayed an unprecedented knowledge of old Russian and folk idioms.

The same year Hapgood published her Russian translations, she also published her translation of the *Meditations* of the French priest Joseph Roux,[8] and the next year, in addition to a large French classic (*Les Misérables*, in five volumes), she published a translation from the Italian of Edmondo De Amicis, *Cuore*.[9] However, no other European language and culture affected Hapgood as deeply as Russian, to which she was profoundly committed by the time she moved to Boston with her mother in 1881. It should be noted that Hapgood also brought with her from Worcester a dedication to the Episcopal Church, to parish outreach into the community through charitable work, and to church unity, specifically its link to the Russian Orthodox Church.[10]

A careful and precise translator, Hapgood evidenced a scholar's appreciation of the text and its complexity. She was proud of her skill and jealously defended her reputation as a scrupulously precise, consistent, and correct translator of Russian texts, customs, and culture. W. R. S. Ralston, perhaps the foremost early translator of Russian folk songs and tales into English, wrote from England to congratulate Hapgood on her excellent renderings in *Epic Songs:* "I have said in each [of the reviews] that the translator has done her work excellently. Only I have had to vary the phrase. I hope that your book will obtain the success it deserves on both sides of the Atlantic."[11]

Hapgood's reviews of her competitors reflected her exacting standards: given the state of early translations, she was rarely complimentary. Her review of the 1886 edition of *War and Peace* (only the second Tolstoy work to be published in America) made a point of the fact that the novel had been translated not from the Russian original, but from a French translation.[12] Hapgood found the miserable rendition to have resulted from "ignorance of French on the part of both translators, as well as to carelessness, but chiefly [from] the headlong manner in which the version . . . has been prepared, in which everything—sense, accuracy, and style—has been sacrificed to speed." She provided numerous examples of "mistranslations and anachronisms" which more than "sustain the translator's well-earned reputation for carelessness."[13]

In her reviews of translations, Hapgood defended the quality of the original works. In "Tolstoi and the Public Censor," written just after her own translation of his article on the Moscow census,[14] Hapgood explained how the Russian censor had mutilated several pieces published in the recent volume of Tolstoy's collected works, especially a fragment of his "My Religion" and "What to Do? Thoughts Evoked by the Census of Moscow." Hapgood allowed herself only a few comments on Tolstoy's recent ideas, provided a summary of the missing parts, and ridiculed the censor. When commenting on Tolstoy's beliefs, her attitude toward his radicalism was respectful, yet amazed, even wide-eyed. After chiding him for "some discrepancies in his arguments on the subject of money," Hapgood commented on Tolstoy's discussion of the poor and charity: "His socialistic utterances upon this subject are delightfully unconventional, but those on cleanliness, which is regarded as a moral virtue, though in reality only valued as a mark of class distinction, are of the most radical sort." In conclusion, Hapgood praised "the strong personality of the great author" that emerged from this volume and reminded the reader that "nothing less than a full translation would convey a complete idea of its contents, especially of the striking Moscow article."[15] It was this "striking" article that Hapgood had translated in its entirety, all 273 pages in the Crowell edition.

The next year, in the fall of 1887, having seen her translations from Italian and French into print, Hapgood and her mother set off for an extended visit to Russia. Shortly after settling in Saint Petersburg, she wrote to Tolstoy to request his authorization for a translation. She had already written him an earlier letter to accompany the copy of her translation of his trilogy and of the epic songs. In this first letter, sent from Boston on August 24, 1886, Hapgood combined admiration for his writings with objections to their poor translations: "Everyone in America is an enthusiastic admirer of your writings. We only regret that you will not write more, and hope that you may give us yet another novel to form a trio with your magnificent *War and Peace*, and *Anna Karenina*. I am sorry that these two should have been so mutilated and badly translated through the French, instead of directly from the originals."[16] Implied is a comparison with her own translations. Concern that Tolstoy write more fiction reappeared in Hapgood's later correspondence with the family.

When her second letter went unanswered, Hapgood wrote again a short time thereafter (December 13) for Tolstoy's authorization to translate any works he had ready. She provided testimonial evidence of her capabilities: "Will you honor me with your authorization? I feel sure that I can do the work in a way that will satisfy you; Mr. George Kennan who visited you in June 1886 calls me *the best translator of Russian now living*. Pardon me for quoting this praise. I like to do whatever work I undertake thoroughly." (Kennan himself had written a letter to Tolstoy which contained unsolicited praise of her translations.)[17] In a lengthy discourse on problems of publishing translations, Hapgood offered her assistance to Tolstoy's friend and collaborator, Vladimir Tchertkoff, in his desire to publish Tolstoy's article on the census. Finally, as the coup de grâce, Hapgood appended a postscript by the noted critic and friend of Tolstoy, V. V. Stasov, who affirmed that she was considered "the best translator today of Russian authors into English."[18]

This letter elicited a response from Tolstoy's eldest daughter, Tatyana, who wrote on her father's behalf, thus beginning the lengthy exchange of letters that would continue for the next fifteen years. This letter, which has not survived, included the authorization that Hapgood desired from Tolstoy together with his agreement to give her what he had ready. In her answer of December 27, Hapgood expressed "thanks to your illustrious father for his authorization to translate his works, and for the promise of what he has now on hand, and also to you for your amiable letter. I had not only heard of your father's book 'On Life,'[19] but that he was also at work on another study in the manner of 'the death of Ivan Ilyich,'[20] and I hope that he will be so kind as to let me have that also. I shall do my best to present whatever he gives me in the best possible manner to English reading people."[21] Hapgood immediately began translating On Life, finishing it in little more than two months.

We know of her rapid progress from a letter of introduction sent to Tolstoy with two acquaintances, Mrs. S. Van Rensselaer Cruger and Mrs. Roosevelt Schuyler, the former an author of novels and short stories published under the pseudonym Julien Gordon, and the latter a writer on architecture for the Century. Hapgood introduced them as having agreed to take her translation "across the frontier." Along with this letter, dated March 10, Hapgood sent Tolstoy some articles on temperance, which she felt might interest him in view of his recent pronouncements against drink.[22]

On receiving the visit and the articles, Tolstoy wrote to his friend, P. I. Biriukov, on March 12: "Yesterday Miss Hapgood sent me articles and two Americans: neither the one nor the other were interesting. Generally, if you can, tell her (1) that her articles are of no interest to me—I know all about this, and (2) that, judging from the corrections I am making to the French translation of 'On Life,' I am afraid that there may be inaccuracies in her translation, and here I am to blame because of my unclear language, and therefore it would be good to check her translation. This, surely, you would not refuse to do."[23] Biriukov, who was in St. Petersburg, communicated Tolstoy's concern to Hapgood, who then wrote Tolstoy to request his corrections (as well as to pass on a letter from Wendell P. Garrison on the nonresistance activities of his father).[24] In the summer of 1888 Hapgood received the galley proofs of her translation, which Tolstoy apparently requested be checked by his friend, the critic N. N. Strakhov. In June, 1888, Strakhov wrote to Tolstoy that he was "delighted with the absolute completeness, the literal transmission of the text, and with the clarity that is characteristic of English" that he found in Hapgood's translation, and that, "Generally I am convinced that your book will appear in America in the very best aspect that one could desire."[25] In a separate letter to Hapgood, Strakhov had offered the same praise for her "splendid" translation.[26] Later, in September, when sending him a copy of her published translation, she reassured Tolstoy that there was but one serious error in the text, and that the copyist and not she was responsible.[27]

However accurate Hapgood's "authorized" translation of *On Life*, her work was seriously criticized by a number of Tolstoyans (unlike the French translation, which was done by his wife, Sofiya Andreevna, and which Tolstoy himself had corrected.)[28] Ernest Crosby wrote to Tolstoy in 1893 that "it is a great pity that your 'De la Vie' is so badly translated in English. In many places it does not make sense. It would be impossible for any one to understand the argument of the book from the English version,"[29] and Tolstoy's avid English disciple, John Kenworthy, also found this translation to be seriously flawed.[30] True, as Tolstoy himself noted, much of the confusion resulted from his own original. Ironically, the most successful attempt to render the work in English was by a Tolstoyan who knew no Russian, Bolton Hall.[31] Nonetheless, Hapgood's translation became the standard in English until Maude's translation forty years later.[32]

Hapgood's persistent requests for new material produced first a description of Tolstoy's "Walk in the Light, While There Is Light," and finally the manuscript, which she received early in 1889, translated and sent to her publishers, who then declined to publish this moral tale.[33] In her letter of September 8, 1888, Hapgood again wrote, "I hope that you will think well enough of me to let me have your new work upon which, as I hear, you are engaged—if, indeed, you have not already finished it."[34] What she had in mind was Tolstoy's *Kreutzer Sonata*, about which rumors had been circulating in St. Petersburg.[35] She received the following response from Tatyana, on behalf of Tolstoy:

[No. 1—September 16, 1888]

Dear Madam,

My Father thanks you very much for the trouble you took of forwarding him the books you mentioned, but he is sorry to say he has not received them yet.

My father told me to write and tell you that he had written nothing new, since his book "On Life," but when he does write anything he will be happy to have it translated by you.

Yours truly,

Tatyana Tolstoy.

The 4th of September 1888[36]

My father's address for packages is: Tula Yasnaya Polyana.[37]

Hapgood had sent copies of her just-published translations of *On Life* and *Sebastopol Tales*.[38] The rumors of Tolstoy's *Kreutzer Sonata* continued, quite detailed, but the work itself remained unfinished; Hapgood never mentioned it by name to Tolstoy, even when visiting him and his family in Moscow in the winter of 1888. Only the next summer did she finally get a commitment to receive the completed manuscript.[39]

In December 1888, when Hapgood and her mother were in Moscow, they visited with the Tolstoy family several times. After their first meeting on December 7, Tolstoy recorded his conversation with Hapgood: she pressed him to explain why he had ceased writing, and when he answered that it was pointless, she pressed further to find out why this was so. He responded: "There are too many books, and now, no matter what books one may write, the world will go on just the same way. If Christ were to come and publish the Gospel, the ladies would try to get his autographs and nothing more."[40] In her own account of this meeting, Hapgood recalled that Tolstoy blamed his earlier condition, before turning to his new Christian principles, on the evil influence of tobacco: he claimed that his "mental and spiritual upturn" began when he stopped smoking. To this Hapgood replied, "Lev Nikolaevich, please, please take up smoking again immediately!"[41]

This insistent, even combative attitude of Hapgood toward Tolstoy continued when they met again. A subsequent meeting was postponed until the Tolstoy household recovered from winter illnesses. Tatyana wrote Hapgood to apologize:

[No. 2—December 26, 1888]

Dear Miss Hapgood,

We were very sorry not to be able to receive you last night, but my father was not at home, and mamma had to attend to my brother, who was very ill last night. Our house is like a hospital for the last few weeks, and the only person we see is the doctor. Mamma was very anxious about my brother, who was very ill last night, but now all danger has passed although one of them is still in bed. I intended to call on you today, but the cold frightened even me.

I hope it will not be so cold on Saturday and we will have the pleasure of seeing you.

Yours truly T. Tolstoy
Wednesday, 14 Dec. 1888[42]

The Hapgoods in fact did visit that Saturday, December 29, and dined with the Tolstoys. The meeting produced only a cryptic note in Tolstoy's diary: "Conversation about the journal, which will come to nothing. And we deceive ourselves. And I felt bad. Then I came out to meet Mrs. Hapgood. Even worse. I'm in a moral decline."[43] Hapgood's account of the dinner gives some idea of what might have contributed to Tolstoy's depression. Hapgood described how she attacked Tolstoy on several of his ideas—charity, assisting others, nonresistance to evil. She made little headway, at one point commenting that "his sensible wife came to my assistance," and at another point that, faced with resistance, she "attacked from another quarter." [44]

The image of the translator arguing with the great Russian novelist and thinker illustrates the special role Hapgood took on herself. What she sensed was wrong or foolish she never hesitated to debunk, even if her victim was no other than Tolstoy. Her duty, as she saw it, was to apply norms of common sense and traditional Christian morality. She gave no quarter to his Christian anarchism and pacifism:

> But he stuck firmly to his "resist not evil" doctrine; while I maintained that the very doctrine admitted that it was "evil" by making use of the word at all, hence a thing to be preached and practiced against. Perhaps Count Tolstoy had never been so unfortunate as to meet certain specimens of the human race which it has been my ill-luck to observe; so we both still held our positions, after a long skirmish, and silence reigned for a few moments.[45]

The next day, Sunday, Hapgood took up Tolstoy's offer to visit Moscow's flea market; their visit to an Old Believers' church was postponed because of the cold (which she herself found insufficient reason—only twenty degrees below zero Fahrenheit). Hapgood's account of this meeting includes a description of her objections to his theories of extreme self-sufficiency and independence. After one more visit with Tolstoy in January, made brief by his ill health, the Hapgoods returned to St. Petersburg. In concluding her description of her skirmishes with

Tolstoy, Hapgood nonetheless defended him against those who considered his ideas "crazy":

> [Tolstoy is] simply a man with a hobby, or an idea. His idea happens to be one which, granting that it ought to be adopted by everybody, is still one which is very difficult of adoption by anybody, peculiarly difficult in his own case. And it is an uncomfortable theory of self-denial which very few

Photograph taken by V. G. Tchertkoff, at Kochety, May 1910.

people like to have preached to them in any form. Add to this that his philosophical expositions of his theory lack the clearness which generally—not always—results from a course of strict preparatory training, and we have more than sufficient foundation for the reports of his mental aberration. On personal acquaintance he proves to be a remarkably earnest, thoroughly convinced, and winning man, although he does not deliberately do or say anything to attract one. His very earnestness is provocative of argument.[46]

Her deep respect, based on his achievements as a novelist, did not extend to Tolstoy the thinker. As long as his philosophy did not clash with her deeper moral sense, she would willingly work toward the broader dissemination of his writings. Faced with a serious conflict of views, however, she refused.

An example of her willing cooperation is Hapgood's translation of "Walk in the Light." On January 17, 1889, shortly after returning to St. Petersburg from Moscow, she wrote Tolstoy of her reaction to the manuscript he had given her: "I have read your *Walk in the Light* and like it particularly because, in it, you bring up and answer, by illustration and words, the objections which other people urge to the life which you advocate. I am sure that it would interest many people in America, where the favorite old theory that every young man should work, and not lead an idle life, is gradually going out of fashion, to the regret of many fathers."[47] She asked and received his permission to translate it,[48] and by March 25 she had finished the translation. In a letter of that date she wrote to Tatyana, "Thank your father from me for the *Walk in the Light* etc. I have sent the translation to N.Y. but do not know of its fate yet! It may be too long for the publication which I selected." In fact, the work was not published, perhaps for the reason stated. Hapgood continued, "N. V. Stasoff gave me to read lately, a short sketch, *Nikolai Palkin*, and suggested that I translate it for America. I did translate it, (lest I should not have another opportunity) but I shall not use it unless your father is willing."[49] In response to Hapgood's request to publish this pacifist tale about the horrors of military service, Tolstoy responded through Tatyana, who wrote (in Russian):

[No. 3—April 1, 1889]

Dear Miss Hapgood,

My father is not in Moscow, but nonetheless I was able to put to him the questions which you asked, and he told me to answer as follows: that he cannot write anything for the American magazine. As concerns "Nikolai Palkin," he says that everything that he wants to disseminate he publishes, and the rest he neither disseminates nor forbids to be disseminated. Therefore, he leaves this absolutely to your decision.

Father left for Troitsy to visit a friend, and Mama has gone to visit our uncle in the country, so there are very few of us left at home.

Mama sends her regards, as do I. Thank you again for the book for Sasha. I cannot say anything about its contents yet since I have not yet read it.

My respects to your Mother,
T. Tolstaya.
20 March 1889[50]

On February 6 Hapgood had sent Tolstoy a request from John Eliot Bowen, editor of *The Independent*, that the writer contribute "a short article or a letter giving [his] estimate of the character of George Washington in the light of the world's history," commemorating the centennial of the first inauguration.[51] On March 29 Hapgood wrote Tatyana explaining that she had sent a book for her youngest sister, Alexandra, and that she had received the letter sent by the four-year-old Sasha. "Nikolai Palkin" was published in 1890 in *Cosmopolitan*.[52]

An example of Hapgood's refusal to translate for Tolstoy was occasioned by his *Kreutzer Sonata*, which she finally received from him directly, after he personally promised it to her during their meetings in Moscow and at the Tolstoy family estate, Yasnaya Polyana. Sofiya Andreevna Tolstoy had extended the invitation to their country home during the Hapgoods' visit in Moscow, and the latter confirmed suitable travel arrangements in a letter of May 28, which also explained a gift of *Nature Readers* sent at this time to the younger Tolstoy children for English practice. Tatyana responded to this letter:

[No. 4—June 8, 1890]

Dear Miss Hapgood,

We have just received the books you sent us and I hurry to tell you so. They have been so long in coming because they have been to Krapivna. When you write, it is always safer to address letters and packages to Toula,—we send there twice a week. For telegrams Moskovsko-Kurskaya zh.d. Kozkovka-Zaseka. We will all be very pleased to see you in Yasnaya and will send to fetch you when you will tell us to. If you have not the time to <tell> us of the day and hour of your arrival, you can always find horses in Toula or Yasnaya,—every cabman knows us there. Only from

Kozlovka you cannot get any horses, although it is the closest station from Yasnaya.

I hope Mrs. Hapgood is quite well and will be able to come down to Yasnaya with you. With respects to her and yourself, I am, dear Miss Hapgood,

yours truly
Tanya Tolstoy
27 May 1889[53]

The visit took place July 9–14, after which the Hapgoods returned for two more days, July 20–21. This protracted stay, unusual for foreign guests of the Tolstoys, testifies to the close personal relations that had developed between them. This family friendship provided an important buffer for the occasional conflict between translator and author.

The week spent with the entire family produced a wide variety of experiences and impressions which Hapgood conveyed in a detailed, vivid account entitled "Tolstoy at Home."[54] Her sympathies throughout the account remained clearly and loyally on the side of Tolstoy's wife:

> Decidedly, the Countess Sophia Tolstoy is one of those truly feminine heroines who are cast into shadow by a brilliant light close to them, but a heroine none the less in more ways than need be mentioned. Her self-denial and courage gave the world "War and Peace" and "Anna Karenin;" and she declares that were it to do over again [i.e. recopy these works] she would not hesitate a moment. The public owes the count's wife a great debt of gratitude, and not of reproaches, for bravely opposing his fatal desire to live in every detail the life of a peasant laborer. Can any one blessed with the faintest particle of imagination fail to perceive how great a task it has been to withstand him thus for his own good; to rear nine healthy, handsome, well-bred children out of the much larger family which they have had; to bear the entire responsibility of the household and the business?[55]

Against this background of moral solidarity Hapgood offers a sampling of criticism of the count's new philosophy, of their disputes and disagreements. She enjoyed baiting Tolstoy and demonstrating the inconsistency of his moral principles. On one occasion, when she found herself mending a series of holes worn in his pocket and he began to get restless and protest, she chided him: "It is plain that you understand how to render services far better than to receive them. Reform. Submit." She described his reaction as "a sort of grim bewilderment in his eye," which she took as a victory on a point which she "had been pining to attack in some form."[56] At another time, during a family conversation on the Shakers, whom Tolstoy greatly admired for their doctrine of celibacy, Hapgood asked how he reconciled this with the conclusion to his recently published *What to do?* that a woman's whole duty consists in marrying and having as large a family as possible. Sofiya Andreevna commented that this was certainly not consistent, but that Tolstoy "changed his opinion every two years." Tolstoy himself stuck to his assertion that "nonmarriage was the ideal state" and "relapsed into silence, as was his habit when he did not intend to relinquish his idea." To this description of the stalemate Hapgood added: "I am convinced he is always open to the influence—quite unconsciously, of course—of argument from any quarter. His changes of belief prove it."[57] On another occasion Hapgood and Tolstoy argued over the innate nature of Russian peasants: he argued for their profoundly nonviolent character and insisted that they rarely if ever commit murder knowingly and willfully. Hapgood insisted that the peasant was just as human as anyone and provided as a counterexample to prove her point the intentional murder of an infant by a peasant in Tolstoy's own work "The Power of Darkness."[58] It was just these topics—marriage and murder—that Tolstoy treated in the work he was completing at this time, *Kreutzer Sonata.*

Hapgood had hoped to receive a copy of this work while visiting Yasnaya Polyana, but it was still being revised. She recalled a few months later:

> One evening last July, during a visit which I made to Yasnaya Polyana, at the Countess's invitation, the Count spoke to me of his story as being near completion, and asked me to translate it when it should be finished. I promised, and inquired whether it was in a condition for me to read. "You may read the last version if you like," he answered, "but I would rather have you wait." His wife showed me sheets of the fourth version, which she was then copying, and advised me not to waste time in reading it, as it was quite likely that he might suddenly see the subject in a totally different light, and write it all over again from that point of view.[59]

By the fall of 1889 Hapgood still had not received the work from Tolstoy, although copies of earlier versions were circulating in St. Petersburg. She wrote to Sofiya Andreevna on October 21, just a few days before leaving Russia, not so much to ask after the piece as to ask if she would consider circumventing her husband's decision to take no profit from the sale of his works: "Your husband asked me, when I was at Yasnaya Polyana, to translate his book when he should have finished it. I shall be glad to do so, as I told him. But, since you take care of the business arrangements, pardon me if I ask you whether payment of some percentage from the sale of the translation should not be made direct to you?"[60] (There was no response from the countess.)

Finally, early in 1890, Tolstoy sent the finished version of *Kreutzer Sonata* to Hapgood in Germany, where she had been staying since late October. She began her translation but soon stopped, unable to proceed with such material: she wrote to Tolstoy that she must decline to translate the work. No doubt she was stopped by the blunt language of the hero, Pozdnyshev, and by his attitude toward marriage and his view that this was his real crime, not the murder of his wife. Unfortunately, this letter has not survived among Tolstoy's papers. However, she explained her thoughts with considerable detail in a review of the work published shortly thereafter, in April 1890:

> At length I received the first copy of the genuine story . . . with the information that, although the substance was nearly identical with that of the version which had already been circulating, and which was said to be in process of translation into foreign languages, the execution had been so altered that "not one stone was left upon another" in some places, while in others whole pages and even chapters had been completely rewritten by the author. My copy was corrected by the author especially with a view to translation, and was, therefore, to be regarded as the only one sanctioned by him for rendering into other tongues, and this version is yet unattainable in St. Petersburg.
>
> Why, then, do I not translate a work from the famous and much admired Russian author: Because, in spite of due gratitude to Count Tolstoi for favoring me with the first copy, and in spite of my faith in his conviction that such treatment of such a subject is needed and will do good, I cannot agree with him. . . .
>
> "Too frank and not decent," was one of the Petersburg verdicts upon this "Kreutzer Sonata." This is so true that, although thus forewarned, I was startled at the idea that it could possibly be beneficial, and, destroying the translation which I had begun, I wrote promptly to decline the task.[61]

Hapgood then assured her readers that she would "yield to no one in [her] admiration for and appreciation of Tolstoi's genius, as displayed in certain of his works." All the more difficult was this decision, she explained, because she was "now morally compelled to appear unfaithful to [her] own former admiration" of the writer. What Hapgood could not elaborate on in print, however, was the additional disappointment of not being able to fulfill her personal promise to Tolstoy to translate the work and to justify the extraordinary trust he had shown by his request and by sending her a special copy of the work.

Not long after her refusal, Hapgood wrote again to Tolstoy to thank him for sending the work. In a letter from Munich dated April 21 she wrote: "I am greatly obliged to you for your friendly feeling and kindness in letting me have the first correct copy of your *Kreutzer Sonata*. I did not feel that I could translate it, but I appreciate your action none the less." She continued, however, in a tone far from apologetic and more like the instructive, corrective attitude typical of her professional demeanor:

> Permit me to say frankly, however, that you make a mistake in allowing an imperfect copy of any of your works to circulate before the correct copy is ready. Some one is sure to take dishonorable advantage and present your ideas to the world in a translation which would not meet your approbation. After that, it is almost impossible to get any publisher to venture on the authorized version. I did manage to get the perfect version of your Moscow Census, What is to be Done?, published, after I had myself translated the imperfect form contained in your published works. But it was only by knowing how to take advantage of certain circumstances, and by sacrificing my own interests.
>
> In the present case, the English translation published at Leipzig appeared at almost precisely the time when I received the accurate copy. This would have prevented my doing anything with it. The publisher who asked me for it immediately retracted his offer, 1°: because, after seeing the Leipzig edition, he was afraid to publish it; 2°: because the Leipzig edition had forestalled him.[62]

Hapgood's publisher, T. Y. Crowell, never issued an edition of *Kreutzer Sonata*. The American market for the work was certainly satisfied, for in addition to the Leipzig edition mentioned here, three more translations were published in the United States.[63] The letter suggests that even had she been able to translate the work, Hapgood could never have found a publisher, and that Tolstoy himself would have been responsible.

Hapgood concluded the letter on a softer, more conciliatory note: "I hope that you will not be too deeply offended with me for my refusal, or withdraw your friendship. It would hardly be quite fair, as you see that, under the circumstances, it was utterly useless for me to try to translate it. I am sorry both for myself, and for you; it must be unpleasant to have one's thoughts published in an unsatisfactory form." In an afterthought, she added: "Is it quite useless to ask for your 'Fruits of Enlightenment'?" It may not have been useless to ask, but it would have been pointless to translate it for just the reasons she had described above: two different translations were published the next year.[64] The only work by Tolstoy that she translated in 1890 was the "Nikolai Palkin" mentioned above.

One of the lost links in the correspondence between Hapgood and Tolstoy is an exchange concerning the meaning of a painting by the artist N. N. Ge (sometimes spelled Gay or Gue, 1831–94) depicting Christ before Pilate and entitled *What Is Truth?* Ge was a disciple of Tolstoy and painted religious canvasses under the influence of his teachings. This work had been removed from a public exhibit by order of the Holy Synod in March 1890. Tolstoy wrote P. M. Tretyakov (whose personal collection became the basis of the national gallery that bears his name in Moscow) to urge him to acquire the work, which he called "an epoch in Christian art."[65] Tolstoy also wrote George Kennan to request his assistance in promoting and interpreting this work during its American

At Yasnaya Polyana, 1909.

23

tour.[66] Hapgood, in a letter that has not survived, asked Tolstoy about the painting, which was about to enter the United States through Boston customs. All that remains of this exchange is Tatyana's notes of Tolstoy's dictated answer to Hapgood:

[No. 5—June 23, 1890]

The meaning of the picture, as my father says, is the following: Christ has spent the night among his tormentors. They beat him, led him from one group of leaders to another, and finally towards morning they brought him to Pilate. For Pilate, an important Roman civil servant, this entire affair seemed to be an insignificant disorder which originated among the Jews and whose essence was of no interest to him, but which, as the representative of Roman power, he was required to put an end to. He did not want to use decisive measures or resort to his right to order the death penalty, but when the Jews demanded the death of Christ with special vehemence, he became interested in the question of why this all came about. He summons Christ to the praetorium and wants to learn from Him how he so angered the Jews. Guessing the reason and, like every important civil servant, expressing it, he insists that the reason for the indignation is that Christ has called Himself King of the Jews. Twice he asks Him: does He consider himself a king. Christ sees in everything the impossibility that Pilate could understand Him, sees that this is a person from a completely different world, but that he is a person,—and Christ in his heart does not allow Himself to call him "raca" [i.e. a term of abuse] or to hide from him that light which He brought into the world, and to the question of whether He is a king, He expresses in the most compressed form the essence of His teaching (John 18. 37): " . . . For this I was born. . . ." "I thought that I could learn something from this tramp about why they are accusing him, but he speaks some kind of bombastic nonsense about truth and one cannot get anything from him. What is he mumbling about truth?" and, having said this, he went out to the Jews. (38, to the Jews). This is the moment which the painting depicts.[67]

Even without a context—without her question and Tolstoy's response—this interpretation provides an illustration of his view of Christ. Pilate is a bureaucrat, concerned with his power first of all, and hardly inquisitive about his subjects. Christ understands that He cannot fully or truthfully convey His own significance: nonetheless He holds no malice toward Pilate, will not curse or criticize him even silently, and out of respect for him as a person gives a short summation of His teaching. Tolstoy sees a nonresisting Christ confronted by the powers of government and organized religion, which is a moment of truth for his anarchistic teachings of nonviolence. No indication survives of Hapgood's reaction to the painting, which is unfortunate in view of her own traditionalist views, her sympathy with Russian Orthodoxy, and her later conclusion that Tolstoy's religious views were such as to prevent her translating his work.[68]

Hapgood tirelessly protected the Tolstoys against the fraud and deceit that she felt threatened them because of their fame. In the area closest to her own interests, the translation of Russian literature into English, Hapgood acted most decisively, even vindictively. She began warning Tolstoy against Nathan Haskell Dole in August 1889. In a letter to Tatyana Tolstoy written August 4, Hapgood wrote:

> Among the letters which awaited me in Moscow was one from your father's friend, W. P. Garrison, about some lies which N. H. Dole had been telling in print. Mr. Garrison reiterated his bad opinion of Mr. D's character, which I mentioned to you, and said that he was delighted when some one answered Mr. D. and showed the public his falseness. Mr. D. could not even attempt a reply. I am sorry that you could not see this letter of Mr. G, in confirmation of my statements. Mr. D. is very false and yet so plausible that he readily wins belief with those who are not acquainted with his ways.[69]

Just what statement by Dole she has in mind is unclear, for the Garrison letter has not survived. Most likely the question centered on who was an (or the) authorized translator of Tolstoy.

Nathan Haskell Dole (1852–1935) studied Russian at Harvard College, after which Hapgood probably met him when he taught at Worcester High School (1875–76). Later he became the literature, music, and art editor of the Philadelphia Press, and then, beginning in 1887, literary advisor to the publishing house of T. Y. Crowell. He was a prolific translator of Tolstoy, having published Anna Karenina (in 1886), The Invaders and Other Stories, Ivan Ilyitch and Other Stories, and Where Love Is, There God Is Also (in 1887), and The Cossacks, Family Happiness, The Long Exile and Other Stories for Children, and What Men Live by (in 1889), all with Crowell. Hapgood had already skirmished with Dole in print over his translation of Anna Karenina:

> Of "Anna Karenina" it is unnecessary to speak in detail. The general remarks which were made in these columns a short time ago with regard to the translation of "War and Peace" apply with equal force to this. It was made directly from the French, not from the Russian, and the proofs begin

in chapter two. The French version is very much cut, not as a concession to a more delicate taste (one passage is omitted for that reason), but in order to shorten the book. . . . But while the American translator follows the French so closely (as a rule) that he even writes *non*, where the Russian *no* is used, he sometimes departs from it without gaining much. *Peignoir* was a perfectly adequate rendering for *koftochka*, which Mr. Dole gives as a *jersey* (jerseys were not invented at that time). . . . The Russian was undoubtedly at hand and referred to, as the preface states, but with the result of confusion rather than improvement in most cases, and a translation from the French, not in a "few passages," but as a whole. It is a disappointment. To quote the words of a Russian who is accomplished both in that language and in English: "It makes the heart bleed to see the havoc that is made with beautiful things."[70]

To this devastating review Dole offered a weak rejoinder that he had not seen the French translation until he was well beyond the second chapter, and in any case he "made no pretense upon the title page of having done the work from the Russian." And he offered "an unsolicited letter from a Russian living in New York," congratulating him upon his success.[71] Hapgood, never one to forget or forgive an injustice, recalled her criticism of Dole's work in a later letter to Tolstoy, when advising him about finding a translator for his *Kingdom of God*. Four years later Hapgood wrote: "Mr. N. H. Dole . . . can translate Russian very badly when he has a French translation to work from . . . otherwise he could not read *un*translated Russian at all, nor manuscript. He is not honest in his work, in any way."[72]

True, Dole's command of Russian suffered badly at times. He wrote the first of his several letters to Tolstoy in Russian (with the assistance, he admitted, of a native speaker).[73] So modest was his control of the language that he could not even write all the letters correctly. He expressed no animosity toward Hapgood in his letters to Tolstoy, quite the contrary. He even sent him her translation of *What Is To Be Done?* and added: "Miss Hapgood by the way is probably by this time in Russia: she sailed some time ago. She is a very brilliant woman."[74] Dole did appeal to Tolstoy on one occasion for equal rights to call his translations "authorized." In a letter of February 2, 1888, he sent two clippings from *N. Y. Critic* and *Boston Traveler* which described how Tolstoy had made Hapgood "the authorized translator of all his works." Dole complained that such a statement, as "an implied repudiation of all the work that has been already done, is calculated to work harm and I am sorry that Miss Hapgood should have set such a story afloat." Dole responded to a (missing) letter from Tatyana Tolstoy: "I can not refrain from writing to tell you how much I was gratified by the assurance in your daughter's letter that my translations of your works were not repudiated by you."[75]

In addition to warning of unscrupulous translators, Hapgood took it upon herself to instruct the Tolstoys on matters of copyright and publication rights to translations. The difficulty stemmed from the fact that Russia had not signed the copyright convention. In a letter of July 16, 1891, Hapgood wrote to Tatyana to pass on this information "to your father; or rather, to your mother, since it is a matter of business." Her coaching was motivated by her concern that

> your father's new books should pay him nothing in America where there is the greatest sale of them, next to Russia, I think. *Someone* makes a profit, and why should it not be your mother and the family as well as an American publisher? I know that your father does not care for the money. But money is necessary in this world, especially with a large family.[76]

Hapgood proposed a complex scheme for translating the new work and collaborating with Paris publishers in such a way that "the American publisher [could] behave as though it were a French book. And for that it is necessary that the book should not be published in Russia until after its appearance here and in France. It must be kept private there." Clearly Sofiya Andreevna, who guarded the rights to Tolstoy's earlier works for the sake of the family, would not have been capable of undertaking such an elaborate scheme.

Responding to this inappropriate, if well-intentioned advice, Tatyana Tolstoy answered with courteous thanks, and also expressed the family's gratitude for Hapgood's gift of a subscription to the English Art Journal:

[No. 6—September 28, 1891]

Toula. 16 Sept. 91

My dear Miss Hapgood,

Many thanks for your kindness in writing so fully about the best means of obtaining copyright for my father's books in the future. I have no doubt the means you suggest would be the best did my father wish to obtain any profit from his books, but he does not. He only desires to circulate them as widely and freely as possible, and therefore it is just as well that they should be a source of profit to the publisher, who has thereby an interest to take them up. At present my father is not writing any new novel, but a tract upon or sooner against war, which is not yet finished.

I have received all the N°N° of the Art Journal, now I have the whole of the year, for which I thank you most heartily.

I am so sorry to hear your mother has been ill and hope by now she has recovered. I have distributed all your kind messages and return you many of my own.

Yours ever affectionately

Tatiana Tolstoy.

PS I could not get any of the groups Abamelek or Stakhovich did of our family, so I send you some done by my mother. They are not very good, but will perhaps remind you of Yasnaya Polyana.[77]

The rebuff to Hapgood's plans was firm, but not enough to discourage her from offering advice again later. The postscript refers to photographs taken while the Hapgoods were visiting in Yasnaya Polyana. Hapgood would continue to write Tatyana and Sofiya Andreevna to inquire about these and other photographs, providing a glimpse of vanity somewhat surprising for a person with her strict moral attitudes.

Hapgood's relations with the Tolstoys intensified suddenly in the winter of 1891–92. Large areas of Russia were suffering from a disastrous famine. Tolstoy and his eldest daughters began their own relief program, and Hapgood joined in the effort from America. From January through July 1892 Hapgood gathered contributions in New York and sent checks to the Tolstoys in an exchange of over sixty letters. Hapgood served as Tolstoy's ambassador to Americans during this campaign, as again her activities extended beyond the literary area.

Failed crops in the spring of 1891, depleted grain reserves, and an exhausted population made it clear by late summer that a terrible disaster loomed for Russia. The central plains of European Russia, sixteen provinces representing its most fertile lands, were devastated by drought—900,000 square miles, extending from the Ural Mountains in the east, west beyond the Volga River, south of Moscow to the borders of Ukraine, with a population of about 36 million, largely peasants—a land area four times the size of France, over one-fifth of the entire European continent. The villages were all but cut off from the outside world during the winter and early spring, and the transportation system was tragically inadequate. Providing food and seed in sufficient quantities seemed an impossible task in the fall of 1891.[78]

After some hesitation over moral questions, Tolstoy devoted himself entirely to the practical task of assisting the starving, disease-ridden peasants. He joined with a family friend and official of Tula, I. I. Raevsky, in a project to establish free food kitchens in villages of Riazan Province. Together with his two eldest daughters, Tatyana and Maria, he set up headquarters at the Raevsky estate in Begichevka, a hundred miles beyond Yasnaya Polyana. By November they had opened some thirty kitchens in twenty villages and were serving fifteen hundred people twice a day.

Left alone in Moscow to care for their younger sons, Misha, Andrei, and Leo, Sofiya Andreevna at first balked at the decision, then joined wholeheartedly in the family effort. She wrote an appeal to the newspapers as a result of which donations of money and material began to arrive, and she busied herself listing contributions, procuring foodstuffs, and shipping them to Begichevka. The countess's appeal also reached the foreign press, which had been reporting on the disastrous famine with increasing frequency,[79] and the quantity of foreign donations began to increase.

Hapgood was single-handedly responsible for a major portion of the foreign contributions to the Tolstoy effort. In five months she collected and sent over seven thousand dollars, an amount especially remarkable because it was mostly gathered from individual donations of five to ten dollars each. On January 18, 1892, she wrote:

> I send you herewith a draft on London for $584 equal in English money to one hundred and twenty pounds, 8 shillings, 3 pence. You can cash it at Zenker's, Rozhdenstvenskii Boulevard. I forget the number of the house, but it is on the hill, not far from the Liubianskaya.
>
> The enclosed Appeal and list of contributors will explain how I got the money for your poor starving peasants, and from whom. I shall have more to send shortly.
>
> Many of these people have written in the most sympathizing manner.[80]

The text of the appeal, published in the *Nation*, read as follows:

A Tolstoi Fund. To the Editor of the Nation:

> Sir. There are, no doubt, many people who would be glad to contribute to the relief of the starving Russians if they could conveniently send small sums and feel sure that they would be applied promptly, directly, and in the most economical manner by some one thoroughly conversant, through long experience, with the necessities of the case and with local conditions. All these requirements are fulfilled in the person of Count Leo N. Tolstoi, the great author and humanitarian, who has already done such noble work among the suffering peasants.
>
> As no postal orders or very small drafts can be sent to Russia, and as

there are serious objections to the use of registered letters for this purpose, I propose to start a Tolstoi Fund. I will gladly take charge of any sums, however small, which any one may wish to send me, acknowledging the receipt thereof at once. As soon as each $5 (five dollars) is collected, I will forward a draft to Count Tolstoi, accompanied by a list of donors. In this way those who wish to contribute may feel assured that there will be no expense attached to the transmission of their gifts, no waste in administering them. From personal acquaintance with Count Tolstoi and his family, who are his assistants in this work, I can answer for it that no one can make a penny go further, or expend it more honestly and judiciously, than they. Each dollar will feed one person for more than a month; hence the smallest offerings will be useful and welcomed by Count Tolstoi.[81]

Since returning from Russia, Hapgood had become known as a personal acquaintance of Tolstoy, his authorized translator and even confidant— an image she nurtured in her writings and recollections of Russia. With her great energy, background in church charitable work, and keen pragmatic sense, she traded on her own reputation to further the cause of assisting famine victims.

This same letter contained a suggestion, however, that exceeded even Tolstoy's sense of practical necessity.

If you are willing to send me some of your autograph Mss. or write me a few lines in English with your signature, I think I shall be able to sell them for a good price, to swell your funds. If they are not sold, I will return them; but I do not anticipate any such ending. You are very busy, I know, but you can help in this way, I am sure, if you can spare the time and Mss.

Tolstoy declined this offer (see letter No. 8, below): the prospect of selling his own literary artifacts seemed too frivolous and vain to be undertaken even for such a worthy cause as assisting the starving peasants.

Hapgood's letters usually arrived in Moscow twice a week, for she sent duplicate checks, as a safeguard against the original being lost (none ever was), and in this second letter repeated or elaborated on the contents of the letter accompanying the original check. On occasion she would request clarification of news stories, as in the case of the report that Tolstoy had been forbidden by the government to gather funds and distribute relief. This news had dampened the enthusiasm of donors, and it had some credibility, given the hostility of the Russian government and church to Tolstoy's activities. In her letter of January 21, 1892,

Hapgood enclosed a clipping from the *Boston Evening Transcript* ("Count Tolstoï has been ordered by the Russian Government to stop his charitable activity") on which she had written:

> It will be very hard to start the subscriptions again if they once stop for lack of some word from your own hand. Americans are liberal, but they are given to believing much nonsense about Russia. If you will just write, in English, a denial of this statement, I will get a fac-simile published in the newspapers, and you will, thereby, save the lives of hundreds, or thousands of peasants, with the subscriptions which will be sure to pour in.[82]

Hapgood repeated this request in her letter of February 5, which elicited the following denial from Tolstoy, expressed in a letter from Tatyana:

[No. 7—February 6, 1892]

Jan 25th. 92.

Dear Miss Hapgood

My father is not in Moscow at the present moment, so I have to answer for him, that the statement in "The Boston Evening" is completely false. He is now in the government of Riazan with my mother and my sister, and is continuing and spreading the work he has begun. He received the draft you sent him and answered you a few days ago. Yours truly

Tatiana Tolstoy.[83]

Tolstoy also apparently sent a cablegram, whose receipt Hapgood acknowledged in her letter to Tolstoy of February 8, but whose text has been lost.[84]

Tolstoy wrote again from the countryside, from the village of Klekotki, to express his thanks for Hapgood's help and the contributions.

[No. 8—February 16, 1892]

Dear Miss Hapgood,

I have received both your letter and the duplicate of the draft for the sum collected by your friends in America. (The draft itself and the list I have received before.)

I am deeply touched by the sympathy of your countrymen with our present distress and beg you to express my heartfelt thanks to your friends for their offerings.

I shall not omit in relieving the starving with your money to explain to

Photograph taken by V. G. Tchertkoff, at Kochety, May 1910 (with V. F. Bulgakov).

them the fact of their receiving help from their unknown brethren in distant America.

As to my autograph you will forgive me if I say that I don't quite like the idea of sending you any. I have never been able to accustom myself to the thought that they would be of any use to anybody, and feel quite unable to look upon them in this light.

I would feel guilty admitting to myself that I ascribe any kind of value to myself, and therefore to my manuscripts.[85]

Please remember me and my family to your mother and thank her for her good wishes.

With many sincere thanks and cordial regards believe me

    Yours truly

    Leo Tolstoy

4 February 1892.[86]

Despite the popularity of collecting famous people's autographs (Tolstoy himself received hundreds of such requests from Americans), his severe assessment of the value of his own manuscripts received unexpected justification later that spring. Hapgood herself attempted to sell the autographs of Tolstoy in her possession to raise additional funds to send to the Tolstoys. The only response to her newspaper advertisement was an offer of five dollars from a Philadelphia butcher, which she declined.[87]

Hapgood's personal relationship with Tolstoy received more publicity through the operation of her Tolstoy Fund, and as a result she often received requests to contact him and convey messages. On March 10 Hapgood cabled Tolstoy and also wrote to transmit a request from the *North American Review* that he write "an article of 3000 words, in three weeks, for the sum of 1200 rubles . . . on the present famine, chiefly descriptive." Hapgood was well aware that Tolstoy did not write on demand—she had already conveyed rejections of earlier requests—but in this case her sense of obligation to the suffering peasants dominated. She expected his refusal: "If you have cabled that you will not, I beg that you will reconsider the matter when this reaches your hands." Hapgood based her appeal on her own knowledge of American charity:

> Ordinarily I would not lift my pen to urge anything upon you, as I consider you to be the best judge of your own business. But that refers to Russia, and to ordinary circumstances. The state of the case here is, that no one has written anything authoritative, from the actual scene of the distress. Terrible pictures have been given—and contradicted. We have all learned to distrust newspaper accounts, even when names are signed to them, because, we are fully aware how incapable of judging the matter are the foreign correspondents, and casual observers. But your name is known and loved and trusted. We are, as a nation, deeply sympathetic and interested, and would give help more largely, I am convinced, if some one whom we could trust would give us a graphic account of the real condition of things.—Now there is no one but you who can do this to our complete satisfaction.[88]

She continued with praise for this particular journal, its "high character, trustworthiness and reputation" and explained that his article would enjoy maximum authoritativeness: "You could never hope to get a better medium for saying whatever may seem good to you about the famine, its causes, its results, and so forth." She closed with an appeal to his humanitarian feelings:

> Pardon the liberty I take; but, if you understand Russia, I, on the other hand, understand America, and what is needful here, for the good of Russia. You will help the brotherhood of mankind by telling the American public what it wants to know, from you.

The appeal was repeated in her letters of March 14, and again in letters of March 21 and 28. Hapgood took Tolstoy's silence as a rejection, and in her letter to the countess of March 28 she again explained this opportunity and its advantages, particularly as a means to counter false rumors and misrepresentations in the press with which Sofiya Andreevna had been contending in Moscow.

Tolstoy had already responded, but their letters crossed in the mails. Having just returned to Moscow, he wrote (in Russian):

[No. 9—March 28, 1892]

Forgive me, please, for not answering your telegram and for only now answering your letter. I received the telegram in Riazan Province, and since I can in no way write for money and even less upon request, I decided that I could not fulfill your request and did not respond by telegram. In addition, the telegram arrived so late because of communications difficulties and I was so swamped with work that I absolutely had no time to answer. Please, forgive me for this. I am now in Moscow, where I came for the river flood season and will stay for two weeks or so. During this time I would very much like to write down my latest conclusions and impressions about the famine and my struggle with it. If I am able to, I would like very much to fulfill your request and immediately upon writing the article, send it to you so that it could be published either in the journal you described or in whatever one you wish, of course, without any financial reward.

I am very, very grateful to you in the name of those towards the alleviation of whose needs your aid is directed, for your energetic and good activity. Our work is going well so far, i.e. we see clearly that our activity is bringing that usefulness that is expected of it and that we so far have not had a shortage of means or helper-workers. On four occasions it happened that we feared we had spread our activity too thin and stopped because we could not anticipate an increase in means. Thus we stopped when we had six kitchens and 3000 rubles. Then we stopped at 20. Then at 60; and now just a few days ago, before I left, when we checked our accounts and saw that we had 176 kitchens and lacked 8000 rubles in order to finish the task, we again stopped and began to cut back. But just as in the earlier cases, upon arriving here I found new contributions (of which yours represent no small part) which cover our deficit, and we can confidently move our task forward. I thank you very much. My wife and daughter will inform you of the receipt of your money. I am certain that it all arrived. If you have not yet received acknowledgment of all of them, this is because the checks have to be sent to the countryside for my signature and back again, which takes much time. In a few days we will make an accounting and then will inform you of the receipt of your contributions. I very, very much would like to write an article and publish it in America, if only as an expression of gratitude for that brotherly sympathy for our disaster expressed by your people.[89]

At this time, in April, Tolstoy did not manage to write anything about the famine, and only later, in June, was he able to send Hapgood a report. The promised accounting Tolstoy sent himself with a short note a few days later:

[No. 10—April 2, 1892]

Moscow
21 March
2 April <1892>

Dear Miss Hapgood
I received in due time your last draft on London for £38 5s 7. equal to $186.70 and repeat my heartfelt thanks for your exertions and the generous contributors.
We are now for a fortnight in Moscow, and all of us not quite well. It is nothing serious, only a cold, and we hope to be able to return to our place in the first days of April. Convey my greetings to your mother and accept my assurances of my sincere thanks and respect.[90]
Yours truly
L. Tolstoy.[91]

Tolstoy returned to Yasnaya Polyana on April 16, and on April 26 he left from there with his daughter Maria for Begichevka.
Sofiya Andreevna remained in Moscow to assist in organizing relief, keeping accounts, and sending supplies. Earlier that year her assistance had included defending the activities of her husband against attacks in the press, notably an attack by conservatives on Tolstoy in the *Moskovskie vedomosti* (*Moscow News*) in January and February. The church and certain government circles considered Tolstoy and his teachings to be a threat, made even more dangerous by the attention, popular support, and gratitude he received for his assistance to famine victims. An article based on a retranslation of Tolstoy's early call to assist in the disaster attacked him as a political revolutionary, and his arrest seemed imminent. (Hapgood had written at that time for confirmation that the rumors of impending arrest were untrue.[92]) Sofiya Andreevna's defense included an appeal to the minister of the interior, a letter to

foreign newspapers asserting her husband's loyalty, and a letter which Tolstoy wrote repudiating the newspaper article.[93] Sofiya Andreevna referred to this incident in her letter of thanks written to Hapgood a few days after her husband's letter above:

[No. 11—April 5, 1892]

Dear Miss Hapgood,

You have done so much to help us in our work that I really do not know how to thank you for the sympathy and the interest you have taken in the distress that has stricken such a large part of Russia.

No country has done as much as America! We have admired so much lately with what energy, good will and haste were sent the ships[94] with the aid for the famine-stricken Russians! If Russia could take example in it from your nice American people, it never would be in such a state, as it is now.

Yes, dear Miss Hapgood, we had lately great many annoyances with the Russian paper: *Moskovskie vedomosti*. If it would not be for our kind Emperor, our enemies would do us great harm! Thank God it is all over now, but I had to overlive a hard time.

Is it not wonderful [i.e., amazing] that a man who has done at present for his country more than any one else, is persecuted more than any other person in Russia. And everyone forgot what Count Tolstoï has done before for his country, what glory his name is for Russia and how hard he has worked all his life only for good purposes.

My husband and my daughters are at present in Moscow for a fortnight, because of the bad roads and the rising of the waters in the river Don. They all send you their love and many thanks for your great interest in their work.

I beg you to thank your mother for her kind wishes, I often think of her with great respect and love.

Believe me, dear Miss Hapgood, yours very sincerely

C-ss S. Tolstoï

PS Thank from me Mr. Wayland for his contribution

March the 25/5

1892.[95]

The reference to the Baptist minister H. L. Wayland concerned funds given to Hapgood expressly for the Stundists, a Protestant sect of German origin in Russia. Unfortunately, as she would write in her next letter, the Tolstoys were unable to locate members of this sect for this special assistance.

In April and May Hapgood sent six more checks, which contained contributions for Tolstoy and some for Sofiya Andreevna. The latter responded with another acknowledgment:

[No. 12—May 4, 1892]

Dear Miss Hapgood,

I have received the two drafts first and second for 13 pounds. Thank you very much for it. You have done so much for our distress, you have shown so much interest, that we shall be always so very thankful to you. My husband is far away in the country at the spot of the famine. He still works very hard for the help, providing lately grains and horses for the people. Maria is with him, but poor Tatiana is ill, and I have to take care of her health here, in Moscow.

I have just read in the papers about the dreadful fire in the theatre of Philadelphia.[96] I hope, that no one of your friends or relations have been there at the moment of this misfortune. What a dreadful sight it ought to have been!

You write to me, dear Miss Hapgood, that Mr. Wayland wishes to send money to the Stundists; but I have written to him that we do not see any; they are dispersed about Russia, but far away from us, and we do not know even the way how to send money to them.

With my most respectful regards to your mother and my kindest feelings to yourself

I am yours sincerely
C-ss S. Tolstoï
April the 22/4
1892.[97]

At about the same time Tolstoy wrote from Begichevka to confirm to Hapgood the receipt of the donations sent to him:

[No. 13—May 6, 1892]

Dear Miss Hapgood,

I think I have acknowledged the receipt of all the drafts that you have sent to me and that you have received them by this time. If I have forgotten to do it please let me know it that I may repair my negligence. Now I received your last draft for forty two pounds s17 d7 in Beguitshewka and I send this receipt to Moscow to my wife asking her to forward it to you because I have not your address. Yours truly, Leo Tolstoy.

<May 6/April 24, 1892>[98]

Hapgood continued to ask for accounting from the Tolstoys, explaining repeatedly that she must have absolute assurance that the donations were received. She appeared to be concerned not only that the system of sending checks was functioning, but also that none of her contributors, however modest the contribution, should doubt that the money was delivered. Again, in response to her urgings in letters of April 25, 27, and May 1, Sofiya Andreevna affirmed the receipt of the latest contributions. In contrast to Tolstoy's terse note, this letter reflects the personal warmth shared by the two women:

[No. 14—May 11, 1892]

Dear Miss Hapgood,

I have looked in my book about all the drafts received from you and Mr. Wayland. Comparing the numbers with those you have sent to me on a separate piece of paper, I found that I have received everything, and nothing did get lost.

I send you my husband's account in the "Russkie Vedomosti" [Russian News]. Perhaps you will translate it for an American paper. Every one who has sent money for the famine-stricken Russian peasantry will see and read how the money has been spent by our family

I will send your little paper [i.e. list of contributions] to my husband, and they will look in their books, if every money has been received which you have sent to Tatiana or my husband.

I am again alone in Moscow with my four last children, and my husband is working very hard providing food, horses and seeds for the poorest in the country, where they live now.

Tatiana is still not quite well; she has lost her health working too hard and not taking care of herself.

The spring does not give us much hope and consolation for the next harvest. It is very dry and windy in many places, and we have no rains at all. No one can do anything against the will of God! But it is sad to see in some places the dusty fields and the downhearted people.

With my best wishes and love to yourself and your mother, believe me yours sincerely

C-ss S. Tolstoï
April the 30/11
1892.[99]

At Yasnaya Polyana, March 1909.

Hapgood was pleased to receive the published account of relief funds[100] which Tolstoy had promised earlier, in his letter of March 28 (No. 9), and she set about to translating it and seeing that it was published. The closing note of despair that the drought was continuing would be repeated in subsequent letters.

Tatyana, despite her weakened condition, decided to return to Begichevka and before leaving wrote a letter to Hapgood to acknowledge the next set of contributions:

[No. 15—May 14, 1892]

Dear Miss Hapgood,
The last drafts we have received from you were for:

2, 17, -
3, 13. 9
42, 17, 7
45, 17 -
2 —

The duplicates often come the same day, as the first cheque, and very often a day after.

I think we have acknowledged the receipt of all the drafts we have received, but to make sure about it I will copy and send you the list of the money received through you when I go to the country where it is written down. If we are often very late in acknowledging the receipt of the drafts, it is because they are sent from Moscow to the country where we live, which is situated very far from the station, where the post comes only twice a week.

I am returning there in a few days, my father and sister are there. They write that the crops this year are so bad, that they fear that next winter there will again be famine. That would be dreadful, — nobody would have any energy left to help as they have done this year.

Have you safely received your photographs? I had a great mind to steal one or two, but I did not dare to.

I hope you and Mrs. Hapgood are well. Allow me to kiss you both and to beg you to believe me yours truly and affectionately
Tatiana Tolstoy
May 2. 92.
Moscow. Hamovniky 15.[101]

In one of the missing letters, Hapgood asked Tatyana to obtain from the Moscow photographer Panoff copies of portraits and groups taken during her visit the previous year. Hapgood acknowledged receiving the photographs in her letter of June 9, in which she described at length how Panoff had tricked her by sending many copies of a picture she did not order. Hapgood then asked Tatyana for further assistance: "As no one cares for any portrait of me except that which has the EYEGLASSES, and as I had only half a dozen of those, I want some more." Indeed, she hoped Tatyana could acquire the negative of this photograph: "If you cannot get the negative, please order me a dozen of that portrait *with the eyeglasses*, and tell Panoff that you will not pay for any others, if he takes the unwarrantable liberty of making them. Also, I think the picture would look better if he cut it off just before the hands are reached. There is just enough of them visible, directly in the focus, to look very ugly."[102] Hapgood was meticulous in all her activities, and not the least when the matter concerned her own image—photographic or otherwise. In this penchant to indulge her *amour propre* she differed from Tolstoy, who in later life considered such concerns (in himself and others) immoral and tried to avoid them.

A few days later Tolstoy wrote a brief note from Begichevka:

[No. 16—May 19, 1892]

7 May 1892
Dear Miss Hapgood,
   I received at once your two letters from 25 of April and May 2 with the draft for £ 20 S. 14 and the other for £ 68 S 13 D. 10, and thank the contributors for it.
   I am very busy just now, and have no time to write about the questions you mention in your letters, and will do so at the next opportunity.
   With cordial regards,
   Leo Tolstoy.[103]

Indeed, he was so busy that he had his daughter Maria write the letter and only signed it himself.

The contributions continued to accumulate, and Hapgood's twice weekly letters and checks continued to arrive in Moscow, and with them comments and advice for the Tolstoys. In her letter of May 5 Hapgood described the dangers of an American impostor, a Mrs. M. Louise Thomas: "Mrs. Thomas has never raised her finger to help Russia, she has not contributed or collected a single penny for your suffering people. But she has begged her passage to Europe and back, on the strength of her lies, and expects to travel everywhere for nothing-gratis—and be treated like a person of great importance, on the strength of the same lies."[104] In her next letter confirming receipt of contributions, Sofiya Andreevna acknowledged the warning:

[No. 17—May 24, 1892]

Dear Miss Hapgood,

I have just received a draft for 18 £., 7 S., 6 D. and thank you very much for this contribution. But every time that you mention the wish of Mr. Wayland, that the money should go to the Protestants, I feel as if it was my fault that I can not send the money to them, as they are very, very far away from us, and we do not know even, if there is famine. I have written the same to Mr. Wayland, but he continues to ask the same thing again. I have also received your letter to my husband, but he will not soon have it, as we are always sending money and foreign letters with some one who goes to him, but not with the post. Your letter about a Mrs. Thomas is also arrived; but I can not prevent her interference, because I am soon going away from Moscow to Yasnaya Polyana, and nearly all my friends are gone away to the country. Today I have sent with my daughter Tatiana my little ones to Yasnaya Polyana. Masha is with her father, who has been ill lately, so that I had to go to see him. Both my husband and Tatiana have lost their health with the hard work, and I wish they should leave it now to other people; they have done enough. The next harvest promises to be worse than last year's. We have not had rain since Easter, all the fields are nothing but *dust*, I saw it myself. Another week of such hot, windy, dusty weather and the starvation will be more dreadful than before!

Excuse the accident [i.e. a part of the page is torn].

It is so sad to see it that sometimes I think it would be nice to die for the sake of not seeing the next year's famine. Today we had a little rain in Moscow, I do hope that it has been everywhere about Russia.

If you will write again to one of us, dear Miss Hapgood, be so kind to address your letters to Toula, but not to Moscow.

With my best wishes to you and my respectful love to your dear mother, I am yours truly

C-ss S. Tolstoï

May the 12/24

1892.

PS. Be so kind, dear Miss Hapgood to write to M. Wayland, that if he wishes to help *only* the Stundists and other Protestants, he should send the money to some one else, because we can not find them out in all Russia, and they are very far from us. The 49 £ are also received.[105]

Hapgood wrote to Sofiya Andreevna (before receiving this letter) to confirm that she had told Reverend Wayland at the outset that the Tolstoys could not reach the Stundists. She concluded her letter of May 13: "In any case, it is just as well that you should not assume the responsibility of distributing money to them, since L. N.'s enemies might make it an excuse for annoying him further. That must be avoided. This will, consequently, be the last money which will reach you from Mr. W."[106] Hapgood continued her vigilance for the best interests of the Tolstoys.

The fear of misappropriation of funds suddenly appeared in Hapgood's letters, after she read in a report of the American minister to Russia, C. E. Smith, that he had received several thousand rubles on several occasions from Tolstoy.[107] Hapgood wrote to Tolstoy on May 11: "I hope that it did not indicate that you had sent him any of the money which has reached you through me. My contributors have given their money to be used strictly by you, or by Russians of your personal acquaintance." She feared that Tolstoy might have given excess contributions to the American Legation or the Anglo-American Chapel for their relief efforts, of which Hapgood wrote: "I approve of neither of them, and would not work for their benefit, or for money to be distributed through them."[108]

Writing from Begichevka, Maria Tolstoy immediately answered Hapgood with a firm denial that any funds had been misappropriated:

[No. 18—June 3, 1892]

22 May
1892.

Dear Miss Hapgood, my father has received your letter and asked me to answer it. My father is very sorry that you can think that he has sent some of the money collected by you for the starving people to the American Minister. He is sincerely thankful for the pains you have taken to collect it, and to the generous contributors, and will always employ it for the purpose for which it has been destined, especially because our work is spreading, and for the last month we are mainly sustained by your American contributions.

With cordial regards, yours truly

Marie Tolstoy.

My father sends you his kind regards and best wishes.[109]

Tatyana Tolstoy soon thereafter wrote from Yasnaya Polyana to confirm receipt of recent donations and to reaffirm that the funds had always been properly spent:

[No. 19—June 27, 1892]

Dear Miss Hapgood,

The last three drafts from you have been for 20, 14/o, 68, 13/10 and 30, 15/0. I don't know from whom you heard about my father giving away the money he received from America to the American legislation [i.e. Legation], but I know that the communication is quite false. All the money we receive goes for the famine-stricken peasants and we try not to trust it to people in whom we have not full confidence.

With kind regards from all of us to yourself and Mrs. Hapgood, believe me

Yours truly
Tatiana Tolstoy.
June 15/27 92. Toula.[110]

Ultimately, Hapgood was able to clear up the mysterious allegation of this misappropriation by going to the source of the story on Minister Smith's report. As she wrote in a letter to Tatyana of July 21, the cabled information was in error and should have read that the money was sent *to* Tolstoy, not sent by him.[111]

Donations to Hapgood's Tolstoy Fund were decreasing and it became clear that it was time to close down her efforts. Together with her letter announcing the end of contributions, Hapgood sent Tolstoy a copy of her translation of his accounting, the original of which she had received from Sofiya Andreevna (see No. 14 above).[112] Tolstoy wrote from Yasnaya Polyana to praise her work:

[No. 20—July 9, 1892]

Dear Miss Hapgood

I received your last letter with the draft for five pounds 18/6 and thank you heartily for the trouble you took in this matter and also the generous contributors. I received also your translation of my article about our work and admired the correctness and elegance of your translation. I am sorry to say that the crops in our place are nearly as bad as they were last year and that I am obliged to continue part of my work next year. I have some money left so that I will be able to do it thanks to your kindness and the goodness of your compatriots.

My compliments to your mother
Yours truly
L. Tolstoy.[113]

Confident not only of her skills but also of her willingness to translate his writings, Tolstoy conveyed to Hapgood another work, "The First Step," in hopes that she would translate it as well.[114] This tract on vegetarianism, moral self-improvement, and Christian self-denial pleased Hapgood. On July 19, 1892, she wrote to Tolstoy: "As you are probably aware, V. G. Tchertkoff has sent me a full copy of your article: The First Step. I have translated it and hope to get it published. I read it with much interest, and I am sure the American public will be interested also."[115] Unfortunately, the publishers to whom Hapgood offered her translation were less impressed than she with the merits of Tolstoy's tract, and the work was not published.[116] Hapgood's praise indicates that she certainly shared some of Tolstoy's moral principles.

In July Tatyana Tolstoy wrote from Yasnaya Polyana, where Hapgood's letter of June 9 finally reached her. In this and earlier letters Hapgood had made it clear that not only were the contributions dwindling, but that poor crops in America made continued assistance unlikely. Tatyana responded, as had her father, by noting that present resources would extend into the next year:

[No. 21—July 23, 1892]

Dear Miss Hapgood,

Your letter traveled after me from Moscow to Yasnaya Polyana, and from there to Begichevka, where I am at present looking after the kitchens, which are yet going on. Happily we have some money left, so that we will be able to continue them during this winter.

I am at present alone here, but my father and Masha will be coming in a week or two. My father and I have both been rather ill, but now we are better. I am very sorry I cannot do your commission to Panoff. I could write to him, but I am afraid he will misunderstand something and will again displease you. If you do not mind waiting some time, I am sure to go to Moscow during the summer and I will see Panoff himself and explain him everything you desire.

My father bids me acknowledge the receipt of the last two sums he received from you, one for 11 1/1 and the other for 31, 15/11.

One of these days I will send you a list of all the contributions we have received from America, asking you to give <it> to some paper to publish. When I will return to Yasnaya Polyana I will send you my photograph, here I have not got one.

Good-bye, dear Miss Hapgood, allow me to kiss you as well as your mother.

Tatiana Tolstoy.

July 11th 92. (Toula. Russia)

PS. Address your letters to Toula, please, - they will always reach us from there.[117]

Relieved of her weekly routine of sending contributions, Hapgood intensified her activity as watchdog over the Tolstoys' best interests. In a letter to Tatyana on July 30 she wrote to ask about a certain Jonas Stadling. The publishers to whom Stadling had offered a manuscript describing his work in Russia on famine relief had turned to Hapgood for verification of his claim that he had "received an invitation from the Countess Tolstoi in Moscow to come over to Russia, and co-operate with her family in the work of relieving the distress among the famishing millions in that country."[118] Although she had no reason to doubt the man's claim, she wrote: "Mr. Stadling has written some articles, which he wishes to publish. . . . But, you understand that if the name of your family is used as guaranteeing his remarks; and if he has not fully understood

Photograph by T. Tapsel, at Yasnaya Polyana, 1909 (with N. N. Gusev).

your father's remarks . . . there may be some more mischief, like that of the Moskovskie Vedomosti last winter." (In fact there was no problem: Stadling, a Swedish journalist, had spent some time with the Tolstoys working on famine relief and wrote about this experience extensively.[119])To illustrate that there were real grounds for concern and vigilance, Hapgood cited a recent case of egregious misrepresentation:

> There was a dreadful case of this grasping carelessness recently—in one of our magazines last spring, where an American woman wrote such a pack of lies and nonsense about all of you, that it made you all ridiculous. She signed herself: "Mme. Dovidoff," and declared that, "ancient family ties and relationships had enabled her to know many things about you, which the world at large could not know!" Having thus "authenticated" her article, she proceeded to retell all the absurd gossip which had ever been current about your father and your family, though she could not even spell so much as CAUCASUS correctly. She was the sister of an Episcopal Bishop, so the editors told me when I ridiculed her, and remonstrated, and made a list for him of 24 lies and misstatements!

The article did indeed make liberal use of current gossip and sensationalist stories of Tolstoy, describing how he "digs and plants and reaps and makes shoes (very poor ones, too, by-the-by)" and "every morning arises with a new maggot in his brain."[120] Hapgood was justifiably incensed.

On August 24 Tatyana responded to Hapgood's letter:

[No. 22—August 26, 1992]

August 14/26 92

Dear Miss Hapgood,

Mr. Stadling's statement is all quite exact, except the word *invite*, which is not quite right. Nobody of us knew anything about Mr. Stadling before my mother received his letter, asking her permission to come and help us in our work. As my father had nothing against Mr. Stadling's arrival, my mother wrote so to him, Mr. Stadling paid a short visit to Begichevka, after which he went over to Samara where he spent several months with my brother Lev, who found him a very agreeable companion. Nobody of our family has anything to say against Mr. Stadling and as much as we can judge from our short acquaintance with him—he is a man in whose honesty one can fully be sure.

I could not answer you before, because I was not at home when your letter arrived.

> With today's post I send you my photo in a costume from one of the places where we had our kitchens in the winter.
>
> Yours,
> Tatiana Tolstoy.[121]

Unfortunately, no such photograph survives in Hapgood's papers.

Hapgood sent the last of the contributions in August, to which Tolstoy responded the next month in a letter written in Russian from Moscow. He enclosed a letter of thanks to one of the final contributors to the Tolstoy Fund.

[No. 23—September 16, 1892]

Dear Miss Hapgood,

As I remember, I received your Russian letter. I also received your final amounts of money. Tanya will inform you about their receipt in detail.

Please be so kind as to send on the enclosed letter to Miss Sara A. Little.

I thank you again many times for all your labors in aid of our suffering fellow countrymen. The kitchens and shelters for children are still continuing even now on this money. The work is now being administered by P. I. Biryukov, whom you know, and I am going there in a few days. The harvest is again very bad, but the area affected by it is smaller. In a few days I will write a report for the newspapers in which I will express everything on this topic. I will be sure to send the printed report to you. Wishing you all the best and asking you to convey my respects to your mother, I remain

Yours,
L. Tolstoy.[122]

Tolstoy's report was sent two months later by Sofiya Andreevna, and Hapgood translated and published it.[123]

True to her calling, Hapgood remained interested above all in Tolstoy's current writing. She received news in this regard from Sofiya Andreevna, who wrote to Hapgood to explain the delay in sending some peasant costumes (which the latter had requested, but had asked not to send quite yet because of a cholera scare in New York):

[No. 24—September 22, 1892]

Dear Miss Hapgood,

I have not sent the Russian peasant-woman dresses, which you asked me to buy for you. They are already bought, but I was expecting a visit of an American gentleman to send the things with him. But the gentleman did not come, so I was just thinking to send you the dresses, when I received your letter. You should not be afraid to have the things from *our* house. Thank God, we have no cholera in our country, even not near it. Once only a woman in the village was taken ill with an illness, which was something like cholera, but she soon got well, and no one else was taken ill.

The Count, my husband, and Tiny [i.e. Tanya] are gone again to the famine-stricken countries. We have a little money left from last year and we have the intention to continue the help to the famine-stricken peasants in the places where help is more wanted. My husband has a friend who has taken upon himself to do the work for the Count, and he will only go now and then to see how everything is getting on. The famine is not so bad in Russia as it has been, and not in so many governments as last year. Also the spot where we shall continue the help this year is not so vast as it has been last year.

My husband was lately very busy writing; he is finishing his work, which he began some years ago, and he began a new one, which possibly may turn into a novel. I would be so glad if he could once more write something in the old style; I mean something like Anna Karenina and other novels. I prefer this to his philosophy.

Please thank your dear mother for her kind remembrance and tell her we all send her our love and best wishes. Accept the same for yourself and believe me yours truly,

C-ss S. Tolstoï
September the 10/22[124]

Hapgood, too, would have preferred Tolstoy to write more fiction rather than philosophy and had so stated on several occasions in print. She wrote to Sofiya Andreevna on October 9, 1892: "I am delighted to hear that your husband is writing once more. I hope, with you, that it will turn out something like Anna Karenina. There is not a man alive who can write as he can, when he pleases. I do not care for his philosophy, because he was not born for that, but he *was* born for the highest sort of pure literature in fiction."[125] In her next letter to Sofiya Andreevna, written October 31, Hapgood announced that she had a plan to sell the magazine rights for the work Tolstoy was writing, if the countess could get him to agree. She put the matter to Sofiya Andreevna:

Let me speak quite frankly to you, my dear Countess. Of course, it is very noble and disinterested of your husband not to wish to make any money from his writings. I know his arguments. But I know also that it takes a good deal of money barely to feed and clothe, in the simplest manner, such a large family as yours. Then, there are the younger children becoming more expensive every year. You must consider them, if you do your duty. Therefore, I have no hesitation in making you this offer, and in telling you that I will do everything in my power to arrange this affair for you, and to get you a handsome price.[126]

The answer Hapgood received must have been a disappointment, for it left no hope for her plan:

[No. 25—November 20, 1892]

Dear Miss Hapgood,

I am sorry to tell you, that I can not do anything for the editor of the magazine, who wishes to have my husband's work. I have never in my hands what my husband writes. His daughters are copying his works, and they do with them what he tells to them, but not to me. It is the second year that we scarcely live together few months, because my husband has done last year his work for the famine-stricken population, and this year he stayed in Yasnaya Polyana, because he does not wanted to be disturbed in his works, and I live in Moscow to educate my two boys and my girl.

You speak, dear Miss Hapgood, about money. My husband does everything as possible for his works. But he has given up lately all his fortune to his nine children. It made a very small part to each of them, but enough not to starve. As for myself, I do my best to live as economically as possible and I feel that I can not do anything to let my husband believe that few roubles more or less in a person's pocket will neither please nor offend God. He will not give up even now, after the last year that money did *everything*, and if not the money—people would starve and be miserable.

The famine in Russia, and especially in the part where my husband has lived last year, is very bad again. We had a little money left from last year, and so we continue to help a little, as much as we can for the money we have got. A friend, Mr. Birukoff has taken upon himself to do my husband's business and to continue his work in the famine-stricken countries.

I am very much ashamed that I have not send you the Russian things you have asked me. It was all ready, but my daughters have found that the things were not good enough and have promised me to get better ones. Now I hope that I will be able to send them to you very soon.

Excuse, dear Miss Hapgood, my bad English; I feel always ashamed to write English letters, I never have learned this language, and am often obliged to answer English letters.

With my best wishes to your kind mother and to yourself, believe me yours truly

S. Tolstoy.

November the 8/20

1892.

PS. My husband's work is not a novel, it is philosophy. [127]

Hapgood responded in a lengthy letter on December 6, immediately on receiving Sofiya Andreevna's. In it she commiserated:

> If your husband refuses to be convinced of the proper value and the respect due to money by last winter's experience, I am afraid argument is wasted on him. I am sorry he is writing philosophy again, for the Editor is likely not to want it. I will ask and write direct to your husband, if he *does* want it. I suppose that would be better than asking you to give the message, under the circumstances as you state them. I am afraid wedded life with a genius is not very easy, even to a woman so clever and full of tact as you. It makes me agree with your husband's theory that the unmarried state is best![128]

The journal in question was *Cosmopolitan*, whose editor, John B. Walker, apparently was not interested in philosophy. He did not give up his quest, however, and later arranged for rights to publish *Resurrection*.[129]

Moscow University Professor of Finance Ivan I. Yanzhul, a confidant of Tolstoy, visited Hapgood in New York in April, 1893, on his way to the Columbian Exposition in Chicago. In December Hapgood had written Tolstoy again that *Cosmopolitan* wished to publish his new work and continued, "I hope you will be able to let me have your new work to translate."[130] Tolstoy sent his new work with Professor Yanzhul along with this note of introduction (in Russian):

[No. 26—March 24, 1893]

Miss Isabel Hapgood. Nassau St. 154 New York.

My friends, Professor Ivan Ivanovich Yanzhul and his wife Ekaterina Nikolaevna Yanzhul are traveling to America. (I envy them very much.) Everything that you can do to assist them in studying whatever may interest them I will consider to be a special favor for me.

Yours truly, L. Tolstoy

13 March 189[3].[131]

Professor Yanzhul delivered to Hapgood *The Kingdom of God Is within You*, Tolstoy's major work on nonresistance, pacifism, and Christian anarchism. It seemed particularly fortuitous that Yanzhul could deliver the work, since Tolstoy hoped he would be able to assist Hapgood in translating difficult passages or, in case she refused, find another translator.[132] His anticipation of her refusal proved correct.

Just two days after receiving the manuscript, Hapgood wrote to Tolstoy:

New York. April 28th 1893
My dear Lev Nikolaevich,

Professor Yanzhul gave me the Ms. of your Kingdom of God. I thank you heartily for your friendliness in selecting me to translate it. It shows me that you feel kindly towards me and value the honesty of my work.

I read it—not all but as much as I could in a few days: as much as was necessary to make up my mind.

I am sorry, but my conscience will not allow me to translate it.

I shall not say anything about it, in print; or in private after it is published by some one else, except what I have said here to you: that I could not conscientiously approve of it, and put my name to it.

I have advised Prof. Yanzhul where to apply to a person who will translate it well. I have warned him, as in duty bound, against Mr. N. H. Dole, who can translate Russian very badly when he has a French translation to work from, that otherwise he could not read *un*translated Russian at all, nor manuscript. He is not honest in his work, in any way. I shall give the Professor and his wife all the help and advice I can to enable them to live comfortably and see what they wish for their work. I thank you for sending them to me.

I am glad to hear from them that you are well. Give my love to your wife and daughters and repeat to them the thanks for their costumes, which I have already expressed in a letter sent by the last steamer.

I thank you again most sincerely for your confidence in me, and truly regret that I cannot comply with your wishes.

Ever faithfully yours,
Isabel F. Hapgood[133]

Hapgood, who had enjoyed friendly relations with members of the court and high officials while in Russia, continued her enthusiastic support of Russian government and church affairs while in New York, energetically representing and interpreting Russian culture and spirituality for her fellow Americans. The central idea of Tolstoy's new work, which applied his theory of nonviolent resistance to governments, was that all states are in essence immoral because they force their citizens to fight wars, to maintain prisons, and to pay taxes. He accused the church of self-interest in supporting government. Hapgood had found Tolstoy's earlier philosophical positions suitable for translation—total self-abnegation in *On Life*, pacifism in "Nikolai Palkin," self-denial and vegetarianism in "The First Step"—but not this attack on all Christian churches of all denominations for distorting Christ's true teaching in order maintain their power. Tolstoy's views of organized Christianity, expressed early in the work, clearly led Hapgood to make up her mind that she could not in good conscience translate it. She did assist in finding a capable translator, Alexandra Delano, who had produced English translations of earlier philosophical stories and works by Tolstoy, including a portion of *What I Believe*, the tract on nonresistance that provides the starting point for *The Kingdom of God*.[134]

Tolstoy replied (in Russian) to Hapgood's letter with regret for her decision and thanks for her willingness to help:

[No. 27—May 18, 1893]

Dear Miss Hapgood,

I received your letter and was very sorry that you have not undertaken the translation of my book. I am very grateful to you for promising to find and indicate to I. I. Yanzhul a trustworthy translator. I need to send a revised ending of the last chapter, but I do not know I. I. Yanzhul's address, and therefore I turn to you with the request to pass on this ending to Mr. Yanzhul or to that translator whom you have recommended to him. Would you allow me to send this ending in care of you and would you be so kind as to send it to the proper addressee?

I beg you to forgive me for burdening you with my request and to accept my gratitude for fulfilling it. All of the family ask that I send you greetings.

With deepest respect,
Yours, Lev Tolstoy.
6/18 May 1893
Yasnaya Polyana.[135]

Hapgood replied immediately, on June 3, "I will receive the altered conclusion of your last chapter, with great pleasure, and will send it at once to the translator." To this she added, however: "Now in return for this little service—most gladly rendered, believe me—let me ask you to answer a letter which I sent you on April 6th last, and to which I have received no reply."[136] In this letter she repeated the request of the editor of *Cosmopolitan*, originally made the previous December: a story of three to four thousand words, for which he would pay three hundred dollars. To this request Tolstoy asked his wife to reply:

[No. 28—July 13, 1893]

Yasnaya Polyana

Dear Miss Hapgood,

My husband is very sorry to let you know, that he can not give any story for the Editor of the Cosmopolitan. He has nothing ready, and he can not work, if he is not *disposed* to do it.

He never wanted to work for money, and so the most generous offer could not tempt him.

Please, convey this to the editor just this way. At present Lev Nikolaevich is out mowing with the peasants in the morning and the evening, and in the afternoon writes, or more exactly, corrects various articles written earlier *On Art* and collected by Tchertkoff.

Taking the opportunity to ask you to convey our respectful regards to your mother and to believe the sincere feelings of your devoted

S. Tolstoy.

PS My daughters are in Moscow at the wedding of a relative, and so L. N. asked me to write to you.

1/13 July

1893

Tula. Countess Sofiya Andreevna Tolstoy.[137]

In September Hapgood wrote to acknowledge this letter and made one last attempt to get the next piece Tolstoy would write. But there was no reply, and with this Hapgood ended her attempts to get any further writings of Tolstoy to translate.

Letters between Hapgood and the Tolstoys became less and less frequent. In September 1894 Hapgood wrote to warn the Tolstoys of a fraud and adventuress, Miss Kate Marsden, whose "Fund for Siberian Lepers" she worked long and hard to discredit.[138] In July of the next year Hapgood wrote again to Tolstoy to ask if he would provide a preface to her translations of works by N. S. Leskov—stories which Tolstoy admired and once suggested to her. A publisher had agreed to bring out the collection if Tolstoy would contribute a preface; Tolstoy did not reply, and the works were not published.[139] In 1897 Hapgood wrote again, this time to ask for a copy of Tolstoy's novel *Resurrection* to translate for a publisher. Her request was circumspect—"After my refusal to translate

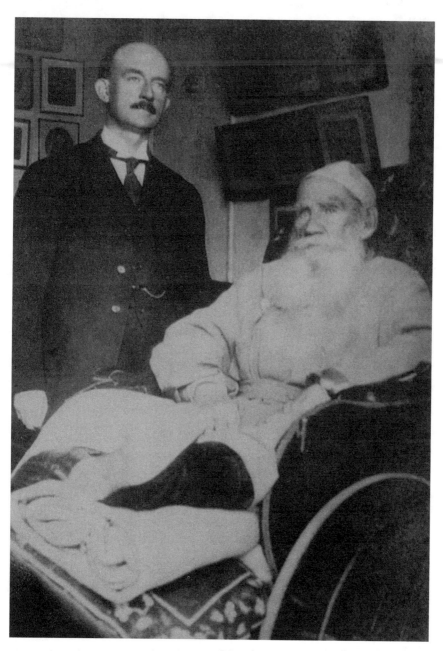

With Henry George, Jr. at Yasnaya Polyana, 1909.

some of your writings, I really have no right to say a word to you about such a subject."—but produced no response, let alone the requested copy.[140]

Hapgood's correspondence with Tolstoy ends, however, not quietly, but with a bang. In 1903, after seeing a Broadway production based on *Resurrection*, she sent clippings of reviews and a colorful account of the anomalies and misrepresentations in the play:

> New York. Feb. 19, 1903
> My dear Lyeff Nikolaevitch.
> I am sending you herewith clippings from the leading newspapers of this city, on the day after the production of "Resurrection."[141] They can hardly fail to interest—even to amuse you—by their agreements as well as their differences. I spoke for a seat weeks in advance—and got it—for the opening night. To tell the truth, there is not much of your "Resurrection" about the play, except the mere skeleton of the tale. It was very well played: so well, that I never wish to behold the actress who took the part of KATIUSHA again![142] Her conception of the part was something infinitely degraded and coarse—very different from your idea, I am sure. (Her father is Keeper of The Tombs—the City Prison—and she was reared in the evil part of the town here). As to its terrible power, there can be no difference of opinion, I should think. That prison scene was the very worst thing I have ever seen—or ever wish to see—on the stage. I think others found it so too. In the last act, the scene in Siberia is intensified by additions: a man is hauled (Pardon the blot! I have no time to rewrite it) off to be knouted, and his horrible groans behind the scenes linger with one like a nightmare long afterwards. They haunt me still. As Russia is made to stand for a sort of public scapegoat, I suppose they thought something like this would be expected by the audience. I do not know how closely the American adapter has followed the French play (with which you must, of course, be already familiar by report). I do know that SOMEONE introduced a lot of nonsense, by way of "local color," I suppose. Twice, mention was made of apple-trees in full blossom, while the brooks were either ice-bound, or the ice was breaking up! The managers here insist that everything is done precisely as in Paris. I take leave to doubt that. The women's costumes, for one thing, would serve very well (except the white cotton nurse's kokoshniki! and the queer aprons), for Swiss or Tyrolean peasants. The ikona hangs out on the door-jam of Pr. N's bedroom; Roman Catholic chants, accompanied by an organ, (in the first and last acts) represent the Easter hymn; the Easter kiss is discharged, bang! square on the mouth—and Pr. N.[143] and the female characters make a lot of flirting nonsense, and fishing for the kiss, which is revolting. In

the Jury-room scene, a samovar, with the brass, extra pipe towering up, and a number of glasses, stand on a side-table. The weary jurors fly thither, and draw FROM THE SAMOVAR DIRECT, something or other! Really, I don't know whether it was intended to be tea or water. It was equally amusing, either way. On the large table there was a framed and glazed article, with some sort of writing on it, enclosed in a broad mourning border, and propped from behind like a photograph frame. The merchant seizes this, and carries it about in his hands—evidently to call attention to it, though he says nothing, so far as I heard, about it. I assume that this represents the "zertsalo"! [i.e., a symbol of authority] (As I have not read "Resurrection," except immediately on its appearance, I do not recall accurately all the minor details. But this MUST have been meant for the zertsalo). They crossed themselves in Roman Catholic style, and, instead of making "ground reverences," one old woman, (in the prison scene), knelt the whole time in front of a candle, perched on a box and a basket, in front of a crucifix, and waggled her body from side to side, in a perfect fervor of devotion, just as I have seen old women do in R. C. Churches! The Easter greeting was given, repeatedly, thus: "Christ is risen!"— Talky-talky-talky, flirty, flirt, flirt: then "Peace be unto you!" as a response!—Do you wonder that I smiled a good deal, in spite of the nature of the play? And as for pronunciation—which, with all the other points, they could so easily have learned aright, here in N.York—they said: "Iwanowitsch," and the like, making as many syllables and as much of a mouthful as they possibly could![144]

The description of the play is quintessential Hapgood: outraged and amused at foolish misconceptions of Russia and Russian culture, yet very much attached to the country and its people.

In this letter she did not mention her magnum opus: a translation of the Russian Orthodox church liturgy. She had mentioned this project to Tolstoy in her previous letter, noting "I presume you will not approve of my work." Surely he did not, nor would he have sympathized with her dream to join the Russian Orthodox church with the Episcopal churches in an intercommunion. She defended this idea and her devotion to it: "It would be a great step towards the establishment of that brotherhood of love and tolerance which you certainly do approve; and I shall be more glad than I can express if I am able to help a little in that fine work."[145] Hapgood's ecumenism produced a work of major significance, her *Service Book of the Holy Orthodox-Catholic (Greco-Russian) Church*, published in 1906.[146] As its subtitle explained—that it is "compiled, translated and arranged from the Old Church Slavonic service book of the Russian

Church and collated with the service book of the Greek Church"—
Hapgood combined and ordered elements of the Russian Orthodox
liturgy so as to make them accessible for English-speaking observers. Now
in a sixth edition, the service book remains in use to this day.[147]

Hapgood had dedicated herself to a cause which took her in a direction
opposed to Tolstoy's Christian anarchism and moral absolutism. In
temperament Hapgood had much in common with Tolstoy. She
understood him, and her sympathy with his fiction and early essays shows
in the accuracy, energy, and veracity of her translations. But when
Tolstoy converted to his new Christian beliefs, Hapgood found herself
unable to translate his works which now conflicted with her own moral
scruples and traditional religious beliefs. So she turned to other Russian
writers and works, and American readers thus lost their best, most gifted
and reliable translator of Tolstoy.

Notes

1. Permission to publish the letters from the Tolstoys contained in the Isabel
Hapgood Papers has been given by the Manuscripts and Archives Division, The
New York Public Library, Astor, Lenox and Tilden Foundations. Permission to
publish and to quote from the letters of Hapgood to the Tolstoys has been
granted by the State Tolstoy Museum in Moscow.

2. Leo Tolstoy, *Childhood, Boyhood, Youth*, trans. Isabel Hapgood (New York:
T. Y. Crowell, 1886). Isabel Florence Hapgood, *The Epic Songs of Russia* (New
York: C. Scribner's Sons, 1885).

3. Nikolai Vasil'evich Gogol', *Tchitchikoff's Journeys; or, Dead Souls* (New
York: T. Y. Crowell, 1886). *Taras Bulba* (New York: T. Y. Crowell, 1886). *St.
John's Eve, and Other Stories, From "Evenings at the Farm" and "St. Petersburg
Stories" by Nikolai Vasilievitch Gogol; From the Russian by Isabel F. Hapgood* (New
York: T. Y. Crowell, 1886).

4. For details on Hapgood's early life and her church activities I am indebted
to the research of Stuart H. Hoke of the General Theological Seminary of New
York City, in his article "A Generally Obscure Calling: A Character Sketch of
Isabel Florence Hapgood" (unpublished).

5. Warren Hapgood, *The Hapgood Family: Descendants of Shadrach 1656-1898*
(Boston: T. B. Hapgood, 1898), p. 257.

6. Abby Farwell Ferry, "Isabel F. Hapgood: A Tribute," *When I Was at
Farmington* (n.p., 1931), p. 80, cited by Hoke.

7. Mary Bronson Hartt, "Hapgood, Isabel Florence," in *Dictionary of American Biography* (New York: Charles Scribner's Sons, 1932), vol. 8, p. 233.

8. Joseph abbé Roux, *Meditations of a Parish Priest: Thoughts*. (New York: T. Y. Crowell, 1886).

9. Victor Hugo, *Les Misérables*. Illustrated ed. (New York: T. Y. Crowell, 1887). Edmondo De Amicis, *Cuore, an Italian Schoolboy's Journal; A Book for Boys* (New York: Crowell, 1887).

10. She had joined All Saints Parish in Worcester, where its rector, William Reed Huntington, began preaching the message of church unity which dominated his career. Hapgood continued to work under his influence later in New York City, when he was rector of Grace Church, in whose parish she actively participated beginning in 1890; see Hoke.

11. New York Public Library, Division of Rare Books and Manuscripts, Papers of I. F. Hapgood, box 4, letter from Ralston of July 13, 1885 (hereafter abbreviated NYPL:IFH).

12. Leo Tolstoy, *War and Peace; A Historical Novel*, 2 vols. (New York: W. S. Gottsberger, 1886). "Transl. into French by a Russian lady, and from the French by Clara Bell. . . . Revised and corrected in the United States."

13. Isabel Hapgood, "Cobbling Extraordinary," *Nation* 42, no. 1082 (1886): 259–60.

14. Leo graf Tolstoy, *What to Do? Thoughts Evoked by the Census of Moscow*, trans. Isabel F. Hapgood (New York: T. Y. Crowell, 1887).

15. Isabel Hapgood, "Count Tolstoi and the Public Censor," *Atlantic Monthly* 60 (1887), pp. 62, 67.

16. Letter to L. N. Tolstoy, State Tolstoy Museum, Manuscript Division, T.c. 219.2 (hereafter abbreviated STM).

17. In a letter to Tolstoy of December 21, 1886, George Kennan wrote positively of Hapgood's translation of *Childhood, Boyhood, Youth*. See *Literaturnoe nasledstvo*, vol. 75, bk. 1, p. 418.

18. Hapgood to L. N. Tolstoy, December 13, 1887, STM, T.c. 219.2.

19. As it was her habit to include bits of Russian in her letters, Hapgood here uses the Russian title ("O zhizni") for Tolstoy's work (which was written 1886–87); her translation was published shortly thereafter: Leo Tolstoy, *Life*, trans. Isabel F. Hapgood (New York: T.Y. Crowell, 1888).

20. Again, Hapgood cites the title of the work in Russian ("Smert' Ivana Il'icha"). Tolstoy had completed it in 1886; the next year it was translated by Nathan Dole and published: Leo Tolstoy, *Ivan Ilyitch and Other Stories*, trans. N. H. Dole (New York: T. Y. Crowell, 1887).

21. Hapgood to T. L. Tolstoy, December 27, 1887, STM, 106 ATc no. 28951.

22. Hapgood to L. N. Tolstoy, March 10, 1888, STM, T.c. 219.2. no. 4.

23. L. N. Tolstoi, *Polnoe sobranie sochinenii*, Jubilee edition, 90 vols. (Moscow-Leningrad: Goslitizdat, 1928–59), 64:153–54. Hereafter abbreviated PSS.

24. Hapgood to L. N. Tolstoy, March 30, 1888, STM, T.c. 216 35.

25. *Perepiska L. N. Tolstogo s N. N. Strakhovym*, St. Petersburg, 1914, p. 371.

26. N. N. Strakhov to Hapgood, May 27 (June 9), 1888, NYPL:IFH.

27. Hapgood wrote in her letter to Tolstoy of September 8: "Owing to A. N. Maikoff being much occupied with his jubilee, he kept the proofs of *Life* for two weeks before handing them to N. N. Strakoff for me. The publisher became impatient at the delay and issued the book without correction. I believe that your friend N. N. S. found very little to alter; hence I hope that this edition will not displease you. All proper changes will be made in later issues. In one case, N. N. S. found that *not* had been omitted, thereby altering the sense. But reference to the original proved that this arose from an error on the part of the copyist. I believe that is the only serious mistake." Hapgood to L. N. Tolstoy, September 8, 1888, STM, T.c. 219 2.

28. Comte Leon Tolstoi, *De la vie, seule traduction revue et corrigée par l'auteur* (Paris, [1889]). On the back of the title page: "La traduction de cet ouvrage est de Madame de Comtesse Tolstoi et de M. M. Tastevin."

29. Ernest Crosby to L. N. Tolstoy, November 17, 1893, STM, 211/25-2.

30. John Kenworthy, *A Pilgrimage to Tolstoy* (London: Brotherhood, 1896), p. 27.

31. Crosby wrote in a letter of February 15, 1897, "My friend, Bolton Hall, has been very much impressed, as I was, by your book on 'Life'—and is anxious to bring it to the attention of the public more successfully than the translator has been able to do"(STM). The result was published in 1897 not as a rendering of Tolstoy's "On Life," but as an independent work: Bolton Hall, *Even As You and I: Parables of True Life* (Boston: B. Hall, 1897). Two years later Tolstoy arranged the Russian translation and publication of Hall's abridgement of *Even As You and I*, which in this form had no trouble passing the censorship: *Istinnaia zhizn'* (Moscow: Etiko-Khudozhestvennaia biblioteka, 1899). It appeared once again in 1903 in the same edition, but titled as Tolstoy's "On Life": L. Tolstoi, *O zhizni*, intro. L. Nikiforov (Moscow: Etiko-Khudozhestvennaia biblioteka, 1903).

32. Leo Tolstoy, *"On Life" and Essays on Religion*, trans. Isabel Hapgood, in *The Works of Tolstoy*, Centenary edition, 21 vols. (Oxford: University Press for the Tolstoy Society, 1928), vol. 13.

33. Hapgood's translation is not found among her papers. The work was published a few years later as Leo Tolstoy, *Work While Ye Have the Light*, trans. E. J. Dillon (New York: United States Book Co., 1890).

34. Hapgood to L. N. Tolstoy, September 8, 1888, STM, T.c. 219 2.

35. For an account of the rumors and manuscript versions of the work which were circulating in Russia, see Peter Ulf Møller, *Prelude to "The Kreutzer Sonata": Tolstoj and the Debate on Sexual Morality in Russian Literature in the 1890s* (Leiden: E. J. Brill, 1988), pp. 39–55, 92–101.

36. Tatyana dated the letter "old style"; dates in the text are given in "new style." In the nineteenth century the "old style" Julian calendar was twelve days behind the "new style" Gregorian, and in the twentieth century, thirteen days.

37. NYPL: IHP, box 4: Russian Papers, R-Y, folder: Tolstoy (Countess Tatyana Lvovna). See note 11 above.

38. Leo Tolstoy, *Sevastopol*, trans. Isabel Hapgood, authorized ed. (New York: Crowell, 1888). When and how Tolstoy "authorized" this translation is unclear, for there is no mention of the translation of these three stories (written some thirty years earlier, in 1855) in their correspondence before this.

39. For details of the rumors and her patient wait for the manuscript, see Hapgood's review, "Tolstoi's 'The Kreutzer Sonata,'" *Nation* 50 (1890): 313.

40. PSS 50:5.

41. Isabel F. Hapgood, "Tolstoy As He Is," *Munsey's Magazine* 15 (1896): 558.

42. NYPL:IFH, folder: Tolstoy (Countess Tatyana Lvovna).

43. PSS 50:15.

44. Isabel F. Hapgood, "A Stroll in Moscow with Count Tolstoy," in her *Russian Rambles* (Boston, New York: Houghton, Mifflin, 1895), p. 136.

45. Ibid., p. 137.

46. Ibid., p. 147.

47. Hapgood to L. N. Tolstoy, January 17, 1889, STM, T.c. 219, 2.

48. Permission was apparently received in a letter from Tatyana that has been lost, written between Hapgood's letters of February 6 and March 25, 1889.

49. Hapgood to T. L. Tolstoy, March 25, 1889, STM, 106 ATc. no. 28953.

50. NYPL:IFH, folder: Tolstoy (Countess Tatyana Lvovna).

51. Bowen's letter of January 21, 1889, was sent by Hapgood, accompanied by a note, on January 25 (old style); STM, T.c. 219, 2.

52. Leo Tolstoy, "Nikolai Palkin," trans. Isabel Hapgood, *Cosmopolitan* 10 (1890): 387–94.

53. NYPL:IFH, folder: Tolstoy (Countess Tatyana Lvovna).

54. Isabel F. Hapgood, "Tolstoy at Home," *Atlantic Monthly* 68 (1891): 596–620, 659–99. Republished in *Russian Rambles*, pp. 148–202.

55. *Russian Rambles*, pp. 162–63.

56. Ibid., pp. 170–71.

57. Ibid., pp. 174–75.

58. Ibid., 185.

59. Isabel F. Hapgood, "Tolstoi's 'The Kreutzer Sonata'," (n. 39 above), p. 313. The review is dated March 29, 1890.

60. Hapgood to S. A. Tolstoy, October 21, 1889, STM, ACT 123, no. 16016.

61. Hapgood, "Tolstoi's 'The Kreutzer Sonata,'" p. 313.

62. Hapgood to L. N. Tolstoy, April 21, 1890, STM, T.c. 219,2.

63. Leo Tolstoy, *The Kreutzer Sonata*, trans. Benj. R. Tucker (Boston: B. R. Tucker, 1890). Leo Tolstoy, *The Kreutzer Sonata*, International Library, no. 1 (Chicago: Charles H. Sergel, 1890). Leo Tolstoy, *The Kreutzer Sonata*, trans. F. Lyster (New York: Pollard Publishing, 1890). The last translation is described as being "from the original manuscript."

64. Leo Tolstoy, *The Fruits of Culture: A Comedy in Four Acts*, trans. G. Schumm (Boston: B. R. Tucker, 1891). Leo Tolstoy, *The Fruits of Enlightenment: A Comedy*, trans. E. J. Dillon, intro. W. P. Pinero. Levell's Westminster Series, no. 27 (New York: United States Book Co., 1891).

65. PSS 65:109.

66. PSS 65:123.

67. PSS 65:333–34. This draft was written by T. L. Tolstoy on the fourth page of a letter from A. N. Dunaev to Tolstoy of June 6, 1890, and is dated on the basis of her note, "Dictated on June 11, 1890."

68. In a letter of January 26, 1891, Hapgood wrote to Tatyana Tolstoy: "I have not seen Gue's picture yet. I have heard that the agent was in difficulties with the Customs House, in Boston. It was a mistake, in my opinion, for him to take the picture to Boston first, for various reasons." Possibly one reason was the picture's overtly secular interpretation, and the strict orthodoxy of Boston's customs officers. On July 16, 1891, she wrote to Tatyana: "You probably know more as to what became of Gue's picture than I do. I never heard a word beyond its being detained in the Boston Custom House. It may have got out and been exhibited here; but it certainly created no sensation of any sort." STM, 106 ATc no. 28984.

69. Hapgood to T. L. Tolstoy, August 4, 1889, STM ACT, no. 123, no. 16018.

70. [Isabel Hapgood], "Tolstoi and Turgeneff," Nation 42 (1886): 389. The anonymous author of this article, if not Hapgood, certainly bears all her characteristic traits.

71. N. H. Dole, Nation 42 (1886): 405.

72 Hapgood to L. N. Tolstoy, April 28, 1893, STM T.c. 219 6.

73. N. H. Dole to L. N. Tolstoy, December 5, 1886, STM T.c. 212 54.

74. N. H. Dole to L. N. Tolstoy, November 23, 1887, STM T.c. 212 54.

75. N. H. Dole to L. N. Tolstoy, February 2, 1888, and April 29, 1888, STM T.c. 212 54.

76. Hapgood to T. L. Tolstoy, July 16, 1891, ACT, no. 123, no. 28961.

77. NYPL:IFH, folder: Tolstoy (Countess Tatyana Lvovna).

78. For an informative, balanced analysis of the crisis and the government's reaction, see Richard G. Robbins, Famine in Russia, 1891–1892: The Imperial Government Responds to a Crisis (New York: Columbia University Press, 1975).

79. In the New York Times over sixty separate articles on the famine were published from September through December 1891.

80. Hapgood to L. N. Tolstoy, January 18, 1892, STM, T.c. 219 3.

81. January 5, 1892.

82. Boston Evening Transcript, January 19, 1892, STM, T.c. 219 3.

83. NYPL:IFH, folder: Tolstoy (Countess Tatyana Lvovna).

84. The cablegram has not survived in Hapgood's papers: she had written Tolstoy on January 21, "I will pay for the cablegram (or refund it to you). Write: 'Hapgood. New York. False/True. Tolstoy.'" STM, T.c. 219 3.

85. Tolstoy wrote this sentence in Russian.

86. NYPL:IFH, box 4: Tolstoy (Letters from Count Leo Tolstoy, 1892–93). First published in Neizvestnyi Tolstoy v arkhivakh Rossii i SShA (Moscow: AO Tekhna-2, 1994), pp. 233–34.

87. "Notes on Tolstoi letters given the New York Public Library by Miss Hapgood in July 1915," NYPL:IFH, box 4 (Russian Papers, R-Y), folder: Tolstoy, Count Leo.

88. Hapgood to L. N. Tolstoy, March 10, 1892, STM, T.c. 219 3.

89. NYPL:IFH, box 4 (Russian Papers, R-Y), folder: Tolstoy, Count Leo.

90. This sentence was written in Russian.

91. NYPL:IFH, box 4 (Russian Papers, R-Y), folder: Tolstoy, Count Leo. First published in *Neizvestnyi Tolstoi*, pp. 237–38.

92. Hapgood to L. N. Tolstoy on February 23 and 29, 1892, STM, 219 3.

93. For an account of the incident (which suffers from some inaccuracies in dates), see Ernest J. Simmons, *Leo Tolstoy*, Vol. 2: *1880–1910* (New York: Vintage Books, 1960), pp. 162–71.

94. Hapgood was instrumental in advising on and organizing several shipments of grain and foodstuffs to Russia. For an account of one of these, see the memoirs of Francis B. Reeves, *Russia Then and Now 1892–1917. My Mission to Russia during the Famine of 1891–1892 with Data Bearing upon Russia of Today* (New York: G. P. Putnam's Sons, 1917).

95. NYPL:IFH, box 4: Tolstoy (Countess Sophia Andreevna).

96. On the fire which destroyed the Grand Central Theatre in Philadelphia on April 27, see "Fire Panic in a Theatre," *New York Times* (April 28, 1892), p. 1; "Seven Dead or Missing: Philadelphia's Fire Worse Than at First Reported," *New York Times* (April 29, 1892), p. 6.

97. NYPL:IFH, box 4: Tolstoy (Countess Sophia Andreevna).

98. Library of Congress, Manuscript Division, John Davis Batchelder. Autograph Collection, 1400–1960.

99. NYPL:IFH, box 4: Tolstoy (Countess Sophia Andreevna). The article mentioned is not among Hapgood's papers.

100. "Otchet ob upotreblenii pozhertvovannykh deneg s 3 dekabria 1891 g. po 12 aprelia 1892 g." [Account of the use of money received from December 3, 1891, to April 12, 1892], *Russkie vedomosti*, no. 117 (April 30, 1892).

101. NYPL:IFH, box 4, folder: Tolstoy (Countess Tatyana Lvovna).

102. Hapgood to T. L. Tolstoy, June 9, 1892, SMT, 106 ATc no. 28964.

103. NYPL:IFH, box 4: Tolstoy (Letters from Count Leo Tolstoy, 1892–93).

104. Hapgood to S. A. Tolstoy, May 5, 1892, STM, T.c. 268 107 no. 38110.

105. NYPL:IFH, box 4: Tolstoy (Countess Tatyana Lvovna).

106. Hapgood to S. A. Tolstoy, May 13, 1892, STM, T.c. 268 107 no. 38111.

107. "New York Chamber of Commerce: Accounting by United States Minister Smith" (*New York Times*, May 8, 1892), p. 20 (col. 5).

108. Hapgood to L. N. Tolstoy, May 11, 1892, STM, 219 4.

109. NYPL:IFH, box 4: Tolstoy (Countess Tatyana Lvovna).

110. NYPL:IFH, box 4: Tolstoy (Countess Tatyana Lvovna).

111. Hapgood to T. L. Tolstoy, July 21, 1892, STM, 106 ATc no. 20965.

112. Hapgood to L. N. Tolstoy, June 22, 1892, STM, T.c. 219 5.

113. NYPL:IFH, box 4: Tolstoy (Letters from Count Leo Tolstoy, 1892–93).

114. Tolstoy had written the work throughout 1891and published it in May 1892 ("Pervaya stupen'" in the journal *Voprosy filosofii i psikhologii*, vol. 13).

115. Hapgood to L. N. Tolstoy, July 21, 1892, STM, T.c. 219 5.

116. The article appeared in English only several years later, in a translation by Leo Wiener in a volume of various religious works that appeared as part of the collected works of Tolstoy, *Walk in the Light While Ye Have Light: Thoughts and Aphorisms. Letters. Miscellanies*, Tula edition (Boston: Dana Estes, 1904).

117. NYPL:IFH, box 4: Tolstoy (Countess Tatyana Lvovna).

118. Hapgood to T. L. Tolstoy of July 30, 1892, SMT, ATc 106. no. 28966.

119. Jonas Stadling (1847–1935) wrote of the famine in Russia, the activity of the Tolstoys, and the ineffective government measures—see his *In the Land of Tolstoy: Experiences of Famine and Misrule in Russia*, trans. and ed. William Rison (New York, 1897). Stadling spent several days in Begichevka, then on March 3, 1892, traveled with L. L. Tolstoy and P. I. Biriukov to the Samara Province, where they worked on famine relief; see his "With Tolstoy in the Russian Famine," *Century Illustrated Monthly Magazine* 46, no. 2 (1893).

120. Madame L. T. Dovidoff, "Count Leon Tolstoi," *Cosmopolitan* 12 (April 1891): 719–24.

121. NYPL:IFH, box 4: Tolstoy (Countess Tatyana Lvovna). On the letter is written in Hapgood's hand: "Note: Mr. Stadling wrote an article for the *Century Magazine*—& the Century asked me to find out about him. This is the reply to my questions. I.F.H."

122. NYPL:IFH, box 4: Tolstoy (Letters from Count Leo Tolstoy, 1892–93).

123. Isabel Hapgood, "Famine: Count Tolstoï's Statement," *New York Times* (November 19, 1892), p. 3.

124. NYPL:IFH, box 4: Tolstoy (Countess Sophia Andreevna).

125. Hapgood to S. A. Tolstoy, October 9, 1892, STM, ACT 123, no. 16018.

126. Hapgood to S. A. Tolstoy, October 31, 1892, STM, ACT 123, no. 16020.

127. NYPL:IFH, box 4: Tolstoy (Countess Sophia Andreevna).

128. Hapgood to S. A. Tolstoy, December 6, STM, ACT 123, no. 16021.

129. He was successful in getting magazine rights to *Resurrection* but was unable to publish the novel without heavy cutting (*Cosmopolitan* was at that time a family publication), to which those in charge of the publication objected. See the letters of E. H. Crosby to Tolstoy of May 28 and October 17, 1899, Tolstoy's letter to Walker of July 10, 1899, and Walker's letter to Tolstoy of October 30. STM, 211 274; 211 276; PSS 72:157; STM T.c. 245 45.

130. Hapgood to L. N. Tolstoy, December 10, 1892, STM, T.c. 219 5.

131. NYPL:IFH, box 4: Tolstoy (Letters from Count Leo Tolstoy, 1892–93). The letter is written on a business card, on which is printed "Léon Tolstoi."

132. See Tolstoy's letter to Chertkov of March 17, PSS 87:182.

133. Hapgood to L. N. Tolstoy, April 28, 1893, STM, T.c. 219 6.

134. Leo Tolstoy, *The Kingdom of God Is within You; Or, Christianity Not As a*

Mystical Doctrine, but As a New Life-Conception, authorized translation from the original Russian MS., trans. Mrs. A. Delano. (Boston: D. Lothrop, 1894). Leo Tolstoy, *What People Live by,* trans. Mrs. Aline Delano. Illustrated ed. (Boston: D. Lothrop, 1886). Leo Tolstoy, *In Pursuit of Happiness,* trans. Aline Delano (Boston: D. Lothrop, 1887).

135. NYPL:IFH, box 4: Tolstoy (Letters from Count Leo Tolstoy, 1892–93).

136. Hapgood to L. N. Tolstoy, June 3, 1893, STM, ACT 123, no. 16024.

137. NYPL:IFH, box 4: Tolstoy (Countess Sophia Andreevna). The first two paragraphs are in English, the last two in Russian.

138. Hapgood to L. N. Tolstoy, September 30, 1894, STM, T.c. 219 6.

139. Hapgood to L. N. Tolstoy, July 16, 1895, STM, T.c. 219 6.

140. Hapgood to L. N. Tolstoy, July 22, 1897, STM, T.c. 219 6.

141. The French stage version by Henri Bataille was adapted for the American production by Michel Morton. The premier took place on February 17 at the Victoria Theatre.

142. The role of Katiusha was played by Blanche Walsh.

143. The role of Nekhliudov was played by Joseph Hayworth.

144. Hapgood to L. N. Tolstoy, February 19, 1903, STM, T.c. 219 6.

145. Hapgood to L. N. Tolstoy, July 22, 1897.

146. Orthodox Eastern Church, *Service Book of the Holy Orthodox-Catholic Apostolic (Greco-Russian) Church* (Boston and New York: Houghton, Mifflin, 1906).

147. See Philip Saliba, "Foreword to the Sixth Edition," in *Service Book of the Holy Orthodox-Catholic Apostolic Church* (Englewood, N.J.: Antiochan Orthodox Christian Archdiocese of North America, 1983).

Four Poems

Mark Rudman

Tell Me Why

I see no reason why the site of this excursus
just had to be Venice.

There are so many other places you might have chosen.
If you had kept an open mind and
used your noggin.

But you always had a hard head.
In more ways than one.

Oh hell, I was in Venice, I stayed at the Gritti—
I bet they wouldn't let you into the bar.

Then you did well on your Rabbi's salary.

It was a tour. I saw more in three days than you'd see in three weeks.

Venice is a tourist trap, and hideously expensive.
You could do so well for half the money in
>   *or*

I like the mists and fog.

Look out the window will you man, Manhattan has enough fog and mist
for two of you. Haven't you often noted, losing yourself in meditation
on the crosstown bus, that in weather like this, damp, warm, misty, that
(utterly accessible) Central Park is like a primeval world, dense, dark,
unfathomable? A place as appropriate to dinosaurs as to ourselves.

Yes.

Then why Venice where, as that poet with the girl's middle name has it,
by late autumn

It doesn't drift like bait any more, this city,
reeling in the days as they surface and flash.
The harder you look the harder the glass
palaces shake. The spent summer hangs

from garden fronds, like puppets thrown
in a pile, crumpled, beyond fatigue. . . .

in lines scribbled down prior to Dachau if I still have my dates in order.

Long before, but I hadn't thought of those heaped puppets in just
that way before.

There's a lot you haven't thought about.
Even by May of 1912
there were too many tourists in Venice
to satisfy Rilke's passion for solitude.

Don't you remember that one reason you chose
to stay in the desert
                              as long as you could,
given the limited decision making power
you had in those tender years—
was to clear your lungs,
to send your asthma
into hibernation
to   breathe — ?

And in addition to your mad wild inexhaustible
love of open spaces,
                              you used each occasion
to drive further and further from the city
limits, you rebelled
             against boundaries.

You and your friend, the one they nicknamed The Phantom, *were*
    never home.
Except to chow down.

The Phantom supplied the Corvair and I supplied the gas.

And you'll remember your father was the one
with the east east east mantra *who*
opposed your finishing high school in the desert

while I—since I was the one who had to drag
you to the doctors when you wheezed—went along
with your wishes.

There was something alluring about the idea of all that nothing
beyond the surrounding mountains.

And yet you longed to return.

All I have to do is say a word and you're back on the street again,
vagabond ragamuffin.

A day of cold rain is no obstacle; it is an enticement, even though
I still get nervous when I detect a slight wheeze in my lungs. Last
week's downpour of light—so dazzling I could hardly shield my eyes
from the glare. Now I'm also grateful for this dark downpour, the
thump of windshield wipers, the blur of traffic lights. I'm interested
to see who's doing what, who resorts to umbrellas, who carries on,
oblivious, lugging shopping bags on Broadway as the wet paper
looks like it will soon detach from the handles and remain on the
street while the carrier continues home, not empty-handed, but
with nothing more to show than handles.

The world rhythmically dying and flaring up again. You're looking ahead
to New Year's Eve when fireworks light up Rome's seven hills.

You're right. There are all the reasons in the world not to go to
Venice. Maybe the fragility of its future provoked me into thinking
differently about history. Here the devastation is so palpable. The
drips and leaks. The rheumatic gutters. The reduction (of life).

It's a place where extremities reveal themselves: where the extreme emotions stand in the foreground.

The pendulum moves from gaiety to language. Where else but in Venice would you find a middle-aged couple, clearly on marriage number two, three, or . . . behaving this way, meandering hand and hand on the Zattere, dressed auspiciously in white, their light hair lit by flares.

What would happen if you kept your eyes open beginning say, tomorrow morning, when you stop for a corn muffin and a cafe con leche at the Rosita beside Straus Park on 107th St. instead of the Rosati on the Piazza del Popolo? Maybe it's a state of mind, not the place . . .

Evening on the Zattere

There's a courtesan, out of Carpaccio. A masked reveler, out of Tiepolo.

There's Canaletto setting up his easel on the Grand Canal.

And Gaudi, another copyist.

It's true, I'm biased toward Tintoretto, his turbulence and agitation: in the "Slaughter of the Innocents" panel at the Scuola San Rocco, he shows a soldier hurling a baby with murderous force from the right foreground toward the center—and yet the baby's white swaddling is painted lightly as white gauze.

I heard he was relentless in his quest
to wrest commissions away from Titian.

Titian was the first choice for everyone
who wanted to be shown in the best light.

Tintoretto was a greedy schlemiel;
indiscriminate. And he lacked the skill
to make his objects and figures look real.

He had to struggle like hell to survive.

He would have painted the gondolas.

But whatever he painted, he made his own.

No one could deny that! And no century
has valued chaos and confusion
more than this one.

I wanted to laugh when I read in the Blue Guide for wanderers that Tintoretto's work expressed an "inner anxiety"; there's something comical about that kind of psychology, when applied to an artist, however self-evident or correct, being expressed in such a pat manner, all the more humorous for being so true.

Venice, a labyrinth of alleys. Palaces out of oriental tales. Everything swirls: skirts, parasols, the water in carafes, in canals, the bodies of the walkers who do not feel their own weight, the air in the baths and temples the gods have abandoned; the robes and draperies shimmering on his canvases.

Here is where I wish you were more adept at cabala. Numerology. You found your way to section five, the number's going to become increasingly significant, you enter fifty lines, and with the door wide open and the secret, the cusp of the enigma staring at you face to face, you're blinded.

(I note you only take off those dark sunglasses when it's dark indoors, or before the screen in a dark theater . . .).

Many have come to a bad end playing with numbers.

*

Sunset on the Zattere. Blaze of blue tile plaque marking the hotel where John Ruskin lived overlooking the Giudecca Canal. My mind wandered to the bizarre preponderance of naked breasts in Italian magazines, still a no no in America. Sam waved at a passing yachtsman. Madelaine sat, graceful, erect and still, taking in the majestic passage of the night, the slap of the waves roused to action by the passing motorboats. A group of teenage boys ran down to the dock where some poles were tied to stakes and lines let out to catch . . . monkfish? The skinny one stripped down to his blue polka-dotted bikini underpants and dove in. And climbed out. And walked up the steps adjacent to Ruskin's house where we were resting, hopped a guardrail, dove in, surfaced, and swam to shore, showing no awareness of the danger. (I guess he hadn't heard about the eye-infection—which never healed—that Kate Hepburn contracted doing her own stunts in *Summertime*.) Less than two centuries ago Byron could swim endlessly in these waters—turning out cantos of *Don Juan* at night on gin—and die of something more worthy of death than an infection accidentally contracted.

You mention breasts.

Just so.

And you mentioned Pavese's name without mentioning the terrific power of the scene in one of his early stories when a woman bares her breasts for an artist. It still has the power to shock even if its contents are unremarkable in themselves by today's jaded, world-weary, "nudity is old hat" standards. I'm talking about a violence and lust that polish, sophistication, even overexposure to the flesh cannot cover up. I'm talking about . . . surprise . . . being taken . . . unaware, like the time you saw the young woman you had known casually and "thought" attractive—but didn't think of too much—until you saw her running around the indoor track in her black tights and tee shirt, sweating, pushing her body to the limit yet remaining graceful and

it's true, sexy beyond the limits I had set for myself that day. I wasn't prepared to see her or be aroused and by the third time she passed I felt, you're right, a surge . . . that in my experience only happens when I'm surprised.

It hasn't happened to me that many times.

It can turn you into a voyeur, no?

*

Love at Last Sight

Years in the same apartment and never
any action in neighboring windows.
But tonight that has all changed: two stories
below, a couple has begun, under
direct light from a standing lamp; lying
side by side they touch each other's faces
tenderly, gently—he feels the down
on her cheek. Puts his tongue in her mouth
and rolls his thigh between her legs as
her hips bend her pelvis arches hard

and he is kissing or biting her softly
behind her ear; they've got a rhythm going now,
even with their clothes on.

It's the best hour. If it weren't dark,
the lamp would not be shining in their room and I would not
have caught her head twisting, her hair falling
across her eyes as she rocked and he reached
under her maroon turtleneck and his hand crept
upwards and she gradually became very still.
I hoped they hadn't stopped because they saw
me at the window: how could I explain my shock
at seeing them and not the vocal coach
in the always well-lit adjacent apartment
put another diva through her paces.

I'd gone to make sure the radiator
was on (it wasn't) when the light
flooding their window caught
my attention . . . and I couldn't look away.
I was in touch with both their heartbeats now.
As she crawled over him, stealthily,
she placed her buttocks on his hips
and gripped. Getting settled
was the most electric part of her dance.
She pulsed in hypnotic cadences,
tensing her buttocks and releasing them,
swooping down to kiss his neck,
whipping her hair across his face . . .

I liked the way she would pause,
collect herself and pull back
the chaos of her hair with both hands
while his pelvis edged her slightly upward
at the thighs. She taunted him
deliciously, tirelessly.
I didn't care if I could not see
the aureoles around her nipples.
I liked the way she leaned forward at the hips
and swept her hair across his lips and eyes.

Midsummer Night in Venice

What's the use of a Midsummer Night's Dream
without trampolines?

A diffuse, undirected aroma wafts through Venice tonight.

Perhaps the gods have not abandoned
these cathedral vaults.
The bells ring on time.
Eternal time.
Now.

Dreams surpassing explanations.

All—bottomless—

for the same reasons.

"There is no falling here . . . "

I have this sense that I am surrounded
by people falling in love with each other again,
familiars finding new qualities to marvel at—
as if they hadn't allowed their gaze to light on
their chosen mates for centuries.

Not years?

No, millennia.

Shadows in the dream green light.
Canal-ripple.

Who did the lightning?

My legs and feet can't keep pace with my desires.

Don't be ashamed. The water's there to foster illusions.

Venice: The Return in Winter

Destination: Venice: The Flight to Milan

This Christmas day the child and I are again
among a half-dozen on the packed
Boeing who keep watch through the long night.

Madelaine sleeps with Andrew Vachss's
Strega in hand, as if in mid-sentence.
And the quick-eyed, voluble

Italian woman with whom I waited
face to face in the vestibule
is now comatose under the blue blanket

she pulls over her eyes. Married to an
American, they live in Austin;
she misses Italy "in some ways, not all.

Nowhere else in Europe, perhaps on earth,
is there another people who still value
the quality of life over the glittering

temptations. I love American movies.
There's no glamor in Italian films and I'm
'up to here' with the poor . . . , always the poor."

Another woman is spread across an entire
middle aisle: her face as raw and harrowed
as one of Breughel's harvesters.

There's something suspect about people
who can fall asleep anywhere.
Three strong swigs of Jameson's and a knockout root-

canal-pain-killer a dear friend lent me
to quell the terrors of this night
flight over the devouring sea

bring me no closer to drowsiness;
besides, do you think the child and I would miss
the "it's free dad!" in-flight movie, and miss

"Tin Cup's" choosing to "go for it"
even though there's wind in his face
and water fronting the green;

or the armadillo meandering the panhandle
alone, backed by an accordion . . . :
"A little bit is better than nada."

Sam's too tall and hefty at 5'2"
and a hundred-and-twenty-odd pounds
to sit on my lap for our return,

but since already it's Christmas day
in our projected time zone
he's in present-heaven and self-proficient

with his new CDs and video games.
He thrills to the first sight of land,
Brussels?, the lights scarce and intermittent

like survivors' last flares.
We're still over France, onetime Nazi strongholds
Vichy and Lyon.

The insomniacs have one advantage
over the sleepers: we can await the white
peaks, immense and various, like islands

above the turfy clouds that cover 360
sky-degrees and be there when black night gives way
to charcoal blue-gray to day-it-self-breaking.

Thousands have passed this way every day
since jet travel took over the skies,
but does that make it one bit

less miraculous?

From *The Negro-Lover*

Joyce Carol Oates

The Way Out

25.

I am not a man for any woman to count on, I am not a man who wants to be loved.

But: love me.

Wanting to surprise him to make him happy. For what makes happy the one we adore makes us happy; what not, not; the universe is a void, an ink-well otherwise.

How many times contemplating stealing for him; in bookstores, contemplating books I knew Vernor would like; priming myself to steal for Vernor Matheius as I would never steal for myself—six-hundred-page annotated editions of Leibnitz, Hegel, Heidegger; commentaries on Wittgenstein's *Philosophical Investigations*; new translations of Nietzsche, Kierkegaard, Jaspers; Ernst Cassirer's essays on the mythic nature of language. Thinking, holding one of these books in my hand, *How happy it would make Vernor, to read this; not thinking, How transparent a ploy to make him love me.*

I never stole any books, I hadn't the courage perhaps, I could not work out how Vernor would respond if he discovered the books had been stolen for his sake; many times he'd expressed repugnance for any form of dishonesty, above all intellectual dishonesty; but also personal dishonesty; petty crime, Vernor believed, requires a petty soul.

The soul enslaved to habits, passions. The slave-soul.

Though I couldn't afford it, though I'd never fully repaid the money I owed, sometimes I bought Vernor gifts, small items out of secondhand shops: a handsome old fountain pen, a pair of onyx cuff links; things for which he had no use, I suppose; for his thirtieth birthday a silk vest in an elegant houndstooth check, on a silvery-gray background gossamer as smoke; when he'd unwrapped the vest he hadn't lifted it from the tissue paper at first, staring down at it, I worried that an item of apparel was too personal a gift and might offend him; but then he took it up, slipped it on and buttoned it frowning at himself ironically in the single mirror above the bureau in his room—"Hmm. Not bad." The silk vest had caught my eye in a secondhand clothing shop in Syracuse, how beautiful it had seemed to me: the elegant fabric, a row of small black buttons; an item of apparel for a gentleman; for Vernor Matheius. He hadn't seemed to mind that it was secondhand, "used"; its label had been carefully removed; to whom it had belonged, what its history was—no one knew. "Why do you buy me things like this, Anellia?" Vernor asked. "You don't have any money." Ignoring this I said, "You look very handsome in your silk vest, it fits you perfectly." He said, reprovingly, "I don't look 'handsome' and it doesn't fit 'perfectly' and I surely don't need a vest. But thank you." Smiling at me, so I believed he must love me, or someone who stood in my place.

Except if he was in one of his moods, in his moods he was another man. But: he wore the houndstooth-checked vest beneath his gray flannel jacket and took me out to dinner; a special occasion, it must have been; not to celebrate his birthday (which he didn't "celebrate"—this was weeks later, in June), nor the fellowship from the National Endowment he'd won; surprising me with the invitation which was the first time (as it would be the last time) we'd ever gone together to a restaurant of any quality, the Brass Rail in downtown Syracuse; Vernor clean-shaven and handsome in his silk vest, a necktie and jacket and the least rumpled of his trousers; I in the black silk dress with the long sleeves and the daring V-neck that dipped loosely to show a portion of my chest narrow and pale as cottage cheese, the very edges of my pale breasts. Around my neck I wore a thin, tarnished gold chain with a heart-shaped locket that had once belonged to my mother (or so I'd been told by my grandmother); my face was radiant with layers of makeup, my eyes shining; it terrified me to appear in public in such a way with Vernor Matheius, as if he were making a declaration about me at last, and about us; we walked downtown, a distance of over a mile, drawing stares on the street; as we entered the restaurant where Vernor had made a reservation he winked at me and pronounced that I looked just right; I looked the part; what part, I asked, and Vernor said the part of a college girl having dinner at the Brass Rail with a friend. In the Brass Rail when we appeared there was a ripple of—not sound but the absence of sound, inheld breath—and the maître d' with a stiff, somber expression wordlessly seated us at the very rear of the restaurant, near the entrance to the restrooms; as soon as we'd given our orders, Vernor reached across the table to take my hand, lifted it to kiss the fingertips; a gesture new to him, and to me; a gesture that both excited me and made me uneasy; for I was aware of other diners observing us; aware of strangers' eyes that, when I turned, shifted quickly away. Except there was a couple at a nearby table who stared rudely at us; middle-aged, white (of course: everyone in the restaurant was white except the busboys in dazzling-white uniforms who were black); this couple whispered to themselves through their meal, and ours; several times I cast the woman a sidelong frown but she continued to stare at me unperturbed, her bright lips turned downward in the way of the Dean of Women expressing profound disapproval, disgust. *You! aren't you ashamed of yourself!* Vernor drank wine, and gave no sign of noticing how we were watched; never had I seen him in any public place so seemingly relaxed, so assured; so aggressively assured; he laughed frequently, a loud jarring-barking laugh; I would have laughed with him but there was something forced and feverish about his behavior; I thought *This is not a man I know, this is a stranger.* Yet how exciting to be in the presence of such a stranger. For much of the meal he interrogated me in his Socratic manner; the relentless questioning that, fueled by wine, can at least be funny, lively; in his eloquent voice, the most musical of his voices, Vernor spoke just distinctly enough to be overheard at other tables; speaking of Heidegger's *Being and Time* which he was reading in German, an "untranslatable text"; in Heidegger it's the "weight" of language that is as significant as meaning; yet the paradox of language generally is that there is no single language, only languages; the tragic paradox is that each of us speaks and hears a language unlike any other. I said but people understand one another very well, sometimes, and Vernor said possibly, but how would you know?—for the conviction that one understands might be in itself a delusion. So strangely then Vernor began to speak of his background, his "ancestry"—Vernor Matheius who had seemed, until this moment, to have no personal history, no "ancestry" at all. He astonished me by saying matter-of-factly that his ancestors, those he could trace, had been the most fortunate of Africans brought to North America as slaves because they'd been sold up into the North, into Connecticut, in the 1780s; and in 1784 slavery was abolished in that enlightened state of the Union; there'd been no significant history of slavery in his background; which was why, he said, smiling, he seemed to have been born with a "free soul" and not a "black soul"; certainly he'd never had a "slave soul." He addressed me as if I'd been arguing with him, and needed to be convinced; he smiled, sipped wine, said, "Why then should I spend my life being 'Negro' for anyone's sake? I have a higher calling." I asked him where in Africa his ancestors had come from, and he shrugged, and said, "'Dahomey'—a place I know nothing about, not even its location," and changed the subject; we talked of families, identities; I realized that never since I'd known him had Vernor gone out of town, or spoke of visiting "home"; he never received mail that I knew of, or telephone calls; as he'd once told me, his home was in the mind; and this seemed quite literally true. I told him that I envied him; I would have liked to have been born with a "free soul" but I seemed to be caught in memories; I seemed to be defined by memories; I could not escape my memories; my dreams brought them to me, like the wind bearing seeds, scent. Vernor frowned at this; sometimes he liked my way of expressing myself, but not this way; bluntly he said, "No. You aren't defined by memory. You define yourself by the mental acts you choose to perform. You are free to choose identity by choosing a course of mental action that excludes other courses." Again he reached across the table to take my hand, awkwardly; he squeezed my fingers hard; as if I were slow, obstinate; as if I needed to be convinced. "I will try to believe that," I said, and Vernor said, lowering his voice, severely, "But you don't try hard enough, Anellia. You disappoint me," and I said, hurt, "I'm sorry," and Vernor said, baring his teeth in a smile like pain, "Anellia, there's something I want to tell you," and my heart contracted in dread *This is why he brought me here tonight, this is the end,* even as I was asking him what, what did he mean, and he said, "Let me ask you: what do you want from me?" and I said, faltering, trying to sound like a girl in a black silk dress with a dipping V-neck, a girl practiced in sexual wiles, seduction, "Only to be with you, Vernor," and he said, still squeezing my fingers hard, as if he felt both pity for me and impatience, "There isn't the opportunity for that, Anellia." As if he were making a statement about the weather; a fact not to be questioned, still less modified; he chose his words carefully as if each word had a price; as he sipped the last of his wine, drained the glass to the last of the darkish-red liquid, conscious of the price of each mouthful. I was smiling, my mouth ached with smiling; there was a roaring in my ears and I could not hear the rest of his words; Vernor's dark, large, fisted hand enclosed mine tightly as if protectively, raised from the table so that the backs of his knuckles grazed my left breast; a caress meant to comfort, not intimidate; there was nothing sexual in the gesture, yet I felt cold, infuriated eyes upon us; I hadn't the strength to confront them, nor even to draw back from Vernor's touch. The maître d' stood above us frowning, disapproving; explaining in a tone of perfunctory apology that our table had been reserved for another party, for nine-thirty; it was past nine-thirty now; we would have to leave as quickly as possible; here was our check, which could be paid at the front. Vernor stared up at the man—a white man in his mid-thirties, elegantly dressed in black tie, with a chiseled-looking face, insolent eyes—and seemed at first speechless with fury, or surprise; then, with deliberation, Vernor pushed back his chair, and stood, tall, knife-blade-lean, the checked silk vest catching the gleam of candlelight, and I got to my feet fumbling, confused; not seeing very well; my eyes blurred with moisture; Vernor was still gripping my hand, saying with icy, ironic politeness, "Fine. We are leaving, and you needn't worry we'll be back."

And there we are walking out of the Brass Rail! I try to see us but there's a blur, a haze, as in a dream that has begun to dissolve; most vividly there's the gray silk vest, and the black silk dress; most vividly the eyes that follow us, the eyes of strangers.

And afterward. Somehow we'd gotten drunk, or I was drunk; in Vernor's bed in Vernor's not-very-clean sheets smelling of both our bodies; in Vernor's arms that didn't close about me but held me loosely rocking me gently out of pity; or maybe I wasn't drunk but in a delirium of crying; couldn't stop crying; and Vernor saying, "Didn't I warn you, Anellia, I'm not a man for any woman to count on," and more softly, "Hey. Look. I wish I could love you the way you deserve, a girl like you," and I was saying, pleading, "Vernor, I can love enough for both." And still I was crying, the ridiculous makeup smeared and melting on my face, my hair disheveled, and Vernor said in that soft, resolute voice, "Maybe you should go away, Anellia. Maybe this should end," and I held myself very still, very still, not hearing.

To purify myself utterly. To become nothing, bare picked white bones. And then I will be free.

26.

Three days later on June 12, 1963, a young black NAACP field secretary named Medgar Evers was shot in the back by a white racist as he stood in the doorway of his home in Jackson, Mississippi; and Vernor began drinking heavily, and got sick; days passed and he refused to leave his apartment, or to dress, or wash himself; he'd told me to stay away from him but I took advantage of his illness, his weakness; every day, sometimes twice a day I went to his apartment where the door might be locked against me and no amount of pleading could induce Vernor to open it or the door might be unlocked and I would enter in dread, anticipation, almost unbearable hope. *Why! why are you doing this, why when I don't want you!* and my unvoiced answer *I have told you: I can love enough for both.* Much of the time Vernor lay in a stupor on top of his disheveled and foul-smelling bed staring at the ceiling with glassy stark eyes beyond irony; beyond even sarcasm; his thin, bony chest rose and fell with the effort of his breathing which was irregular as if forced; as if breathing had become an act of will, and that will tinged with angry reluctance. *Vernor? Vernor?* I would whisper leaning over him, or sitting beside him and touching his damp forehead with the flat of my hand; like a sick, irritable child he might shove my hand away but like a sick, irritable child he hadn't the strength to keep shoving, resisting. Of Medger Evers he said contemptuously *That's what happens when you step into history: you get erased from it.* There were times when he ranted, swore; in a fury of sobbing he trashed his room, threw down books and papers; tore down the marmoreal likenesses of Socrates and Descartes which I discovered in tatters on the floor, never to be pieced together again; in the effort of lowering shades over his windows he'd ripped them from their rollers and they dangled in strips and shreds, which I removed; there was broken glass underfoot, there were cigarette butts, ashes; the room stank of beer, smoke, and of scorch; there were myriad burn marks in the bedclothes; I worried that Vernor would burn himself up in his bed, set the entire apartment building on fire in his fury.

On his desk that looked ransacked the portable Olivetti remained though shoved back askew, a sheet of paper partly ripped from it; on this sheet of paper there were many XXXXXXXs and only a single paragraph legible—

Axiom: if (following LW) the propositional sign is assigned a projective "relation" to the world does it therefore follow that the use of the perceptible sign of a proposition (spoken or written) is a projection of a possible situation? (See LW, 3.11)

I understood only that "LW" was Ludwig Wittgenstein; I did not dare inquire about the argument itself, which must have been a part of Vernor's doctoral dissertation; for Vernor was in no mood to indulge me. My task was to care for him, and this I did with energy, resolution and good humor; I would be his nurse, and he would see how I loved him, and did not judge him; for you do not judge the sick, you nurse them back to health; you nurse them back to sanity; you nurse them back to their true selves; I brought Vernor food to prepare for him; on his worst days, he had no appetite, food disgusted him and he could tolerate only soup; a thin broth of a soup in which I cooked sliced vegetables; I was a woman in an old tale, a legend in which a love potion is mixed with a man's food; an unsuspecting man's food; I thought I would cut my finger with a paring knife and allow a drop or two of my blood to fall into the soup for Vernor; so frequently did I fantasize this, I came to think I'd actually done it; perhaps in fact I had done it; but no crude wish-magic would work on a man like Vernor Matheius. I had to be content with being tolerated in his presence; I had to take pride that he would eat what I prepared for him at all; I convinced him to eat a piece of toast, two pieces of toast; it was a triumph for me the morning I convinced him to eat a boiled egg, and toast; I sat beside him at the tiny Formica-topped table that was his dining table and watched as he ate, his face ugly as if distorted with grief; grief indistinguishable from rage; rage indistinguishable from grief; he wore a filthy undershirt, and sat hunched, breathing harshly, almost panting, beads of oily sweat on his forehead and his eyeballs starkly white, furious; rarely in his sickness did Vernor wear his glasses; his gaze upon me, when it fell upon me, was intimate, intense and accusing *I'm sick to death, my guts are sick, God damn you let me alone, can't you see I detest you, your cunt, the color of your skin repulses me.*

I was not sick but Vernor's sickness pervaded me like a sweet, cloying odor; unresisting I entered into his delirium as sometimes (if he did not repel me) I lay beside him on his rumpled bed gripping his hand; curving his fingers around mine so that it was as if he were gripping my hand; his long steely-strong fingers enclosing mine; as in the restaurant nudging against my breast; my breathing quickened, or slowed, with Vernor's breath; we lay together side by side like carved funerary figures in a suspension that would have looked, to a neutral observer, like peace, tranquility; love's aftermath.

Why? why are you doing this!
Because I can love enough for both.

In gray-soiled underwear Vernor Matheius lay on his bed, like a fallen prince amid gray-soiled sheets; he smoked cigarettes, letting ashes scatter and fall into the bedclothes, and onto the floor; when, late one afternoon, hazy June heat pervading the apartment, he rose on shaky legs to take a shower, I took heart; I thought *This is a turn, he will be himself again* and so it seemed to be. Six days and six nights had passed since the onset of his sickness; his abrupt and mysterious collapse; six days and six nights since the murder of Medgar Evers in that pattern of mad accelerating cruelty and violence against civil rights activists that would culminate, in April 1968, in the assassination of the Reverend Martin Luther King, Jr.; in that future blowing toward us like a dark, ravening wind. *When you step into history, you get erased from it.* I did not think at that time *When you exclude yourself from history, you get erased from it* for at that time I was thinking solely of Vernor Matheius; while he was out of the room I hurriedly began to clean; stripped the soiled bedclothes from the mattress with the intention of taking them to a laundromat; I would add Vernor's towels when he finished showering; I would add as many of Vernor's clothes as he would allow. I found a broom, and swept the filthy floor; emptied dustpans of cigarette butts, ashes, crumpled papers and bits of dried food and dirt into a brimming wastebasket; collected the empty beer cans and others that had accumulated; carried the trash downstairs to a bin at the rear of the building. *As if I live here. I live here, with Vernor Matheius.* I wished I'd encountered another tenant of the building so that I might have behaved in a calm, matter-of-fact way. So that I might exchange hellos, comments on the weather. In the muggy June heat I was strangely energized, excited; I took childish happiness in such simple, direct physical tasks as I would never have taken in cleaning my own now largely abandoned room in the residence hall. A mocking voice lifted in a thin soprano *Negro-lover! Nigger-lover!* and more masculine guttural voices but I did not glance around for of course there was no one; no one observed me; no one passed judgment on me; I was alone.

Upstairs in Vernor's apartment while he was still in the bathroom I set about restoring order on top of his desk; his desk I'd so admired, now in a chaos; except for the Olivetti, everything had been knocked about; I hoped to rearrange numerous scattered papers (pages from Vernor's dissertation?) into their original neat stacks; but I could not make sense of them, and gave up. Stealthily then I slid open one of the filing cabinet drawers; the filing cabinets were made of pale green battered-scratched aluminum; Vernor had bought them for five dollars each at a bankruptcy sale of office supplies; the drawer was crammed with manila folders containing more papers, notecards; some of the folders were meticulously neat, and others were not. I knew I should not be looking into Vernor Matheius's folders yet I couldn't resist; here was a treasure trove of old, yellowing papers, neatly typed outlines of books of the Bible including such obscure books as *Jeremiah, Hosea, Philippians*, and *Thessalonians* as well as most of the books of the New Testament; in a large and passionate hand not immediately recognizable as Vernor's were written in columns the names of magical-Biblical figures—*Moses, Jacob, Joshua, Elisha, Job, Jesus, Mark, Paul, Mary Magdalene*—as if these names belonged to individuals known to Vernor Matheius. In other folders, farther back in the drawer, were more notes and outlines; theology, philosophy, ethics; most of these written in a bold, rapid hand, no more than a dozen lines to a page, as if thoughts had spilled out Vernor's teeming mind out onto the paper, scarcely contained in language. I smiled to see his college papers: neatly typed, held together with rust-stained paper clips; with such titles as "The 'Problem of Evil' in Milton's *Paradise Lost*," "The Concept of 'Virtue' in Epicureanism," "The Concept of 'Mind' in Bertrand Russell"; if there were red marks on these papers, the marks indicated enthusiasm, praise; Vernor Matheius's grades were uniformly A and A+. I tried to summon up a younger, vulnerable Vernor Matheius, an undergraduate hoping to impress his professors; how difficult to imagine arrogant Vernor Matheius perceiving himself in a position inferior to anyone. Then staring into another folder I'd carelessly opened, at what appeared to be razored-out pages from magazines and books; an essay on Plato's *Laws* removed from an issue of the *Journal of Philosophical Inquiry*, Fall 1961; a chapter from a study of Spinoza; a chapter from a study of Kant; several diagrammed pages from an essay on symbolic logic; had Vernor Matheius removed these from magazine and books not belonging to him? *But he would not do such a thing! Not Vernor Matheius!* Peering now into another folder at the very rear of the drawer, almost hidden from sight; packets of badly wrinkled letters and snapshots; some of the older snapshots were in black and white, the rest in bright color; I was staring at brown-skinned strangers, and at Vernor Matheius in their midst; he was a younger man than I knew, in his early twenties perhaps; tall, lean, unsmiling standing beside a plump, happily smiling young woman with an infant in her arms and clinging to her leg and, laughing at the camera, a boy of about two; an attractive young woman with full, fleshy lips and a wide nose; a beautiful little boy with Vernor's narrow features; the snapshot had been taken out-of-doors in a grassy rural setting, a woodframe house in the background; it had been taken in a season of flowering fruit trees, forsythia and dogwood; there was a preacherly look to Vernor in his tight dark suit, white long-sleeved shirt and dark tight-knotted tie; a tie I recognized; the very tie he'd worn with the silvery-gray silk vest; his eyeglasses were not wire-rimmed but black plastic; he was standing just slightly apart from the smiling others staring moodily at the camera and beyond the camera as if already he were edging out of the frame, planning his escape. On the back of the snapshot was May 1959. *So he's married, has been married. Has a family, children. So he lied.*

I let the snapshot fall, my hands were trembling. That familiar sickening rush of blood into my ears. In that instant my love for Vernor Matheius contracted like an outstretched hand closing into a small hard fist.

There was a sound behind me, Vernor's bare feet slapping against the floor; I felt the vibrations of his footsteps before I heard or saw him; his fingers gripping my shoulder, shoving me away from the opened filing cabinet; and he slammed the drawer shut, and cursed me—"God damn you, Anellia! Get out of here!" His face was contorted in fury, and in chagrin; his wire-rimmed glasses, the lenses still faintly clouded with steam from the bathroom, were askew on his face; his skin had darkened with blood. I pushed at Vernor's hand to protect myself—he was shoving me, hard—I pushed at his bare chest, as he was crowding me; he pushed back at me, and caught the side of my face with the back of his hand; his hard, flying hand; I cried out, ducked and stumbled for the door; he cursed after me as I ran away, panting and sobbing on the stairs as a low, stricken, despairing voice called after me like a wail of grief I pressed my hands over my ears to keep from hearing. *Get away get out of here don't ever come back fuck you! fuck you white bitch!*

27.

> By space the universe encompasses and swallows me up like an atom;
> by thought I comprehend the world.—*Pascal*

Yet: I sat hunched hugging my knees at the foot of the stairs staring out at the rain; it was hours later, very dark and steadily raining; a steamy mist rose from the pavement; how long I'd been sitting there entranced with grief, how long I'd been away from Vernor raging after me and returned at last wet from the rain, my hair dripping in my face and my clothes soaked, I could not have said; I had lost a sense of time; though hearing the tolling of the clock in the bell tower of the Music College every quarter-hour, like a giant pulsebeat; yet unable to comprehend its meaning. The night sky was opaque, utterly lightless; a heavy sky, a suffocating sky; I was no longer crying; I had ceased crying; I thought *I will never cry again, no one will ever have the power to hurt me again*; and this would be so. I felt Vernor's fingers gripping my shoulder, I saw again his look of rage, disgust, yet guilt; I had peered too deeply into his soul for him to forgive me; I had gone too far; he had loved me or had almost loved me or had begun to allow himself to consider that he might love me or in any case he had begun to allow himself to consider that he might allow me to love him without irony; and I had destroyed that, I had destroyed my own happiness; I had destroyed the purity of my love for him; I had destroyed Anellia, who was such a fool. It was Anellia's hair dripping into her face, Anellia's thin arms, legs pressed tight against her body in an effort to keep from shivering convulsively in the chill rain; Anellia whose soul quavered at the very edge of extinction; about to be sucked into the void, which was nothingness; for what was there after all except atoms and the void, which was nothingness. Yet I saw with certainty what I would do: I would return to my room and throw my pathetic-glamorous secondhand clothing onto the floor, in a heap; I would cut it to pieces with a scissors, as once in a burst of angry joy I'd cut my long tangled hair; stepping out of my costume-clothes, stepping out of my suffocating hair, like a newborn creature; I would snatch up the silver belt that fitted my small waist so exotically and I would tear at it until the carved medallions broke apart and clattered to the floor; my heart beat hard with the certainty of all I would do, and would never regret doing; I would join demonstrators marching and chanting and waving handmade signs; I would join CORE, I would join SANE; I would be fearless though terrified inviting jeers, threats from white faces, thrown objects like beer cans, rotted fruit, rocks and scraps of lumber; I would expose my heart, as I would expose my body; I would be vulnerable, I would expiate my guilt; I would remake myself another time, empowered by loss, grief. No longer Anellia. Waiting to see who I might be, after Anellia.

And there came at last Vernor's voice down the stairs. And it was a voice of sobriety, chagrin; a voice still tremulous with emotion; a raw voice, a voice of hurt, dismay. "Anellia, is that you? Jesus." And my heart continued to beat calmly with the certainty of what I would do, and what I would not do; what I would not ever do again; and I did not turn to look up at Vernor Matheius. I would not turn to look up at Vernor Matheius. Slowly then like a drunken man or a sleepwalker he descended the stairs; gripping the railing, he descended the stairs; I guessed he was barefoot, and only partly dressed; he'd pulled on trousers, possibly a clean t-shirt; he was breathing quickly, panting. On the step just above me he paused, he was looking down at me, I had a childish fear that he would kick me in a sudden eruption of fury; but he said, "Anellia, you shouldn't be here. You'll only be hurt," and there was a pause as if he had more to say but he said nothing, and I said nothing; he stepped down then to sit beside me so I eased aside to make room for him as if it was the most natural thing in the world for us to sit together in the dark, in the rain; Vernor lit a cigarette, and expelled smoke through his nostrils, and after some minutes of silence said, "I don't have a black soul. Because I don't have a black soul, I don't have any soul at all." I said quickly, "I thought you didn't believe in 'soul.' I thought you didn't believe in personal 'identity.'" He said, "I don't. The way a color-blind person doesn't 'believe' in color because he has never experienced it." There was bemusement in this remark, and sadness; a sadness I'd never heard in Vernor Matheius before. I said, "You have a family? Children?" and he said, "No longer," and I said, "What do you mean, 'no longer'?" and he shrugged and said nothing and I said, my voice quavering with indignation I hadn't known I could feel, "You left your wife and children behind? Where are they? How could you do such a thing, Vernor?" and Vernor said curtly, "It's none of your God-damned concern who or what I left behind me or who or what I am. Or what you or anyone else expects of me." And I said nothing, but I did not acquiesce; and Vernor sucked at his cigarette, and released clouds of stinging smoke; and it crossed my mind light as a feather blown by the wind that I would not miss this: the stinging smoke, the stink of cigarettes: I would not miss this at all. We watched a car pass in the rain, splashing through slick gleaming puddles; there were rivulets of water rushing down Chambers Street, down the steep slope from the university hospital complex. And at last Vernor said in a flat, clinical voice, a voice from which all romance and pretension have drained, "My ancestors I told you about. They were from Dahomey, they were tribal people, they were captured and brought to North America as slaves in the 1870s, but they'd been slave-traders themselves for decades. This was a secret imparted to me when I turned twenty-one by my mother's grandfather who was a minister. That my ancestors, his ancestors had sold other Africans, other tribes, to white slavers." I was staring at Vernor in disbelief; in shock; this was a man out of whose mouth revelations emerged; I'd believed I could predict him at last, and yet I could not have predicted him; never could I have predicted the sorrow in his voice, and the resignation. Yet there came his wry, bitter humor, his grimacing grin and sidelong squint as if after all he and I were allies in this predicament; this problem; as if the problem of Vernor Matheius were an intellectual puzzle we might contemplate together and attempt to solve; like ardent students of philosophy devoted to analyzing, assessing, defining truth; enjoined in a single passionate quest for truth which is after all the philosopher's life-work, a labor that transcends personal happiness. He said bitterly, "Why judge them? My so-called ancestors? They were human beings and like all human beings they were cruel, xenophobic; they were primitive people in a tribal society and members of other tribes aren't perceived as fully human, or significant, in such societies; you can kill them, you can sell them into slavery, you can practice genocide, like the Germans of the Third Reich, and it's 'natural'; it's 'nature'; it's instinct. So my ancestors sold their brother and sister Africans into slavery and they flourished for a while until it was their turn to be slaves. White men's trading ships sailed from Liverpool, England, to the west coast of Africa and traded textiles, arms and other cargo for black men and women; the ship sailed across the Atlantic to Jamaica where the black men and women were traded for sugar, which was brought back to England to be sold; the ship sailed from Liverpool to the west coast of Africa and loaded up with black men and women; and so on, and so forth; it was a lucrative business, there was a seemingly inexhaustible supply of black men and women, everyone flourished except those with the bad luck to be designated as 'slaves.'"

Vernor spoke flatly; his was a recitation of mere facts; incontestable facts; yet every syllable was damning; every syllable was a shriek. Gently I touched his arm and said, "Vernor, you aren't your ancestors, any more than I am my ancestors," and Vernor said, "Then I'm no one. I don't know who the hell I am," and I said, "Why should it matter?" For wasn't there a dimension of pure rationality, pure logic and a language pruned of all sentiment, all history, wasn't such a dream possible? And Vernor said, for even in a moment of tenderness and exhaustion Vernor Matheius was a man to have the final word, "Yes, why should it matter? Yet it does." How strange, how uncanny to be sitting beside Vernor Matheius on these stairs just slightly rotted, just slightly giving beneath our combined weight; a couple sitting together outside their apartment building perhaps, one of them smoking, gazing out into the rain; summer rain in thin slanted skeins blown along the pavement with a look of antic excitement. There came a faint sweet tolling from the Music College tower, more chimes than I could count; it must have been midnight. How strange, how uncanny and how wonderful, what happiness flooded my heart as on the eve of my twentieth birthday I sat beside Vernor Matheius on the lower steps of the outdoor stairway of the shabby stucco apartment building at 1183 Chambers Street, Syracuse, New York on the rainy night of June 18, 1963.

If you'd driven by, and seen that couple, wondering who they were, they were us.

Three Poems

Rachel Hadas

The Banquet

In both dreams about my father he is alive again, but in a public place: first in an auditorium after the lecture in a clump of people and then at a banquet where I'm an anonymous guest if I'm a guest at all.

My presence is either an embarrassment or else transparent.

In the first dream, although he acknowledged me I was one of a group surrounding him, so I had to wait in turn to congratulate him for the brilliant lecture.

But he was also me—talking to strangers, admired, greeted, distant.

In today's dawn dream he was at an official university banquet trying to persuade the carefully chosen administrators there of something. He was not the master of ceremonies, he was one more honored guest, but also somehow responsible for everything.

He got drunk with attention and began to be indiscreet, too emphatic, it was reported to me later.

Feta cheese crumbled visibly in his open mouth like a stigma of greed, but it was in the mouths of others as well. Still, things were becoming desperate.

And then offstage he was removed from the scene.

Offstage? As from a messenger in Greek tragedy I heard about it from my mother.

And I think it was I who broached the hard questions one after another: *Is he in the hospital? Did he have a stroke? Can he speak?*

and to each question the answer was the wrong one, the bad one, as I had known and she had known I would know it would be.

There was no chance, then, to say goodbye. He was removed invisibly, neither alive nor dead.

Not having been present, I lacked even the slightest sense of what the people with him there in the banquet hall had seen or exactly how when and why in detail it all happened.

Which is all minutely accurate, true of the actual death of my father as it was reported to me or rather as it never was reported in any detail at all.

So when people are thinking about how their secondhand Toyota truck with its 300,000 miles and its many journeys and various repairs is an emblem of their lives,

or—my own favorite—when they take stock of every stitch of clothing they're wearing, every piece of jewelry or scar, bruise, burn, cut, prosthetic device, or love bite, exactly where and when and how they acquired it,

they might remember also to try to conjure in memory or recreate from eyewitness reports what the death (at which they were not present) of someone they loved might have been like.

But we have a built-in lack of curiosity, to say the least, about these matters; we are hardly permitted to get to the bedside, and we're not in a huge hurry even if we are permitted, and even if we are there then often we cannot bear to remember or perhaps are not even meant to remember precisely what it was we saw.

Thus when my mother died around noon the doctor called by two to tell me but the machine was on and he left a message on the machine for me to call him but did not—apparently doctors are trained not to—leave word why I should call him,

and when I did call him at three or four his service could not get through to him and the upshot was that I went to visit my mother early that mild May evening and found her bed made up, spick and span, empty in an empty room.

I had forgotten all this—it was almost five years ago—or rather was evidently storing somewhere a perfect memory of it but I had forgotten I remembered. Who wants to remember? And who wants to forget?

But my dreams remembered, although in this dawn's dream my mother appeared characteristically only in the ancillary guise of messenger to tell me about the death of the protagonist as if she were not herself worth remembering and mourning in the dream as one who had also subsequently died.

The other disturbing detail was that at the beginning of the banquet, which—have I already said this?—was some official function sponsored by Columbia—

early in this dream feast the figure in the hot seat, as it were, was not my father, it was my husband,

but he slipped away at some point midmeal as soundlessly as later in the dream my father, who had replaced him, also did,

though not, I hope, I fear, for the same reason, mortal exhaustion and terminal illness.

But the silent oiled automatic merciless quality of this disappearance—these twin disappearances—made me lonely for him on awakening and apprehensive,

love entering, as so often, late through a door marked Exit,
    the white world of the morning, the blank windows of day rich with the fading splendor of a dream about loss and silence,

leaving me as I woke with a clear image (but was it from after or before I opened my eyes?) of a shining white-painted ceiling and in the middle of it the nipple-like carved protrusion of an ornate floral arrangement,

the kind of ornament one might stare at while flat on one's back in bed or on a stretcher or on the floor

but also reminiscent of a wedding cake or any sort of centerpiece on a banquet table,

Miss Havisham's moldy wedding cake and the spiders silently rushing over it and over the ragged yellow-white lace tablecloth flashing through my mind at this point.

But not only was I unsure whether it was a dream vision or something I saw when I woke up or had seen at some time earlier, the day, the week, earlier in my life before;

I also had no way of knowing whether it was the last sight that had met my father's fading eyes at the very moment when he was felled at the white dream banquet

or for that matter whether in the dream this nipply thing had been seen by my husband as he was silently wheeled off the scene and replaced by an older man whom the same university had sheltered, Alma Mater, and worn out,

and I did not assist, French *assister*, to be present as at an event, but "assist" in English has a simpler, more active meaning,

I was not there to help them.

The Caravan

in memory of Dulcie Holden Maynard
1955–1995

A blank dreams do their best to fill,
or smashing like a fist,
her lack maneuvers nightly
to make itself more space.

As if room for grieving
were only found between
the cracks of our continuing
campaign to love our own!

The urge in the grip of mourning,
the wish in the teeth of loss
is to retreat, fold inward,
and shrinkingly embrace

our dear ones, cherish all the more
our version of the life
lost by just the person
occasioning this grief.

Dulcie, so abruptly
erased from summer's map,
whom I remember bending
to children on her lap,

moves on now—we all do—
in the great caravan
composed of both the newly dead
and what still seems our own.

Painfully and slowly,
the pull is nonetheless
away from what we thought we knew
and loved to someplace else.

The Week after Easter

Saturday. Suburban funeral.
Emerging into skimpy April sun,
"of course what all this means is vertical,"
said my companion.
She sketched a swift diagonal
from heaven to hell—

gesture that left it up to me to trace
the arc in my imagination.
Golden forsythia haloed half the place,
but close up something dark was in slow motion:
a receiving line, inching along.
All this was horizontal. She was wrong.

Lift up your heart, the funeral mass advised.
My heart slid sideways as I eyed each face—
so many terrestrial creatures poised
at a mortal crossroads. East or west—
which way were we to head,
buttonholed by the living and the dead?

One bee last Sunday, drunk with its success,
negotiated blossoms in the park
where I was stretched out motionless
in blazing sun; who woke up in the dark
Monday morning to tattoos of hail,
magnolia blossoms battered in the gale.

Dramatic weather? Just a pale reflection
of Holy Week's impassioned allegory.
Hot on the heels of the Crucifixion,
the Resurrection salvages the story
and rescues history. Last yields to first,
the best redeemed—enabled—by the worst.

Silvery lilies, trumpet-tongued, proclaim
their clanging gospel to the air.
Exactly at this crux of space and time
believers throng toward a single stair,
a narrow window opening—a gate—
ladder to heaven. Quick! Do not be late!—

and vanish. We who opt to stay below
survive and flail,
coping with spring's successions: flowers/snow;
sunbath on Easter Sunday/Monday, hail;
the agitated season's swoop and veer.
Tuesday noon, eyes narrowed from the glare

of sun on ice, I venture out in search
of solace? celebration?
Both, it seems; the florist's, atheists' church,
being my destination.
The warmth, the fragrant moisture . . . I breathe deep,
tugged by anxiety and stroked by hope.

People I love keep falling from the scene.
Their histories melt away like winter ice
in synch with leaves routinely turning green:
changes that must be faced. But both at once?
Arms full of flowers, I linger in the sweet
air inside, then move toward the street.

From *Incisions*

Gabriel Motola

1. Shazam!

Because the woman is the vessel in whom is contained and through whom flows the history of the race and thus, so Jews contend, determines the kinship of the child, the mother must be descended from the faith while the father, who carries out the law, need not be. Thus blood carries truths language cannot translate. Born in the Bronx of a Sephardic mother and father, themselves born in the Ottoman Empire, in which their families had lived for hundreds of years, having been exiled by their native Spain whose language they still spoke and sang in the same ancient manner even if they wrote it in Hebrew, Daniel Peirera, the ancient lineage flowing through his veins, understood the language but did not speak it, read the Hebrew but neither spoke nor understood it. His name a reminder of the history of his ancestors, a history his own parents barely understood, Daniel read and spoke and wrote English, the language of the living. Forced by her parents to leave Greece because a non-Jew, a young naval officer, fell in love with and wanted to marry her, threatened to kidnap and take her away from Salonika to parts of Greece where Jews did not live, Daniel's mother at age sixteen or seventeen, arrived in New York in 1921, excited by the new land, not afraid of the new language, knowing Greek and French as well as her native Ladino, having witnessed from an upper floor window as a girl of four or five by the light of the moon the burying of an egg which contained her maiden aunt's madness for reasons only known to the Jews of ancient Iberia, having forgotten as she stepped off the gangplank the face of the Greek naval officer, whose passion was responsible for her arrival, whose white starched uniform, made more dramatic by the casually fluttering tasseled brocade, she would always remember. Taken in by an aunt who was not mad and an uncle who was lascivious in New Brunswick, New Jersey, too remote from New York City where, after sewing skirts all day, she would be able, uninhibited by the strictures of a too loving mother and father, to tango and Charleston all night in still white Harlem dance halls with young men of different religions and nationalities, where the Babel of languages resonated, bursting passions laughingly applauded, differences deliberately blurred. Isabella Abravanel, having insinuated to her mother's first cousin and her husband, whose two grown daughters were married, living on 116th Street and Madison Avenue that her mother's sister's husband was too affectionate with her when her aunt was out, she was able to move in with them and be exactly where she wanted to live in New York City. Working in the sweatshops on the Lower East Side with other Jewish and Italian seamstresses who labored over their Singer sewing machines for ten hours to earn a dollar, who laughed and sang because they were young, free of their tiny villages, of domineering fathers, of suspicious brothers and handpicked suitors, where with other teenage girls who worked, but not so fast or adroitly as she did, on machines that sewed a hundred times faster than their mothers' gnarled hands, Bella, as she renamed herself, because it suited her view of herself, the view others had of her, sang loudest and most beautifully both in Spanish and Italian, satisfying all the other girls, even if they didn't understand or hear the words to the songs, who saw open before them the same clear blue horizons, their bent necks and crooked fingers yoked to the whirring thread that bobbed through the needle that stitched the material into skirts. Bella laughed and sang, took pride in her ability as a maker of skirts, an operator, the trade she had learned from a French seamstress her father had hired for her when she was a girl in Salonika. Bella always recited to her children the story of how her father paid for her lessons in gold, pieces of gold that Daniel saw falling from his unknown grandfather's hands into the hands of a seamstress whose Gallic haughtiness was met by his Semitic certainty shaken nevertheless by his daughter's insistence that she be made a dressmaker, not a lifeless student poring over books. Proud of her ability to create, to fashion, to make a skirt or dress, a jacket or coat from rolled yards of multicolored fabrics, proud of her *bendichos manos*, Bella later became ashamed of her struggle to read a newspaper, to write a letter to her parents and brother and sisters, of her inability to figure the simplest calculations, to multiply the number of skirts she created by the price of the skirt so that she wouldn't be cheated by the owners of the sweatshops. Daniel had to do her figuring, starting when he was a boy not yet thirteen, to whom she increasingly turned, his father the night manager of a 42nd Street diner, his sisters good enough for cleaning and shopping and cooking but not for the mental calculations that demanded precision to the penny. And though she lamented the fact that her lack of education prevented her from becoming a star, a fashion designer, a woman of substance, Bella, the beautiful one, took pleasure in her melodic voice, in her creative eye, in her children, especially in her son who had the looks and intelligence, the seriousness and discipline that characterized her own father whose name he carried, because her husband's father had had the same name, perhaps the only fortuitous circumstance that graced the union of Isabella Abravanel and Yeshua Peirera. In satisfying the Sephardic custom to name the first born son after the living paternal grandfather, Yeshua, trembling with pride during the circumcision ceremony, their family and friends in attendance, their glasses of homemade raki raised high, loudly proclaimed the name of his son to be that of his father. But when Bella crooned her son's name in his ear she knew it was her father's.

Having fled Istanbul to escape being drafted into the Turkish army, Yeshua Peirera hardly spoke of his father and mother whom he left there with the one remaining sister—his two other sisters having gone to Casablanca and Jerusalem, his two brothers to Lima, Peru and Havana, Cuba. Unlike Bella, Yeshua never spoke of his childhood, of his father's employment, of his mother's cooking. Handsome, self-assured, and voluble, Yeshua wooed and won the beautiful Isabella who took his superficiality for nonchalance, his stubbornness for character. Proud of her beauty, her singing and dancing, her cooking and sewing, Joe, arrived at after Yeshua became Joshua which became Joseph, brought home friends and coworkers to show her off. He brought flowers and candy to his Bella who objected to his extravagances but bragged to her family and friends how her husband showered her with love and affection. Working in a grocery store, in a luncheonette, squeezing orange juice and grilling hot dogs, Joe strove to climb the economic ladder, thinking that the climb to the second rung from the bottom was a mighty achievement, wanting his wife to exalt in his success as an assistant night manager in a twenty-four hour hot dog stand in midtown Manhattan, those beneath him consisting of two men, a compulsive gambler, an unmarried Cuban in his late fifties, and a nineteen-year-old Greek, recently arrived, who was sent by his family so he could bring over his three younger brothers who would then all work to bring their parents and two older sisters. Joe relished his job, working for the Ventano brothers, Sephardim who had arrived a couple of years before Joe did, and now had six bustling hot dog stands—two in Manhattan, three in the Bronx, and one in Coney Island.

There was no telling how much money these brothers would earn before they reached forty. And Joe was already, at twenty-eight in 1930, an assistant night manager during the depression when other men were unemployed, having to wait on soup lines for a handout, something Joe would never allow his family to suffer. He would work twelve hours a day, six days a week, for his thirty dollars a week plus tips and look forward to the time when, in the not too distant future, he would own his own restaurant, fancier than a hot dog stand, and become a rich man, more generous than the ones he knew and more gregarious, sharing his wealth with, and patting the backs of, those not so fortunate as he, having not only wealth but a wife like Bella who, though now still working in the sweatshop in order to put aside her salary so he could run his own business, would never have to work again. She would take care of their sons, four sons so Joe would not only be assured of a place in Heaven but also have proper heirs to carry on the huge food empire that he, before having reached forty years of age, would have created.

In 1931, their first daughter was born, and Bella stopped working. Eugenie, named after his mother, was robust, playful, spoke and crawled. In her fourteenth month, she developed pleurisy. The rabbi renamed her Sarah to confound the evil spirits as well as to gain additional support from God. She had to have an incision, a large scar in her back, so that the pus could be drawn from her lungs. Fearing for her life, Bella cried and prayed, prayed and cried, but Joe remained strong. His faith in God and in his mother's name assured him his Sarita would recover. And as she did, the weeks growing into months of slow recovery, Joe was vindicated: his mother's name made God heed his prayers. Bella cried for joy but the joy was mingled with fright as she gazed at her daughter's sallow complexion, her diminished energy, the dimmed light in her once bright, black eyes. Joe tried to reassure Bella. Although her energy was less than what it was, she would, as the doctor in the clinic said, recover fully. Even her wandering, her vacant stare, he pointed out, seemed to occur less often. But hypochondriacal Bella knew her better than anyone and took her even as an adult to doctors who confirmed her good health but could not explain to Bella the vacancy in her daughter's eye. Even if renamed and reborn, Sarita was still Bella's daughter and she sang to her every day. When Señora Hazan, the ancient woman who smelled of incense, whose print and tasselled shawls draped over her broad shoulders and covered her huge bosom, who spoke only Ladino, who was regarded as a seer even by Dr. Behar the only Sephardic medical doctor in the Bronx, was again asked to visit their apartment on Washington

Avenue so she could look at Sarita, now that she was six and Daniel three, she said there was nothing wrong with the girl. That she was able to see things differently, that she was capable of strange powers which would develop as she grew older. And again Bella was reminded of her aunt who was cured by the burying of the egg near the sea in the light of the full moon, but Bella didn't know the language of the strange chant which might not have worked in any event in the Bronx since there was no sea and the moon never seemed full. Daniel scoffed at Señora Hazan, even at three, because he knew his sister relied on him. Señora Hazan glared at Daniel when he, having been ignored for too long as the attention focused on his bigger sister, punched his sister on her back where he knew the incision was. Señora Hazan shouted at him and then, when he returned a fierce look to the equally fierce old woman, she pulled herself up and, turning to Bella, said something in still another language which Daniel didn't understand. But Bella shrugged her shoulders in embarrassment to the old lady as if she could do nothing to Daniel who was so young and who was so loved by his older sister.

In fact, Daniel wondered why Sarita loved him since he was born to amend the error of her existence. Because he could focus clearly and rationally on things, he knew what was important and what was not. From their earliest ages, except when they danced, when she was in control, when she helped him move to the rhythm, Sarita obeyed his every glance or word not, as was the expectation of their father and mother, because he was male and she female, but because Daniel knew things which she never did. And Daniel, even as he helped her to see, let her know that he could never forgive his parents for his not being their first born. Sarita would have gladly given him her birthright, but he, having long since arrogated it to himself anyway, nevertheless resented the accidental nature of things that mocked his sense of order. Rachel's birth, three years after his, helped to mollify him, since he did become an older brother confirming his sense of the creation. He regarded the move in July of 1941, a few months before the war forever changed the United States, to a five-room apartment on Morris Avenue, situated in a better neighborhood than their three-room apartment on Washington Avenue, as a commemoration of his seventh birthday. Walking four abreast, Rachel in his father's right arm, Daniel's hands held by his father and mother, his mother holding Sarita's as well, walking through the large courtyard to their new apartment building, Daniel felt a surge of strength course through his young body, felt a peace which surpassed his young understanding of things. Here in this place he would somehow be able to correct what it was that had gone wrong. Because Rachel, named after Bella's mother, and Sarita were to share one room while he was given his own room, he realized that the wrong was on its way to being corrected.

And since he started a new school and had new friends and had new clothes and books, books that could help him discover what it was he needed to know to correct the wrong, he was excited in ways that he'd never been before. He and his father had read books with pictures. Comic books that Daniel liked to look at. And as soon as he learned to read, and he read so well that he was placed in a special class, he discovered through the comic books what the country they lived in was really like. Yellow-haired, freckle-faced Archie and yellow-haired Betty and black-haired Veronica and Jughead, in the funny hat, these were real Americans living in the middle of the country, in the center of the country, the real heart of the country. Where there were no apartment buildings and no trolley cars or buses. Where teenagers drove jalopies while the rich, spoiled, black-haired kid drove a sleek car with new tires and a radio, but who was always beaten by Jughead and Archie who loved and laughed in living color. Bright yellows and oranges and reds in the corner soda fountain where they were always able to find a friend to talk to, to have a malt with. But Daniel knew that here at the edge of the country, where the Atlantic Ocean led to the old country, where when summering in Coney Island during the war they had to pull down black-out shades at night so the German submarines that were patrolling the waters could not see them, where there were crowds of people of all kinds: the Japanese family who operated the ski ball alleys, the first Italians to sell pizza by the slice, the Germans who sold wurst and beer at the large open-air, boardwalk restaurants, and the Jews, Nathans and Shapiros, Cohen's Baths, and the amusements parks where Yiddish was heard as often as English, where even blacks worked. This city was where all the others came and were held. Daniel and his family moved from Washington Avenue to Morris Avenue because too many black people were moving in. But here in Coney Island the blacks worked as porters and haulers, barely seen or heard. There was even a black kid, Frances Johnson, in Daniel's second-grade class whom he remembered all his life because on the first day of classes, when the teacher asked Daniel where he had moved from, he replied "Washington" which she thought was Washington, D.C., but when she asked him why his family moved, he said in a loud voice, "Because too many coloreds were moving in" and he smiled innocently, looking at Frances, not seeing his color but a boy from the old neighborhood. But the first grade teacher, Mrs. Wielderstein, angrily told Daniel to take his seat. And as soon as Daniel realized the error of his remark, he was glad he had made it, though there was no evil intent or prejudice in it, because he assumed that Frances felt the sweet poignant pain of the special person, like an incision in the back, singled out for special attention, not to be trusted, which Daniel, a Spanish Jew, a double curse, began to feel as he heard his parents in hushed tones speak of what was going on to Jews over there, in the old country. And even in the school, in the yard or in the halls, where the Irish and Polish kids would beat up Jews because they had killed sweet Jesus, their Saviour who, Daniel later learned, was Jewish just like most of the children in his class, and wondered why Jewish kids were beaten if Jesus himself was Jewish. A few Armenians and Poles, Italians and Irish, but mostly Jews. Not all Sephardic Jews, whose parents spoke Spanish, but Jews whose parents spoke Yiddish.

The special class for very good readers. But no kid in the class was like Archie or Jughead because no kid in the city was like them. And because the city, the Bronx was a place where an Archie or a Jughead would not be safe, there was a need for Superman and Captain Marvel and Batman. The trinity who Daniel reluctantly but inevitably came to recognize as the heroes necessary to the safety and well-being of the city dweller. Even before his Bar Mitzvah Daniel realized grown men read books without pictures and therefore refused to discuss comics with his father, who never stopped reading the comics. Insensitive and boorish, Joe felt pride in being able to read in English, though he had been in the country for over twenty years and had not progressed to real books. Daniel knew his father could not understand why he favored Captain Marvel over Batman and Superman—since even his friends preferred Batman and Superman who were, after all, city heroes, rising over tall buildings, driving fast cars through the mean streets of the metropolis. But Batman and Superman merely changed clothes to become who they were; they never metamorphosed the way Billy Batson did to become Captain Marvel: "Shazam!" A mysterious word which had to have been from a time and place different from the here and now, a mysterious word which must have been one of many such words which could, Daniel believed, transform him too into a Captain Marvel who could soar through the sky. All he need do, he told himself, was to find the life-transforming word by reading the old books that were copied by the scribes. Like what the old shamanic woman did for his grand aunt by the light of the full moon. He discovered one such word in the fifth grade, believing himself to be one when he was called one by his teacher, Mrs. Fitzpatrick, the gray-haired old lady who treated all the children with warmth and respect, even though most of them were Jewish, children of immigrants who barely spoke English. She called Daniel her scribe because he read quickly and wrote diligently, because he volunteered to go to the board, proud to see his writing so prominently displayed, capable of being seen by all. And so he never forgot the word, *scribe*, and how it described what he would do, read and write in the old languages. Finding the way to the word with its magical powers would transform him not only from a boy to a man not like his father, not like Joe the squeezer of oranges and slinger of hot dogs, but like the scribe who wrote not what he had originated but what he had copied, not even knowing or caring who the original writer was, concerned with the faithful copying of the words whose meaning even the scribe himself may not have known, may have been afraid to know, but if not afraid, if willing to decipher meaning then he might transform boys into men, men into gods, capable of creating their own meaning.

Which is why Daniel could not tolerate his father's attempts to talk about, to try to laugh with him about Dick Tracy or Terry and the Pirates, his father not particularly interested in Archie and Jughead, Billy Batson and Captain Marvel. But like Daniel's friends, especially fat Ikey and bespectacled Sammy, Joe was a fan of Batman and Superman, particularly if they were performing their feats in a special, double issue, its thicker than usual binding giving the comic book a weight it ordinarily didn't have. But Daniel knew even at an early age that bindings don't give weight to meaning or significance: Art must be stripped of comics, its heft judged through history and philosophy, its worth structured through words and feeling, its beauty redeemed through rhythm and form. Art, he learned later, revealed the only two exits to the labyrinths of life: sex and death—the only subjects tantalizingly touched on but never probed in the comic books. Holding up a double Superman issue in his left hand, Joe pointed to its cover with the forefinger of his right hand, hands to which always clung, however faintly, the cloying smell of vanilla syrup and oranges, hands abnormally enlarged by the squeezing of hundreds of oranges every day, ten to twelve hours a day, six days a week. Sitting at his secretary bookcase, the desk shelf opened beneath its glass-covered bookshelves, the ornate if flimsy wooden curlicues over the glass failing to give it the substance that originals of such a piece of furniture must have had, bought for him by Bella with money earned at the skirt factory, Daniel looked up to see his father in the doorway of his room pointing to the cover of the double Superman issue, Superman's right arm out-stretched as he soars high above the Empire State Building, Lois Lane lovingly looking at him as she is held by his left arm. Startled, interrupted from studying his Torah portion for his Bar Mitzvah, Daniel was momentarily confused as he saw his father standing in the doorway of his room holding up a comic book. The untranslated Hebrew words still floating from right to left in confusion before his eyes, he saw his father's grin fading, his father's quizzical eyes deepening in pride, as he lowered the comic book, no longer caring to know if his son had read the latest double issue, pride now lifting the father, the ancestral pride of the shared secret tongue still studied by the son so that he too could follow in the footsteps of all the fathers to the Ark, so he too could recite his portion and thus enter into the covenant of the fathers. Seeing the sorry attempt to conceal the comic book, frustrated by the words he could not translate but which he would have to read, Daniel glared at Joe who, smelling of stale cigars and acrid oranges, interrupted his concentration, his rhythm. And the father, seeing the rebuttal, straightened up, about to back away when the son, guilt ascendant, began to smile in recognition, as Sarita, having heard the sudden silence in the house, hurried out of her room to head off problems her father would create. Nearly sixteen, her unbrushed black hair wavy over her shoulders and back, framing her olive skin, her full lips, deepening her black eyes, Sarita pulled the father and the son from each other onto herself. Her neck and throat bare, her full breasts heaving under her thin blouse, her body tense, she controlled the moment.

"Poppa!" She paused, saw the limp comic book dangling from his dangling hand. "Can I see that when you're finished?" A smile spreading over her lips, the smile of the old world woman learned from her mother, given to the man, the smile of grateful submission, the smile of innocence confused with the vacancy that penetrated the marrow, the smile of fervent acceptance that Daniel was the chosen one, the son and brother, the hope and the destiny of them all. Even when they were younger, when he was eleven and she was fourteen, when she was still teaching him to dance, she let him lead, though he was never as graceful and rhythmic as she. She who, like her mother, could sing and dance to the music which he felt in his breast but which he could not make as did his mother and sister. After they had practiced their steps to Xavier Cugat's rumba on the new Emerson radio-phonograph console, their parents having taken the baby out for a walk, she throwing him out then pressing him close as was done in the movies with Fred Astaire and Ginger Rogers, after they had gone to their separate rooms, he walked unannounced into her room as she, unaware of him, stood gazing in wonder at her changing body in front of her dresser mirror. Mouth agape, he saw her waist-high nakedness, saw under her left shoulder blade the incision which he had always known but which now seemed grotesque and mysterious, a ragged imperfection to which adhered a substance and meaning of its own. He, whose eleven-year-old fingers and hands still felt her incision, wanted to probe the scar; she, barely conscious at fourteen years of age of her fully defined breasts. Even at eleven years of age, he wanted to scrutinize the scar, jealous of it, of its power to attract and transfix, insisting to her that he be allowed to touch it, to run his fingers and hands over it. And she who had always felt ashamed and defiled by it, even in front of the doctors, who as a child insisted on wearing a tee shirt even at the beach, who always covered it up as an adult with wide-strapped bras, she took his left hand with her own across the front of her body and stretching it behind herself, his bare arm brushing then pressing hard against the black nipples of her breasts, she guided his hand and fingers over the cut. Releasing his hand from hers, from the uncomfortable position of being held fast, he moved behind her and, her long hair tickling his arms, placed both his hands on the cut and lingered there, his fingers, like a blind man's, running over it, seeing in the mirror as he did so a smile spread across his sister's face, her eyes closed, her head tilted back.

Her countenance changed suddenly, as father and son, father and brother, brother studying to become a man, gazed at her, as sensuous as it was innocent. And, as if aware of having succeeded, her face darker, her sensuality more severe, an instinctual awareness that the collision she had averted in them might now devolve onto her, to be the victim of both, felt rising within her the fear and resentment she could only mask with that tentative smile, the smile that acknowledged vulnerability and desired compassion.

"Pop," an impatient glance at his sister before returning to his father, his voice uncertainly cracking into manhood, Daniel muttered, "I was studying." Outwardly ignored, though her sex defining and threatening them both, she remained rooted to her spot. His blood rising, his massive hands down at his sides, Joe saw himself the common enemy, the cause of the alliance of his children. He was now imitating his own father who had extracted obedience and respect from his seven or eight children in the same manner that all fathers in Istanbul extracted obedience: from using the belt to merely snapping it. Joe too had beaten his daughter— no matter her age. The crime was clear. His dumb brute hands had reacted to her having taken his tips earned from serving others.

Screaming in pain, the six-year-old girl alternately denying she had done wrong and pleading for forgiveness for wrongs done, for having imitated her mother whom she had seen taking needed loose change from his pants pockets while he slept. And three-year-old Daniel in fear of those brute hands, in fear of them tearing the skin, causing incisions, shrieked with his sister, causing Bella to run in, to grab Sarita in her arms, to protect her from Joe, her hatred for him first apparent to the children. Almost a decade later, the brute hand now held the double issue comic book, Superman and Lois Lane soaring blissfully above the city, while Daniel and Sarita remained still in suspension.

"Today I am a man."

Holding the looseleaf, lined paper in both hands, Daniel read aloud to friends and family the handwritten speech Rabbi Algava had written for him in English and in Ladino. In the large hall, rented in the old neighborhood, near Crotona Park in the South Bronx where the Sephardim first lived when they came from Turkey and Greece, from lost corners of the extinct Ottoman Empire, bringing with them the language they kept alive for hundreds of years but which their children would not speak, which their grandchildren would not understand, Daniel addressed the assembled throng first in that antiquated, awkward Spanish and then in the comfortable English of the Bronx, giving the same speech in both languages. The crowd seemed enormous though there weren't a hundred people there. But when he spoke they all listened. All the men and women, boys and girls, paid attention and that attention was, he realized, what made him a man.

"Today I am a man." The Shazam of the Jews.

Identifying himself in time, identifying time in himself, Daniel celebrated the words that shushed friends and family. They shifted in their seats around the aroma-rich tables laden with stuffed grape leaves and Calamata olives, with Salonika peppers, radishes, and sticks of celery, with round Italian and long French breads and with baked phyllo pies filled with feta cheese and spinach, with pitchers of iced water and Coca-cola, with clear bottles of homemade raki. They laughed as they took him in, the little boy who would be a man, they laughed at the squeaky voice and the scrubbed face, at the hermaphrodite asserting manhood. But then they hushed themselves, the men and the women, the boys and girls, as Daniel uncertainly repeated the words that silenced them all: "Today I am a man." The same words had been uttered millions of times before and would be uttered millions of times again but, like "once upon a time," the words continued to instill, despite the puniness of the utterer himself, wonder and awe. And, he delighted in the concomitant revelation, words themselves determine as well as describe: the Word defined the beginning of being—In the beginning was the Word. Shazam! In Hebrew from the holy parchment at the synagogue, in Ladino and English from the yellow legal paper in the rented community room, Daniel read the words that bound him to the covenant of his people, even if he could not understand the mysterious Hebrew and could not speak the ancestral Spanish. Daniel swayed, however, to the Turkish music that blared from the phonograph, the music his people salvaged from the vestiges of the Ottoman Empire. Accompanied always by the chanting of their Hebrew prayers, a thousand years of subjugation split between the Iberian and Ottoman Empires, the Sephardic Jews sang their Spanish songs and danced their Turkish dances. A middle-aged, costumed couple in Turkish garb, hired especially for the event, the mustached man an oud player and his wife in a gold brocade purple dress who played the tambourine, wailed and sang songs in both Turkish and Ladino as Bella rose from her seat to the cheers and clapping of the men flushed with raki. Alone on the dance floor, arms extended above her head, her fingers snapping in time to the Turkish music, her head gliding from side to side as if detached from her grinding and undulating torso, she made her way to where her son was sitting, coaxing him with movement and gesture to join her in the dance before the now roaring revelers. Unable to deny so public a request, Daniel rose, and in the dance and song of a country he'd never seen, in imitation of his sister who had taught him the dance, moved in perfect unison with his mother. Arms extended above their heads, their bodies warily circling each other, they twisted themselves so that while their bodies were back to back their faces were not. And as the guests shouted and clapped, sang and stomped, Bella sinuously made her way to where her husband and daughters were seated, Daniel and the crowd expecting her to pull her husband to join in the dance. Instead, Bella pointed to Sarita to come to the floor to dance with Daniel while she, pretending exhaustion, plopped down next to Joe who was holding Rachel in his lap. Sixteen and glowing with pride, her long black hair swirling about her olive face, laughing with joy at her brother's coming of age, the guests loudly whispered their piteous laments in Ladino over *la hermosa hija* who could move so gracefully but who still had the innocent eyes of a five- or six-year-old girl, the girl who danced like Scheherazade, like the belly dancers of the Pashas, like Rita Hayworth of the silver screen. Her arms over her head, snapping her fingers the way her mother taught her, her *bendichos manos,* Sarita danced with her brother who, hands over his head, had often danced with her alone in their house, had felt his own stirrings as she held him in her arms so he could follow her steps, encouraged by her whose perfect rhythmic and graceful instinct he could not reproduce. But here on the floor at his Bar Mitzvah, Daniel danced with his sister to the delight of the guests, to the delight of their parents. Increasing the tempo, the oud player stroked and strummed his instrument while the singer, imperially swaying in her Ottoman costume, beat the tambourine with the heel of her hand. Unable to keep seated, the music yanking him forward, arms upraised, fingers snapping, Joe led Bella and ten-year-old Rachel to the floor so that, bodies gyrating, faces beaming, arms upraised, all the Pereiras danced for their screaming and clapping guests and for themselves.

Shazam! Today I am a Man.

But the picture of the Jews, led by the terrified young boy, not yet a Bar Mitzvah, whose large cap shadowed his pale, wide-eyed face, arms upraised in surrender to unsmiling Supermen, more powerful than Captain Marvel, with bayonets affixed to their rifles, became a permanent negative in Daniel's mind in 1947. Aware of the fact, now that the war was over, now that the Germans had been defeated, that had his mother not left Greece, he too, with all her family, he, the boy, arms upraised, would have led all the men and women, all the children, to their death in a dance without oud, without tambourine, just the hissing of the gas as they showered, naked and trembling, without water. And having read his Torah portion on the day of his Bar Mitzvah, on the day he became a full member of the tribe, family and friends in a lost corner of the Bronx rejoiced in song and dance to Daniel and— Shazam! Next Year in Jerusalem—to the land of ancestral memory. Shazam! Death and resurrection. Six million souls sprinkled among the sands blooming the desert into Israel. Shazam! Today I am a Man. Shazam!

Shazam! I am!

Shazam! I am! I am!

2. Learning Disabled

Not a gap, not a rip in the soul's veil, the vacancy in Sarita's eyes was a parting, an opening beckoning its completion. At twenty-one, she was finishing her third year of college, struggling to satisfy the academic requirements of her professors most of whom knew that her knowledge came from a life lived on perimeters, so they overlooked, as City College professors often did, her academic weakness because they perceived sensitivity and understanding that books could not teach. Majoring in art, in sculpture and ceramics, in the molding and shaping of clay and wood, in defining and redefining plastic and steel, Sarita through eyes and hands was granted a joy her mind could finally see and feel. Her straight A's in all her art courses, all the studio courses, offset the C's received in academic courses. Her grades, which her parents were indifferent to because unaware of what grades signified, her A grades that she earned and the C grades granted her because of kindnesses and favors without her knowledge or asking averaged a B minus which she nevertheless was disturbed by, not because she cared for grades, for other peoples' evaluation of her, but because she feared that her brother and sister would be contemptuous of her, of her kind of intelligence. Of course they pitied her, but even their pity would turn to scorn as they continued to function at the top of their classes. She regretted her brother's contempt while she feared her baby sister's, whose own steely, black eyes never flinched, never revealed a pool of clarity.

Rachel, now fourteen, ready to graduate from Wade Junior High School, having named herself Ricky, without a scar or blemish on her face or body, whose wavy, black hair reached her shoulders, whose face was more perfectly formed than her sister's, having straight and even teeth, smooth and soft olive skin, knew at fourteen years of age that she was beautiful and intelligent, knew that she would, like her brother, succeed in ways that her father dreamed but could never achieve. The favorite of her father whose love for his baby daughter melted but never fully extinguished his desire for sons, Ricky made Bella and Joe proud but even at fourteen she knew there existed between her brother and sister a bond that excluded her, that separated her from them. And she knew that that bond was created out of weakness, out of Daniel's vacillating pity for Sarita who could not fathom all that went on about her, that her childhood illness left her brain even more than her body scarred in some subtle way. Ricky was jealous of her older sister's possession of Daniel, her handsome older brother over whom all her friends oohed and aahed. But Ricky was at the top of her class and even though only fourteen, seven years younger than her sister in college, she was able to discuss Sarita's school work with her, even though Sarita thought she was just talking about her courses and not asking for help, Ricky would go over words that clouded meaning for Sarita, go over concepts that words made confusing, more so in history and philosophy than in mathematics and biology, which would have been more perplexing to Ricky had she not

111

long been aware of Sarita's unpredictable, even uncanny, mental prowess which even her professors somehow or other recognized.

Having no friends despite efforts made by many boys and girls throughout her school years to be that to her, reclusive Sarita had no one other than her brother and sister with whom she could or would discuss her school work. But Sarita would never ask Daniel or Ricky for help. Never. She would talk to them about school, about college, but just to let them know what it was like. Not to get help. And she enjoyed college, she said. Not that Sarita was unfriendly which is why many classmates took pains to try to get to know her, to go out with her or to take her out, but which no one, male or female, succeeded in doing. She was always accessible, smilingly indicating a tentative but private warmth, which those around her would try to feel, try to be covered by but which remained distant, like a glowing coal, its heat visible for miles but suffusing only the air it consumed. Joe and Bella were pained by Sarita's isolation, especially Bella who was so outgoing, so gregarious, who reveled in the praise heaped on her when she sang and danced, who thrust herself forward to garner attention even from strangers on buses or subways, whose incessant extroversion made Sarita smile and Daniel cringe but which served as a model for Ricky. Unlike her baby sister who had many or her brother who had few, Sarita had no friends she brought home or to whose homes she went, preferring the company of her family to that of strangers. In school, when she had to be with fellow students, Sarita was usually silent, speaking only when spoken to, smiling to accompany her self-conscious responses. Her silence was received by her fellow students as a sign of a special depth of understanding, of an intelligence and insight that schools refused to recognize or that they tried to do away with since such intelligence couldn't be measured and categorized by tests that schools were capable of devising. Always gentle and kind to her fellow students and to her teachers who admired her beauty and recognized her special talent, despite her being different from them, from not being complete, Sarita was unaware that her very omission made her all the more attractive and desirable, believing instead that her difference was a fault, connected to the incision in her back, done to remove the poisons that threatened her life, but taking with the poisons a vital portion of being, a breath or spirit she had to rediscover and recover unto herself. Not interested in clothing, wearing little or no makeup, Sarita patiently endured but ultimately ignored her mother's pleas to put on more lipstick and rouge, to allow her to make clothing for her that was more stylish like other girls her age. Wearing simple skirts and blouses that were loose fitting but which unintention-nally accentuated the fullness of her figure, Sarita made herself up so as to be comfortable, to deflect attention, but in so doing attracted more to herself, but the kind of attention that was laced with admiration and respect.

Not fully aware of the impact she was making on other students, though glad to be accepted by them, Sarita was feeling within herself an independent being beginning to bloom in the third year of college, the first two years an inner torment because of the threat of disgrace through failure. Recognizing through the molding of clay and the restructuring of plastic and steel the possibility of reinfusion, Sarita experienced a joy she never knew was possible. Her hands spoke, her eyes heard. At school, she garnered respect from fellow art students and professors because of creations that promised a new way of seeing. One student in particular, Marcus Singer, a strapping if diffident and gentle young man about the same age as Sarita, was especially drawn to her. Studying painting, he was in a couple of her art theory classes and because he was so unobtrusive, so quiet and introspective, Sarita didn't mind if he joined her in the lunchroom or when she walked to the subway. But when he hinted that they go to a movie or to a museum together, she told him with an embarrassed but grateful look in her eye that she never went out with anyone except members of her family, a situation he nodded his understanding of.

At home, her family shared in Sarita's enthusiasm, her new found joy. Bella exalted in the pieces Sarita brought home, praised and exhibited them throughout the apartment, though except for the early clay busts of Lincoln and Washington Bella had no idea what the three dimensional shapes in plastic and steel, stretched and pummelled before being returned to a rounded fullness, were supposed to mean. Having often made her children's clothing, transforming yards of raw material without patterns into fashionable jackets and skirts and pants, Bella bragged that her daughter's bendichos manos, her blessed hands, her artistic ability, came from her, from her own ability as a seamstress though, unlike Sarita's, her creations were useful and easily identifiable. Shrugging his shoulders to his wife as he held in his hand one of his daughter's molded shapes of clay, transformed by the annealing fires of the oven into a silky, an ivory smoothness, oval shaped but twisted, its sinuous declivity so intriguing that his huge hands, accustomed to the rugged but yielding skin of oranges, could not stop hefting it, probing it, could not put it down, Joe, embarrassed by the hold it had over him, wondered aloud why she didn't make him an ashtray. Wondered aloud what it was he was holding. And Sarita, thinking he was asking what she called it, the name she gave it at the insistence of her professor who was stunned by its primitive grace, but who couldn't come up with a title because words were not what she created, who shrugged her helplessness at her young professor, an artist himself, a guest professor whose reputation was already secure, who prodded her for a name, a title which would confer upon it not only dominion but also distinction, said she couldn't make a decision. So the visiting professor, Jacobo DiGiordano said, "Indecision" or "In Decision." And Sarita laughed and said "Incision" which the professor liked best of all. And that is what she said it was, and Joe, hearing the word as if from a distance, again said, "Ashtray." But Daniel reminded his father that he wondered what it was called and The Wonder was as good a name as any. The Wonder, at which the whole Peirera family smiled in agreement. The Wonder it was.

At nearly eighteen, ready to graduate from the Bronx High School of Science, unlike Sarita who went to Walton High School, an all-girl school where she did passably well, Daniel was at the top of his class, already admitted to City College though he could have applied to and certainly gotten into Columbia and other prestigious private universities, could even have gotten a scholarship or fellowship but which would have set him apart from those, like Archie and Jughead, Betty and Veronica, who belonged by virtue of birth and custom. Delighting in his sister's new found creative ability, Daniel was himself infected by her never before experienced enthusiasm that promised direction and focus, but he knew too that he would still have to be responsible for her, that she would never be able to provide properly for herself. At City College, he would be with his friends who, like him, were bright and studious and Jewish, able to have gone to the private schools but content to go where they would be with their own, able to get as good an education there as anywhere. Besides, Daniel reckoned, being at City College would enable him to help Sarita, even though she always resisted his offers, getting angry if he even asked if she wanted help with History or English or whatever. Lately, he noticed, she seemed particularly disturbed by a term paper which she refused to talk to him about but which she apparently needed to do for her last required English course, one which she had put off taking as long as she could.

At the end of April, still not sure how to indicate or even to do the research for the paper, and not wanting Daniel, a senior in high school, to involve himself in it, Sarita went for a conference to her English professor's office which, like all the other faculty offices, was located on the top floor of the four story building that housed the English department. In his early thirties, Dr. Jonathan Marek was intense and ambitious, confident of an intellect that was equally analytical and insightful. Fair-skinned and of medium height, his shoulder-length, wavy brown hair, his gold-rimmed spectacles emphasizing rather than concealing his brown piercing eyes, his slightly hooked nose, all made for rugged good looks that complemented a penetrating intelligence and self-confident manner. He wore, in compliance with his professorial persona, a brown tweed jacket, dark corduroy pants, striped shirt and beige woolen tie. Having made a 2:15 appointment on Thursday afternoon to see him, Sarita at 2:10 was walking alone on the darkened corridor of the fourth floor. Except for a student who passed her on his way to the staircase and for a few open doors to faculty and departmental offices, the floor was deserted especially in comparison to the floors below on which students and faculty milled about near their classrooms. Nervous at finding herself in such an area, where elongated shadows were cast by hanging light bulbs, nervous at the prospect of still not understanding what Dr. Marek wanted, Sarita felt her heart beat faster, her legs heavier as she looked at the numbers on the closed doors wondering if she was heading in the right direction, wondering if there was a Room 432 on this floor. Hearing footsteps behind her, she spun around and saw in the distance a student who must have come out of the English department office. She wanted to ask if he knew where Room 432 was, but she was unwilling to call attention to herself, to her uncertainties. She turned back, continued walking, her legs feeling heavier, wishing now she had let Marcus come with her, seeing the corridor bend at a right angle, unhappy about having to turn an unfamiliar corner onto an unfamiliar place. She could go back, tell Dr. Marek in class that she felt sick, could not attend the conference but would stay after class to get the information. But she knew, even as she continued walking, that such a retreat would be wrong, that she would suffer from her fears. And as she neared the corner, she saw a brightness, a reflection of light. Her heart lighter, her step quicker, she turned the corner to see in the middle of the hall the open door to Dr. Marek's office casting a huge swath of light onto the corridor, onto Sarita as she stepped into it, felt bathed by it.

"Eugenie! Come in!"

Sarita stood by the door, reassured by the smiling Dr. Marek sitting at his desk in his shirtsleeves, looking at her through his gold frame glasses, but momentarily stopped by his having called her "Eugenie," the alien name she distantly recognized as her own, the birth name she was known by at all her schools, the name on all official documents, the name even Marcus used since she never told him what she was called by her family as if doing so would violate some unuttered decree. And hesitating, momentarily pausing at the door, draped by a loose skirt and a cotton blouse her full body outlined by the darkness behind her, her hair falling onto her shoulders, Sarita returned to him an uncertain smile. His eyes fixed on her, Dr. Marek sat up straighter as the pen in his hand drooped against its paper. "This is," he spoke after a moment, beckoning her with a motion of his hand to take the seat facing him against the side of his desk, "the first time you've come to see me, isn't it?" Her nervousness preventing her from speaking, making her as always tongue-tied, though she did not stammer, did not falter, since doing so would reveal her inability to master words, to call them up at will, the way Daniel and Ricky could so easily do, Sarita nodded a yes, smiling politely so as not to show any disrespect, but the look in her dark eyes both distant and yearning. "What can I do for you?" he asked, leaning back in his swivel chair. Her books in her lap, staring at him, then looking away from him to the large window behind him which opened onto the deserted green of the campus, then back to him, smiling, then not smiling, she said, "It's about the term paper." "Oh, yes. I thought so." He made himself busy, pulling out his roll book, looking through it apparently to see what Sarita's standing in the class was. "Mmmm. Mmmmm." He repeated, staring at his record book, looking intensely professorial. "You've been doing passable work," he said finally, his tone indicating forbearance, "but I know," he tossed the roll book on his desk as if its touch offended him, "you could do better. Much better."

Much better? Much better?

The thought terrified Sarita. She was doing the best she was capable of. How could he not know that? She tried so hard. At home, she was able to work at her own speed, to pace the floor, to look up words for their meaning and spelling, to make sure verbs and subjects agreed, that sentences were complete, not fragments. And on the papers she did at home, sometimes without her having to ask him, Daniel would look at them and suggest improvement, and Sarita did well. But in class, without the dictionary, the grammar book, without the freedom to pause and reflect, to stretch and clear the mind, under the pressure of time and place, she foundered. Words got stuck, they repeated themselves, preventing others from being called up, of thinking of others. Of whole sentences. The words scrambled, confused her, frightened her. They got stuck in her mind. And repeated themselves over and over again, like a broken record, the repetition only gradually making itself known to her when the others looked at her expectantly then impatiently, the repetition turning the vacancy in her eyes to anxiety. She looked at Dr. Marek, feeling herself breathing hard. He smiled at her. She leaned back in her chair, giving herself time as she had learned to do, to prevent the repetition, to prevent the repetition, from causing confusion, she leaned back in her chair, brushed her hair from her forehead with her left hand so as to give herself a moment to say that she was really doing the best she could. She paused to catch her breath when he said that he realized most students did better when they weren't under any constraints of time and place. In fact, he himself did better work when he wasn't under the gun, so to speak, when he wasn't under any time pressures so he certainly understood the difficulty she was having. But the fact is, he went on, most of us whether we realize it or not have to perform under pressure. Think of Hemingway, Dr. Marek leaned forward, placed his hands on the desk, with his insistence on grace under pressure. In addition, his voice dropped to take her in his confidence, the disparity between work she did at home and what she did in class was too great, she must bridge the gap somewhat. And, she wanted to bridge the gap, seeing his eyes trying to take her own but which were already startled by the allusions to grace and pressure, searching her mind for a memory of grace under pressure in herself or in her family, searching for grace she felt the vacancy beginning to return but she returned her eyes to his, seeing him say he would be glad to help her since she seemed much more mature than most of the other students he was teaching. Hemingway, she said, Hemingway, remembering the story read, the woman killing her husband with a gun, under the gun the man did better even though he was killed. The short happy life . . . short and happy, even though he was already a grown man, he was happy for a short time. She turned to Dr. Marek, placing her hand on the desk so she could touch wood, to get strength from the wood, Hemingway died from the gun, remembering what he had told the class about Hemingway. Hemingway, yes, Dr. Marek beamed at Eugenie since she remembered something about Hemingway from earlier in the term.

"You can do the term paper on Hemingway, if you like. Perhaps some aspect of Hemingway. You can compare Hemingway to another author, like Mark Twain."

She loved Huckleberry Finn and Tom Sawyer who reminded her of Archie and Jughead, but better and more substantial than the comic book characters. She loved to read about children or teenagers, she told Dr. Marek, but she had no way of explaining to him that the term paper was overwhelming, that the term paper with its thesis statement, with its prescribed way of taking notes, of citing primary and secondary sources, of footnoting, of creating a bibliography of books and articles. . . . She looked out the window.

"I could," his head back, Dr. Marek threaded the fingers of his left hand through his long hair, "help you. You seem more mature than students your age so I can help you. I mean," he laughed, "I know you won't tell the others that I'm giving you extra help. I know you won't tell others. You don't seem to talk much to the others. To other students. So my helping you won't be broadcast all over the campus. . . ." In an apparent gesture to seal the alliance, he put his hand over hers. "Help . . . ? Help me . . . ?" Wide-eyed, her bosom heaving, unable to finish, to tell him she didn't need extra help, she clutched at the hand that covered hers, she didn't need extra help. She was not stupid because she sometimes struggled with words. "Yes, yes," he looked into her eyes, wild now with passion. "I'll help you." "But . . . but . . ." she pulled her hand from his, bringing it to her bosom, "I just need to know how to do, need to know how to do the term paper. The term paper . . . the research. I'm having trouble with research. . . ." She wanted to give him back his words—footnoting and bibliography, note cards and thesis statement, mechanics and format—but the words failed to come. "Look," his hand still on the desk where she dropped it, "I'm just interested in your—in the student's ability—to understand, to interpret literature, to interpret the text. Research is a tool but . . ." She couldn't follow him. The text seemed to be the same as literature, but the text was a book used in school. Text and texture, search and research. Words within words. Words changing words changing meanings.

She looked at him, saw his mouth moving, saying things meant to help her. But help panicked her as much as that which required the help. "Look," she heard him say, "you can interpret the Bible if you want. Any text we read in class. Adam and Eve . . . The story of Joseph . . . The Exodus. . . ." Again he leaned forward, staring into her distant eyes, his outstretched hand on the desk grasping the air. The Bible she knew. She knew the story of Adam and Eve in the garden, of Moses leading the Jews out of Egypt, the Book of Ruth, and much more. She could see the biblical figures struggling with God, with their sons, with their brothers, with each other, with their enemies. Abraham and Isaac, Cain and Abel, Jacob and Esau, Moses and the World. She loved going to Hebrew school with Daniel, to read from old books how the world began, to read in those old books rules that her people still followed. But Sarita was glad girls weren't bar mitzvahed. Standing before the Ark reading from the Torah portion would have been her struggle with God. She was happy to listen and read in English without having to worry about remembering who was who. "Adam and Eve . . . Joseph in Egypt . . . ?" she repeated, a smile beginning to form on her lips. "Of course," Dr. Marek said, "you would interpret the story from a literary rather than a religious point of view. You could, for instance, include Thomas Mann in your bibliography. . . . " Her eyes clouded, her parted lips froze: a bibliography for the Bible. "What's the matter?" he shrugged. "There's so much on the Bible. Why do you think it's been so popular? Even if you don't believe in the Book as being the Word of God as I don't. . . . " he straightened up, pulled his hands close to his chest. "Think of Adam and Eve in a different way. As children about to become grown-ups. Think of the entire episode in the Garden of Eden as a children's story for men and women whose only entertainments are eating and drinking, song and dance, storytelling and sex. Don't look so shocked," his professorial tone and bearing began to waver, a hint of conspiratorial familiarity intruding. "That's right, sex. Those were people five thousand years ago. Same as us."

He glanced at the open door and returned to her. "Think of Freud, of the psychological interpretation. . . . " "Freud?" her heart beating rapidly, she remembered the name, remembered her psych course, discussions of childhood behavior and sexuality, of unnatural desires disguised in dreams that released demons, classmates voluntarily reciting their fantasies and their nightmares. She looked around, words failing to come, words of release. "Yes, Freud," he went on, more animated. "Adam and Eve and the Serpent in a Garden where everything is available? Does that sound plausible? Who are they? Real figures made by a God above? Real figures? Some would say so. But there are other ways to look at this work." She could feel him bursting with insight and energy, with power and understanding. "Think of Adam and Eve as a boy and a girl, as adolescents about to become a man and a woman. "'Do not eat of the Tree of Knowledge of Good and Evil,"God said unto them, for "if thou eatest thou shalt surely die.'" Die! They would die if they ate an apple? Death because of knowledge! Death if they partook of the knowledge of good and evil!" He smiled hard at Sarita who shrank, recoiled in her seat, her hair flowing around her shoulders, her eyes wide, like a bird suddenly caged. But she listened fascinated, his words holding her. Partook, she marveled at the old word, but continued fascinated at the sudden lecture: "Why should one die from knowledge of good and evil? Isn't that what we've been trying to teach for the last five thousand years?"

He pushed his chair back, straightened himself up, staring into her dark eyes. "So we can look at this another way. Adam and Eve become aware of themselves as man and woman. The still erect Serpent seduces Eve into biting into the apple, who then seduces Adam to do the same. After eating of the Tree of Knowledge of Good and Evil, Adam and Eve become aware of their nakedness and try to hide from God in shame. But no one can escape the eye of God; He finds and punishes them all. The once proudly erect Serpent, now limp and defeated, will have to crawl on his belly, and become the enemy of Eve—'between thy seed and her seed'! Can you imagine?" he shook his head, stood up as if unaware of Sarita's presence, and began to pace the office. "What seed does a serpent have that can appeal to a woman? Listen." He looked at her again. "The Serpent, Freud would agree, isn't a cigar. Why a serpent? Why'd the writer choose a serpent? Because a serpent could easily symbolize a penis. That's right, a penis. Don't look so shocked, Eugenie," he laughed, shifted uncomfortably on his feet. He went on. "After it seduces Eve, the woman, it is no longer erect. Since the Bible was written by men who lorded it over women, women are punished by having to bear children in pain even while their husbands rule over them. And Adam's punishment? He has to labor in the fields to support his wife and children. Think of that! It's a fairy tale describing what happens to boys and girls when they grow up. Boys and girls become aware of time, of their differences, of their lustful desires. . . . " Her heart pounding, her mind scattered, her eyes unfocused, her stomach churning, she rubbed her legs and thighs against each other under her full skirt. Obedient and respectful to her father and mother, to all her elders, to all the doctors her mother took her to so as to cure the vacancy in her eyes, smiling at them as if to say that she, even if not fully understanding their utterances, nevertheless respected them. And so, a pained smile of uncertainty on her face, Sarita looked up at Dr. Marek whose gaze was upon her. "Do you follow me, Eugenie? Eugenie? Do you hear me? You seem distracted. Try to relax. Don't be so nervous."

He took a couple of steps and stood at her side. His fingers threading her hair, he rested his hand on her shoulder. She stiffened. "A research paper," he removed his hand, "is really not so difficult. It's just time consuming. But if you work on the Bible—maybe the New Testament, some aspect of it you study in church." "I'm Jewish," she said. "Jewish?

Jewish?" He stepped back. "Eugenie . . . Eugenie Pereira? That's not a Jewish name, is it?" "That's my name. It was my grandmother's name. She was Jewish. I am Jewish. My family is Jewish." "Oh . . . you're . . . Are . . . are you Sephardic? Are you a Spanish Jew? You're Sephardic."

He stepped closer to her. "Did you hear that?" he asked. Sarita looked at him, having heard nothing. Nothing. "What?" she asked him, afraid of an unheard sound, looking up at him, her eyes wide. "That . . . that . . . listen. Footsteps down the hall. Probably a student." He looked at the open door. "A student down the hall, probably. Looking for a faculty member to help him with his work. Or maybe with his program for next term. That's why," he looked at her, "I like to be far from the English department office. Students are always looking for faculty members to help them with what they should do on their own." Sarita didn't follow him. She was here to get help from him. He had told her to come for help. He walked to the door, peered out, looked both ways, then quietly closed the door. "We won't be bothered if the door is closed." Sarita wanted to leave. She no longer cared about the research paper; she would ask Daniel for help. Dr. Marek was scaring her. She felt herself breathing hard, her mind beginning to scramble again. Unable to articulate sense, unable to form thoughts that could release, ease the fear. So many times she felt this. Unable to stop it. The words refusing to come, to release her. She heard his steps behind her. "There are many stories in the Bible," she heard his now soft voice directly behind her, "which you could examine, do research on. Come up with an exciting paper. Joseph and Potiphar. Judah and Tamar . . . " Her heart pounding, knowing he was behind her she concentrated on the names he uttered. Names she didn't know. Joseph. Only Joseph's. Only Joseph. She wanted to turn, to run. Seek Daniel and. . . .

His hands, weaving through the thickness of her hair, resting on the back of her neck, gently massaging. Behind her. At her back. She stiffened. Words stuck in her throat. Breaths were coming fast now. Words tangled now. His thumbs under the collar of her open blouse gathered the material. Her blouse was being tugged, pulled . . . pulled up. Please, stop. . . . Doctor, stop. Doctor . . . looking at . . . revealing the incision. Her chest heaved. Heaved. Shaking. Blouse being lifted. Her arms fell at her side. Her books spilled from her lap onto the floor. She tried to rise but couldn't move. Words began fading. At her back. Fading. From the back. Her back . . . her legs rubbing hard, her thighs squeezed tight against each other. She moaned. Hands now on the skin of her back. Doctor . . . Please not on the skin . . . No! Ohhh . . . Oooh . . .

Nooo. Not the back, Doctor. The back. No! Eyes wide, head turning from side to side. She fluttered. Standing in front of the faceless doctor who was holding her, preventing her from falling. Lifting her arms. Standing. Leaning. Fluttering. Fluttering to a halt. Fading. Into blackness. Stopped. Words stopped. Unable to see or hear words in the blackness. Wordless now. Words pierced. Time pierced. Pierced and was silent. And was black before the dim light returned. Time passed. Now looking up at the doctor, his dark face made still darker by the bulging whites of his eyes, Sarita sprawled in the chair at the side of the desk felt dizzy felt disheveled, felt unclean. Bella was right this time. Sarita had to wear clothes properly, dress herself with more care, sit properly. Bella knew how to dress. Sarita sat up, straightened herself, smoothed her skirt, saw her books on the floor. "Eugenie . . . Eugenie . . . " Dr. Marek whispered, his hoarseness filling the empty spaces. "The paper," she said, avoiding his strange eyes, the strange look in his eyes, "the research . . . " "The paper . . . !" Relief in his voice, he shouted, "Look . . . don't worry . . . " Ignoring him, picking up her books, her eyes focused clearly on the books, she went on, "I can ask my brother. Daniel's very good. He's an excellent student. He knows how to do research. Bibliography . . . footnotes . . . research. He's good with words. . . . " Back to him, she took a few short steps to the door, her books in her left hand, her right slowly tucking her blouse in her skirt. "Thank you, Doctor." "Eugenie . . . Eugenie . . . . " his trembling voice, filled with fear, with sorrow and pity, barely penetrated the thick air of his office. She opened the door onto the dim corridor. Forced to pause a moment as she narrowed her eyes to sharpen her focus, she stepped noiselessly into the silence that stretched along its darkness.

Rivalry

David H. Lynn

Jeremy's father would never lay a hand on him. Nor, of course, would he touch the younger children, Caryn and Luke. But to Luke this seemed an afterthought—Jeremy was the oldest, his father's favorite.

In his own absolute safety Jeremy had grown marrow sure and entirely unconscious. But Luke happened to be watching his brother at the moment when the truth first struck him—Jeremy—as odd, as astonishing. That he should be beyond reach. This happened on the same day when their mother murmured to him, "You should stand up for me—you shouldn't let him."

Mama wasn't crying any longer. She didn't sound angry or accusing, merely matter-of-fact, as if this too were a truth Jeremy had known all along, or should have known if he were any kind of son. Luke saw his brother's shoulders stiffen as the strangeness of his situation occurred to him.

The calm, the exhaustion, the relief of a battle just past lingered in the air, an acrid smoke that was sharp and familiar. Their mother showed few visible signs of the blows she'd taken before her husband's fury flung him out of the house, blood flowing down his own cheek from a deep gash at the corner of the eye. This his wife had inflicted with a wild flail of her nails even as he'd cornered her at last, having pursued her slowly, relentlessly from room to upstairs room of the old house. Dr. Rosen's face was red, his brow trembling, spit flying, tie flapping over his shoulder. "Whore," he bellowed. "Tramp."

The sound of his rage filled the rambling farm house, more terrible to the children cowering and watching from a bedroom even than the physical blows thudding against their mother. At last he'd stormed from the house, leaving her sobbing in desolate triumph. She was younger than he and darker, lonely and calm and strong.

Her eyes were puffy from weeping. Her lips were puffy too, though not from weeping. Gingerly she bathed her face with cold water while Jeremy watched from behind, studying his mother's features in the mirror above the basin. In turn, Luke and Caryn watched from the doorway. Caryn's hands were picking, picking at themselves as she didn't quite study her mother, her heavy reddish hair flopping every which way.

"You should stand up for me," Mama said, "you shouldn't let him."

Luke saw her words strike his brother. Mirrorward, she was staring directly into Jeremy's blue eyes, which grew dark and broody. Her own jaw was clenched. Luke sensed that she understood very well what she was doing.

Jeremy's face slowly twisted into a dark scowl. With sudden terror Luke wondered whether his brother, tall now and lean as willow, would lash at their mother himself for pointing out his shortcomings? Would he hit her? Would he cry? Luke almost shouted out to warn Mama. But Jeremy controlled himself. Or no, that wasn't it, it wasn't control: he folded the anger and hurt and shame round and drew them into himself. They writhed in his throat and disappeared. And Luke, still watching from the safety of the bathroom door, panted with relief as Jeremy turned and thrust past him, his face stony, his eyes on something very far away.

Their mother lowered her face once more to the basin. Again and again she heaped the water against her skin, until Luke felt the hollowed-out numbness cold in his own flesh.

*

"Dammit—can't you stop? Jeremy. Listen to me. Don't push him any more." Their father, exasperated, pale, pleaded with the boy.

Without any direct acknowledgment, Jeremy shoved Luke roughly against the ball return. Then, pushing him aside, he heaved a full-sized bowling ball off the rack, wagged it contemptuously in his brother's face, and turned back to the lane. But the ball was too heavy for him. It skidded out of his hands, lumbering awkwardly down the lane. At least it avoided the full humiliation of the gutter. Two pins waggled and collapsed. Lips pressed thin, Jeremy turned nonchalantly and wiped his fingers on his pants.

As usual at this hour they were the only ones in Strike-'n-Spare Alley, Jeremy and his father, and Caryn and Luke. Half the lanes were cloaked in a darkness that wasn't quite cool, though it shielded them from the dust and blinding light of an August Sunday afternoon. But the warmth pawing at the hangarlike building from outside kindled a stench of spilled beer, dirty socks, mildew.

Jeremy, impatient and irritable, had seemed to be wading chest-deep through mud as he selected the bowling shoes with a large "9" on the back. He was preoccupied, seemed to be listening to a faraway sound, preparing himself. Standing behind, waiting his turn after Caryn, Luke had sensed growing danger; Jeremy's temper could ignite as quickly as their father's.

These Sunday afternoons at the bowling alley were one bead of a rosary (their mother was Catholic and the metaphor was one she'd mockingly chosen), counted off from week to week, of what a surgeon could imagine to share with his children. Monday through Saturday he'd be gone before breakfast on the long commute to his hospital in the working-class neighborhood of the city, returning only after their bedtime if he managed to make it home at all. So Sundays he salvaged for his children. Once or twice a month they'd drive to a movie. A ball game when the weather was good. In desperation they'd spend a day at home watching colorized movies or golf together on TV.

The three kids hated it. They dreaded these forced holidays with all their hearts and yet pretended to enjoy themselves for their father's sake. Did Dad know that? Luke sometimes wondered. Did he realize that their enduring the stiff, lonely hours was an act of love? Had he come to hate the stink of the bowling alley as much as they? Or did his more general misery overwhelm such specifics?

*

Early that morning Luke had tugged on jeans and a shirt and slipped past Jeremy's bed to the stairs. His father, up for hours out of habit, had finished his coffee, was just clipping the leash on Parson, their springer spaniel. Half a year earlier the dog, runt of a puppy and nearly blind, had scratched her way through the back door screen, hungry, wounded, desperate with cold. Meanwhile Dr. Rosen was lying ill in his own hospital, nearly dead from meningitis. Caryn had (secretly at first) adopted the pup, nursed her, and together the family smuggled her weeks later into the hospital room as a surprise for their father's convalescence. He'd lain stupefied as Jeremy gave birth, tugging Parson out of the belly of his jacket and settling her on his father's chest. That they could break every rule so brazenly! (But he hadn't wanted to yield the dog up when time came for him to rest.)

Crouching in the shadow on the stairs, Luke hesitated until he'd read his father's mood. The doctor was wearing pants from a discarded suit, too baggy for him now and hanging loose on their suspenders. His shirt sleeves were rolled to the elbow. Absently, pondering something else entirely, he was bending over the dog, scratching her ears and snout. Luke noticed how sparsely his father's hair had grown back after surgery had peeled his scalp open and saved his life. A purple seam still marked the ragged border, a tattoo that had been forced on him. His father was an old man—that's what came home with a stinging clarity—he could've, should've been his grandfather.

Jeremy sometimes told stories of a time when his Dad would take the stairs by twos, would toss a ball once, twice before rushing off to his patients, would stay up late drinking whiskey with friends and still be fresh in the morning. But this was all legend. Luke couldn't remember or share. For him the sour reality had been a series of illnesses stealing his father's youth away. The murmured possibility of death sealed off anything beyond the near horizon. (Can you teach me golf in the spring, Dad? Jeremy had asked. If I'm still here, his father replied, gouging his three children with anguish.)

And his rages—wild, uncontrollable. What touched them off? Your father sometimes is sick that way too, Mama explained. This verdict offered both an excuse and an all-encompassing blame. She'd bite her lip, pick at it till it bled, look away.

Out of his head. That was a phrase Jeremy had tossed off to his brother and sister. Never to anyone else though—there'd be no admitting. Luke didn't understand. Somehow his father imagined things about what his wife did while he was working. About other men, about wild fun and secret meetings. It was crazy. Was it crazy? Of course it was crazy. But Luke also sensed that Mama kindled him: she coaxed his rage alight, a way of taunting the older man she'd married and now spent so much time nursing.

This morning Luke, wary, spied no hint of temper. His father seemed tame, if a bit distracted. Jeremy and Caryn still lay asleep upstairs. Mama, asleep or not, remained hidden in the big bedroom. His father was stroking the dog's head, flapping the leash against his leg as if trying to remember something. Luke slipped up against him and the doctor absently patted his second son's head too.

Together they set out into the early morning light. Rising out of the creek below the house and its small stand of willows, last remnant of a larger wood, the sun was gathering itself, waiting to unfurl the full weight of summer across the sparse flanks of countryside. Luke smelled the faint dew on the grass even as it was drawn off into the air, hovering like an echo.

His father apparently had no particular destination in mind for their stroll. He'd bought this small farm when it was surrounded by other poor farms and alfalfa fields. But just in the last year or so suburban developments had begun to harry it on all sides, gradually sealing the old house and five remaining acres in on themselves. From time to time the doctor, city boy himself, walked along the roadway, through the lanes and fields, as if measuring a campaign already abandoned.

Heat blossomed stealthily as they turned out along the main road. Dust and gravel spread away to the left. Freshly spilt asphalt was melting into a black goo in the other direction. Hardly hesitating, the doctor swung them into the worn channels and along the rills of the hard-packed yellow dirt road. But it wasn't long before perspiration broke across his brow to disorient him. Halting, he gazed toward a far bend where the gravel had been washed away by melting snow and spring rains. Parson tugged at the leash, whining. At last Luke seized his father's hand and gently tugged them round, a small boat piloting a larger, more awkward craft.

As they limped down the lane Mama was standing in the doorway, a sentinel, her hand raised. She was smiling now with relief as they approached. As Luke released his father's fingers he felt a small and secret squeeze. Startled, he glanced up.

*

"No more," their father warned. "Listen to me, Jeremy. That's enough."

"Or what?" the boy demanded, slapping at Luke's ear and shoving him hard to the deck. Caryn, darting forward, tugged at Luke's hand to draw him clear.

"Or what?" the doctor repeated in disbelief. For an hour now, teasing his brother, plucking and pinching him, Jeremy had also been harassing his father, goading the old man, taunting him.

Luke pushed Caryn's hand away. Flushed and sweaty, he lay sprawled on the hard apron behind the alley lanes. A blaze of hatred swelled in him. His father didn't care that it was Luke who was wronged, just that Jeremy was defiant, challenging his authority. Jeremy didn't care either, didn't even notice.

Luke rose to a knee and, sprung by a scalding anger, he leapt at his brother. Clawing, swiping at Jeremy, he yearned only to hurt him, to make him notice.

The older boy brushed aside his first wild blows, hardly aware of the assault, then turning to it with a harsh laugh as Luke's kicking and swinging and lunging began to annoy him. Stepping clear, Jeremy flicked a fist and caught Luke under his right eye. It staggered the younger boy.

Tears welled up, blinding Luke. Pain flared to match his fury. It throbbed in his face and he ignored it. He welcomed the hurt as a kind of gift, a discovery of what he could endure. Again he launched himself at Jeremy. He scrabbled at him, desperate to share the gift. The anger, the pain, the rush of exhilaration lifted him so that he could hardly breathe. He was soaring.

Jeremy winced under his brother's fresh attack. Again he jabbed, harder this time. His fist smashed through Luke's arms, landed on his mouth, cut him, splayed him suddenly onto the floor. Blood dribbled through Luke's lips as he tried to rise once more.

But in that same instant a blow caught Jeremy on the shoulder, slipping with a glance off his head. Not even a blow, a gesture, a despair. Together, astonished, Jeremy and Luke and Caryn realized that their father had struck him. For a single long moment they all remained very still, frozen in a new orientation, a new dance step suspended in the air. This was what Jeremy had been after all along—Caryn and Luke suddenly grasped that too—and he could gloat now, martyred. Their father stood above them, startled with himself, white with an anger already exhausted.

Jeremy's lips tightened into a sneer as he turned away, breaking the spell. All of Luke's fury drained at the sight and he felt very cold. He realized for the first time that Jeremy was nearly as tall as his father if not as heavy—he could have hit back but didn't deign to.

"I told you, I begged you." The doctor spoke at last. He was shaking his head. Shrunken and frail, short of breath, he seemed baffled by what had happened, by what he'd done. But his eyes were heavy with resignation, as if a prophecy had borne itself relentlessly true. Beads of sweat dampened his thin, graying hair to his scalp. "I told you. Why'd you have to keep after your brother that way?"

Jeremy broke away free and clear, blue eyes aflame, face stern but with a barely masked giddiness. He was already tearing off his bowling shoes and heading toward the counter. He was wounded and righteous and triumphant.

Luke remained on the ground. His father pressed a handkerchief on him and he was wiping at the blood where his teeth had gashed his upper lip. Awe at the passion that had swept him up had replaced the rage itself. He also felt guilty. As if somehow he'd done more than simply dance his part, as if he'd actually choreographed the terrible dance by insisting on his own right to be noticed.

*

"What's wrong?—What's happened?" their mother demanded. Silence and dismay hung like a shroud over her family as they drifted into the house earlier than usual. Sullen, not answering, Jeremy pressed past her and fled to his room. Behind her, enveloping them now, were the smells of a Sunday dinner prepared while the house had been blessedly her own.

"Jeremy picked a fight with Luke. That's all." Caryn, middle child, spoke up quickly, trying to shut all else out and gather peace. Luke nodded and held up the bloody handkerchief. Together they wanted to end the matter before their father arrived.

But he was already behind them, shaking his head. "I hit him," he declared, his voice too loud as if he were trying to be heard over his own disbelief.

"Hit who?" demanded his wife. She was biting her lip.

"Jeremy. I hit Jeremy." He was already holding up his hands to ward her off, her words. Something had been settled for him and, helpless, he was surrendering, though perhaps to no one but himself. "No—I know. It's time. This isn't possible." He shuddered, as if the house were shockingly cold.

Luke saw an equal disbelief flood his mother's dark eyes, a surging horror. "You hit him?" she cried softly as if she couldn't let the fact go. "What did he do? How did he make you?"

But her husband had already turned away and was climbing the stairs, puffing with speed and effort. He disappeared and it seemed that they—his wife, Caryn, Luke—could not, dared not move until he came into view once more. When several minutes later he did reappear he was carrying a valise and his medical bag. "I'll send for the rest," he said.

Caryn had settled to the carpet, dark red hair hanging over her face as her hands picked and picked. Luke watched, always watching, and he wished desperately now that some of the rage or some of the pain that had buoyed him beyond all caring in the bowling alley would return to console him. In his right hand he cradled the faint pressure where his father had squeezed his fingers that morning, only that morning.

His mother hadn't moved from the front hallway. She was shaking her head as if to make sense of fragments, of nonsense. Luke had never seen her arms wag so awkwardly. Her husband walked heavily to the door, but this time neither of them managed to speak. As it closed behind him she seemed to shrink, suddenly aged too, diminished. Craning her face up the stairs she called, "Jeremy. Jeremy!" But to this command her son did not respond.

Recitation

David Wagoner

He had to say a poem. Others before him
Got up and said their poems. Some of them
Remembered everything they were supposed to,
And some of them cried when they couldn't get the words
Right with their lips as stiff as Popsicles.

One of them didn't say anything, just stood there
And stared at his mother on the edge of her pew
Nodding and staring back, and one nice girl
Told about flowers and looked like one and smiled,
Making her hands go up and down like petals

And butterflies, and everyone murmured
And whispered how nice she was. Then his own mother
Led him by the hand up the three steps
And let him go by himself on the flat part
To the middle place where he was supposed to turn

And face the people. He was supposed to say
The poem he'd been told in his left ear
At bedtime for a week. It said he was sitting
Down on a bumpy log, being as grumpy
As he could be, while a little bullfrog

Called from a bog, *Cheer up! Cheer up!* and sounded
So funny, the boy in the poem had to laugh.
And *he* was supposed to laugh, but he wouldn't do it.
He'd seen a frog and a bog, had sat on a log,
But frogs didn't sound funny, and though he remembered

Everything he was supposed to say to these people,
He didn't want to say it. His mother was looking
Sad and his father inside his Sunday suit
Was turning red, and just when they all thought
He wasn't going to say it, he said it

Loudly in a slow sarcastic sing-song,
And they never asked him to recite another.

Three Stories

Kevin Casey

Where Dad Lived

I look at the postcard and find it difficult to understand what I think. The scene is totally familiar yet I view it with a certain apprehension as if I know that when a cloud moves or a branch creaks or a lorry drives away, something worrying will happen.

The front of the postcard is a monochrome photograph captioned "The Round Tower, Kells."

Do you know about Round Towers?

They were built between 900 and 1100 A.D. for the purpose of defending monastic settlements and stand, tall as lighthouses, mysterious in their lost usefulness. The Tower in Kells no longer has the typical conical roof but is otherwise in remarkably good condition, a testament to the construction abilities of its builders.

The postcard must be forty years old. There are three lorries parked on the side of the street, heavy and ponderous, like vehicles from some forgotten war, with tall slatted sides that suggest that they have carried animals into the town on a fair day. I can remember seeing cattle herded against the church wall close to the Round Tower and near to where the lorries are parked. Perhaps I even saw the lorries on an afternoon when school was over and I ran, my satchel heavy on my back, to see the drama of the fair. On the day that the photographer from Raphael Tuck & Sons Ltd. arrived in town I might have been there, somewhere outside the stare of his lens, watching or waiting.

I collected postcards when I was a boy and the view of the Round Tower would once have been in my big, green album. Years later, when my younger daughter had her own collection, I gave her the album. When she lost interest and the postcards were on their way to the attic, I rescued that view out of some sense of nostalgia, and was touched to see that she had written "Where Dad lived" on the back, in a child's careful, early joined writing. It was as if I had once lived in the Round Tower and survived for centuries like some figure in a fable, peering out across the plains of Meath for the first sight of hostile invaders. I suppose that, for her, the entire scene was impossibly dated and that the street that I knew and the Tower that had been there for so long looked contemporaneous, a lost world, somewhere that was over a very long time ago.

I want to understand that scene, to enter into it, to go back there again, to walk up Canon Street past the Tower and the buildings that once defined the outline of my world. I pass the house of my mother's friend, always known as little Mrs. McCarthy, deaf and inquisitorial, and the brooding clouds in the postcard are moving slowly across the sky over Loyd where there are town allotments and a paupers' graveyard. Will I go out to the river? What am I doing here? I seem to be motivated by a force much greater than memory. I feel the wind of an autumn afternoon across my face as I walk around by the Fair Green and down Carrick Street toward the cross. This is an old town and the streets curve erratically, up and down hills, with irregular steps before the doors of houses and curious windows set into thick walls. I pass lanes that I had not been allowed to visit when I was young and which I now feel no interest in investigating and the houses of boys with whom I had been at school. I can anticipate these in ways that surprise me, even guess at the color of a door. It has got colder and there is the sound of a bell from one of the churches. I seem to imagine that a bus has just pulled away from the curb and turned around the corner toward the Navan Road.

There is a middle-aged man coming toward me, walking quite briskly. He is dressed in a gray tweed overcoat and is wearing a felt hat, pulled a little jauntily toward his right ear. His walking stick is a heavy blackthorn with a silver ring and a bulbous handle. He is staring straight ahead, undistracted, making good progress. I watch him and it takes me some time to realize that it is my father, whose grave I should have visited. He is walking down Maudlin Road toward the bridge over the Blackwater, the river in which a close friend of his drowned so many years before. I want him to see me but he appears to be preoccupied, a mysterious figure. He walks away out of sight, along the empty streets of the town in which both of us once lived.

Alarms

Once upon a time the sound of the suburbs had been the voices of his children playing or the rhythmical scrape of their skates on the paths or the clash of their bicycles being dropped on the steps before the door as they ran in to plead for ten or twenty more minutes playing time. He remembered evenings that stretched imperceptibly into dusk, the new road losing its definition, shadowing into a landscape of possibilities congruent with the pretenses being enacted by the children in their play. These evenings had doubtless acquired, through nostalgia, an importance that had not been evident at the time, but they defined an era when the road and most of the people who lived there had been young.

As the children grew older, the definition of the road became less certain. Some families moved away. There was something a little threatening about the FOR SALE signs and the presence of removal vans, fracturing an atmosphere that had once seemed indivisible. The children had discovered different horizons. They traveled in to the city or to the houses of new friends from school; their voices were no longer so evident in the evenings. A number of retired couples bought some of the newly vacated houses. They were gentle presences, gardening with more care than their predecessors, anxious to salute anyone whom they met during their arthritic walks to nowhere in particular. Stoner was sometimes guilty about the antipathy that he felt toward them. He guessed that it was because of the memories that they evoked of his father's decline into parkinsonism, shuffling like they did and appearing vague. It was difficult not to fear the mystery of their decline, the other dimension that they appeared to occupy, the incomprehensibility of their landscapes.

An elderly accountant died and his widow moved into a retirement home overlooking the sea. Two doors away, a man who had once had a high media profile as a psychiatrist developed Alzheimer's disease and would sometimes wander aimlessly and helplessly like a small child, from road to road, nodding and smiling at people whom he met until his wife would find him and guide him back to their home. They moved to an apartment near to a hospital and to the center of the city. Both houses were bought by younger couples whose young children were suddenly a rejuvenating presence on the road. Their excited voices were like happy memories; they enacted the same games and familiar customs, reaffirming the enduring importance of ritual. Stoner enjoyed the energy that their play brought back to the road.

The new occupants of the houses invested in burglar alarms, devices that had been little used in the area before then. Small red or blue metal boxes began to appear above hall doors like badges of honor as if to proclaim the superior value of whatever was inside. The sounds that they made, unexpected and insistent, became a feature of the road. Their shrill ringing was invariably assumed to be an aberration rather than a proper warning; neighbors came out to stare disapprovingly at the houses but never sent for the police. Many of the alarms would switch off after ten or twelve minutes but a few went on and on until somebody with a key arrived to restore peace.

Stoner's wife, a biologist with a growing reputation, was preparing a paper for a conference on the global politics of ecology. She sat in front of a computer screen in their bedroom, tapping at a keyboard, obviously excited by the force of the ideas that she was finding. It was a summer's evening and a dead heat had gathered gradually in the house like the threat of something about to happen. Then an alarm of a new and particular shrillness sounded from somewhere close by, intruding like a scream.

"Oh for God's sake!" his wife said to Stoner as they stood on the landing, rigid with the act of listening. "If that's one of those cheap alarms that don't switch themselves off I'll never get this work finished in time."

The noise went on persistently, seeming to fill the house with something even more evident than heat.

"I'll go," Stoner said, "to see where it's coming from."

He walked down the road. The ringing had an intriguing quality of bi- or trilocation. Sometimes it appeared to be coming from one of a small square of houses at the bottom of the road, then, seconds later, it was as if it had shifted around the corner to a parallel terrace of newer houses. He pursued it like someone in an old story, beckoned on by a temptress, pursuing fate. It was getting late; the colors of the hedges had darkened or become insubstantial and shadows were strewn across the path.

A teenage boy and girl were kissing each other passionately, their hands moving across each others bodies urgently as if engaged in an act of survival. He looked at them with some envy, remembering a time when emotion and desire had been so easily expressed and yet so deeply experienced. The girl was no older than his younger daughter, slight and immature in her denim jacket and jeans but she behaved with a sexual confidence that was a little shocking to Stoner. He attempted not to look at them but it was difficult to ignore the force and fusion of their drama.

A short distance away, he located the alarm on a house that was obviously empty, its curtains open, the rooms unlighted. He had no idea who lived there and stood, a little helplessly, as if he could think up some formula that might will the sound to cease. There was something alien about this part of the road, the unfamiliar garden, the staring windows.

Suddenly, he remembered an occasion that he hadn't even thought about for years. It was a New Year's Eve, just weeks after his twentieth birthday. He was in the room that he had rented on the north side of the city, alone and not without self-pity. He hadn't been invited to any celebration and the girl whom he had asked to accompany him to a dance or to dinner had made some perfunctory excuse. The window of his room looked out onto a back garden full of old apple trees that moaned in the breeze. At the bottom of the garden there was a railway line and then, farther away, a prison, its walls and tall chimneys bulking darkly against the sky.

At midnight, he heard the sound of a bell from some distant church. He opened the window and the air was suddenly filled with urgent and persistent clanging sounds coming from the prison, staccato and rhythmical beatings that he guessed, after a few minutes, were being created by the prisoners hitting the pipes in their cells with some metal objects. The sounds gradually died away.

He was surprised at the power of the memory. He stood looking at the empty house and for a few seconds it was as if the earth exhuded an immense weariness. Then, abruptly, the alarm stopped ringing and the girl laughed and the road returned to being more or less the way that it had been.

The Hill

Months later, as he thought about it, during the extended weeks of an unusually warm summer, Stoner was unable to recall the occasion on which he had first become aware of the girl.

It could have been one morning, when he was driving his daughters to school. That was a real possibility. Or perhaps it had been later in the day as he walked along the suburban road that curved slowly downhill toward the old and almost unchanged main street of the village. There were certain familiar figures who were often encountered at these times; a few of the inhabitants of a home for old men, shuffling to or away from the diminished center of their lives, or women out walking their dogs or people coming home from work. She must have emerged from a kaleidoscopic anonymity to become recognizable, but the process would have been so gradual, such an unpredictable compound of chance and choice and coincidence that nothing would have marked its occurrence.

He had become aware of her as a tall, dark-haired girl, not beautiful, not even pretty but with an attractively athletic stride and a tendency to stare straight ahead as she walked, as if uninterested in anything other than the pace of her own progress. It may have been the intensity of that concentration that had marked her out to begin with. It hinted at a self-containment that was sufficiently unusual to notice and admire, a subcutaneous confidence that transcended the usual demeanors of the suburbs.

There was something inexplicably exotic about her. It was probably nothing more than that walk, yet after he had seen her on a number of occasions he became aware of the pallid angularity of her face. This paleness was accentuated by her long, black hair, brushed back to form a severely defined straight line above the smooth descent of her forehead. She had the look of someone from another country, a visitor from an area of the earth where faces were created with an unusual depth of definition, the cheekbones high, the chin decisive, the eyes dark and deep-set.

He became familiar with her routine, not because of any deliberate surveillance but because of the coincidence of their timetables. Each weekday morning, at almost exactly the same time, she walked toward the traffic lights in the main street of the village. She tended to wear long, black dresses or loose-fitting trousers so that the shape of her tall and intriguing body had to be imagined rather than observed. He would look at her covertly as he drove past or, if stopped at the traffic lights, watch her in the rearview mirror, coming toward him, framed by the indistinct morning faces of his daughters. She would turn left into the main street as he drove straight on toward the school. He was not a very good judge of age but guessed that she was in her late twenties.

After a few weeks, he admitted to himself that he was looking forward to seeing her. It was as simple as that. He had come to rely on the experience as if it had some definable significance; he felt deprived if he missed any of those moments of assumed intimacy. The day was changed a little by the disappointment of not seeing her.

He knew that this was foolish, that he had invented her as a child might invent an imaginary friend, but this insight did nothing to curtail his need. Her elusiveness added to the range of her attractiveness. She enticed by her failure to realize that she was occasionally observed.

He experienced some guilt about his attitude. His interest, although unknown to her, was unmistakably predatory. He looked at the faces of his daughters in the mirror and wondered how they would react if they knew what he was thinking.

One lunchtime, as he was walking to the village, he saw her coming toward him, dressed in familiar clothing, a long black dress and a black tee-shirt that featured the logo of a successful, local rock band. He panicked. He considered crossing the road to avoid her but the traffic prevented him from doing so. He could have turned and walked back toward his house but she was so close to him that this option would simply have drawn him to her attention. As she walked past, without even noticing him, her unfamiliar perfume surrounded him like some tangible expression of his desire. He would like to have turned to look after her but walked, instead, to the village, a little diminished by the experience.

On the following Friday afternoon he saw her locking the front door of an office in a small house near to the end of the main street. She was accompanied by three other girls, all talking loudly, and by a small man with a large stomach and an undistinguished mustache who seemed to be overwhelmed by their company. They went into a nearby bar. Stoner checked the brass plate beside the office door. It was for a firm of insurance brokers. He was surprised that she was involved in something so utilitarian. He had thought of her demonstrating expertise in a more complex profession with clients captivated by the extent of her allure.

He followed them into the bar and found a stool near to the end of the counter where he could see her reflection in a mirror. She was drinking lager, the long, slender neck of the bottle held between thumb and forefinger. One of the other girls was talking effusively and the man, who had taken off his jacket and loosened his tie, was nodding in agreement. They were too far away for Stoner to hear what was being said and, as he watched, the reflection was gradually dimmed by clouds of cigarette smoke.

He became aware that she walked home every lunchtime. This was surprising. She lived farther away from the village than he did and would have to spend most of her lunch hour walking to and from her home. He wondered about this; its inexplicability became a part of her enigma. It meant, however, that he could see her, if he chose to do so, several times during the day.

Once, as he was about to enter a news agents', he almost bumped into her. She was holding a tabloid newspaper and a packet of cigarettes and looked startled for a second until he stepped back to allow her leave the shop. She acknowledged this movement with a smile, a small tightening of the lips. It was the first time that they had looked directly at each other, so the moment assumed an intense importance for Stoner. He noticed that she had a very faint scar at the corner of her left eye. This detail was like a deepening of intimacy, a hint of perverse pleasure. When he next saw her, walking away from him toward the village, he was surprised to feel possessiveness assume the pressing dimension of a newly acquired skill.

Now that she might remember the encounter in the doorway, he became more cautious. He did not want to be seen but on two or three occasions he thought that she looked into the car with a slight frown of recognition. This was disconcerting. He experienced a sense of loss as if he had abandoned an initiative and become vulnerable to accusations of harassment. He decided, with some sadness, to change aspects of his routine and adjust his timetable to avoid seeing her. The unexpected result of this was that he encountered her even more often; collecting a trolley in a shopping center, standing waiting for a bus, looking at the cover of a magazine, walking along a road where he had never seen her before. These sightings, each of which provoked a shock of surprise, were even more satisfying. There appeared to be something inevitable about them, a force of fate or coincidence transcending the predictability of planned encounters. Each morning, he wondered where and when he would see her. The anticipation became an important part of the day.

There was a field behind the shopping center, a sloping patch of green that must once have been part of a farm before the suburb engulfed it. Stoner often crossed this field, taking a short cut to the public library. At its highest point, there was a weathered tree stump. When his daughters were small they would clamber onto it then jump and rush, screaming, down the hill to where he stood waiting to catch them, hot and breathless, in his arms. There were summer evenings when they seemed never to tire of this activity, repeating it over and over again in a ritual of anticipation and excitement.

He was walking to the library one Saturday afternoon when he saw a boy aged three or four climbing onto the stump. After taking a few more steps he saw that the girl was standing at the bottom of the hill, her arms spread wide. He stopped, shocked, as if he had blundered into a scene too intimate to be witnessed. The boy ran down the hill, screaming, and she caught him, scooping him up in her arms and pressing him tightly against her body as he wriggled and laughed. Then they walked away together, hand in hand.

Stoner went home. He never saw her again. Perhaps she changed her job or went to live somewhere else. He didn't really wonder about it. It was one of those things that didn't matter all that much.

Still Life

Elliot Figman

I take the objects I love and arrange them

> *brown egg*
> *white pitcher*
> *yellow bowl circled*
> *with periwinkle blue*

All objects find their home,
all objects are seated.

All pose, like Aunt Martha
with Aunt Rose;
the early, formal days.

The elegant cup casts an elegant shadow.

Who's to say the love of objects
pales beside the love of people.

The objects on the table are so peaceful;
I think about their lives.

The mind arranges itself
endlessly, slowly;

it will put the bowl
wherever it wants.

And who is looking at me?
What finite place is mine?

When We Parted

Tom Wayman

I was brought
to an offshore island
—one of those rocks that lift abruptly from breakers
to an impossible height, a mesa
in the desert of the sea.
On top, sparse soil
allows the growth of a few cedar and pine
and clusters of grass that bend with the flood and ebb
of ocean light.

And I saw from my perch
a fjord hillside with a settlement
along the water.
From the ridgeline above,
a flow of blocky, jumbled ice
descended, a glacier
that ended just higher than
the village's row or two of homes
and larger structures, dock
and pilings.

I observed a glitter of silver
threading between the sharp angles
and squares of the town:
a meltwater creek
that increased
second by second.
The runnel widened

until the banks on which houses stood
threatened to crumble.
A section of the glacier's lower edge
collapsed,
soundlessly at this remove.
The river eroding the village
surged faster, larger.

I knew I must alert
someone who could help.
I strode to the island's edge
and panicked.
I was far over
the miniature whitecaps on the sea.
I could no longer recollect
how I had been transported here:
by hang glider? Other wings?
I could not jump
from this elevation into the waves.
Nor could I clamber down
the sheer rock walls.
Even if I did
I had no boat.

The view oceanward was
magnificent: tiny combers rolling
to distant white clouds. Salt wind
ruffled my hair.
But I was sick
at the prospect of the drop
into space
on every side, as across the inlet
a glacier
and human order
washed away.

The Guitarist

David Breskin

for Bill Frisell

The guitarist goes home to the old home
where his father died. Gutbucket hospital

blues, loose change of cousins wandering
on the porch, call-and-response holler

of undertaker: this is the score of January
airplane, Carolina rain. Why some gigs

turn out the way they do is mystery
science theater of road, food and sleep. Why

certain notes attack other notes—certain
cells attack other cells—is not answered

in woodshed or studio, or on the phone
while mother gently weeps, but lies instead

against the grain of fret and neck unknown.
Slow amoeba of solo, with feedback,

against and inside the thrashing time
of drummer's snare and tom, ventures a guess.

Anaphora chorus, cilia of grace
notes swimming with echo: each piece constructs

a better place, like silence above
shouting. The guitarist carries his axe

with him at all times, into the forest
of funeral, into the Douglas fir

and weeping willow, live oak, sycamore,
because in the end your chops are all

you have against the skirling tone-deaf world:
hammer, pluck, chord, gouge, pedal, ring, sustain.

Finch Nested

Kathryn Winograd

I

Finch nested, I could not help myself
pulling down again and again
       that half globe of earth
studded by petunia, purpling flag
of the heart's bowl.

I disturbed air. I lessened heat
sometimes my rooting there
       pitched like a wound
in the eye's seed
in that dark helmet of finch head,

bird I waved into the green
unfolding. What does it mean then
       to have taken into my hands
this potted plant with its nested finch
as if it were you

or yours or this whole
long winter, your flowers of winter,
       and to hold on to it
as if you were standing at some river now
forgetting everything

and me, saying over and over again
before the mind sits only the world?

II

Everything we do is alone,
in loneliness, such
       quiet.
Here, I say to my daughters
again and again, *three blue finch eggs*

and now it is not you,
but your mother I hold
       and already my hands,
their long bones you have given me,
bend as hers did in her leaving,

their whiteness
like the first stars in the hard
       light we cling to.
Thumb size, blue tombs of the sky,
our falterings, paradisical, freckle,

here are the shells
the singing bone leaches
       in dark genetic storm, small bird pulse.
And now we watch the crossing over—
sac of the body, the vein's web, bird blossoming.

III

Resurrection. My father.
I wanted only to save them, what
       my quiet watching
had already damned, finch fled now,
and I, like some Christ with a Q-tip,

filling its nestlings with sugarwater.
They opened their mouths to me,
       all beak and dark throat,
soundless what spurs the mother.
And then the black bulge of their hearts

stopped.
How the world blurs—
          my mother weeping, wood
of my ailing father
burgeoning, all those black clusters

of trees, how can I name them,
like shrouds their branches
          in the winterlight
spilling down and the snow crusted and finch,
I mean, cardinal (the betraying

brain, oh, wounding) burning
where my father—
          Bird-Blossomer,
River-Swallowing-Snow—
already walks.

Grounded

Kawita Kandpal

Close your wings, bright angel!
They expose me to light which I have
not as yet learned either to absorb
or avoid. It only threatens me,
do you understand? And it hurts.
Ernest Sandeen

I've watched you uncomfortable
beneath goose down clouds.
They weigh heavy with your perspiration.
Feather quills pinch and poke out
a quilted cave to outline your form.
These feathers feel like tumors
they found bristling
inside your liver, you say.
I offer you food and drink,
distraction to push you up
into another day's sunrise.
My mouth presses words
like marriage and future
grandchildren into your cheek.
You want me to take down
the hanging bird feeder outside
the bedroom window. Those birds
split seed, squawk, and scatter.
This talk of feathers and nests
has made you tired.
Some have even tried to fly in,
mistaking the window for sky,
you say. At evening's end, I help
you lift your arms upward
and downward to keep muscles

from stiffening. It is then you refuse
to look at the moon.
You say your body will become that
stone which swells and stiffens
in the night sky. I want to tell you
that these hands of mine will
roll back stones from your cave.
Your body will rise
without feathers.

The Competition

Rachel Levine

For S. P. L.

The glaciers were busy
doing their glowing blue work,
drip-dripping into the rivers.

The rivers were busy
smoothing rock, enlarging their banks
in their humble rush to the sea.

The grapevines were busy
drinking from the dark earth
reaching and curling under the sun's warm hum.

Johann Sebastian Bach was busy
composing six new concertos for the Marquess Brandenburg's
competition.

The six new concertos, a fine horsehair bow
laid gently, quickly
back and forth across the strings of our souls,
each one a varied and glorious instrument in the orchestra of the court.

The hummingbirds and yellow-jackets are busy
maypoling our thumping hearts round
with Bach's harpsichord, flute and violin sounds,
and the music lifts us, we rise from our steady plod toward
decomposition. We are busy. We do.

O golden apple! O Paris!

Now, the rivers have long forgotten
the name of the composer the Marquess chose
but it was not Bach, with his six new concertos.

Killer

Catherine Seto

In the electric aura of the circus tent, 1975, a man was pedaling on a bicycle. His title, *Dai Yut*, Main Cyclist of the Beijing Arts Ensemble, filled him with majesty and laziness—he was busy making eyes at the two seamstress sisters standing across from one another. The older sister was by the stage door, framed by mesh curtains, and the younger one, the one that insisted on being called Miss Fu Lam as if she were much older than her twenty years, was leaning against the front row rail of the audience. Fourteen of his fellow performers, wearing head-to-toe turquoise satin, began clambering onto the cycle without compassion, gritty slippers pushing down on the crown of his head, a knee thrust up into the hollow of his throat, fingers poking at his eyes which were still fastened on the sisters. The audience waited for the finale, the moment in which everyone burst out their arms and twitched their fingers to create the image of a shivering, almost frightening, human peacock. But before this moment occurred, the man pedaling the bicycle, Han Li, lost his footing—the chain catapulted into the audience, and down everyone went, collapsing like a house of cards.

The older sister, Kitty, only remembered the house lights going off—or was it her hands covering her face that masked the tragedy?—and the whoosh of the crowds' screams coming at her in a tidal wave. It was Miss Fu Lam who was sure that in Han Li's last moment, he saw things no human had ever seen, the world backward, an aerial shot of his buttocks and the back of his heels. She saw her love's neck become twisted, broken beyond oblivion in the boomerang of the handlebars, his eyes opening with life in one second, arrested by darkness in the next.

They were packing a trunk within the empty guest house in the city of Nanjing, throwing clothes and fighting while the rest of the circus remained at the arena. The younger Miss Fu Lam wanted to take an ugly stallion figurine that Han had once given her, but Kitty wrestled it out of her. "We take nothing of his with us," she instructed. "If you try and take it with you, I'll beat it upside your temple, Little Sister. I will."

"Where is the boat?"

"Where do you think—by the water's edge." All her life, Kitty had seen the illegal boats, nondescript vessels by day that moved stealthily across the waters at night. Across the ocean rested a world without ancestral spirits, where she could die in peace. Even Han had said a human's worth was the significance of his death. And his crushed spirit was a sign, she was sure of it—Han was telling her to move on, nodding at her with his rouged cheekbones.

"Without Han, the ensemble is all downhill. And without the ensemble, we're nothing," Kitty said. She knew Miss Fu Lam needed to be convinced in some way. Her sister's presence was radiating through the room again—they both rubbed sandalwood over their skin, but it was Miss Fu Lam's sweat that made her smell intoxicating. A terrible urge tickled away inside of her. "And besides, do you want Han's spirit to haunt you?"

"What do you mean?"

"He was always a moody man, now think of his spirit. You took his life, he'll never forget it."

Miss Fu Lam shook her head.

"Your beauty made him weak, he lost his focus."

"You were standing there too!" Miss Fu Lam's neck snapped back, then forward. Her bright, pink lips were flapping away, "Why not you, you're the one with snake eyes, death glare eyes, hypnotic eyes."

"You made him look, Little One, standing there with your nipples— who's the one Mother always said had naughty hips. Who's the one everyone says can make the dead spit, just by pouting her lips?" Kitty had her finger pointed at her sister's breasts.

Miss Fu Lam gave a snort through her nostrils, she looked down at the floor, ashamed. It was true what their mother said, though she said those things half boasting to be modest about her daughter's beauty by shaming it. But she remained silent. Something about the way her sister presented things always rang true one way or the other—and it *was* his eyes she caught in the end, the sight of his mangled body falling to the stage, and the front wheel of the bicycle that rose above the bodies, slowly turning.

It was decided by Kitty that Miss Fu Lam was the killer. It was accepted by Miss Fu Lam's silence. The two sisters hadn't even kissed the man, one could not claim him over the other, but their shared admiration was partly why they remained together and not enemies. The sight of him, on board a unicycle with his beaded sleeves raised into the air, sent the both of them into schoolgirl antics, giggling themselves into hiccups. Kitty emphasized to Miss Fu Lam that she could not control her body, and the sight of her shape caught in lights was like a golden fruit halved—what man wouldn't lose his concentration? They would have to pay the entirety of what little savings they had for an illegal boat and start fresh elsewhere, something Kitty had been planning and saving to do anyway— working as low-life seamstresses for the circus was torturous, it was a sign wasn't it, Han's death? She put her arms around Miss Fu Lam who was now crying on the bed.

"Listen to me," Kitty said in her most convincing voice. "These days, everyone is blaming everyone. The leaders on their deathbeds are escaping into the afterworld and it's filled with restless spirits."

"I don't want to go. There's nothing there I want."

"You won't be a killer in America. Nobody will know."

"You loved him too."

Kitty closed her eyes and embraced her large, rounded body and said, no, he was not looking at me, *sa gnan*, I do not have snake eyes.

They hid out for the night on the crowded platform of the harbor boat and by morning they were out of Nanjing, passing Kowloon and across the deep marine of the Pacific. It was a miracle they survived the gales that fueled and gave supernatural powers to the water that washed overboard, spinning the boat, throwing it off course so that instead of heading to America, the driver soon announced they would be shooting for one of his brothers' boats in Canada. They ate dried, salted perch and sour relish, and when that ran out, they ran a net into the water and ate the coarse, bristly seaweed. They relieved themselves by squatting on the part of the deck which was not railed, and Kitty thought she would pass out each time a man stood and watched her with interest.

Han Li came to her in a turquoise satin outfit—he appeared on the rails in the middle of the night when she opened her eyes and the nightmare poured out of her. He was just this quick and flamboyant when he was alive. When the ensemble was on the road, asleep in the RV, he had shuffled between the two sisters, flirting and touching their cheeks with the back of his hand. When something in his costume ripped, he never took it off, insisting that they patch it up on the spot with him standing there. Kitty had felt his powerful, muscular pedaling thighs, the glimmering blue sheen as he turned his leg toward her, his wiry hair sticking out from the rip. She imagined dying in his arms, smothered in the slippery material, his slippery grasp. She heard him on the boat, calling to her somewhere beyond the rails. He said it was safe to die.

In the moments when the rains came, and the decks began filling with water, Kitty's heart pounded furiously within her weak body, so hard she thought of throwing herself off if the boat did not go down itself. Once, she rested flat on her back on the deck and inched her way forward so that her feet and then her legs slipped beneath the rails and were flapping in the wind.

"Stop it," Miss Fu Lam called out.

"I'm just resting. And if we drown, I want to be free. I don't want to be caught in the sewage drain."

"We're not going to die, if that's what you're fearing." She went over to her sister, and nudged her with her foot. When Kitty refused to move, Miss Fu Lam grabbed her wet hair and pulled her back. "If you do this again, I *will* kill you."

For Miss Fu Lam, it was easier, being a killer on a boat that seemed doomed. She accepted this, *naw sat sai,* I killed a star. And if it really were true, then there was nothing worse, the boat could plummet them all into the water, and she would know it was Han giving her punishment, or ending her misery. She used to imagine how his touch would feel, his dark, bony face pressed to hers and the sound of his voice, the sound of a wounded dog as he kissed her down every inch of her body, worshipping it. With each passing day, she was more ready to accept life or death, and something in that made her invincible.

Kitty was weakening every waking moment. She lay flat on her back in the belly of the boat where it stunk of piss and mold, closing her eyes and thinking she could not bear it for another second. One day, she opened her eyes and her strong little sister was holding her hand—it was toward the end of nearly two weeks, and Miss Fu Lam was guiding her off of the ramp into a drier boat docked a mere ten miles from the Toronto harbor. In this boat, they were given hot *bo lai* tea, dry sheets to wrap themselves in, and assignments for places where they could find work without needing permits. The two sisters looked at each other, both afraid to smile, for what if something happened to this boat and they drowned just miles from land, Han looking down at them from the afterworld, cackling?

A year had passed since Miss Fu Lam and her older sister Kitty fled Nanjing when they heard of Mao's death. They were working in a garment warehouse on Yonge and Bloor in the heart of Chinatown, and had enough money to rent an apartment with its own running toilet with an enamel, mint green seat. They read about his death on the front page of the Toronto Sun at the corner of what was then the new Chinatown, fighting over the page that held the photograph of the Chairman's grizzly, half-glum smile, the heavy folds of his eyes angling up to make a triangle shape of his face. There was a downpour and it washed the hair spray out of Miss Fu Lam's perfect hair and it dribbled down her sweater, some of it splattering on her new heels where the fuschia color started to bleed away. She looked at Kitty who had grown fatter and exposed a triple chin when nodding. Miss Fu Lam proceeded to curse her out, blaming her for their being in the middle of Dundas Avenue on a rainy day when they could be in Beijing mourning their leader and being blown to bits with dust.

"Water brain," Kitty scolded. "He'd be riding bicycles all over your head if you were still there."

"To hell with you, it wasn't my fault," she said.

"It was decided."

"Well then, fine, if it'd make you feel better than fine—I'd be tortured by him. To hell with you." Miss Fu Lam continued cursing as she ran down the street, screaming at the top of her lungs, "*Sai gung*, I never want to see your ugly face again!"

Up until that moment, Miss Fu Lam had been unhappy in Toronto. But the rain had cooled her skin, and she went into a noodle shop where she let the steam of the broth move across her face. She enjoyed running from her sister in the rainstorm, it was oddly soothing to have all the hair spray washed from her. She wandered the streets for hours in the dark: being a killer made her a foolish brand of unafraid. She finally stopped into a flower shop and bought a red gladiola that looked like a stick of fire, making her laugh.

Kitty went back to her apartment and put on her brocade slippers and fell asleep with her hands folded neatly beneath the puddle of her cheeks. In the middle of the night, she felt her sister's palm stroking her hair, which was still wet, and the sound of her voice, *gnaw fon lai na*, I'm back again.

It was always this way. Miss Fu Lam never followed through with her threats. The heat rose and throttled her mind for awhile and she'd have to break away, choosing to sneak back conscious, wide-eyed, when the rest of the world at an ungodly hour was not. She returned when she knew Kitty was dreaming—this was what calmed her, sneaking back into the little apartment so that she could watch her older sister's eyeballs dart from side to side under their lids. She knew the nemesis of Kitty's dreams. She accepted again her sister's accusations. People told them they should have been twins, or their souls should have been combined to make one child, a great son, who would have amounted to something. This was how they knew without speaking to never contact their family again when they left to join the Ensemble and tour all of China in three metallic, pill-shaped RVs. This was how they knew the sort of crazy love they had fallen into with a man best described as a stranger.

Miss Fu Lam peeled lichees for her sister at the kitchen table, and then she left for her own room, ending the night. The night was clear, the breeze pushed in from the slit of the window and rolled over her face and her open eyes, and she was haunted by Han. He did not appear in her dreams like he did for Kitty, he kept her awake, he sometimes haunted her in the day when she walked down a street and saw a ring of bicycles tethered to a tree where the only thing she could do was fix her eyes on the red bricks of a Victorian house and pray. Sometimes, when the sight of bicycles became overwhelming, she went over to them and would push the first one down with her foot until all of them rested against each other in a severe and slanted shape. She would hike her skirt up and run down the street, grinning with mischief.

As for Kitty, she put her head back down on the table, drifting, dreaming: of Mao and Han Li, seated before a great, mahogany table, peeling lichee nuts for one another. Mao was explaining that it was the act of peeling that he was after, not so much for the taste of the fruit which was tart during the spring season. They were good friends. Han nodded and then he looked up at the ceiling which broke wide from the weight of a bicycle, crashing down on and killing him. Great leaders and entertainers were one in the same, Han screamed through laughter. What do you have to live for, he shouted at her, be brave and die. And he fastened his gaze on her face, and entered her through her irises. It was true, she thought, she was dead in her family's eyes the day she left. She had joined a circus and created costumes made only to be soaked with sweat, to fade beneath floodlights, torn by the bodies that molded them. She had fallen asleep on a platform bed beside her sister whose smell was raw, waiting for desire.

The next day, Kitty rode the elevator. It was her favorite thing to do when she was not piecing corsets at the assembly, ascending the elevator to the top floor maternity ward of Hope Memorial—not for babies, but for the view, which overlooked the Toronto harbor. It was a cold day, and she chose to stay inside of the building rather than go out onto the observation deck. She looked out through the glass and it was fascinating to her, how indistinguishable things were made by the water, unable to gauge whether Nanjing was above or beneath or east or west of her, whether the biting gales that swooped off the surface had any of China's breath to them. The babies bothered her, especially the ugly ones with their crooked mouths quivering with noise. She was watching their rubbery limbs snap and twitch in their mothers' arms, and she was glad that her own mother had said to her that she would be too fat, too plain, too abysmal to make her womb attractive enough for a baby to bloom within it. Her womb was a dark house, a charred and unwelcome pit.

"Miss, what are you doing?" The nurse asked. She was wheeling a cart filled with bed linens, and she was staring at Kitty, who had managed to stick her knee out over the ledge of the window.

"I dropped my wallet."

The nurse went over to the window and looked all the way down where the cars were nothing but dots. She looked at Kitty, whose face remained expressionless. The wind was blowing her short hair back, and her eyes were as dark and impermeable as a magpie's. "What in the world are you trying to do?"

Kitty couldn't answer. The windows in the maternity ward were small squares, made that way for safety. She had realized that when her leg was dangling in free air, and the rest of her body waited to be twisted, then shot out, that she was too fat to be pushed all the way through.

The nurse put her in an office and locked the door. "Where is your husband?"

"I don't have one."

"What about your parents?"

"They're dead."

"Who is close to you, anyone I can reach?"

"Han Li," she answered, smiling.

"And where can I get a hold of him?"

"He's dead. I killed him." Kitty smiled and tucked her hands beneath her legs. "No, I am just kidding."

She didn't know what Han had been thinking, why he had ever flirted with her and stared at her heavy legs as if they were the loveliest things he had ever seen. He was the only man who adored her. Before Han had become the main cyclist, he was part of an eleven-formation that made a neat pyramid and rode around the ring several times. His ego was smaller, he wore a plain white shirt and asked Kitty to iron it only before performances. Then he got the idea of a record-breaking fourteen-formation—members gashed arms, bruised ribs and mashed toes trying to perfect it. She was backstage on the night that it was perfected, as frightful a sight as it was. He ran backstage and embraced Kitty, lifting her thick body into the air. He wanted fancy costumes from then on, he wanted them pressed and ironed everytime they left a member's body. *Yes*, she murmured, *whatever you want. Gnaw oi lai*, he adored her, this was what he said, the foul pig, and then he told Miss Fu Lam the same thing.

He was spoiling Toronto for her, which she would have loved completely for its flowering parks and red streetcars, had not everything she did in the day end up as a nightmare of Han: the bright sun appeared in his mouth when he opened it to kiss her, the baskets of tangerines along Kensington Market were force-fed by him into her gorged stomach until the acid hissed with delight. She thought of overdosing on iodine. There were bottles of it on the shelf behind the nurse. She gave a heavy sigh because it wasn't working, he had followed her across the Pacific.

It became routine that on the weekends, Miss Fu Lam took long afternoon walks outlining the perimeter of Chinatown, always stopping at flower shops smelling mums, letting the petals pucker to her nose. She wore her long, black hair tied back into a bun the size of a fist and bound her breasts with a length of cloth against her body. She was careful not to put her hands on her hips, drawing attention to them when she stood on street corners, or carry a posture that would make them swing when she walked. Still, the butchers waved at her through their steamy, square windows, and the men playing dice on the streets called out to her, *lang nouy*, pretty thing, *bay gnoi niep lay*, let me pinch you where it's wet. What was left of her sadness was the notion that in this place, Han could not be felt. Even the sight of bicycles provided her with just a streak of shivers that soon went away. He was not here on this Canadian land, he could not be reached. He was in the red afterworld, cluttered with fragrant, silk-spun hills, and it was on a cloud that hung an eternal distance above the stretch from Beijing, to Shanghai, to Guandong.

On the day Kitty went to visit the hospital, Miss Fu Lam was visiting the flower shop on the corner of Chinatown next to the movie house where she spotted a plaster angel fastened at the canopy. The face of this cherub was Han Li's at the flash before the lights went out—his face, like this angels, possessed no pupils, no shadow, just a lucid, pale look indicating the world had come to an end. She stood frozen at its presence, until the owner was nose to nose to her.

"*Surng mai mah*, do you wish to purchase it?"

"Its face is haunting. No, I'd be crazy to want it."

"Well, you have a pretty face, it looks like you."

She said nothing.

"Let down your hair, it will be wavy just like it."

"Are you crazy?"

"I'm going to give it to you for half price."

"'*M sai*, no need to."

"You'll be doing me a favor, see the crack along its hand?" He twisted the giant cherub off the hook and cradled it under his arm. The owner was young, and skinny—almost as skinny and handsome as Han was, but his neck was thicker and his skin was a light naples-yellow hue.

Miss Fu Lam looked right at him, and then she slowly undid her hair, searching and plucking out the bobby pins. He was leaning nervously forward at her, and she leaned against the wall. She felt her *minop* grow taut, and she decided she was going to sleep with this man, whether he was married or not. The feeling erupted like a spark. She left with his phone number printed on a receipt, and the plaster angel cradled in her arms.

She was sitting in the apartment, in the armchair beneath the picture window. The radiator was broken and hissing, and she changed into a summer dress filled with silk-screened butterflies all the colors of bubble gum. The phone rang, and when she picked it up, it was the exasperated voice of the nurse. She dove into her heels, draping a sweater over her shoulders, and ran down the street to catch a streetcar.

At the hospital, her sister waited in the pysch ward wearing a tissue gown. "They made me swallow a tray of orange pills," she told Miss Fu Lam. "They think I'm mad."

"She's not crazy," Miss Fu Lam said, turning to the doctor.

"No, she's not," he said. "We found out she really did drop her wallet out the window. But I'm concerned about your sister— she'll need routine therapy. It's not normal behavior."

Miss Fu Lam nodded. She looked over at Kitty who nodded along with her. They rode a taxi back, both pressed up against the windows, stifled by the silence. When they returned back to the apartment, Miss Fu Lam tried sitting in the kitchen, trying to smooth out her summer dress which was wrinkled as if she had slept in it, the butterflies askew on the sky of blue silk. She was in the process of making tea, mixing fresh chrysanthemum petals with dried ones, flushing them with sugar water.

"They said they thought you were trying to jump," Miss Fu Lam said.

Han had seen the world backward before he died, perhaps her sister was trying to do the same.

"*Tse zien*, ridiculous." Kitty was leaning against the stove, inhaling the smell of boiled flowers. "Why did you let your hair down? You look like a *gai nouy*, hooker."

"Everyone wears their hair like this nowadays."

"Well, it looks different on you. You look indecent."

Miss Fu Lam squinted at Kitty, wondering if her sister had come all this way just to die. "I don't want to hear it."

"It's true. And the dress, it shows your nipples."

Miss Fu Lam felt the heat rising within her again, and she went into her bedroom. She ran to her drawers and in distress pulled down her stockings and her underwear and found the slip with the pink rosettes embroidered into the straps. She rode the streetcar all the way from Jarvis to Spadina and found herself at the door of the flower shop again. When she saw the warm light fill the windows, her heart gave a sigh, and when he appeared, she did not hesitate to follow him upstairs into his little flat smelling of Tiger Balm. A half empty vial of it was by his night stand, and she dipped her fingers into it and went right up to him and smeared the menthol jelly down his neck and under the band of his undershirt. The strength of it made her eyes water, but she continued on, wrapping her arms around him and pressing the balm in circles against his back and down the smooth bone of his spine.

The next morning, she asked his last name.

"Hui," he replied. "Tat Ken Hui."

"My family calls me Miss Fu Lam as a joke because I am the youngest and I always wanted to be older," she said. "Though I wouldn't want to be my older sister."

"Do you care for your sister?"

"I do."

He nodded, as if he understood.

"Well, we don't speak much. She has a blackbird mouth sometimes, it gets loose and says horrible things. I'm tired of that, I'm tired of being horrible."

"Horrible to her."

"Yes, that's a good way of putting it."

There was an awkward pause between them. His eyes lowered in shyness, and she lifted her head up and said, "You know, the next time we do this, it would be nice to make use of your flowers. It would be nice to get rid of the ointment stench."

He stared at her in disbelief, *the next time*, still shocked by the fortune of her body curled around his. "The red mums are the most fragrant, and hothouse magnolias," he managed to blurt out. "We can burn them with incense."

Kitty lifted the plaster angel up by its wings and wondered if this was what spirits looked like in this part of the world. This angel was pale, chalky, it looked sickly to her. She was lying in the courtyard of the apartment building. Weeks had passed since she dropped her wallet at the hospital. A rounded hedge had broken her fall and she was lying in the dented mass of leaves and broken branches. She cursed at herself, the apartment was on the second floor after all, and falling served as nothing but a joy ride. Her back was twitching, but she managed to rise to her feet. The angel was looking up at her, its nose broken off so that it now resembled an animal. The sun was going down and it washed a glow of resin over the lawn. A sense of dread fell over her, imagining her death ordinary, occurring in her sleep or when she had grown grisly and old.

"I am insignificant," she said to the angel. She scoured the grounds for its nose.

The angel did not reply.

"I was just sitting there on the ledge," she explained. Her feet were swinging back and forth and the angel was beside her. She had fallen first, then pawed in the air and caught the angel's head and took it down with her. She fell with her arms outstretched, balancing the sculpture. The impact was filled with darkness, and she wondered if this was what Han had seen before his glorius death. She started to cry when she opened her eyes and saw pedestrians roaming about on the sidewalks. They flashed through the slits of the black iron fence that circled the courtyard and passed her.

Miss Fu Lam wondered if Kitty became accustomed to opening the door of her sister's room and seeing nothing but a mammoth angel perched on the dresser. She wondered if Kitty would find its features equally as mesmerizing. She got up and peered out Tat Ken's picture window, imagining it was her own, the one in her apartment which faced the street and the rush of streetcars that dragged haloes of black wire sparking. She imagined her sister wandering back into her room seeing the empty bed, and the single wrinkle that fell across the sheet. The light in the hallway would cast a line of shadow that would creep up the back of her nightgown, disappearing into her dark hairline.

"Why not move the rest of your things here?" Tat Ken asked.

"There's nothing left, really."

"And Kitty?"

"Oh yes, there's Kitty left," she laughed.

The next night, and the night after that, Miss Fu Lam fell onto Tat Ken's sheets with the flower petals ground beneath the cover of the mattress. She opened her mouth and let him kiss her, his body pushing into her until his hands went up around her back and grasped her shoulder blades. And one nameless evening, she opened her eyes, and Han was gone from her. She remembered hearing Tat Ken shake the ash from the incense, placing it onto the wall altar. When she lifted the sheet and brought it down over their bodies, she inhaled in the hot delight, the luxuriant sweetness that was caught around them. Their limbs were entangled, and the flowers were everywhere, pressed into their pores, the petals stuck between toes. She would not return back to Kitty. She would not ask what Kitty was dreaming. The window above her head was sooty in the night, and she laced her fingers in the dark with his. She drifted into sleep knowing every variety of flower that was buried beneath her back, *hyacinth, hothouse magnolia, japonica, orange blossom* . . .

Over the Moon

Blake Maher

The paper birches were doing battle. They thrashed and shook their leaves, the wind blowing helter-skelter. I stared into the hole, Sang one step behind me, my loose shirttail clutched in his thin hands. It was more than a hole really, a rectangular pit the size of a small cellar—the trap we called it—its opening thatched with a crisscross of dead branches. The two of us had dug it the week before.

"Anything?" Sang whispered nervously over my shoulder. I doubted there would be, certainly not what he hoped for. He pushed back his hair, silk smooth and black, the kind of hair I imagined back then that all Vietnamese children had. Circling Sang's hips was the plastic cowboy holster the Taylors had bought him and, around his neck, on a single strand of twine, hung a fat clove of garlic, a charm that I'd promised would keep away the Sasquatch. Because of me, he was frantic one would kill him.

I pressed my finger to my lips. "Shhh! It hates the sound of your voice."

He drew a toy gun from his holster, waved it anxiously. "I am not scared! I shoot it up! Bang! Bang!"

"Stay back," I warned and began pulling branches off the opening.

The trap, of course, was empty, a great earthy void below us, and seeing this Sang relaxed his grip on my shirt, though his left eye continued to twitch. His hand drifted upward and he pulled out an eyelash. "It is almost noon—yes, Ricky? I must go back now. The Taylors will come soon." Since he'd arrived in Stillwater, Sang had gone on day trips with the Taylors almost every weekend, though he was living with Nanna Deplanques, a relation of my father's with whom I was staying too while my parents were away. Sang's boarding there was temporary, to last only until our parish found him a good home. I pictured him in a nice house with smiling parents and, knowing Sang's luck, a great dog. Probably goddamn Lassie. Though at eleven I was a year younger than Sang and small for my age, I stood almost a full three inches taller than him. He had miniature hands with tiny little wrists as thin as bamboo shoots, and his skin had a translucent delicacy that made it seem as if he might dissolve in sunlight. On his right cheek was a scar, a circular burn mark the size of a quarter.

I pushed the branches back over the hole. "I bet they won't adopt you," I told him.

He looked uneasy. "You don't think?"

I shook my head emphatically, though in truth I thought his adoption by the Taylors was inevitable. Everyone loved Sang. His onyx eyes and high musical voice charmed all the adults we knew. He was also kind and well mannered, two things I wasn't, and even back then I could see that it was these qualities—not his foreignness as I tried to convince myself—that drew people to him. Still I felt envious of all the attention lavished on him. Men my father's age rumpled his hair and rummaged in their pockets for half-dollars to give him; women went all motherly when they saw him, cooing and fussing as they pulled him onto their laps. Worse for me still were his weekend visits with the Taylors, visits from which he always returned laden with gifts.

"They say they will buy me a fishing pole and take me to the Saint Lawrence River. Maybe I will not go to Texas now. Maybe I will stay here instead," Sang said.

I vibrated with resentment.

I sniffed the air, pretending I'd caught a hint of some foul scent.

Sang grabbed a rock from the pile of stones we'd excavated from the hole, his dark eyes darting back and forth, the rock poised. The wind tore through the trees, showering a spray of pine needles onto his hair. "You smell something, Ricky?" His nostrils quivered. So did his voice. "You smell a Sasquatch?"

The week before while out in the woods, Sang and I had seen a humongous black bear off the trail near Nanna's. Through a screen of pine boughs, we'd watched it lumber menacingly through the trees, its dark shape moving toward us like something from a bad dream. It stopped beside a young birch tree and then, bawling out a horrible tin sound, began shaking the trunk until the tree groaned and cracked and fell. Even after the bear ambled off, Sang had stood staring after it in silent terror-filled awe. "Shit Almighty!" he'd whispered. Like my family, Nanna lived in the Adirondack Mountains, and Sang's fear of the strange sounds and smells and animals there was acute. He never seemed so out of place to me, so completely dislocated as when we were out exploring the woods, pretending we were Iroquois or Algonquins. The machine-gun chatter of a raccoon or a deer suddenly bolting through the trees always made Sang freeze in panic. After the bear had disappeared, he'd grabbed my hand. I'd smelled something sharp and slightly sour—fear. "What you call that?" he'd asked, squeezing my hand until my knuckles went white. I'd reached out and pinched him hard. "Sasquatch," I'd said and he'd shivered visibly as if the word itself were evil. He'd asked if it was dangerous and I'd nodded with conviction. "It eats little gooks like you. Sucks the flesh off their bones. Good thing we're down wind—otherwise you'd be dead." I'd gone on to describe horrors of flaying and decapitation so gruesome that the next day Sang had appeared before me with a shovel in hand. "I will catch it before it catch me!" he'd announced.

As we followed the trail back toward Nanna's, Sang fell in step behind me, scuffing his feet the way I did. "Ricky?" he said, stopping, "you think Nanna Grace will sell her house like Rose Marie say?"

I grabbed a stick from the path. "I told you not to listen to Rose Marie, Sang."

"But she say Nanna will leave."

"Ignore her, man. Rose Marie doesn't know beans." I squinted through the trees, out over the clearing to Nanna's house, an old, white wood structure that sat like an aging queen on a bluff above the lake, its long glinting windows reflecting onto the black water. It was the kind of weather in Stillwater that seemed to make everything move more slowly—the temperate wind, the swaying of trees, the slow slap-slap of the lake against land—but instead of feeling calmed by the tempo, I felt restless, impatient in knowing that each hour would drag by in the same dull, predictable way. I thumped my stick against a hollow tree.

"Where are you going with the Taylors?"

Sang gave me a wary glance. He scratched a mosquito bite on his elbow. "Amusement park," he said quietly. I pictured him plunging downward on a rickety roller coaster, his mouth wide with pleasure, his body pressed safely between Mr. and Mrs. Taylor. The park was a local tourist attraction, the kind of noisy, hectic place that children loved and adults hated. Full of junk food and overpriced trinkets—a place I had only been to a few times with my parents though we lived just on the other side of the lake.

When I banged the tree again a cluster of bugs swarmed down the trunk. "I bet you won't like it there. I've been a million times. It's boring and smells like the dump. Most of the rides there are for babies."

Sang plucked another eyelash from his eye.

I warned him of the dangers of such delicacies as cotton candy. "It's poisonous," I said with authority. "It makes you sick if you eat it. I knew a kid who died from it last year. He couldn't stop throwing up blood."

Sang stood wide-eyed. My word was gospel. He glanced back to where the trail was swallowed up by the trees. He fingered his holster. "They have animals there?"

I pictured the petting zoo at the amusement park, the goats and pigs and harmless hutched rabbits. I shrugged. "Some."

He plucked out another eyelash, let it fall and twirl to the dirt. "They have Sasquatch?" he asked.

Except for what I'd overheard Nanna telling my mother earlier that summer, I didn't know much about Sang's life before he came to Stillwater. He was from a small village on the Bantangan Peninsula where his parents had been killed, their farm shelled by U.S. forces; he hadn't seen his younger sister since a battalion of American soldiers had loaded them and a bunch of other villagers onto separate trucks and driven off; he'd had a younger brother too, an infant who had died with the parents. Besides that there was no other family as far as anyone knew. Though I thought he was lying, Sang insisted that the burn mark on his cheek had been there for as long as he could remember. I wanted to believe it had some exciting wartime origin.

Before coming overseas, Sang had spent several months at an army compound near Saigon where an American GI, a twenty-one-year old Texan named Hank Mitchell, had befriended him. In a snapshot he'd shown me, Sang was seated on the hood of a mud-splattered jeep, a combat helmet pushed up on his broad forehead; next to him was a young American soldier dressed in regulation olive pants and t-shirt, his body leaning casually against the jeep in a pose of practiced arrogance, a posture I've always since associated with soldiers. Hank—as Sang identified the soldier—was making a peace sign, his lopsided smile seeming to insinuate some private joke. To me Hank looked like every other GI I'd ever seen, but to hear Sang tell it, Hank had hung the moon: Hank lived on a ranch—Hank owned horses and guns—Hank lived for glory like a Hollywood cowboy. Sang swallowed everything Hank had told him, hook, line, and sinker. He talked about him incessantly. "Hank say to me 'You will make good cowboy, Sang. When I go home I will take you with me and you will be my boy. You will be John Wayne, Jr.'" While even back then I knew this was unlikely, I still begrudged Sang even the slimmest chance that this might come true, that Hank might take him to Texas and provide him with some kind of fairy-tale life.

At the time my own parents were off on what they half-jokingly referred to as their fourth second honeymoon. For them second honeymoons had become an almost annual event, patchwork efforts to mend the existing tears in their marriage before they were beyond repair. Usually my older brother and I were shipped off together, but this time he'd gone to Cape Cod to visit my mother's family while I'd been left behind at Nanna's.

In retrospect, I see that Nanna, who'd always been something of an eccentric, was starting to get a little senile. She collected random things—doorknobs, pine cones, discarded pen husks, old shoelaces. Sometimes she even forgot my name. If I entered a room unexpectedly, she would often look up at me with a slightly bewildered expression on her face, as if my arrival had somehow dislocated her memory. The inside of her house was cluttered with all sorts of junk—colorful rocks, oddly shaped pieces of dried wood, anything at all of interest she came across— all of it strewn about haphazardly, the counters and shelves dripping with old dog leashes and rusted picture frames. Once I'd wandered into her kitchen to find her standing before the stove, holding a collection of dirty thimbles, dropping them one by one into a pot of boiling water. She'd become flustered when she saw me watching and accused me of spying. Didn't I know better, she'd scolded me, hadn't my parents taught me not to sneak around like that? Unsettling as they were, such outbursts were not common. Usually she was generous and giving. Over the years she had opened her home to a slew of needy kids, Sang being only the latest in a long line.

That Saturday, after Sang had gone off with the Taylors, Nanna and I sat at the old Steinway in the parlor. At my mother's insistence, I had been taking piano lessons from Nanna for almost a year. As I banged out an awkward C scale, she corrected my hand position. Rose Marie, Nanna's middle-aged daughter who was visiting from Tampa, sat on the love seat opposite us, flipping through the property listings Mrs. Taylor had left for her. Rose Marie greatly admired Mrs. Taylor's career as a real estate agent. A real modern women, she called her. The week before Rose Marie had driven up from Florida to escape the sweltering heat and had not seemed overly pleased on her arrival to find two young boys underfoot. In conversation, she referred to me as "Cousin Ricky," as if she had been born and bred in the Old South, not northern New York state, and whenever Sang was out of earshot she called him "our little alien." She made it sound as if he were from the moon.

"It can't hurt to think about it, Mother." Rose Marie glanced up from the listings, her skin so deeply tanned that all her features seemed to blur together, her eyes and gold earrings the only points of reference for the rest of her face. Since her arrival, she'd been on a campaign to get Nanna to sell her house, to move down South closer to her. No winters, no snow, no icy roads, she said. No frozen pipes, no thirty-below-zero temperatures. But Nanna wanted no part of it. Her life was here, she said. What would she do in Florida? Play Parcheesi with a bunch of other widows?

"Summer is the best time to show," Rose Marie went on now. "All I ask it that you talk with Mrs. Taylor about what's happening around here, what kind of prices people are getting. Don't give me that look, Mother. I'm not saying you should sell tomorrow—but you're going to have to face facts sometime. This house is getting too big for you all alone."

Nanna stopped tapping the beat out on my wrist. "Good Glory, Rose, will you just stop. I don't want to have this conversation again. I hate it when you talk like I have one foot in the grave."

Rose Marie lit a cigarette and shook out the match. She exhaled an exasperated cloud of smoke. "Mother, don't get yourself all worked up. All I'm saying is that you should be considering your options. The market is good right now. You could make a tidy sum, get a cozy place on the beach. Listen to the waves, relax. God knows you deserve it after a lifetime up here. Why on earth anyone lives year-round in this forsaken wilderness is beyond me. Mother, look, all I'm trying to do is have a little bit of foresight." Nanna began tapping my wrist again as she grumbled something about preferring hindsight. Rose Marie thought Nanna was too old—too old to be living alone, too old to be driving her ancient Buick around the back roads, too old, I'd even heard her say on a number of occasions, to be watching Sang. She thought someone else from St. Mary's should act as his guardian. Someone who wasn't old enough to be his great-grandmother.

"What's happening with our little alien?" she said. "Any decision yet?"

"You're the one who's become so chummy with Mrs. Taylor. I'm surprised you don't know." Nanna pushed my wrists down into position. "Flatten the backs of your hands, Ricky."

"Really, Mother—I've just asked her a few questions."

"Well, I don't know what they've decided—and what's more, I don't care," Nanna said sharply. "Father O'Brien is in charge of those things. They were cleared by the agency. Seem like decent folks. It's a shame she can't have her own. The boy is an older child—that can be an adjustment—but I don't think they're gun-shy. At least there's no hurry. He can stay with me as long as need be."

In the mirror behind the piano, I could see Rose Marie's reflection changing like an image in a fun house. As if the lower half of her jaw and chin had turned to putty. Her eyes widened. "Mother," she said, her voice sliding upward. "You sound as if you want to adopt him yourself."

Nanna continued counting time out loud.

"Mother?"

Nanna didn't respond.

"Mother, you are seventy-eight!"

Nanna slammed her hands on the keys. "I know how old I am for Christmas sake! Don't talk nonsense, Rose. Of course I'm not thinking of adopting him." Her voice quavered. "I just feel bad is all. He's such a sweet little boy."

Rose Marie walked stiffly to the window, her dark dyed hair pulled back so that it gave her the severe dramatic look of an old ballerina. Her cigarette sent up a stripe of smoke. Outside the wind rushed over the glinting wave tops, making them surge shoreward.

The conversation ended there and Nanna directed her attention toward my lesson. As we finished, Rose Marie approached us, fishing something out of her cardigan pocket. "I almost forgot. I picked up the mail when I was in town this morning. This is for you, Ricky," she said, handing me a postcard. On the front was a picture of wide white ocean beach, a touristy man and a woman seated on the back of a giant artificial fish, riding it across the ocean like rodeo stars. ". . . and you should see the one that got away . . . " my mother had written beneath the picture in her smooth sloping hand. The back read: "Having a great time. Hope you are, too. Be good for Nanna. We'll be back on Sunday. Love you." I handed it to Nanna.

"Mother, promise you won't get angry at what I'm going to tell you." Rose Marie turned and glided back toward the window. "I asked Kimberly—Mrs. Taylor—if she would come by a little early tomorrow. I asked if she might have a word with us about the house."

Nanna's body went rigid. Her right arm began to twitch. I thought she might bang her hands down on the keys again, but instead she pivoted toward me on the bench, opening her mouth as if she was about to speak. Except that no sound came out. Nothing. Instead her mouth remained open—a dark gaping hole—then her eyes rolled back slightly so that just the whites showed. They fluttered for a few seconds, then they rolled back down—as if she were in a trance. After a minute, she turned over the postcard in her hand, bringing it up so close to her face that it was almost touching her nose. Her hands were shaking.

"Nanna?" I said.

Rose Marie turned. "Mother?"

Nanna reached out tentatively, set the postcard down. "Isn't that lovely," she said. Almost as if she hadn't seen it at all.

The evening news flashed over us as Sang lay on the floor beside me, staring at the television, his new baseball glove beside his head. At that age I would have preferred just about anything to sitting through the news—another hour of adults blabbing at me, the screen filled with pictures of hippies and protests and Nixon's guilty face—but Sang insisted on watching each night. I'd noticed how he'd become more attentive whenever a story about Vietnam came on, but when I asked him what he was looking for he just shrugged.

Earlier he'd recounted his trip to the amusement park, telling about each ride he'd been on, imitating how Mrs. Taylor screamed as the Octopus had flung them skyward—how she'd barfed her brains out afterward. And then he'd unveiled the biggest surprise of the day, the baseball glove Mr. Taylor had bought him, a fine deep leather mitt with a well-padded pocket and an imprint of Mickey Mantle's autograph. I looked at it with envy. I thought it was about the most beautiful thing I'd ever seen. "Mr. Taylor says I will be the next great player," Sang had chattered enthusiastically. But during the news, he'd become increasingly quiet. His eyes were closed and he was humming quietly, a high-pitched angular song I'd never heard.

When I pulled his new glove onto my hand, he sat up. "Mr. Taylor say he will take me to see the Yankees in New York City. Maybe next year you and me will be on your same ball team here."

I tossed the glove aside as if I could have cared less. "Maybe," I said. Then I looked at him. "Nanna is going to talk to Mrs. Taylor about selling the house, you know." He stared back at me without blinking. "I got a postcard today from my mother," I continued. "She said my father caught the biggest fish anyone's ever seen in Maine."

Sang tugged the glove on. It was too large for his small hand and I felt a quick thrill of satisfaction. He caught me smiling and looked at me as though he were trying to decide something. Finally he touched his lips together delicately and spoke with a careful deliberateness.

"Cotton candy is very good," he said.

I felt as though I'd been kicked in the gut. My voice stuck. "You'll get sick."

Sang stood up. "You are a liar," he said, his voice brimming with anger. "You lie about everything. Cotton candy is good. It is not poison. I love it." He started for the front door, but then turned back and glared at me with something akin to hatred. "There no such thing as Sasquatch. Mr. Taylor says that you make it up. He says you are just trying to scare me. You are not my friend!" he yelled and slammed the door. I watched him run across the lawn, into the woods.

The truth in Sang's words made me feel somewhat guilty—but also vengeful—embarrassed at having been caught in my own deceit.

I got up and followed Sang down the trail, walking quietly, carefully, not sure what I planned to do, but not wanting him to hear my approach. Maybe I would sneak up on him, I thought, scare him a little to even the score. Fifteen yards or so before the trap, I spotted him up high on the limb of a tree, his legs astride the branch as though he were riding a horse. He was singing the same strange tune he'd been humming inside, the words in Vietnamese, not English. I stepped off the trail and crouched down out of sight. After a while he stopped singing and began talking out loud instead, using two different voices, the first an imitation of an American man with a thick southwestern accent, the second his own.

"You like to come live with me, Sang?"

"Do you have horse?"

"No."

"Can I shoot guns?"

"No."

"Drink Whiskey?"

"No."

"You have a pot I can shit in?" He began giggling.

"Yeah-yas," he drawled.

"OK then. I come be your boy."

He laughed harder, swinging and lifting himself off the branch as his legs flew backward, his hands set squarely before him. But after a minute his laughter subsided. He lay his head down on the branch. He squeezed his eyes shut, hugging the tree.

"Hank is dead," he said in the first voice. Then he began to cry.

My stomach felt as if it had dropped out; I wanted to slip away, without being noticed, but as I made to leave, an explosion of sudden sound—like a flock of birds taking flight or the sudden rush of rain—burst from behind me. As I swung around, an eight-point buck crashed out of the thicket. I saw the corded muscles in its neck, its white tail flashing as it leapt. I heard Sang scream as it bounded toward him. The buck sprang into the air again and for a moment it seemed as if could fly, as if it might just keep soaring upward. But then, just as suddenly, it came down again. And as it landed there was the sick splintering sound of sticks and branches giving way.

Sang jumped down from the tree and rushed to the pit. I ran out from where I hid and stood beside him. Below us, the deer slowly struggled to its feet. It blinked up at us, swaying side to side, stunned.

For two hours we tried to free the deer. We brought rope from Nanna's shed and tied lassos in hope of somehow encircling the deer and hoisting it out. We extended branches, waving them before it as if its hooves might be miraculously transformed so that it could climb out hand over hand. We even attempted to dig an access ramp, but a thick tangle of pine roots made it impossible to dig more than a few feet. While we worked, the deer paced below, snorting, thrashing its antlers back and forth. Pawing the dirt. Every few minutes, in a desperate attempt to get out, it would rear back and throw itself against one of the side walls. Exhausted, filthy, Sang and I headed back to Nanna's as night fell.

We discussed the possibility of getting help, but every idea only made us seem more culpable. Even an anonymous call to the forest ranger's would lead directly back to us.

"My parents will kill me if they find out," I said as we walked. "My mother loves deer. She puts out food for them to eat in the winter. My father doesn't hunt anymore because it makes her cry."

Sang pulled out three eyelashes at once. "Mr. and Mrs. Taylor will not like me. They will say I am a troublemaker." We walked the rest of the way in silence.

That night my mother called to say that she and my father would be returning to Stillwater the following evening. When I asked her if they'd been having a good time she sounded tired. "Yes, Baby. Things are fine."

"How is Pop? Let me talk to him."

There was a sound like sheets being folded. "He stepped out for a minute, honey." My mother waited for me to speak. "Honey, you still there? —Ricky? Can you hear me?"

There was a pause as I held my breath. "We caught a Sasquatch today," I whispered.

"Your father's fine, Ricky."

"It looks like a deer."

My mother laughed. "Don't worry, honey. We're fine," she said. "We'll see you tomorrow."

After everyone had gone to sleep that night, Sang climbed out of bed and began pulling on his clothes. The house creaked and shuddered in the wind. I took the flashlight from beneath my pillow and aimed it at Sang, encircling him in light.

"Where you going?"

He fumbled with his holster buckle and squinted at me. "Sasquatch," he said.

I pushed back my blankets. "Liar," I said, getting out of bed too.

As we neared the trap we switched off the flashlight, and for a moment everything was silent as we stood under the cover of night, nothing to be heard but the lull of the trees, the distant sounds of the lake. But then out of the dark—out of the trap—came a noise, an unearthly sound that made me shiver, a desperate high-pitched whinny that until that night I didn't know a deer could make. Sang took the flashlight from me and pointed it into the trap. The deer stared up at us, dazed, eyes glimmering wetly. There was very little room in the hole and the buck's antlers had deeply gouged the dirt walls. The deer made the strange sound again, then rearing up, it bolted forward, colliding with the wall. I heard Sang sigh.

"My sister," he said quietly, "she is afraid of the dark. She would be scared living here." He lifted his free arm and pointed it directly at the deer. "Bang," he said. After a moment he turned away and headed down the trail. I stood listening to the trees, to the deer's heavy breathing. It grew louder and louder until I couldn't stand it any longer.

I found Sang sitting by the shore. I waded through the high reeds, out onto the sandy strip where he was tossing stones into the lake, rings rippling the water so that the night's reflection wobbled on the surface. The sky seemed oddly luminescent. Looking up, I saw the northern lights, their pale dusky bands fanning across the mountains, a few columns at the furthest edge tinged softly pink. Under this light the lake looked like a pool of pure silver. I told Sang to look, but he wouldn't. I explained to him what my mother had once told me about the northern lights, how they were lights from heaven. Behind us, I noticed one of the windows in Nanna's parlor was lit, and as I stared at the squares of light extending across the expanse of lawn I was filled with an overwhelming longing to go back inside, a desire so strong that, even now, years later, my heart still races at the recollection.

"Someone's up," I said. "We should go in."

Sang didn't respond.

I touched his shoulder. "Sang, c'mon."

He pushed me off. "Go away," he said, turning his back to me.

As I walked toward the house, I felt angry at Sang for not coming with me. Alone and anxious. Halfway there I turned back toward him. "Gook!" I called through the dark. Then I ran to the house.

It took a few minutes for my eyes to adjust to the light inside, but as they did Nanna's figure came into focus over beside the piano. She was barefoot and wearing her nightgown. She had pink bunion pads on some of her toes and wore a hairnet. In her hand she held a hammer—and before her—on top of the piano—were a wooden spoon and a long carving knife. Next to them a bottle of aspirin. Oblivious to my presence, she clutched the aspirin bottle, trying to open it, her eyes tight with frustration. It startled me when she looked up, spoke, her words tumbling out with such weight that it seemed as though they had fallen through a very long hole. She raised the hammer behind her head. "I can't get this Goddamn thing open," she said. Then with surprising force, she brought the hammer down. The bottle spun wildly, clattered to the floor. And Nanna stood there, staring as if she didn't know what in the world had happened—or where in the world she was. I hurried to her side, unwrapped her fingers from the hammer. I set it next to the knife and wooden spoon, opened the bottle for her and shook out two pills. As she sat on the piano bench, she gazed at her upturned hands for a long time, then, using the piano for support, struggled to her feet. She walked to the window and looked out at the sky, at the lights shearing down, and stood without speaking. Her lips moved silently. She shivered and hugged herself, rocking heel to toe. "Aurora borealis," she said softly. Stepping toward her, I asked if she was OK. She turned and gazed at me as if she were surprised to find me there. She looked around the room, then back out at the sky. After a moment she nodded solemnly. "I'm over the moon."

The next morning Sang and I brought the deer vegetables and fruit, unsure what it would eat. For an hour we sat beside the trap, trying to come up with a plan to free the deer, but neither of us could think of a thing. Sang squatted beside the pit, chin resting in his upturned palms.

"We have to tell," he said finally.

I imagined the trouble I'd be in with my parents. "What about the Taylors? They won't like you if they find out," I reminded him. "Aren't you going somewhere with them today?" He nodded slowly. I hesitated. "You'll ruin everything if you tell them." He unfastened his holster, then lay down on his belly, extending his arms over the pit so the belt dangled down. Lying there in the dirt, Sang looked so strange it seemed that I didn't even know him. I pictured him beside a young girl about his age with dark straight hair and black eyes. "Sang, I'm sorry," I said. "I'm sorry I lied about the Sasquatch."

He let the belt slip from his hands. It circled as it fell, coiling and uncoiling. He hung his arms over the edge as though he might throw himself in next. "Forget it," he said. "You did not scare me. I know what is what. Sang is not stupid."

Before the Taylors picked him up that afternoon, Sang spent an hour getting ready. He combed his hair again and again, parting it carefully on the side instead of letting it fall forward the way it usually did. He asked if he could borrow my pocketknife and painstakingly cut and cleaned his nails. He scraped the mud from his shoes and put on his one white dress shirt, buttoning it up to the very top button. When he asked me if he looked all right, I was tempted to say something mean, but the vulnerability in his eyes made me just nod.

"Why, Sang, don't you look nice," Rose Marie complimented him when she stepped into our room a few minutes later.

"Don't!" he shouted, slapping her hand away when she reached out and touched his hair.

Rose Marie stepped back in surprise as he fastidiously began combing again. She turned to me. "Richard," she said, "make sure you're all packed for your parents. Check under the beds for socks and anything else you might have left." I thought she would be glad at my leaving, but her face seemed more weary than anything else. She told us she had set out lunch for us, then asked if, after we'd eaten, would we mind playing outside until the Taylors arrived. Nanna was lying down, she said, she needed her rest.

I thought of the night before. "Is she sick?" I asked.

Rose Marie smoothed her slacks. "Just worn out, I think. She doesn't know her own limits."

Out on the dock after lunch, I kept thinking about the deer, that maybe we should go check on it. Though I didn't want to have to look again. At those big blinking eyes. "How long do you think it can live in there?" I said, sticking my foot in the water.

Sang stared intently across the lake at the uneven spine of mountains. Out on the water a group of Boy Scouts were canoeing by, laughing and fooling around, splashing each other as they paddled by. An older boy of about fifteen stuck his paddle in the air and waved.

"Are you still going to tell?" I asked.

But Sang didn't answer. He just stared at the canoe, at the boy waving.

When the Taylor's arrived, Mr. Taylor joined us out on the dock while Mrs. Taylor met with Rose Marie. He told us that Mrs. Taylor would be a few minutes—business, he added, winking. He had blond hair and a fuzzy mustache that turned up when he smiled. After we ran out of small talk, he suggested we play catch while we waited.

"Sang, how would you like to stay overnight at our house next weekend?" Mr. Taylor asked as he tossed him the ball.

Sang held his new glove out before him awkwardly. He swatted at the ball, missing it. He stared at the ground, at the ball there. "I have to ask and see," he said. "Nanna Grace might not like it."

Mr. Taylor said they could visit the museum at Blue Mountain, maybe even go waterskiing. Had Sang ever done that? Sang shook his head, picked up the ball and threw it, a poor throw that landed only a dozen yards in front of him. "We've got a bedroom for you with a bunk bed like cowboys sleep in."

Sang trotted to where the ball lay. Closing his eyes, he threw it as hard as he could, but this time it flew off wild to the right, landing in the weeds near the shore. Mr. Taylor retrieved it and lobbed it to me. "Watch Ricky throw," he advised Sang. "Bring your arm back, then snap from your wrist. Step and throw." I caught the ball easily.

"Maybe I could sleep over with Sang," I suggested.

Mr. Taylor smiled. "Now there's an idea—though maybe we out to let him try it by himself a few times first. Who knows, maybe he'll like it so much he'll want to stay for good."

I pitched the ball at Sang. Mr. Taylor laughed when Sang jumped out of the way. He told Sang not to be afraid of it. "It won't hurt you, Sport. Just stay in front of it. Open up that pocket a little more."

Sang's throw to Mr. Taylor made it less than halfway. Sang stomped his foot. "Shit almighty!" he swore. Mr. Taylor didn't react, but tossed me a high-fly that I caught on the run. I glanced at Sang who was frowning. His glove hung off his hand like some instrument of torture.

"Here, Sang," I said. I reared back and threw it at him as hard as I could. He stood bravely facing it down, but the ball caught him on the shoulder and knocked him to the grass. He jumped up and flung off his glove. "You stupid!" he screamed at me. "You did on purpose! I hate you!" He ran at me, his fists raised to fight. From the look on his face I thought he might kill me, but Mr. Taylor caught him from behind, wrapping his arms tightly around Sang. Sang swore again and again, hiccuping with anger, repeating that I had hit him on purpose. I didn't like him, he said, I wanted to hurt him. Mr. Taylor told Sang he had to learn to be a good sport, that it was part of the way games were played here in America. Mr. Taylor sat on the ground, holding Sang between his legs, rocking him. He told Sang not to worry, that he would teach him to throw. By this time next year, he said, Sang would be the best little ball player in Stillwater.

"No," Sang sobbed. "I will not. I will not be here. I will be in Texas."

Mr. Taylor looked confused. "Texas?" he said.

Shortly afterward, Sang left with the Taylors. From where I sat on the dock I could see Rose Marie walking the three of them to the car; I could see the house and the drive and the land all around it—and I could see Nanna as she stepped out onto the porch, walking into the head wind. She crossed to the rounded stairs at the far end of the porch and stood on the top step, staring off at the lake, her thin house dress luffing behind her like a sail. As she looked over her shoulder at where Rose Marie stood chatting with Mr. Taylor, her expression suddenly changed. Her face drew in on itself. She glanced around in distress. Seeing me below, she waved me toward her.

As I approached her, she grabbed my arm. "Who is that man?" she whispered.

I was out of breath from running. "Who?" I said.

She pointed up the drive to where Mr. Taylor stood with Rose Marie. She narrowed her eyes. "The man with Rose. I don't like the looks of him." She gripped the porch rail tightly, the wind blowing back her hair so that it trailed behind her like wisps of smoke. "I don't care what anyone says. Rose is too young to date."

I looked at her. "Nanna, that's Mr. Taylor."

She glanced back at them, mouthing his name as if she couldn't quite place it. She closed her eyes, then opened them again, clutching my arm as if she were about to fall. Her eyes watered as she repeated the name. The wind blew straight on.

Sang would not talk to anyone when he returned. He wouldn't answer any of Rose Marie's questions. When she asked him for a third time if anything special had happened with the Taylors, he told her to mind her own bee's wax and ran outside. She lit a cigarette and tapped her fingers on the counter, smoke swirling around her. She picked up the phone. "Ricky, keep an eye on our little friend until I get to the bottom of this."

I knew I'd find Sang at the trap. As I approached, he didn't acknowledge my presence but stood at the edge of the hole, his eyes fixed on the deer below. He took a handful of small stones from the pile beside the trap and let them roll off his hand, into the pit.

I was sure he had told.

"What happened?" I asked.

He wiped his eyes with his fists.

"Don't the Taylors want you anymore?"

He looked up at me, his cheeks smudged with dirt, and shook his head. He pulled another rock from the pile, cradling it in his hands. "They want me," he said, his voice muffled by emotion. "They want me forever." He jammed his heel violently into the ground, then raised his hands over his head and threw the rock into the trap. The deer began to snort and buck, thrashing its antlers.

"Shut up, you stupid!" Sang hollered.

The deer reared back and threw itself against the dirt wall. Sang picked up another rock the size of a small pumpkin. "Shut up!" he screamed, hurling the rock down. It hit the deer with so much force that the animal's knees buckled and it fell. After a few seconds it struggled unsteadily to its feet. Sang grabbed another rock and flung it down. This one hit the deer's head and it fell again. Sang threw another rock, then another. And another.

Stumbling back to its feet, the deer pawed frantically at the earth. It raised its head. Its eyes were large and glassy and desperate, as if it knew there was no escape. It gave a terrified high-pitched whinny of fear.

I stared at Sang and he stared back. He took two more stones from the pile. He handed one to me.

"Sang?" I said.

He threw his stone. He looked at me. "There is nothing else. We have no choice."

My parents were tan and healthy-looking, my mother's light freckles more visible across the bridge of her nose, my father's teeth whiter, his eyes more blue than I remembered. They talked with Nanna and Rose Marie, telling about the Maine coast—lobster and seals and sunny skies. I watched closely, searching for any sign of discord. Every so often my eyes would catch Sang's and we would both look away quickly, reminded by each other's eyes of what we'd done.

Before we left, my mother unwrapped a large ocher-colored shell she'd brought back from the beach. It was striated, iridescent, and caught the light as she handed it to Nanna.

"The minute I saw it, I thought of you," my mother said, smiling. She tucked her hair behind her ears. "It's just the kind of thing you're always picking up."

Nanna held it before her. She looked confused, as if she weren't sure what to do.

Rose Marie passed a weary glance at the overflowing shelves. "Just what she needs," she said, not bothering to hide her irritation. My father coughed and my mother blushed. An uncomfortable moment passed before my father said that we needed to hit the road.

Rose Marie made her goodbyes from the kitchen, but Sang and Nanna walked out with us onto the back porch. A cluster of moths fluttered aimlessly in the bright spotlight shining on us from the eaves. My father shook Sang's hand. He said that he was sure Sang had gotten stronger since he'd last seen him. He made Sang flex his bicep and pretended to be astonished by its size. My mother knelt down before Sang. "It's nice to see you again," she whispered, pressing him to her and kissing his cheek. "I have a feeling we'll be seeing a lot more of you."

I slid into the back seat of our car, my parents into the front. The upholstery smelled like the two of them, my mother's faint perfume and my father's scent of boats and water. I breathed the smell in deeply as my father put the car in gear.

"I told you that you shouldn't have brought that sea shell," he said as we started up the drive.

My mother sat beside him. Silent.

"Well, I did, Claire—" my father said defensively.

"Cal, don't," my mother said. "We just got back—"

"I didn't mean it like—"

"Like what? Like you were right and I was wrong—"

"Don't start getting sarcastic, Claire—"

"I'm not the one who started this—"

I closed my eyes and listened to my parent's voices, the familiar rise and fall of their words, the welcome pattern of their fights and our lives. I sat for a moment and let the sound settle safely inside me and then, breathless with relief, I turned so that I knelt facing the back window where I could see Nanna and Sang still waving from the porch. The night was almost black, but the outline of their shapes, illuminated as they were by the porch light, remained starkly visible, backlit so that they both seemed suspended in the night, both of them separate, both distinctly alone, unmoored and floating vagrant. Two bright beacons with nowhere to go, two bright stars who had lost their heaven.

Decadence

Brian Bouldrey

Wally motioned to Petra under the water: I want to tell you something. He was treading water and he was so tall that the further elongation from his flippers brought him thrillingly close to the fire coral. Petra lifted her head and pulled out her snorkel, the only concession she'd make with so much marine action swirling around her.

"It's a yellowtailed damselfish," Wally said.

She was grateful. It was her new favorite fish, she said when they first jumped in on this second day of snorkeling on the island. It was blue-black with a bright yellow swallow's tail, and, best of all, it looked like a night sky full of stars limned the—what was it?—damselfish's back. A perfect name, and of course Wally knew it. Petra looked as grateful as she could with a goggled mask parenthesizing surprise on her face.

She did love him. Even after five years of marriage, she thought him terrifically handsome, sensibly so. Wide Northern European face, strong chest, tall, hazel eyes that she swore changed color now and then. Each morning, his beard had grown into two satellite's-eye views of hurricanes, one on both spots where the jaw hinged on the skull. Full of facts: "Did you know that Luther Burbank was so successful in strengthening plant species that the dictionary carried a verb, 'to Burbank,' meaning 'to improve'?" he told her once. "What would the verb, 'to Wally' mean?" Petra asked out loud. "To intimidate with reason," Wally volunteered.

He was already underwater, investigating a manta ray.

As casually as she could, she glanced toward the beach. There he was: Edward, who hadn't even taken his shirt off, making some mysterious maneuvers across the sand. Was it some sort of religious ritual, Petra wondered. Has he been learning New-Agey meditation practices in therapy?

But Wally drew her attention, surfacing again. "I don't know whether you've noticed, but the snorkeling here is ten times better than it was in Vieques. Lots more live coral."

She nodded and dove. No, she hadn't noticed, but that didn't make her feel terrible. Ten times better than paradise was hard for her to calculate like Wally could. She also supposed that all this pleasure made her gluttonous, greedy.

All this pleasure: dipping below that perfect Giotto-blue surface, she was just in time to see some clown-lipped parrotfish, three brown spotted trunkfishes, and a school of royal gammas, their heads a tart orange, as orange as a hunting license pinned to a coat, their back ends Jolly Rancher purple. That's about all she knew in the way of names, except for her New Favorite, the yellowtailed damselfish, the Queen of Night-on-Her-Back.

It's a fairyland, she thought, a Midsummer Night's Dream. She hummed herself the ebbing lullaby of Britten's opera version of that Shakespeare, Petra's and Wally's favorite. Floating on the reef like this was a lullaby, too.

On the dusty road down to the beach, an adorable little local boy, shiny black with long legs and arms and wearing his school uniform of blue shorts and tie with a short-sleeved white shirt (oh!, in late January!) scrambled home, obviously eager to get out of that straitjacket. Petra had said, "Let's steal him and take him home!" and Wally, playing jealous Oberon to the baby-finding queen of the fairies intoned, aria-like, "Ill met by moonlight, proud Titania!" and they both laughed.

But Edward did not laugh. Edward thought they were being racist. "They're not for ownership any more," is what he actually said.

For somebody who essentially called them bigots, Edward certainly was nervous around the locals. "Did you lock the doors?" he said whenever they headed for the beach, a needless precaution.

And when Wally stopped to pick up a hitchhiking woman and her baby, Edward completely freaked out. "What are you thinking about?" he wanted to know when they'd dropped her off at the next town, after sitting sullenly next to her in their rent-a-heap for fifteen minutes.

"Edward, *tranquilo*," said his cousin. "That's how it's done on thee eye-lahnd." Wally was trying to get the local accent: birds were boids. Murder was moider.

"Even I have to say I'm surprised at how friendly everybody is," Petra said. "I'm so used to angry black boys and here, here everybody wants to help you. Everybody is always waving."

Edward had snorted. "I think that waving thing is a test. They're all talking about the new tourists at the cottage and wondering when we'll be gone so they can rip us off."

"Well, I think it's nice," she said, not wanting to argue about it.

While treading water later, after the encounter with the school of damselfish, Petra confessed to her husband, "Wally. I think it wasn't such a good idea to bring Edward along. He doesn't seem to be having a very good time." She caught herself doing it again: registering a complaint by pretending to be the recipient of the complaint. Wally always knew that when she said, "I think he doesn't like me," it really meant, "I don't like him."

But it had been her idea when they were back at home in San Francisco. Edward's boyfriend of seven years had died half a year ago. Wally was his only relative in the city and the only one Edward didn't completely dump when he let his family know about his lifestyle (Edward's word, not Wally's). Petra begged Edward to come on this trip with them.

"Why now?" Wally wanted to know. "Why not in the summer when we go to Barcelona, where he could busy himself with cute Catalan boys named Jordi and Pep? Besides, we'll be here for him at Christmas time. By the time we're on the island, the holiday suicide season will be over."

"That's where you're mistaken," Petra said, "statistics say suicides are actually higher two weeks after Christmas, because depression creeps up on you, see? It's like vertigo—you're not afraid of a high place until you've had time to think about it for a while."

Creeping Vertigo. That's what changed Wally's mind, he knew what she meant. The more they flew in airplanes, the more the sound of the landing gear coming up caused their palms to sweat. They held hands during touchdowns and liftoffs.

All Wally and Petra did was travel, actually; when they weren't on the road, they were making plans for the next trip. They loved being together this way, and while Petra loved Wally, lusted for him too, she adored the way they were like best friends when they had packs on their backs. Best friends, or, when they wanted to do a little play-acting, he would set up a dangerous situation from which he gallantly saved her. Each destination was an elaborate fantasy rescue operation.

Petra didn't mind. "From the moment we fell in love," she'd explained to Edward on the plane ride down here, trying to make him a closer friend, "Wally said he wanted to show me the world. He said he saw the planet like a big lawn that had to be mown, and wherever he stepped was where his lawn mower made trails. I loved that." Wally wasn't completely happy unless they were "out mowing," and she was perfectly happy journeying with him.

She explained to Edward the way it all worked. "Each year we make three different kinds of travels. There's The Journey, like a week of hiking in the mountains. Then there's the Big Destination, you know, sort of like a cultural junket, lots of research beforehand, museums, memorials, history. And then there's The Decadence. This is The Decadence."

"And you thought of me," Edward rolled his eyes.

"No, no. That's just what we call it. Sitting on the beach, cracking open coconuts, lots of big fluffy rum drinks. That kind of decadent."

But here on the lee side of the reef, watching all these angelfishes, elkhorn coral, and—what was that?—a school of voracious tubular trumpetfishes, Petra thought of what she meant by "decadent."

She had almost forgotten all this sea life from the trip to Vieques, the myriad of textures and colors, the sheer haute couture of it all, and when Wally reminded her that it was much better here than their last trip, she knew she had forgotten. "I always come to expect things," she told Wally and Edward when they met on shore. "I feel so greedy I want more and more."

Edward, looking Edwardian fully clothed and in long pants, hopelessly trying to keep sand out of his perfect cuffs, had guarded their towels and beach reading. Who knew who'd come along to rip them off? He answered her with, "More more more. And look where it gets you. You are burnt. Red skin is damaged skin."

While she toweled off short fierce legs (inherited from her mother, a Scot, and her father, a Serb), long leonine brown hair, healthy skin that might have shown up on some experimental painter's canvas as green, she said, "I remember when I was a girl in Sunday school we got the story of Moses delivering the Israelites out of Egypt. I was always mad at those guys. I mean, hadn't they just seen spectacular plagues? Frogs from the sky, locusts, a river of blood? Hadn't they survived a big bloody Passover? Didn't the Red Sea part? What about that God damn pillar of fire? What did they think all that was? And then Moses slips off for a few days up Mount Sinai to get the Ten Commandments, and what do they do? Melt down all the gold and make idols and worship them. I never understood.

"But now I do understand. It's about how beautiful things are so miraculous that you can't believe you saw them once you've walked away from them for a minute or two. It's just impossible. And you haven't got any names for it, because it's all new. You get this kind of Beauty Amnesia"—she was proud of her made-up term, almost as good as

Creeping Vertigo—"But then when you see it all again"—she thought of her damselfish—"it comes back to you. All I want to do is apologize for forgetting it."

"Put this on," Edward said, reaching to her with a tube of number thirty sunblock, "or have you forgotten what it's like to be fried, too?"

Wally heard her, though. "I think you forget because you don't have any of the names for things. I mean, if the Israelites had words for all those miracles, maybe they would repeat the stories of them to each other and then they'd remember. Who knows what miracles happened out there in the desert that we don't know about."

All miracles are local, he explained. If a refrigerator fell from the sky, how would the Israelites have explained it?

She thought to herself, who can keep faith with paradise?

Their island house, charmingly gingerbready on the outside, was a little ordinary on the inside. They'd rented it from a Canadian man with youthful aspirations to pop music stardom, and the house was the final resting place for an old hi-fi, tasteless records, big leather couches, macrame hanging planters, and a swag lamp that Edward had disassembled for safety's sake. There were three bedrooms, two upstairs and one down. Petra and Wally slept together upstairs and Edward stayed down.

Later, Wally walked into town to buy some groceries and also brought back a writing tablet for Petra. "You should keep a journal," he said, "of everything you see. Look in the guidebook and find all the names of things. Then you won't have your Beauty Amnesia."

Petra liked that idea. She got the guide out and looked up all the fish she'd seen. Then she described them her own way, how one had a tail shaped like a pennant or the flag of some undersea nation, green, red, yellow. How another's scales were the exact same color and pattern as her mother's kitchen linoleum back in 1974.

And trees, she wrote, our house is surrounded by banyans, palms, hibiscus, primrose, umbrella trees. I saw a speckled lizard who ran with his tail all curled up. I saw a bald eagle. Wally and I came across a barracuda as big as he is. I know I shouldn't be scared, but he followed us, and the more I splashed to get away, the more he wanted to be near me. Wally drew him away but I was too spooked to get back in. Wally said dolphins were as big as barracudas but I said dolphins gamboled while barracudas patrolled. Wally showed me the section on dangerous sea creatures and the barracuda wasn't even listed, but fire coral was.

Edward saw the section on the dangers of the sea and oh he just loved that. Can't get enough. I suppose he'll never get in the water with us now but at least he's got something to do while he's vegetating on the beach.

God, he's like a fop in a Forster novel, all carefulness. I made the mistake of calling him Eddie and he corrected me right there, it's Edward, not Eddie, and you could just imagine him gathering up his skirts. I talked to Wally about it and he said gay guys prefer their full name, Robert, not Bob, Edward not Ed, because they've had a long life of indignity, and this gives them a little dignity. Well, I said, if you wake up one day and say you want me to call you Walter, shall I file for divorce?

If Edward feels so insulted by a nickname, he certainly knows how to dish out the insults. We're in the grocery store and all he can say is "We've got better stuff at home," or "you can't get good coffee here," and he doesn't even see what he's doing to the lady at the checkout. Oh, I'm sure they get it all the time from ugly Americans, but still.

He's homesick, Wally says, that's how people deal with wishing they were back in familiar surroundings. "We got one of those, it's not as good here as it is there." It's just a way to deal.

Homesick for what, I want to know. Everybody he knows is dead now, except maybe his cat, and I like cats, but that cat is so icky. In any case, Wally is right. Edward has rearranged the furniture in our rented cottage so that it looks like his San Francisco apartment.

After writing all this, Petra dutifully named all the coral she'd seen in the ocean that day. She wrote this as her first entry in the tablet and felt very satisfied. By the time she put it down it was after eleven and both of the boys had fallen asleep. The sliding glass door was wide open and in two days the moon would be full. Even now it cast shadows and illuminated piles of chubby clouds. "God, and it's not even buggy here. Sheer decadence."

In the morning, she came down to find Edward furiously swabbing the kitchen counter. "Somebody left coconut syrup out after the piña colada party," he sniffed, "and I woke up to a huge swarm of ants and flies."

"Oh, that would be my fault," she said, but it didn't seem to do any good apologizing. She decided to pitch in with the cleanup and grabbed another dishrag. In the garbage she could see all the grapefruit, lemons, and oranges they had poached from the abandoned house up the hill the day before. "These seem all right," she ventured, holding up a grapefruit.

"Who knows what laid its eggs in all that crap. We can't just leave things out and we can't rinse things off in this water, it's contaminated."

"Edward," said Petra, "is your immune system compromised? Because if it is . . ." she suddenly trailed off. Although she highly doubted his health was at risk, she had suddenly realized this was a very inappropriate thing to say, and she was sorry.

He smiled and kept scrubbing the counter.

After breakfast, Petra packed the swimsuits again, and the masks, flippers, and snorkels. She also packed her new journal and a pen, wrapped in a plastic bread wrapper to keep them from getting wet.

Edward did not pack his suit but made every move to show he was coming along. "You don't have to come if you don't want to, Edward," Petra said. "We don't want to bore you" (another version of "I don't think he likes me").

"Don't mind me," he said.

They went to the Caribbean side of the island today, where the water was calmer. In the shallows, a fisherman had dumped five smallish thresher sharks that had been caught in gill nets.

"It's like a bad omen," Edward said.

The barracuda from yesterday had slowed down her zeal. She'd been fearless before, but every time the sandy bottom was disturbed, she felt her heart race a little. She saw a small ray and two sea turtles. There were schools of yellow fish with turquoise stripes and she let herself remember an art class where she learned that before the invention of the prism, people believed that all the colors came from blue and yellow. The sand was gold and this sea was blue—maybe it was true.

To rest, she and Wally climbed up on some rather painful coral that was smooth in some places but viciously sharp in others. "Not coral, but karst," Wally corrected her. There were tide pools with dozens of skittish crabs, anemones, and urchins just beneath the surface. "Nature, red in tooth and claw!" Wally exclaimed. He told her he'd been following a handful of angelfish when something big swung out from under a reef and swallowed one of the pretty things whole.

Petra was remembering a big hairy wolf spider she'd seen on the road, which she didn't bring up because she didn't want Edward to become an impossible basket case. And this coral really hurt to sit on! Fire coral! Barracuda!

"You are getting a bad sunburn," Wally warned. "Maybe you should swim back and get a t-shirt or something."

"God, you sound just like your cousin," she said, not budging.

"Why are you so rough on him, Petra? He's been through hell, you know. What would you do if I died?"

When she kissed him on his mask, it meant both reassurance and protest. "I wouldn't walk around like I had a stick up my butt," she said. "And even though I'd miss you terribly, I'd do my best to get a hobby."

Wally conceded by the way he gasped: "What does he do all day?"

189

"He's probably reading my journal right now," she said, but as she said it, she decided it was true, and she thought of all the nasty things she'd written about him. She put up a saluting sailor hand to block the sun's glare, and she could just barely see him, crouched in the shade, watching their things.

"One more dive for me," said Wally, poking her arm experimentally, to show her how red she was, "but you should call it a day."

Petra made a point of going ashore at a spot further down the beach and tiptoeing up behind to catch Edward reading her journal. As she approached, she could see he was plainly reading. Then she felt like she shouldn't do this, it would be too embarrassing for everybody. But when she got a little closer, she realized he'd been reading a trashy paperback novel.

The three of them walked home along the side of the main road. Cars drove on the left side on this island, even though the cars were American and had steering wheels on that side too. It was as confusing when they walked as when they drove, because the road was curvy and there were many blind spots.

"You should try and paddle around with us tomorrow," Petra told Edward. "It's really pleasant. And when you stay out for a long time, you sort of keep that bobbing-around feeling, so at night when you go to bed you lay there and you feel like Mia Farrow in *Rosemary's Baby* when she's dreaming of the devil coming to impregnate her, and even her new Vidal Sassoon haircut isn't going to save her."

She thought he might like a little campy allusion like that, since he was gay. Apparently, he'd never seen *Rosemary's Baby*, because he said, "I'd hate to be out in the water so long that I got as red as a lobster."

Not swimming, not old movies—what hobbies did he have? After a couple of nights, Petra noticed the one thing Edward liked to do that fell into the category Decadent Vice. There were poker chips and card decks in one of the drawers upstairs and he brought them down and put them on the table. There were other games, too, Rack-O, Uno, Yahtzee, dominoes, Monopoly. Petra couldn't stand this sort of crap. Wally said he'd play but Edward said it was no fun if just two people were playing. This was another reason for Edward to dislike Petra, she was sure of it.

Over dinner the following evening, Edward leaned back in his rattan peacock chair. "Walter, may I see our return flight itinerary?"

Walter? "In a hurry to go home?" Petra wondered. Oh God, he really did read her diary.

"My God, there's a three-hour layover in Las Vegas," he marveled.

"I know. Isn't it awful?" said Petra. "I just don't get the whole gambling thing. I mean, look at me, I like indulgences. Things that are wonderfully bad for you. A good stiff drink. A steak, medium rare. Sex. A feather bed. Rock and roll. Even cigarettes, though I don't smoke. But gambling? I just can't approve. It doesn't have any sensual satisfaction." She thought of her great aunt Karen, whose trailer smelled like floor wax, who hit every bingo hall in town, a different one for each day of the week. What a pig.

Edward didn't take the bait. Wally, for the first time in a long time, gave Petra a disappointed, even dirty, look. She could feel her body begin to throb from shame and sunburn, the same feeling she had when Wally had buried her up to the neck in beach sand on the first day of their stay, that weird pounding of the body.

Edward sighed. "I have the best luck with those airport slot machines."

After punishing Petra by ignoring her for a while, Wally came into their bedroom and tried to cozy up to her. This was usually the way tiffs ended between them. But Petra said, "Wally, he's reading my *diary*."

"Oh come on," said Wally. "Diaries are fair game. Unless you've put it in a hiding place, they're public property, like postcards."

She wanted to agree, but she was too mad, and irritated by sunburn.

"Look Petra, he's a fussbudget, I agree. But this is the way he's used to taking care of people. Hoover was sick for so long that the only way he knows how to show his love is to be a nurse."

"I'm trying to make him see I don't care that he's gay, but he takes it all wrong."

"If you mean that *Rosemary's Baby* crack, well, that was some shameless sucking up, and he probably clocked it."

"Oh, you're one to talk," she recoiled. "You know how to play the gay card whenever it's convenient."

"The gay card?"

"Yeah. You walk by him in that skimpy swimsuit and you know he falls all over you. I'm just his rival."

"If that's some kind of compliment, it's too obscure," he said, sitting up, sauntering out of the room.

Of course she was terribly burned that night. No matter how much aloe she slathered on her skin, she felt herself radiating heat. She took aspirin, forfeited her piña colada, chopped up cucumbers and put them over her eyes and still, in the end, she asked Wally to sleep in the third, unoccupied bedroom so his own body heat didn't overwhelm her.

She lay on top of the sheets and felt small breezes wafting in. She distracted herself from the throbbing by thinking of being Mia Farrow in

Rosemary's Baby and then by writing in her diary. *Mangroves, Australian pines, date trees with bright red fruits. Citrus, all sorts. The hibiscus I want to plant in my garden at home. Just to make tea.*

The moon was nearly full. Downstairs Wally was making all kinds of food, just because he had the time to do it. He was experimenting with the local fruits and fish.

Outside in the night, she heard the sound of some exotic bird. It had a pure, clear, long sound that eventually tapered off into a less lovely croak. Petra was reminded of their cuckoo clock back home that had broken one time. Wally had taken it apart deftly, almost eagerly, and though he had fixed it as deftly and eagerly, she discovered in the process that the cuckoo sound was made not by air through a whistle, as she'd once (when? youth? sentience?) decided, but through two pieces of wood being rubbed together. Unlikely and somehow disappointing: she'd hoped that all machines imitated animal functions. Now this night bird sounded, there at the end of its cry, like the croaking of dry wood splints rubbed together.

In the morning, she found the house dead quiet, but the glare at the window suggested that she'd overslept. Petra went into the spare bedroom and found Wally gone. She rushed down into the kitchen. Edward was playing solitaire. He was drinking coffee with tons of sugar and milk. He had the radio tuned to some easy listening station.

After her adrenalin trundle down the stairs, Petra tried to recover or reenact her groggy disorientation, as a kind of nonchalance. She yawned. "Where's Wally?"

"At the beach. We were worried that you'd had too much sun yesterday so we wanted you to stay inside today. I told him to go ahead and I'd keep you entertained." He was running his hands over the waxy surfaces of the cards laid out.

She held her breath a moment, and then she squealed, scooping up the solitaire layout and flinging them outward. "I am not your damn patient!" Hearts and spades fluttered around like a party.

Feathers, dollar bills, all helicoptering down. She watched him not get angry. In fact, he looked like he was quelling ecstasy. He was taking *sensual pleasure* from those *damn cards*. Edward took a long draw on the coffee cup and said, "You're a game board thrower, aren't you?"

"What? What?"

"You always finish a board game by not finishing, by throwing all the pieces."

In her mind flashed a comic montage of chess pieces, checkers, mah jong tiles, Monopoly money, Go pebbles, all the stupid, cold, purely fateful signs that she was losing, all upset and in midair. "Yes, of course I am! Because they're stupid!"

He didn't say anything until he'd finished his coffee. "I know which beach he went to. He took the car but if you don't mind walking, I'll show you where he is. He showed me on a map."

Petra wanted to say something mean but she weighed it in the balance of five more snarling days with Edward, and of not snorkeling today with Wally. "Okay. Let me get my things together."

By the time she'd gathered her gear and a towel and put on her sandals, he had cleared up the dispersed cards and washed out his coffee cup, which sat alone on the drying rack on some kind of perfect slant.

Just before he locked up the house, she peered over his shoulder into the house and realized that the furniture had been arranged back to the way they had found it on arrival.

They walked down the gravel driveway to the road. "Now where is this place?"

Edward drew out his map of the island. "It's this one called Surfer's Beach."

"Oh, Edward," Petra wanted to cry. "That isn't close! This isn't walking distance! Can't you even tell? That's twenty miles away. We'll have to hitchhike."

"Hitchhike? No. No hitchhiking. The Club Med bus goes up and down this road. We can wait for their bus." Already, three cars had passed by, their drivers waving merrily.

"That bus starts a mile back, in town. That's just stupid."

"I'm not hitchhiking, Petra. We'll get dragged into some back field, raped, and killed."

She tried hard not to lose her patience. What oddly ran through her head was, if he's so insistent on using his full name for the sake of dignity, how could she know if he was making fun of her? He calls Wally Walter, but Petra is just Petra. She said, "Fine, Edward. I'm going to get a ride. You can take the bus if you want. I'll see you there or I'll see you at home."

Edward shrugged. He could be so careless when he didn't care. He started walking in the direction of town. He was pocketing the map. She watched him for a minute or two.

Then: "Your whole life is a dark gray mess, isn't it, Edward? And you'd like it to be a mess for everybody else, too. Well, screw your tight-assed vicious unhappiness. Screw *you*, Edward, you big fag!" It came out panicky and shrill without him to hear it. Edward had already disappeared around a bend in the road.

Suddenly alone, for a moment she thought the world was silent. When palm fronds blew in the wind, she thought, they shivered. But it wasn't cold here in paradise, it was warm—washcloth warm—and "shiver" wasn't the right word. They quivered like harp strings, vibrated like piano wires or the coils in a doorbell mechanism. When cold is removed from the act of shivering, then, what is left? Music. *Sure.* When the stars twinkled, that was a kind of music.

A car pulled up. It was a station wagon with some of its chrome stripping loose. A man, so dark and oily she didn't see his features at first until her eyes adjusted to the inside of the car as she leaned through its window, wanted to know, "Where would you be goin, missy?"

Now she saw that he was wearing a short-sleeved shirt and tie, with some kind of name tag. His radio was playing that crazed revivalist preacher stuff. She couldn't even begin to tell what the radio guy was going on about. "I'm going to Surfer's Beach," she said.

She thought he said, "We're there, then," and she climbed into the front seat beside him. All the seats, the separate arm rests, even the dash were covered in thick plastic. It was hot and the stuff immediately stuck to the backs of her legs. He said, again, "Where's that at?"

"Oh, I'm sorry," she said, "I thought you'd know—it's a straight line, isn't it?" There'd be a sign. The island was long and narrow with only this one main road. She'd studied it enough to know there was little opportunity for getting hopelessly lost. "It's twenty or thirty miles down the road. Are you going that far?"

"All the way to the end," he smiled. "I'm Marvin."

"Petra," she said and closed the door. He accelerated and she thought, Marvin, not Marv. "My friends call me Sugar," he added just then. They'd been repaving the road, so loose gravel sprayed everywhere, making him seem more of a dare-devil than he probably was. She noticed the car needed steering fluid, it cried out on every turn. Nothing but heaps on this whole island.

As if reading her mind again, he said, out of the blue, "Theys foity-poicent tariff on out-os from thee states. You can't have a new car unless you rich."

"Where are you going this morning?" she said. She flashed on Edward and his tight butt cheeks sashaying down to the Club Med bus stop.

"To choich, goil," he said incredulously. Where all Christians should be, went the other end of that sentence. She thought of telling him she was Muslim, and she was going to the place where she'd be closest to Mecca, it being Ramadan and all. Or that she was Jewish and her sabbath was over. Or that she wasn't a Christian at all, but a Catholic, which was the truth. "I'm going to the beach," she said, "My husband's waiting for me there."

The man chuckled and accelerated a little. "Oh-ho, you husband."

"Yes! He thought I was too sunburned to go with him but I'm feeling a lot better." The land on either side was low and swampy and filled with mangroves.

He did that low chuckle thing again.

"What's so funny?"

"Well, just look at us," he said. "We all know what goes on in thee States. Here I am a big man" (it was true, she hadn't noticed how big he was, all folded up into the driver's seat) "and you a goil hitchhiking. And here I am telling you to go to choich like a good Christian, and you are going to some rawndayvoo with you so-called husband."

It was about then that creeping vertigo set in. Her sense of danger began to grow, probably provoked by Goddamn Edward. But now she wanted to know if this man, this stranger was all the Christian he said he was. Was he playing an obscure game of humiliation? That whole Christian-harlot thing? Did that turn him on? And anybody who was told that a lone girl let herself be picked up by a lone man, regardless of his age, creed, color, or sexual orientation, was just asking for it.

"I'm soary, missy," he said. There went that uncanny, spooky mind-reading thing he did. "Why don't you have a Vita-Malt?" he pointed to a six-pack of something under her feet. What was this? They looked like beer bottles—God, was he trying to get her drunk? "It's good for you!" he exclaimed, "Lots oav vitamin B."

He reached into his pocket—for what?—and rummaged around. He pulled out a second key ring that had a bottle opener hanging from it. He handed it to her and she nervously fumbled open the Vita-Malt, then took a quick swig. God, it was vile stuff. "Mmm," she said, "never heard of it."

"It coams in ginger, too," he smiled. Her stomach was upset and her skin was burning. She should have stayed home, Wally was right. And now she had to drink this nasty bottle of Vita-Malt. "I never could understand you people in thee States drinking that rute beer you all so proud of. Taste like medicine."

What the hell did he think this tasted like? She looked at his speedometer. They'd been going steadily slower. They were in an area where there weren't any houses, just salt marshes with mangroves. No roads intersecting, just this one. The radio preacher was getting even more annoyed, or excited, or something.

There was nothing to do but remember every hitchhiking horror story she'd ever heard and drink the Vita-Malt. She could tell they'd gone about eight miles. Cars would pass them now and then: why was Marvin letting them pass?

"Do you have a family, Marvin?"

"Friends call me Sugar," he reminded her. "My goil woiks on one of thee other eye-lahnds, for thee money. Good money. More tourists."

"Yes, there isn't too much industry here, is there, Sugar?" She had had a conversation with Wally about the economics here, so maybe they could talk about that. "Some farming, some tourists, what else?" They'd come into a stretch with abandoned cinder-block silos overgrown with vines. In a whoosh, the Club Med bus roared past them. It surprised her, she hadn't heard it approach behind them, and when it passed on the unexpected side of the car, it made her pulse race, the way it had when she encountered the barracuda while snorkeling.

And of course, there he was: Edward, peering primly down at her from one of the windows. He waved, sort of, and she didn't wave back—what would Sugar think if she started waving at buses? That she was looking for rescue? But everybody waved on this island. Everybody was friendly. What she really wanted to do was mouth the word "help" to Edward, but she didn't want to create a scene. As if to make her more unhappy, Edward simpered, as if to say, "Ha, ha, I'm going to beatcha."

"I used to woik on thee farms round here, but they gone now. Woiked every kind of farm, except chickens. Nasty things, chickens. For years I lived on thee other islahnds, for a long time I lived next to a choich, all that singing and practicing thee singing, I had to go to sleep listening to thee singing and thee preaching. Now I can not sleep without thee noises. I have to listen to thee preaching and thee singing to keep myself calm." He turned up the radio just a touch, to emphasize.

After the radio got louder, they both used it as an excuse not to talk any more. It was another twenty minutes before they got to her turnoff.

"Well, what do you know!" she said trying to sound like it had been an ordinary drive. "Thanks so much, Sugar!"

He didn't slow down. "This is no way to thee beach, goil," he said, but she knew he knew that she'd had enough. After all this was over, she would realize that he was slow to consent because he was worried about her, out here on the open road. "Let me take you to thee next town, at least," he said.

"Hey, no! My husband is out there! He's expecting me!"

"Nobody ees expecting you, Petra," he said her name for the first time, which was supposed to sound earnest and concerned but just sounded creepy. "You say your husband thinks you at home."

"Just please," she said, "I'm missing my turnoff."

Marvin didn't say anything, he only pulled over. She thanked him. "Don't forget you Vita-Malt," is all he said after that, and then he pulled out. Some of the loose gravel kicked up and stung her shins.

In both directions, as far as she could see, there were mangroves and no houses. She couldn't see the ocean on either side of the road. It was still a half-mile walk to Surfer's Beach. She realized that she didn't have any sunblock, and there were no big chubby clouds to shade her from the sun, no breezy coconut or date palms, no banyans, Australian pines, or umbrella trees. She couldn't even remember what such trees looked like. All she could know were crappy scrubby mangroves.

Another heap whizzed by, without hubcaps, making her heart pound. It came up from behind her, so nobody waved, and it stung her legs with gravel.

She started walking. She'd be fried by the time she got where she was going, there'd be blisters on her shoulders, white on red. That would make her look like a yellowtailed damselfish, the fish she had promised herself to fill an aquarium full of when they got back to San Francisco.

No Last Names

Leslie Pietrzyk

1973

What I didn't like about AA was how everyone drank all that coffee. And how it had to be black, like they were telling you, I'm a certain kind of person because I drink black coffee. It happened that I preferred my coffee black, but I wasn't one of them, so I dumped in sugar, loaded my cup with powdered creamer, sipped slow to choke it down.

And I hated the room in the church basement where they met. The floor was the colorless tile of a high school classroom, so when you stared down at it, your stomach knotted the way it did when the teacher used to say "Pop quiz!" The room was stuffy, and there was an old piano that someone was always pounding on before the meeting, thinking they were a better player than they were. Or maybe it needed tuning.

There were about a hundred things I hated about AA. I hated how everything had numbers, like twelve steps and one day at a time and ninety meetings in ninety days. How the parking lot was gravel, so I nicked up the heels of my shoes. How you never knew if the basement door was unlocked or if you had to go around to the side, and whichever way you guessed, you got a locked door. There were a million things. Maybe the worst was how it was like confession in church back when I lived in Detroit, the same dry silence lingering uselessly between words, the same weight, the time-moving-backward-never-ending trap I'd already escaped once.

I kept going to AA because I'd told my husband I would for three months, and when he didn't believe me, I decided to prove him wrong. Hi, my name is Beth and I'm an alcoholic.

Only my name is Sophie.

The morning the kids and I were packing up the car for the annual summer trip to visit my mother in Detroit, Jimmy got me alone and put a folded piece of paper in my hand. I smiled, thinking it was maybe a lovey-dovey note about how much he'd miss me—we were both trying that hard lately—but it was a phone number. I didn't have to ask; his words spilled like liquid, how great that I was finally getting help, how important it was to our future together, how he was proud of my new beginning. Finally I put my hand over his mouth and said real slow, "Whose phone number?" and in the pause, my hand got warm from his breath so I took it away.

"It's the AA office in Detroit," he whispered so the kids wouldn't hear. His eyes moved far away, and I looked to what he saw but it was nothing. "So you can find a meeting," and that's when he looked straight at me, his face open like a book with a picture you don't want to see. He'd decided he couldn't ever trust me again; with his face that way, he didn't look like a husband anymore, just a man I once knew. But it was the sun, because when I stepped back and stopped squinting, he was the same Jimmy, just more worried-looking.

"Vacation doesn't count," I said.

"It counts," he said.

"I'll be fine."

"You're not fine here," he said.

Amy walked by with two pillows that she tossed into the back seat. She made that flippy noise with her thongs, slapping hard on the pavement, and Jimmy and I stopped talking. She paused, then said, "We're almost ready to go," as if she were the one driving, as if she were in charge.

I folded the piece of paper as small as it could go. "You're right," I said to Jimmy. "Vacation counts." Then I slipped the phone number into the zippered pocket of my purse.

"OK." He knew the word was wrong but he didn't know any others. "OK."

I kissed him on the cheek. "You need to shave."

"Sophie, this time I mean it," he said.

I nodded, patted my purse, nodded again.

"I love you," he said, like it was a reminder. I probably would've thought more about that, but I needed to get in the car and get moving. Never mind that it was only Detroit at the end.

Another thing I hated about AA was how there was one pipe that made this pinging when anyone ran water in the bathroom sink, exactly like ice clinking in a glass. A lot of us stopped washing our hands because of it, but there was nothing we could do about other people in the church, people at different meetings, and the more you tried not to notice that ping, the louder it was, and I mean *exactly* like ice.

The drive up from Phoenix was fine; we stayed in Holiday Inns, even though the kids begged for Howard Johnson. Amy said HoJo pools were better, but I knew it was because Holiday Inns had lounges, and I could just hear Jimmy telling her, no Holiday Inns. But I was good; I sat by the pool and flipped pages of magazines while Amy and Cal squabbled and dunked each other and begged me to come swimming with them.

I was so good. Before the kids went to sleep, I sent Amy with the ice bucket and she didn't want to go, but finally I screamed enough and she went, and as the kids slept, I sat at the funny little motel desk and watched the ice melt to water in the plastic bucket. And the next two nights were just like that first one, and then we were in Detroit and I was calling long-distance to let Jimmy know we'd arrived safely. When he wanted to know how I was, I said, "Fine, good," and then he said, "Let me talk to Amy," only he asked for her too soon, too suddenly, so I knew exactly the questions he wanted to ask her. "She's asleep," I said, and what could he say then? Wake her up? and the conversation crumbled to pieces that didn't connect, and when I hung up the phone, Amy came out the kitchen door and said, "I wanted to say hi to Dad," and I just said, "Sorry." She opened her mouth like there was more, but I guess there wasn't, because she closed it and went back into the kitchen.

The next day was Sunday, and in Detroit, Sunday meant 10:15 Mass. My first-ever Sunday in Phoenix I woke at noon and wore pajamas all day just because I wanted to, and that's how I knew I'd left home. In Phoenix, when I heard church bells, I didn't also hear "hurry-hurry, Sophie, you're so slow, are your feet stuck to the floor?" All I heard was ringing, and it wasn't long before I didn't even hear that.

So I woke the kids by apologizing that we had to go to church. "We have to do this for Grandma," I said. "Church is something she thinks is important," and I kept talking so the kids wouldn't grab up silence to fill with their fussing. Amy tried to butt in; I cut her off. "I don't want to hear any more; we're going to church and that's that," and I headed for the bathroom to put in my hot rollers.

"I *like* church," Amy called after me.

"You don't have to lie," I said, hair pin clenched between my teeth. "I thought church was a waste of time when I was your age."

"I like when we're early and the boys are lighting candles with that long, skinny torch," Amy said. "And when they jingle those little bells that sound like wind."

"I like those chairs they sit in," Cal added.

"And pouring water over the priest's hand."

I came out of the bathroom, my hair half-rolled. "Did you ever wonder why there aren't any girls up there?" I asked Amy. "Why it's only boys?"

"Mo-om," she said, turning so I could button the back of her dress. "It just is."

"Don't you think you could ring those bells as easily as any boy?"

She looked at Cal who bent to tie his shoe. "I guess," she said.

"Well, doesn't that make you mad?" I asked.

She shrugged.

"It made me really mad when I was living here," I said.

"Don't you like the pictures of the people in the colored windows?" she asked. "Or the songs? Or anything?"

All my aunts and my mother said the two of us looked alike, but it wasn't something I could see. She twisted a strand of hair between two fingers, put it in her mouth, let it slip back out.

"I'm hungry," Cal said.

"I bet Grandma has pancakes for breakfast," and they went downstairs, Cal because pancakes were his favorite food and Amy because, even though she was only eleven, all our conversations now were like those of two people who'd just met on a train and were trying to be nice because they saw a long trip ahead of them.

What else did I hate about AA? That I never knew what to wear to the meetings. Was I supposed to put on a skirt and heels—and look like some moron housewife hooked on cooking wine? Or patched jeans and a t-shirt with holes under the arms—like a bum stumbling in off the street? No one thought about those kinds of questions.

My mother glanced at her watch as I walked into the kitchen, but she kept drying the breakfast dishes. I was right about the pancakes; she'd set aside a plate for me, but there was no time to eat—not that I wanted such a heavy breakfast—so I held the plate over the garbage and let the pancakes slide in. My mother still didn't say anything. I dabbed maple syrup off Cal's cheek with my finger, pushed Amy's hair out of her eyes. Then I poured some coffee.

My mother hung her dish towel over a cupboard door and looked at my feet, at the chipped polish of my toenails. "Sandals to church?"

I had been planning to get my shoe bag out of the car, but instead I said, "Sandals were good enough for Jesus." When she didn't say anything, I added, "Don't you think God has better things to worry about than what I'm wearing to church?"

"Same old Sophie," she said, shaking her head. How many million times had I heard that?

"Do you want me to change shoes?" I asked.

"You do what you want," she said. "You always do. Go on outside, kids, we'll be there in a minute." She took the plate out of my hand, washed and dried it quickly, then pushed through the side screen door, letting it slap behind her. Just a pair of stupid shoes. I blew on my coffee to cool it.

"Did Jesus really wear sandals?" I heard Cal ask.

"Flip-flops?" Amy asked.

My mother laughed. "Jesus lived in the desert, and I suppose desert people wore sandals."

"We're desert people so maybe Mom's sandals are OK," Amy said.

The church bell started clanging, startling me. "Hurry, Sophie, we'll be late!" my mother called.

"Just a sec," but they started walking without me.

So I dumped my coffee down the sink and filled the cup with water, leaving it on the counter. I hurried to catch up to them, and when I got there, Cal was saying, "Once Mom threw her shoes into a hotel fountain at a wedding. Then she danced in her underwear."

"Shut up," Amy said. "That was one time. And you weren't even there, so how do you know so much about what happened?"

"I saw the picture before Dad ripped it up," Cal said. "The police came."

"Everyone thought it was fun," I said. "All my friends thought it was hilarious."

"Weren't your shoes ruined?" my mother asked.

"It was one pair of shoes," I said. "We were having fun."

"Shoes cost money," my mother said.

"We were having fun!" and I couldn't raise my voice, so I kept it low and tight: "That's the point of the story; that's why I threw the shoes in the fountain!"

"I couldn't be so wasteful like that," my mother said, and I wanted to stand and scream until she understood, that of course *she* wouldn't but *I* would, and that I had, and I'd do it again, because the way I remember, it was fun; everyone laughed when the police came and I was standing in the fountain with the water bubbling like champagne, and we were all laughing, and I was somewhere all my own I'd never been before, a place I'd discovered.

Maybe my mother didn't want to hear what I was going to say, because she started telling me about the wonderful new priest, and how the women in his former parish in Ohio used to make him kielbasa and sauerkraut for Sunday dinner, but now he said Detroit women fixed the best kielbasa. Every last detail about the kielbasa and the new priest filled up the rest of the walk to church.

I had to talk at AA, so I told them about what happened at the fountain, going to the police station with some cop's too-big sweater wrapped around my body and how my husband didn't remember it all funny the way I did, and how copies of those pictures kept coming in the mail with no return address, and how our friends started calling me Bubbles because they said champagne went to my head (guess they didn't know about the gin and tonics). I talked about the hangover the morning after and how I demanded that everyone leave the house because they were breathing too loud; as soon as they were gone, I cried for hours, missing them, sorry I'd been so mean. I decided to bake a cake and I tore through every kitchen cupboard looking for a mix, but there weren't any, so I thought I'd make one from scratch, but we didn't have any eggs, and all there was to make was oatmeal, and when they got back that night, Jimmy said, "Why's this cold oatmeal on the counter?" and I screamed at him because he should've known why.

I'd been to enough AA meetings to know I was supposed to be sorry about the whole thing, the fountain and the oatmeal and the shoes, but after I finished, I felt a smile where one wasn't supposed to be, because, damn it, the fountain had been fun—my friends applauding and the cop car's red light spinning round, me spinning with it; as soon as I smiled, there were murmurs, frowns, glances exchanged, and the leader sighed. So I added, "I never found out which of my friends was sending those nasty pictures."

Then it was someone else's turn. "Hi, my name is Joleen, and I'm an alcoholic," she whispered. "I'm here because last Saturday night I set my baby on fire by accident, and he died yesterday."

That's something I hate about AA: all those pathetic, sad people, and how now all they've got going is trying to out-pathetic, out-sad each other, and me sitting there, afraid it might rub off on me, knowing that if it did, that's when they'd really listen to what I have to say.

The priest was younger than how I think of priests, and he even told a funny story in his sermon; he had a nice, embarrassed kind of laugh, like maybe he knew a dirty joke or two. He was just chubby enough that I could imagine him caring about good kielbasa. But it was still church, still one man who thought he was God trying to tell me what to do, and when afterward my mother lingered to light candles for my grandmother and my father, I headed to the back of the church to wait.

The bulletin board was an inch-thick jumble of scraps of paper pinned on top of each other, and smack in the center was "AA Meeting Every-Day in You're Church Comunity Center 8 pm." I read the words over and over, correcting the spelling and punctuation in my mind, rewording it to make it more discreet, less abrupt, and when I finally looked away, Amy was standing beside me, her arms folded loosely against her chest, head cocked to one side.

Finally she said, "Grandma's ready," but she kept looking at me.

I pointed at the bulletin board. "Parish picnic sounds fun."

"You hate picnics," she said.

For a moment I couldn't remember if I did or didn't.

"Grandma's waiting outside," and she sounded like someone who wasn't a daughter.

Outside, my mother waved us over to meet Father Lipinski. "Sophie lives in Arizona," my mother said. "Where it's a hundred degrees in the summer."

"I'd like to visit the Grand Canyon someday," Father Lipinski said.

"It's absolutely beautiful," I said. He watched me as if he knew things about me that he wasn't supposed to know. I imagined my mother talking about me to him, my mother whispering secrets in the confessional booth. "I enjoyed your sermon."

"Thank you, Sophie," he said. "Often people mention they enjoyed the homily and then through our conversation, I realize they weren't listening to it. Very humbling."

All I remembered was the funny story. My smile tightened.

"I never want to reach that point where because I'm standing in front of a group of people I assume I have something to say that's worth listening to," he said.

"Very wise," my mother said, nodding that way she had, slowly and deeply.

"Is it really true that God is always watching us, like how you said?" Amy asked suddenly. "Is that like a spy?"

"Like a friend," he said. "Like someone who cares about you."

"Can I ask you something else?" Amy said.

"Of course, dear." He smiled at my grandmother as if he knew that these children didn't go to church and were living like sandal-wearing heathens in the desert.

"Could you pray for me to get a horse?" she asked, her voice dwindling into a whisper.

My grandmother and the priest laughed and looked at each other again, same story: This is what happens when you raise children who don't go to church every week.

I said, "Amy, we talked about the horse, and you understood why we can't get one for you."

"I know you and Dad can't," she said. "But maybe God can."

My mother laughed again, and winked at the priest, and I could just see this being the funny story in next week's sermon. He said to Amy, "God has His own reason for everything, Amy, and if you don't get a horse, I think maybe there's something He's trying to tell you. It's hard for you to understand now because you're so young, but someday you will. I'll pray for you, Amy, I'll pray that if you don't get your horse, you'll come to understand why not. And I imagine one day you'll see that sometimes it's better that God doesn't let us have everything we want."

"You listen to him, Amy," my mother said. "Father Lipinski is such a smart man."

Silence stretched so thin it had to snap. This is what I didn't like about church, Detroit, my mother. This is why I brought my children here only once a year. It wasn't so awful simply to want a stupid horse.

But Amy thanked him, her forehead wrinkled like she was actually thinking about what he'd said instead of dismissing it as crap. Someone else was tugging at the priest's sleeve, so we said good-bye, my mother promising to bring by some pierogi on Wednesday.

As we walked home, my mother said to Amy, "There's a new petting zoo at the park; we'll go see the ponies after dinner."

Amy nodded, keeping just a little bit ahead of us, her head bent low, and she walked the way I used to, stepping on the cracks, scuff-step, scuff-step. Back when I walked like that, what I was thinking was how one day I'd be somewhere so far away no one could ever find me and bring me back.

The next evening, Jimmy called from his office. I sat in the chair by the phone table and listened to him talk through static that sounded like wind blowing a long way away. "What have you been doing?" he asked. I told him about going to church and going to the pathetic petting zoo in the park down the street and how the animals were crammed inside too-small cement cages and a kid near us got bitten by a goat, about all the cousins and aunts and cousin's children who kept asking how hot was it *really* in Arizona. "What else?" he said, and before I could answer, he said,

205

"You promised this time would be different," and his voice cracked apart like the shells off hard-boiled eggs, and maybe he started crying because he didn't say anything else, and all I could do was whisper that the church had a meeting tonight at eight and that I would go, and I kept whispering on and on—same words, same promises—and it was easier to talk to him without seeing his face, without seeing how he didn't believe me; it was the way confession should've been, over the phone, not you pressed deep in a dark booth, tight enough so you could hear each wheezy breath the priest pulled in or pushed out. My sentences spun like cobwebs in the corner, and finally Jimmy interrupted: "Don't you understand that it has to change, Sophie, it has to be different now," and didn't he know I wanted things to be different, too? Back then it was the two of us dancing cheek-to-cheek in fountains while everyone laughed; it was me and Jimmy driving out to the desert to howl like coyotes at New Year's Eve midnight; it was us at a party that went from Friday night to Saturday night to Sunday morning. Was having fun so bad?

But I told him I'd go to the meeting, and then he wanted to talk to Amy, and there was a staticky pause where I felt him wondering if I'd have the nerve to say no. "Hang on a sec," and just before I set the receiver on the table, he exhaled a long, heavy breath, like someone had been holding him underwater. "So far she's fine," was the first thing I heard Amy say, and whatever the rest was, she turned away so I couldn't hear.

All the women at AA brought those little packs of Kleenex. Before the meeting started, they rustled through their purses, arranging the tissue pack on top. When someone started to cry, it was a race to see who could get out their tissue pack first.

I thought about not going. But that's what he'd think I'd be thinking.

Getting out of the house felt the way it used to, when I lived here and too many people had to know where I was each minute of every day. When I mentioned taking a walk, Amy wanted us all to go. When I said I had to buy gas for the car, Amy remembered the station that gave out the free glasses was closed for vacation until Wednesday, and my mother nodded. The three of us watched the clock on the mantel chime for 7:45; of course the longer it took me to get out, the more it wasn't the stupid meeting. Finally I told them my cousin June had asked me to stop by some night to help her sort through old pictures and clippings to put together a scrapbook for the high school reunion committee.

"Want me to come with you?" Amy asked. "I like old pictures."

"I'll be out too late," I said, shaking my purse, listening for the rattle of car keys. "You can look at Grandma's pictures."

"What time will you be home?" Amy asked.

"Late," I said.

"How late?"

"I don't know, Amy, ten or eleven. Maybe later," and I shook my purse again and again. "Where are my car keys? Where the—where are they?"

Amy pointed to the end table by the couch. "Where you left them," she said, and I grabbed the keys, poked one finger through the key ring and held hard.

"See you guys later," and it felt like I was running out the door, though I forced myself to walk slow, to think slow, to breathe in only slow, deep breaths, but once I was outside, once I was down the front steps, I ran to the car, forgetting that they'd hear my sandals slapping the pavement through the open windows, and all I did was run fast, faster, I didn't even bother with the car, I ran down the street until the blood pumped hard and wicked through my body, pounded into my brain and I heard it in my ears. Escape was how I remembered, letting go of everything at once.

When we craved alcohol we were supposed to pick up the phone. The idea was we'd talk apart our desire, hold it back, force it into conversation. The reality was they'd talk while I'd think about the last drink I'd had, how I didn't know then that it was going to be the last, and how if I could have it again, I'd sip it slow, I'd stretch it out a week, two, longer; maybe I wouldn't take the final sip so I'd have it always waiting for me.

It could've been the church basement I usually went to; the cigarette smoke was like columns in the room, and a woman with crooked teeth was brewing the second pot of coffee as I arrived. "We're just about to start," she said as she poured coffee into a styrofoam cup for me. "You said black?"

I took the cup, used a plastic spoon to scrape crusted sugar out of the bowl; the creamer was solid so I gave up on that.

"How long have you—?" the woman started.

I cut off her question because they always sounded like an inspirational poster when they asked. "Twenty-seven days," I said.

"You'll want to sit over there, dear," she said, pointing to the far table. "Herb will be guiding the discussion. He's a wonderful man; in fact, back when I started coming, he was—"

"Thanks," and I flashed one of those smiles that feels fake but you hope doesn't look it and headed to the table; I sat in a chair between two empty seats so no one could talk to me, stared into my cup of coffee, watched the steam twist and rise until the coffee cooled.

Herb started the meeting, and it took about two seconds to figure out he was the blah-blah-blah type who thought he was more interesting than he was. He had a bad laugh, sort of a donkey-monkey combo, like the kind of high school teacher everyone in the class imitates as soon as he goes out in the hall. By the time we started introductions, I'd stopped paying attention, started thinking about Jimmy and what he was doing, whether he was home tonight or invited to someone's house for dinner because he'd been using that "poor old bachelor" routine, and how the wives we knew liked to show off their gourmet cooking when someone was over and there were always things that flamed or were jelled in aspic or were prepared in special cookware that was used only for that particular dish like a fondue pot, and how our friends had grown up in places where people knew how to pick really good bottles of wine to serve with these kinds of meals, and how now I was supposed to say, "Just water please," and the way their faces looked the first time they heard that, the looks that flashed from one to another across the table, across the room, me and Jimmy pretending not to see, and how the water tasted dull and empty, like what there is when you take away the scotch; and how at my mother's house when I said, "Just water please," she said, "No milk? Your teeth will drop out. Your bones will break," and she wouldn't stop talking until she'd poured out a glass of milk for me and I'd gagged it down, imagining it was an endless, icy martini with two olives, like the kind Jimmy made that our friends raved over. He soaked the olives in gin in the refrigerator—that was the secret. If I brought olives home from the grocery store now, Jimmy ground them down the garbage disposal.

"My name is Andrew, and I'm an alcoholic." Smile, clap, put that listening look on my face, think about standing at the refrigerator and eating those olives at three in the morning when everyone was asleep. But this voice wasn't like the others; it wouldn't let go, so I looked at the man speaking. It was Father Lipinski, sitting one chair over from me. His fingers fiddled with a crumpled napkin as he spoke, and he watched them as if he had no idea they were moving, no idea how to hold them still. "I'm continuing to learn," he said. "It's great comfort to know that you're watching out for me, that you understand where I've been." He had been watching his fingers so intently that when he looked up, I was too surprised to glance away. I wasn't sure he'd recognize me, but then he gave a tiny nod, like someone who doesn't want your secret but suddenly has it forever. He looked away, continued: "This last week has been more difficult than some. But isn't it the struggle that makes us stronger, better people? God gives us only as much as we can bear."

Someone murmured "Amen, Father," and he flushed red, lifted one hand in protest.

"In this room I'm not a priest," he said. "I'm just a man learning how to live one day at a time, like the rest of you."

"Well put," Herb said, and I was next.

I cleared my throat. "My name is Beth, and I'm an alcoholic." It's what I always said—first name, no last name—and it sounded fine, except that I was still looking at Father Lipinski, and as I spoke, I remembered that he knew exactly who I was.

"Hi, Beth," everyone chorused.

Father Lipinski wasn't any older than I was, but he was a priest, so he felt older; or maybe I felt younger, I felt fourteen, as if I were back in Detroit when Sunday meant 10:15 Mass and Saturday meant 4:00 confession, and, despite the screen between us, our priest always knew who I was, even when I disguised my voice. He was old and wheezy, every breath scraped out seemed a struggle for him, and I thought about what would happen if he died while absolving someone; would that count? I'd make up sins to confess—giving him something interesting to listen to instead of the endless round of women like my mother and grandmother and aunts who maybe at worst let "sweet Jesus" slip when they lifted a roasting pan without a hot pad. I made up sins that were exotic and extraordinary, sins filled with biblical words like "coveting" and "adultery." I claimed I'd kissed my math teacher more than once in an adulterous way; or I said I incestuously coveted my cousin who wanted to be a priest. Other times my imaginary sins encompassed moral dilemmas: I'd stolen fifty dollars from a cash register but I gave it to a bum on the street; or I'd taken a convertible for a joyride but while I was driving around, I rescued a child from a burning building. The priest sighed and said, "Fifty 'Hail Marys' for your disrespect. Fifty, five hundred—you don't say them anyway, do you, Sophie? If your mother knew . . . ," but he couldn't tell her—confessions were bound to secrecy. It was something that made me laugh, a way to get through one more Saturday—how many hundred more before I was out of Detroit forever?

I got big laughs with my friends in Arizona over that story.

But I didn't tell them about walking out of the confessional booth and the light coming through the stained glass windows like soft breath and the organist in for practice holding the notes too long and too slow; there was nowhere to look, no one to look at, only down at my feet, only the scuffed floor. "Hail Mary" was in my head, but I'd be damned before I'd whisper the words, not even "Hail Mary, full of grace," not even "the Lord is with thee," because I could give a shit; it was what I did to survive Detroit. I was on my way out as soon as there was somewhere to go. I wasn't these people, my mother kneeling, hands clasped together, her lips moving, eyes closed; I wasn't someone trapped into one way of being, one way of thinking.

I looked at the strangers sitting around the table, at Father Lipinski watching me, concern spread across his face. "You don't know me," and there was nothing more to say, so I repeated myself.

"Honey, we're here to help," a woman my mother's age said. She unzipped her purse. I didn't need her stupid tissues.

I stood up, pushed the chair back, pushing, pushing; it was something to hold onto, and it made a long, loud scrape against the floor. "I don't belong here," and I hurried toward the door.

"Beth!" Father Lipinski called after me. "Beth! Come back. Sophie! Please!"

It was like hearing another language from somewhere you'd been once. I wasn't going back; I knew exactly where I would go—and what I'd do once I got there and how I'd feel while I was doing it, and the sound of my feet tromping the stairs was the rhythm of a whispered prayer, so I started to run.

There was a bar on about every corner in Detroit, so it took me about two seconds to get to one. I'd been to this bar before, in fact, maybe on the last trip, or the trip before, or who the hell cared. Five or six men lined the stools inside, the kind of men whose fathers had spent out their lives sitting at this same bar. I took a stool along the far end, facing the mirror behind the bar, and the gin finally going down was like ice melting into a cold, hard stream, something that carves gullies down the face of mountains, and it was just that feeling, no more.

It was the kind of bar where they wouldn't talk to you until at least your third drink. Even then, no one had much to say; and what they said was spoken straight ahead into the mirror. Or staring at the television that played some cop show with the volume all the way down, so all there was was silent shooting and long quiet car chases; it all seemed so peaceful, so faraway. It was what I loved about bars, that silence—the only sound the whir of the revolving fan, the whoosh as the stirred-up air hit your face then moved away—it was being in the one place where all anyone expected you to do was order yourself a drink.

When I was partway through my fourth drink, a boy came through the open door. He was about Amy's age, but he didn't have that shy, looking-all-around look that most kids have when they're in bars; he nodded at the bartender, lifted his hand in a general greeting. A couple men nodded at him in the mirror. "Hey T," the boy said to a fat man with each hand around a Stroh's. "You seen my dad?"

The man tilted his head. "In the can," and the boy hopped up on a stool. The bartender pushed over three chunks of lime on a napkin, and the boy sucked on them one after the other, scraping off the pulp with his front teeth. Someone should've told him that would eat away the enamel. Finally the fat man said to the mirror, "How's school going, Bobby?"

The boy said, "Summer vacation."

We all turned at the creak of the bathroom door. The father was fastening the last button on his jeans, shoving his hand down deep to tuck in the front of his t-shirt. When he saw the boy, he scowled and rolled his eyes, slapped the back of one hand into his palm. "You following me?"

The boy took the last lime out of his mouth, dropped the rind on the bar, spoke into the mirror. "Mom's waiting at home."

"She can French-kiss my mother-loving ass," and he laughed, got the rest of them laughing, too, slow at first, then louder and harder.

The boy's face reddened. "Come on, Dad," and he slid off his stool, his feet thumping heavily on the floor, heavier than you'd think a kid would be.

"'Come on, Dad,'" the man mimicked in a prissy voice. "'Come on, Dad.' Don't you know nothing else to say?"

"Time to get home." The boy reached for the man's arm.

"Who the hell are you, telling *me* what to do!" he screamed. "I'm your goddamn father!" He shoved at the boy who stumbled backward, knocking into a stool. "Why're you always spying after me, you little piss-ant?"

The boy rubbed his elbow, looked toward the bar. "Hey T, how's about giving me a hand?" A moment later, he added, "Please?" I looked down into my glass; the ice was about melted, and I lifted one finger for a refill. Someone had scratched the initials A. R. into the varnish on the bar.

The father said, "Get on home to your Mommy."

"Please don't miss Mom's birthday," the boy said. "I got a cake."

"'I gotta cake.'"

"It's OK that you missed my birthday and Katie's, but not Mom's. Please?"

"I said get!" and he raised his arm and stepped toward the boy, who spun away sideways and ducked. "Go on! Mommy's calling!"

The boy's shoulders hunched as he walked along the bar, head down. I hadn't noticed the bruise under one eye, and how he kept his elbow tucked close to his body. No one looked at him or his father or even at the mirror, and there were just his footsteps, then his voice, "See you later, Dad," then more footsteps, then nothing.

"What?" the father said, stepping over the chair he'd knocked down. "Fill me up."

Someone shifted their weight and a stool squeaked; maybe it was me. The bartender turned up the volume on the television, flipped through a couple channels; "Tigers won," he announced to no one in particular.

I hated the way people talked at AA, as if they were never-fail, 100 percent, all-the-way right. As if we were too stupid to remember the flip side to our stories. Jimmy turned that way, not remembering how we used to stay up all night with our friends and cram into someone's car and tear the three hours down to Mexico to eat *chilaquiles* and drink tequila while the sun rose. We'd pick up a bottle cheap for the ride back, everyone screaming when I bit the worm in half between my front teeth, Jimmy— my boyfriend before he was my husband—kissing me hard and wet and tight as he whispered something I never remembered the next day.

Every time I glanced down the bar at that man, I saw the boy instead. He wasn't any older than Amy, but already he had that kind of face, the got-to-get-out look I knew. It was more than the awful father; it was Detroit, it was gray skies pressing you in, it was being worn down into someone you weren't. Just looking at that boy you knew he woke up nights sweating, terrified he'd lose the race of getting away before turning into his father.

Two more swallows of gin—by this time I'd stopped bothering with tonic—and I remembered somewhere else I'd seen that face. It wasn't like I was forgetting my kids' birthdays or anything like that, but maybe I should do something nice and extra-special. Something fun to get Amy's face looking more like a kid's and to give her something to talk to her father about besides the spy report on what I was doing.

I finished the last bit, jiggled my ice, thought about having another. The boy's father slumped low on his stool, one hand loose around a shot glass, a couple lime rinds scattered by his elbow. When he saw me watching him in the mirror, he toasted me, beckoned for a refill. The bartender set the bottle up on the bar, not taking his eyes off the television. "Those bastards," someone said, too tired-sounding to mean it.

"Lady, what're you staring at?" the boy's father asked.

"Sorry," I mumbled.

I put down some money for the bartender then headed for the door. Even when I knocked into a table, no one turned. "I know my kids' birthdays," but I didn't say it loud enough that anyone could hear.

Outside, moths circled the street lights, and the air was heavy and drippy, something you want to wring out and throw away. I walked faster, passing the church, its narrow windows looking like eyes that weren't all the way open but weren't all the way closed—like when you're fifteen and coming home after curfew, and you're not sure if your mother sitting on the couch is awake or asleep so you tiptoe and she doesn't move, but the next morning she glares at you over oatmeal and whispers, "Don't think I don't know about you; you're coming to confession with me this afternoon," and nothing you could tell her or a priest would explain where you were or why you were there—because you were downtown, sitting on the hood of a boy's car, counting the headlights crossing the bridge to Canada. Even the boy you were with was only along because he wanted to kiss you.

I stood under a circle of light, swatted at a couple moths. I wasn't that father at the bar, but I wasn't my mother either. How could I make my kids understand what that meant? That your life could be more than praying to God and waiting and learning lessons. That maybe you just wanted a horse—or to watch the bridge—or to dance in a fountain—just because you did.

I decided Amy should get a horse.

I decided she should get one now.

I picked up my pace and headed toward the park and the new petting zoo and where the horses were; there were so many there, and they were crammed too many to a pen—what'd they think they were, sardines?, and I thought that was pretty funny, so I laughed and walked faster. In fact there was a sign on the wall—Amy had noticed it: adopt a horse, or something like that. The zoo had too many, obviously. The whole getting-a-horse thing would be easy: all I needed was a rope to tie around its neck, and I was clever enough to realize that the detachable strap from my shoulder bag would do fine.

There weren't many lights at the park, but the moon was big. Besides,

I'd been coming to this park since it had opened—I knew it well, especially since things never changed here: where the hoods hung out to smoke, where the easy girls went with their boyfriends. The petting zoo was in the far corner, and though it was new, it was already as tired-looking as the whole park—as if it had been designed that way.

The front gate was open, but of course it was more fun to climb the wire fence (certainly my mother had never climbed a fence); partway up, I pulled off my skirt and let it flutter to the ground. How much more comfortable—and cooler—and even more unlike my mother—to be wearing just a slip. Swinging my legs over the top, I jumped to the ground and landed soft like a cat.

I was right near the goats, and a couple came bleating over to the fence, following me as I walked, but my daughter didn't want a dumb old goat. She wanted a horse named Blaze; it was all she talked about since she was seven; she'd be surprised to wake up tomorrow and see a horse in the yard. I couldn't decide whether I should tell her to share Blaze with her brother or not.

After the goats was the duck pond, with the chicken house over on the side. Then rabbits, then the deer pen, and finally the yard where they kept the horses, next to the horse ride set-up that Amy went on six times in a row, thanks to my mother buying a whole booklet of tickets for her. No more corny twice-around-the-ring horse rides for my daughter, a soon-to-be horse owner.

I climbed over the wire fence and started calling, "Here horsey, here horsey," whistling, "here Blaze," and one horse actually turned its head. I closed my eyes and held out my hand; its lips pressed rubbery against my palm. "OK, Blaze," I said, "come on with me," trying out that soft, soothing I-know-what-to-do-around-animals voice that worked on "Wild Kingdom," and Blaze made a chirpy noise and seemed happy enough to let me loop my purse strap around his neck.

The gate was hard to figure out in the dark, and I whispered as I fumbled with the latch. "You'll like Amy," I said. "She's been wanting a horse for I don't know how many years, and she's going to love you to pieces. We'll feed you apples and grass and what else do you guys eat? Sugar cubes? Carrots? Whatever you need. Tamales, if you want them! We've got a nice little yard for you down in Arizona—" I paused, thinking how was I going to get a horse to Arizona, but didn't U-Haul rent trailers? "Maybe when it's nice Amy can sleep outside with you in a sleeping bag and when it rains, you can go under the carport, or whatever. Anyway, I know you're going to like living with us," and it all sounded so nice and so wonderful—

exactly what Amy wanted—and the gate swung open, and I led Blaze outside, past the deer, past the rabbits, the chickens, the duck pond—where the horse took a little drink and I almost fell in—and finally past the goats and to the front gate, and we were on our way, clomping along the cement path to the main sidewalk, and I'd forgotten my skirt, but I just couldn't wait to show the horse to Amy—I'd wake her up if she were asleep, because this was just too good, too exciting. Your own horse! That's what I'd say, as I'd lead her down the stairs to the front door where she'd stand on the porch and see the horse nibbling grass in the moonlight, and I'd be so good that I wouldn't even look at my mother, wouldn't say or even think, How's that for answered prayers?

Most houses were dark as Blaze and I walked through the neighborhood. I tried to keep him on the grass so the clatter of his hooves on the sidewalk wouldn't wake people through their open windows. I felt like Santa Claus, except that Santa Claus never actually brought horses to little girls; how many times had I told Amy stories like Santa couldn't fit a horse in his sleigh or Santa thought a bike would be more practical? After she found out about Santa, I just said no.

The porch light was on at my mother's house, and so was the front room light, which was unusual this late, but maybe she'd left them on for me.

I led Blaze to the tiny front yard. "Look at this great grass," I said. "She waters it every Wednesday," and sure enough the horse leaned over and started nibbling, and I couldn't wait: "Amy!" I screamed. "Amy!" Let the neighbors see what a wonderful mother I was! "Look!" and Amy was at the screen door in front, and as soon as she saw me, she came onto the porch, pulling shut the heavy wooden door. When she saw Blaze in the yard her mouth dropped open, and then she quick slapped it covered with one hand, then let her hand fall away.

"What happened to your skirt?"

"Look!" I said. "Your very own horse!"

"Where have you been all this time?" She was about one notch away from yelling.

I pointed to Blaze. "Your horse."

My mother yanked open the door. "Do you want the neighbors to hear?" she hissed.

"Do you like the horse?" I asked.

"It's a pony, not a horse," Amy said.

She was supposed to be hugging Blaze by now, climbing up on his back, thanking me again and again, but she was still on the porch, arms crossed.

She was wearing the nightgown with the pink flowers, the one that was too small for her, and there were circles under her eyes that I hadn't noticed earlier.

"What have you done now?" my mother said through the screen door, her arms folded like Amy's, except tighter against her body.

"I got a horse for Amy," I said.

"Why is this animal chewing up my front yard?"

"It's what Amy's always wanted," I said. "A horse." My words felt slow and heavy, like they were coming from somewhere far away. It was so clear to me. "This is what mothers are supposed to do. Right?" I opened my arms to Amy, letting my purse fall to the ground, dropping the strap that was around Blaze's neck. But Amy didn't move, so I came closer, to the first step. "Right, Amy? You wanted a horse, didn't you?"

She looked straight up into the awning, blinked real quick.

"What are you going to name him?" I asked. "I think it's a him. Maybe it's a her. Blaze is a good name for a him or a her. That's the name you like, right?" She didn't answer, so I asked again. "Right?" and I walked up the steps to where she stood, barefoot, crying. "Isn't Blaze a good name for a horse?" I asked.

"Oh, Mom," she said, rubbing her eyes with the back of one hand.

"Isn't it?"

She nodded, then pushed through the door, past my mother.

"What were you thinking?" my mother said. "Where did you get that thing?"

"'That thing' has a name," I said.

"Where did it come from, Sophie?" She said each word slowly, distinctly, like she was afraid I wouldn't understand her question.

"The petting zoo," I said.

"You stole it?"

"I'm adopting it," I said. "Amy wants a horse so bad." It was all so simple.

"Come inside," she said. "Everyone will see."

"See what?" I sat on the step. "A mother who wants her daughter to be happy."

"You didn't go to June's house like you said."

It took me a moment to remember. "I did too."

She shook her head. "We called."

"We?"

"I called. June hadn't seen you all night." My mother's voice turned soft.

"In fact, she didn't know anything about a scrapbook or a high school reunion."

"Amy told you to call, didn't she?" but I didn't really have to ask the question to know the answer.

I watched Blaze eat grass, tear-chew, tear-chew. He looked happy to be out of that awful petting zoo, happy to have been adopted by people who appreciated him. Amy would ride Blaze on trails through the desert; they'd see the wildflowers bloom in spring and watch forks of lightning shatter distant mountains. She'd say to me, I can't imagine my life before you got me Blaze; she'd say, He's like part of the family now.

"That animal better not go near my rosebushes," my mother said.

I could've spoken the words for her, because I knew she'd say them. A horse had appeared in the front yard, and she was worried about rosebushes. It was my whole life in one sentence. I asked, "How long did Amy wait before she told you to call, ten minutes? Fifteen? She's worse than Jimmy."

My mother looked at the house across the street, where an upstairs light went on, then went off. "I didn't raise you to be like this, lying, sneaking around at night, stealing ponies from the park, going to bars. You should be ashamed of yourself, Sophie."

"Plenty of people have a few drinks," I said.

She shook her head. "Not people like us. Not this family."

"I got Amy her horse, didn't I?"

She shook her head again, longer, slower, like a machine just starting up, just getting its rhythm.

"Stop doing that!" I screamed. "Listen to me! I'm not one of those people; I'm not like that! I'm not what you think." I slapped my palm again and again on the pavement near where I sat until blood ribboned up through my torn skin. "I just want to be who I am." The words sounded stupid and lost.

"Who you are?" she scoffed. "Good people like us don't do that. I'll tell you who you are, Sophie, you're nothing but a—" and she paused, leaving me just enough space to say the only thing that would keep her unspoken words dangling.

"So's your precious new priest, Mother; I saw him at AA."

The horse neighed and shook his head back and forth. I watched my mother's face as she tried harder and harder not to let it move. Now, she wouldn't be able to stand near him without secretly sniffing his breath; any time he laughed too loud or too long, she'd wonder; fixing Sunday dinner in his kitchen, she'd poke one hand all the way to the back of each cupboard, feel around, pretending she was looking for baking soda. What she'd tell him in confession would be measured out differently because the man who judged the secrets wasn't perfect after all. She wouldn't want to think all this about him, but now she would.

Amy returned to stand behind the screen door. "The police are coming to get the pony."

"The police!" I said.

"I looked up the number in Grandma's phone book."

"But it's the horse you wanted!" I said. "It's Blaze!"

"Mom, that's Fred from the pony ride. He's like twenty years old."

My mother slid her arm around Amy's shoulder. "Thank you, honey." She sounded tired, like an old woman. "I'll wait for the police. You go on up to bed."

Amy opened the screen door, walked to where I sat, knelt next to me and held out her hand. "Come on, Mom," she said. "Time to go to bed." She waited one minute, two minutes, maybe three, her hand steady. I listened to her breath move in and out, faster than my own, softer.

A goddamn pony. Not even a horse. Even now, already, she was too big for a pony.

The bones in her hand felt tiny. My hand filled hers, overflowed. I didn't know how to say I was sorry and really mean it, so I didn't say anything, just let her lead me upstairs to my bed, where I belonged.

Back in Arizona, I told them my name was Sophie. "Hi, Sophie," they said, like somehow they'd known exactly who I was all along.

Among the Missing

Dan Chaon

My mother owned a lakefront cabin, not far from where the bodies were discovered. She watched from the back porch when the car was pulled out of the water. She could hear the steady clicking of the big tow chain, echoing against the still surface of the lake. Brown-gray water gushed from the windows and trunk and hood as the car rose up. The windows were partway open, and my mother's first thought was that animals were probably in the car also: suckers and carp and catfish and crawdads— scavengers. The white body of the car was streaked with trailing wisps of algae. She turned away as the policemen gathered around.

There was a family in the car: the Morrisons. A mother and father, a seven-year-old girl, a five-year-old boy, and a baby, a little boy, thirteen months old. They had been missing since late May, over six weeks, and the mystery had been in the papers for a while. People around town reported having seen them, but no one had taken much notice. They were a typical family, apparently, no different from the hundreds that passed through during the summer months. Lake McConoughy was the largest lake in Nebraska, one of the largest man-made lakes in the entire Midwest, and it drew not only locals but also vacationers from Omaha and Denver and even farther. When the police came around with the pictures, people thought they had seen them, but they couldn't be sure. The investigation was bogged down by our town's uncertain memory. It didn't occur to anyone to drag the lake, especially since reported sightings continued to come in from as far away as Oklahoma and Canada. Most people believed that they would turn up, and that there would be some rational explanation—despite the claims of the grandmother, who lived in Loveland, Colorado, and who had first reported the family missing. She felt foul play was certainly involved. Why else hadn't they contacted her? Why else had the father, her son, not returned as scheduled to the real estate office where he'd worked for ten years?

Before the bodies were discovered, my father had a theory. He said that it would eventually come out that the father had embezzled a large sum from that real estate company. Sooner or later, he said, the authorities would catch up with them, they would find them living in a big house under an assumed name in some distant, sunny state. "Or maybe," said my father, "maybe they'll never catch them." He paused, a little taken with this romantic possibility. "Maybe they'll get away with it," he said.

When he heard they'd been found, he seemed almost bitter that the idea he had repeated and embellished turned out to be so far from the truth. "It just doesn't make any sense," he said, and glared darkly down at his hands.

The two of us were out at a local bar, a place called the Fishhead that he frequented, and he was already several beers ahead of me. He was slurring a little.

"I just can't fathom what could've happened. How do you drive your car into a goddamned lake? And how do you get it out there as deep as they got it? Even if there was a drop-off?"

"It's freakish," I agreed. I sipped my beer. "A real tragedy," I said.

My father shook his head: I had failed to get his point. "Do you know," he said. "Every one of them was still buckled in. That's what Buddy Bartling told me, and he was there. The woman was driving, and she was strapped in behind the wheel. It just doesn't make sense. You know, if the water had been icy cold, it would have been just, Bam! Hypothermia. But it wasn't that cold."

"Hm," I said. It sounded like he was concocting a new theory, and I waited. The barmaid came over and asked how we were doing and my father tapped his empty glass.

"You know what gets me," my father said. He cocked his head at me, squinting one eye, and lowered his voice. "What gets me is your goddamned mother. Here this happens not five hundred yards from her cabin. But she sees nothing, she hears nothing. That's just how she is. You know it. I mean, it's nothing against her really. That's not what I'm saying. She's your mother, and she's not a bad woman."

"No," I said. He was drunk, I thought. I felt the alcohol moving thickly through my own body, and I couldn't follow where he was going. I gave him the same one-eyed squint.

"You would think," my father said, "a person would think they would've hollered. Those kids. They had to have screamed, don't you think?"

"I don't know what you're saying," I said, and he hunched his shoulders.

"I'm not saying anything," he said, but his eyes had a strange intensity. "It's just a shame there wasn't someone else in that cabin other than your mom. That's all I'm saying. They would have found those folks a lot sooner."

My parents had been separated for almost three years by that time, though they'd never officially divorced. They had "parted ways," as my mother said, some time during my sophomore year in college, I wasn't even sure when. No one told me. My mother moved out to the cabin, and my father remained at the house in Ogallala.

I didn't quite understand the situation. My mother said that it had to do with his drinking—though, to me, he didn't seem to be an alcoholic, at least not in the way that you read about. He never did anything outrageous or abusive. He just drank beer or an occasional glass of whiskey, the same as he always had, and generally all that meant was that he was a little out of it after about nine o'clock at night.

My father felt that it had to do with the difference in their age. My mother was ten years older than my father, and once I had left home, he said, the differences had become more difficult. It was hard to get a clear answer from him. He hinted that it had something to do with menopause (what he solemnly called "the change o' life"). She'd just—changed, he said.

Nevertheless, my father was out at the cabin regularly. All their finances were still intertwined, and whenever he got a check for work (he was a carpenter) he came out and gave it to her, rather than deposit it himself. It didn't make much sense to me.

The morning after our conversation at the bar, I woke to the sound of them arguing. It was an almost comforting noise, familiar to me since childhood, and lying there in half-sleep I might have once again been thirteen years old, or ten, or seven.

"Damn it, Everett," I heard my mother say sharply, and I smiled because the phrase was so familiar, and because I knew it would make him blush and grow sullen. His real name was Everett, but everyone called him Shorty—he was five foot five, a compact, wiry little man—and some time in the distant past he'd come to see this nickname as a kind of badge of respect, and "Everett" as an insult, a sissified embarrassment. Even my mother used it only in anger.

I heard my father mumble back at her, a low stubborn sound. He was terrible at arguing, he always lost (even when he was right), and mostly he was reduced to petty, childish comebacks. He used to flip up his middle finger at her. "Sit and spin, Darlin'" he would say. For a while, this was his favorite final word.

By the time I came into the kitchen, they had lapsed into silence. He was sitting at the table, moodily sipping his coffee, and she was at the stove, frying eggs, wielding her spatula with venomous precision.

"Morning," I said, and my father raised his eyes and nodded. My mother said nothing. She flipped an egg and the grease crackled.

"I'll tell you something," she said after a moment, without turning from the frying pan. "If you're going to be drinking and carrying on until all hours of the night, you can stay with your father."

My father and I exchanged glances, and he rolled his eyes a little. The issue was sensitive, since the choice of who I stayed with meant that one of them would feel slighted. The truth was that I mostly chose my mother, for selfish reasons—she cooked, and I had easy access to the lake. I kept my face neutral.

But no one said anything more. My mother set plates and silverware in front of us with an irritated snap of her wrist, and I saw plainly that their argument had been about me. It was an extension of earlier fights they'd had, when he'd taken me to bars before I was of legal age.

"Do you want toast?" my mother said, and I nodded.

"Yes, please," I said humbly. "With butter."

"There's oleo on the table," she said, and put two slices of bread in the toaster. "There's a knife by your plate to spread it with. There's no butter in the house. I don't buy it anymore."

This was her "all-I-do-is-serve-people" tone of voice. And it was true, we sat and she waited on us—"hand and foot," as she liked to say. On the other hand, if I were to attempt to fry my own egg, she would be right behind me, watching and making critical, disapproving faces. If I tried to get my own silverware she would say, "What are you digging for?"

In retrospect, I suppose that it was that morning when I first began to get a strange feeling about her. I realized that she must have an inner life—that she was a person who thought and felt and had memories and desires like the rest of us. But I sensed that there was something changed and hardened about that inner life. We had both become mysterious to one another, and I was aware that she wasn't particularly interested in my adulthood. I was still her son, naturally; but at some level, I was also something else—an invader, a grown-up mind that was beginning to commandeer the body of the child she had loved so much.

I don't know if I was an adult, really. That spring, for a variety of reasons, I had come close to failing my final semester of college, and, at the last minute, had managed to talk my adviser into helping me get an emergency withdrawal. I took incompletes in all my classes, and, two weeks before graduation, packed up my stuff and drove home. I left on the same weekend that the Morrisons disappeared.

I took a job at a video store in a little mini-mall near the lake, some five miles down the shore from my mother's cabin. When I was a child, it was simply a gas station and convenience store which sold canned goods and bait. But over the years, it had expanded; now, in addition to the video store, there was souvenir "shoppe," a McDonald's, and a Domino's Pizza. It irritated me, a little. "They" were taking over the lake, I thought, though I wasn't sure who "they" were—new people, I guess. I spent my days feeling scornful and superior to the kinds of movies most people rented.

Everyone was talking about the family who had died. My boss told me that there had been a number of reporters around, and even a television news team from Denver. It was all a mystery. Had they simply run off the road, and perhaps been knocked unconscious before they hit the water? Had foul play been involved somehow? A pale fat man in cut-offs told me that he'd heard they'd been drugged, that it had been a mob hit—which, if true, never appeared in the papers.

What did appear that morning was an unnerving, posed studio portrait of the Morrisons, grainy and badly reproduced, on the front page of the *Star-Intelligencer*. They were all grinning for the camera, even the baby. The mother sat in front, holding the infant in her lap; the seven-year-old girl, plump and obviously proud of her waist-length hair, sat on the right; the five-year-old boy was on the left, his hair sticking up a bit, "a rooster's tail," my mother used to call it; the father was behind them, with one hand on each of the children's shoulders.

Looking at their photograph, you couldn't help but imagine them all in that car, under the water. I saw it as a scene in a Bergman film—a kind of dreamy blur around the edges, the water a certain undersea color, like a reflection through green glass. Their bodies would be lifted a bit, floating a few centimeters above the upholstery, bobbing a little with the currents but held fast by the seat belts. Silver minnows would flit past the pale hands that still gripped the steering wheel, and hide in the seaweed of the little girl's long, drifting hair; a plastic ball might be floating near the ceiling. Their eyes would be wide, and their mouths slightly open; their skin would be pale and shimmery as the inside of a clamshell; but there would be no real expression on their faces. They would just stare, perhaps with faint surprise.

I thought of all the times I'd been swimming in the past month, and I felt a vague need to scrub myself again, as if that vision of them had seeped into the water, as if the existence of those unknown bodies had left a film on my skin. My mother had gone through the freezer and thrown out all the fish she'd caught that summer, for the same reason: it seemed contaminated. I was sickened to remember the catfish—a scavenger—that she'd caught a few weeks ago, and that we'd eaten, breaded and deep-fried, one Saturday evening.

People who knew where my mother lived would ask about it. I said that she didn't hear anything. I wasn't back from school at the time, I said. I would talk about how strange it was. It didn't seem logical; maybe the police would be able to figure out what happened. I honed small speeches for reporters, or news cameras, but I was never interviewed.

The police had stopped by to talk to my mother the day they'd found the car. She said they'd asked a lot of questions but wouldn't go into specifics. All she could tell them was that she hadn't heard anything. I could picture her sitting there on our old cabin sofa, the policemen across from her. I could see the stiff, official way she held herself, her careful monotone when she spoke. She felt as if she were being judged—like she was one of those Kitty Genovese people, who sat in their apartments and ignored the cries for help while a woman was murdered in the courtyard below.

She really was that type of person. It wasn't that she didn't care; it was simply that it was hard for her to take the initiative in a situation that wasn't her business. She would have assumed that someone else had already done what needed to be done.

When I came home from work, I only briefly mentioned the things I'd learned: the photo in the paper, the television news team, the speculation I'd heard. She rested her hand against her forehead. "Oh, oh," she said softly. She shook her head, sadly, and was silent. Then she asked me if hamburgers were all right for dinner.

At the time, this weird juxtaposition, her insistence on switching to the mundane, seemed like pure irony. Sometimes I thought that she was so repressed that she was more or less blank on the inside—or, at very best, one-dimensional, her consciousness a space where simple commands were given and executed: "Eat. Sleep. Make food for offspring. Sleep again." Perhaps an occasional emotion or idea would flutter through, briefly, and then disintegrate. If anyone could fail to be curious about this horrific event, it was my mother.

This was our life together: dinner, dishes, perhaps a video I'd brought home from work, which she usually fell asleep in front of. When I asked her what kinds of movies she liked, she shrugged. "Oh, I don't care, really," she said. "They're all about the same to me. Half of them don't make any sense, anyway." When I pressed her to name a film she'd liked, she at last came up with *Wait until Dark*, about a blind lady being menaced by criminals. I brought home some thrillers after that, which she watched dispassionately, but with interest—sudden deaths, killers hidden behind doorways, screaming women pursued down endless halls. When it was over, she always claimed that she knew how it was going to end.

Looking back, I realize that this was my last chance to get to know her. I would never again live at home—apart for occasional visits at Christmas or Independence Day. Sometimes I can't help but think that if I'd only been paying more attention, I might have been prepared for what happened to her later. It might not have happened at all, had I been watching for the signs that I can now only search my memory for.

But back then, whatever puzzles my mother's inner life presented were not nearly as interesting as the mystery of the Morrison family. I called my college friends and talked to them about it, feeling a little indignant that it hadn't been picked up by the national news. "It's pretty amazing," I told my friends. "It's almost like there's no rational explanation, you know?"

I walked down to the site of the accident and examined it for myself. Here was the place where the car had inexplicably gone off the road. They must have been going fast down that curving dirt road—in the dark, one would assume, though no one knew. They had to have been going so fast that the young, man-high saplings didn't slow them down. They flew over an embankment—since surely, if the tires had hit the strip of sand between the low cliff and the water, they would have stopped, merely bogged down in an unpleasant but eventually hilarious situation. Somehow, the car sailed over the sand. It hit the water and sank. The lake was shallow for several yards before it dropped off swiftly. Somehow, the car got past that, too.

"But don't cars float for a while before they sink?" one of my friends asked. He was sure they did. And even then, there would have surely been time to roll down the windows, even while they were submerged, there would have been time for at least some of them to escape.

When I walked along the edge of the road, there were no signs of any accident—no tire marks at the edge of the ditch, not even a broken sapling. Of course, almost two months had passed; the elastic trees had straightened, summer plants had grown wild, rain had smoothed the ground.

As I came back to the cabin that day, walking along the line of shore, I saw that my father's work van was parked in the driveway. He had probably stopped in for lunch. I came up the beach-side steps—which my father had built many years before—padding barefoot, quiet though I didn't necessarily intend to be. I could hear them talking in the kitchen. The sliding glass door that led from the kitchen to the deck was open, and their voices floated out, clear and disembodied as I approached.

"Call her up," my mother was saying. "Tell her that if she doesn't pay you this week you're going to take her to court."

"I have half a mind to go out there and take down the whole damn addition, two-by-fours and all."

"You should."

My father laughed. "Can you see the look on her face?" he said, and my mother chuckled deeply.

"I'd like to be there to see it," she said.

I sat down at the top of the steps to listen. They were always at their best when they were talking business, making plans and strategies. I couldn't help but feel sad, hearing them. It could be like this, I thought foolishly, we could all be friends, sitting around, joking, talking easily. That's what it could be like.

"She probably thinks I owe her something," my father said.

"Do you?" My mother said coldly.

"No," my father said. "Not really." He cleared his throat.

"Well, then," my mother said.

After that, they were quiet. I heard a plate being set down on the table. I got up and went inside.

They both looked up, startled. "Hey, Bud," my father said. "What have you been up to?"

"Nothing," I said. I watched as their expressions tightened, as whatever they were talking about was buried away, out of sight. I was coming to realize that I didn't really know them very well. Somehow, twenty-two-year-old Shorty had fallen in love with my mother, a sharp-tongued, thirty-two-year-old telephone operator. Somehow, they'd stayed married for twenty years, and then, abruptly, somehow they'd decided to give up. It didn't quite make sense, and I looked at them, for a minute aware of the other mystery in my life.

"Do you want some soup?" my mother asked, as if I were a customer.

Looking back, I wish that I'd gone about finding answers in a more systematic way. I don't even know if "answers" were what I was looking for at the time. Mostly, I was thinking of myself—where would I be at thirty-two, forty-five, fifty-five? How did people go about falling in love, getting married, having jobs, families, living their lives? I wanted to frame my parents' lives like scripts—plot, conflict, motivation, theme—anything that could be easily analyzed, anything that might give me a clue about how to proceed, or how not to.

Perhaps this was what I thought of as my mother and I sat on the deck, as we often did on hot nights. We sat, smoking cigarettes, staring out at the dark shape of the lake—at the lights of houses on the other side, at the soft brightening and dimming of fireflies in the air, which reminded me of the way the lit end of her cigarette would glow more intensely when she breathed in, and fade when she exhaled.

I can't remember that we talked, though we must have. Perhaps we spoke of the weather, or whatever mundane daily activities we'd gone about; maybe we joked about the "news" in those supermarket tabloids she liked to read. I believe that was the year Princess Grace of Monaco died, in her own mysterious car accident. We might have discussed that.

But it was the things that we didn't talk about that seemed most present. I wanted to know what she really thought of me; what had really happened between her and my father; what she was going to do with her life now. But it was if we were deep underwater—those conversations drifted over the surface, far above us, like the rippling shadows of rafts and swimmers that fish might notice, and startle at.

I said, "So . . . what are your plans for the year?"

"Oh," she said, and sighed. "I don't have any idea. I'll probably just do the same old thing. Live here in the house, and take care of your dad's books" (she meant his finances), "and try to get by."

She was silent, as if the process of "getting by" was fraught with secret perils. A couple of kids came running along her stretch of beach, laughing and calling out, their flashlights bobbing like will-o-the-wisps. We watched as they ran off toward the spot where the bodies were discovered. The lights dipped and swayed as the kids ran past, growing smaller in the distance.

"That part of the beach is going to be haunted," I said. "Don't you think?"

"What do you mean?" she said sharply.

"Oh, you know," I said. "The way people make things up. When something like that happens."

"Hmm," she said, suspiciously. "Well, that's the way people are," she said. "Full of stupidity." She looked at me as if I might be one of them, a spy from the world of the ignorant. She tilted her head back and breathed out a long trail of smoke. "I don't think about it," she told me, firmly, and frowned. I thought, as she gazed out toward the water, she looked troubled. The tall cottonwoods alongside the house trembled a bit in the breeze. She stubbed out a cigarette and lit another one.

This was the way my mother had always been, as far as I could remember, though you don't notice it as a child—or at least, I didn't. It seemed the natural course of things. I can't really guess what her life was like, from day to day. I recall only little things, mostly. I remember how, when she took out her curlers, she would let me put my fingers through the holes in those tight, tubelike curls. I would stretch her hair out to its full length and then watch it bounce back, perfectly, into its hollow shape against her skull. Then she would brush her hair until the curls turned into a kind of bubble around her head, perfectly round, like a helmet. She would hair-spray it until it was stiff. This was her late-morning ritual. She would drink coffee and watch television, or do crossword puzzles. When I wanted a hug or kiss, she would give it to me.

I don't think she was ever vivacious. Her laughter, if it came, had a grudge underneath it. I have seen early pictures of her and my father where she appears to be laughing, yet still she seems self-conscious about it, glancing a little off to the side, uncomfortable. She is never especially pretty in these younger pictures—there is too much hardness and cautious ambivalence in the set of her features. It is my father who seems to have a glow about him. You can tell in his face, in the way he looks at her, that he is in love. He is a little in awe of her, it seems—as if she is an older sibling who will always, always outdo him, but he doesn't mind.

In the middle years of my growing up—between, say, nine and thirteen—she was depressed a lot. I knew why. I was told why. It was because of my sister, Lori, who died.

Lori wasn't actually a real sister, though that was what my parents always called her. "Your sister," they said. She was a stillborn baby whom I never saw. My parents had a grave for her, though, with a little headstone which they decorated with flowers on Memorial Day. There were, I learned later, a number of miscarriages between me and Lori, though none of them got very far along. Lori, on the other hand, was one of those flukes. She strangled on the umbilical cord, and there was nothing, apparently, the doctors could do.

I remember the time when my mother tried to kill herself. No one ever spoke of it as such, but at that age I was old enough to put it together. I recall the ambulance coming to our house, the men trying to put her on a stretcher and her just aware enough to struggle with them—flailing her arms when they lifted her, her mumbled protests through lips that seemed claylike and unnatural, moving like a badly dubbed Japanese film. "No, no, no," she said. "No, no." I think now that she must have taken an overdose of pills.

My father and I were at the Fishhead one night, talking. He wanted me to play pool, and though I'd never been any good at any sort of game, I agreed. I figured it was something I owed him, something a father and son should do together.

"That's all right," he said as the cue ball I'd hit drifted in between the colored balls it was meant to strike. "Good try," he said, as he squeaked blue chalk onto the end of his stick.

I don't know why this should have called up an image of my mother in extremis, but it did. Perhaps it was the way he glanced over his shoulder, edgily, worrying that someone might laugh at my ineptitude. Perhaps it was simply that we had been talking about her.

"You remember what she was like when you were a kid," he said. "She was something else, then, boy! You might not have known it. She was intense."

"Intense?" I said. An image sparked in my mind—her, struggling with the ambulance drivers. Where was my father at that moment? Standing aside? Watching? I couldn't remember. He leaned over the pool table and ran the stick between his fingers.

"I don't know," he said. "She keeps a lot of things bottled up inside her." He struck, sending a striped ball into a pocket. He stared as it vanished. "Ah, Markus," he said. "You know I tried to be a good husband to her. You know that I tried to be good to you both. I was a good dad to you, wasn't I?"

"Sure," I said. "Of course."

He was a little more drunk than usual, I thought. He was looking at me in that crafty, sidelong way of his, as if he had a secret and was trying to decide whether or not he could trust me with it. He'd squint one eye and fix on me with the other, sizing me up. He might say something interesting, if he had a few more.

"You feel like having a shot?" I said slyly.

He shrugged. "I wouldn't mind," he said.

I went back to the bar and brought back two glasses of bourbon, neat. He was in the process of finishing off our second game. He named the pocket for the eight ball, defeated me again, and then took his glass of whiskey, clicking the glass against mine with a muted pride in his victory.

"You need some more practice, my son," he murmured teasingly.

Little did he know that I had scored a small victory of my own—for as soon as we sat back down at the bar, he began to rub his chin ruefully, studying his own reflection in the mirror behind the rows of liquor bottles. "I've been thinking," he said. "You know what I think? I think she did it on purpose, that woman."

"What?" I said. I was still thinking of my mother.

"That woman that drove into the lake," my father said. "I think she did it on purpose. She had it planned out, you see? That's what they're not getting. She had it planned out. Maybe the husband was in on it, too, I don't know about him. But she definitely knew what she was doing."

"Dad," I said. "Why would someone do that?"

There must have been something snotty in my tone of voice, because he snorted as if I'd offended him. "Why do people do anything?" he said. He looked at me, a slow, drunken film over his eyes, a sad and scornful look. "Do you think you can say why people do what they do? They teach you that in college?" He stared at me thoughtfully, and later, when I was older, it was something I recalled, that expression. It was the stare of a man who has realized that he doesn't know his son, and his son doesn't know him. He shrugged. "Ah, well," he said.

"I just asked," I said. "I'm not doubting you."

He put his hand to his forehead, soddenly. "I'll tell you a story," he said. "You probably don't remember this, you were just a kid at the time. You remember when Lori was born?"

"Yes," I said.

"You know, your mom—she was real upset. She was having a rough time of it. Women go through a lot of bodily changes when they give birth, hormones and that. You've been to college, you probably know more about it than I do." He paused for a moment, and I shifted self-consciously.

"No, not really," I said. "I didn't take that kind of course."

"Mm," my father said. He gazed down, running his thumb over a wet circle on the bar's varnished surface. "Well, anyways," he said. "She was depressed. You know that. We struggled with it, I felt like . . . I had to watch her. You didn't know what she might do. She . . . well, she was at a point where she was a danger to herself. You remember. But it was hard. She had never been a weak person, you know, and . . . I wasn't . . . I can't say I was doing so well that I could be the person for her to lean on. I never thought I'd have to, you know, Markus? I thought she'd always be herself—like she was.

"I'll tell you," he said. "I think about this one night. She wasn't sleeping much then, you know, and I don't know what woke me up but I suppose I heard her out there in the kitchen moving around. Those days you had to sleep like you were half-awake, in case something happened. She'd tried stuff.

"So I got out of bed, you know? Maybe I was still part in a dream. . . . it must have been sometime after midnight, which was not all that unusual for her back then, she'd wander around at all hours. But I had a funny feeling. And so I got up and I sort of—called to her, but she didn't answer. So I went out to the kitchen and then I could smell the gas from the stove.

"She wasn't herself then, Markus," he said apologetically, though I was just sitting there, my face neutral and attentive. "She wasn't even there, not really. I could see that. She was just standing, looking at the burners of the stove. I guess she'd blown out the pilot light. I could smell it pretty strong. And then I saw that she had a cigarette—it wasn't lit—she had a cigarette in her mouth, and she was fingering her lighter in her hand, waiting. Thinking about it. I don't know what I said. I think I said something like, 'Honey, don't.'

"I don't know what I was thinking. I don't think I panicked at all. I guess—I don't know, when she finally looked up at me, there was part of me that wanted to let her go ahead and do it. I loved your mom a lot, and she had those eyes. Those eyes, boy—I could do a lot of things when she looked at me a certain way. I just thought—a part of me thought—well, why not? Everything has gone to shit. Do you see what I'm saying? It's just a matter of a second. Like that family. The Morrisons," he said, cynically. "The big goddamned mystery people. That's what we would have been. They would have writ it up in the papers, like 'Family of 3 Dies in Mystery Blaze,' or some crap, and they would have yammered and gossiped and wondered . . . "

"But," I said. "She didn't do it. She decided not to do it."

My father gave me a tight smile. "I reckon she didn't," he said. "We're still here, aren't we?"

I felt my skin prickle. Would I have awakened when the air caught fire? I wondered. I saw myself, myself at nine, sitting up in bed as a red-orange cloud rushed into me, the flash of a single synapse. Would it have hurt? What would it be like, to suddenly cease to exist? I felt my back tense at the image of that bright red burst, that blotting out. What about me? Weren't they thinking about me at all? But I didn't say this.

"What stopped her?" I said at last. "Why didn't she . . . ?"

My father shrugged. "That's all I'm saying. It's a second. I don't know. We might have looked at each other for a minute or five minutes—who knows? But then she just—turned off the stove. Walked over and opened a window. There wasn't any . . . big scene. I don't think we ever talked about it again."

"Why not?" I said, and my voice felt hushed and ragged. I stared at the neon letters above the bar, which spelled out BEER.

"What was there to say?" my father said. "What do you say about something like that?"

Years later, I would try to replay this conversation in my mind, thinking it might hold some clue. I can only make up his words, though they sound honest in my imagination. I can picture my drive home that night—I parted ways with my father, awkwardly, on the sidewalk outside the bar, standing near our cars, and there was a moment when we might have hugged but didn't. "Goodbye, see you tomorrow!" "Goodbye, sleep well!" I must have gotten in my car and put the key into the ignition and my hands on the wheel. The night must have been dark, maybe with a little rain, and the thick trees along the roadside were heavy with foggy moisture, and the yellow line in the middle of the slick highway kept dividing, pulling apart like blurry amoebas beneath my beery gaze.

All of this must have happened, but what I really remember is the image of my mother with her lighter and the room full of gas. I remember a particular faux-velvet red nightgown she would have been wearing. I can see her naked, bony feet against the black and white kitchen tile. I can see my room, when I was nine years old, the taped posters and drawings of robots on the walls, the microscope, the rock polisher, all of that stuff is vividly imprinted. I remember television shows I watched more clearly than I recall what was going on between my parents.

My mother was asleep when I got home and would have been angry to find me, stumbling in drunk at all hours, as I'd promised not to. But she didn't wake. I distinctly recall standing over her bed, watching her. The quilt was pulled up to her neck, and she was breathing deeply, loosely, her mouth slack and vulnerable and innocent. Her knees were pulled up near her belly. Rain made a sound like sleep outside the window. She didn't appear to be dreaming. It was quiet.

I want to tell you that something else important happened that summer, that the mystery of the Morrisons was solved, that I finally understood my parents' relationship, that my mother herself became suddenly clear to me. I want to say that I finally confronted my mother, shortly after the conversation with my father in the bar, that we had an in-depth conversation. I wanted to—I meant to talk to her.

Meanwhile, I was very busy at the video store. I was going back to college in the fall, and I had to decide what I was going to do. I had this enormous, virgin expanse of time in front of me that needed to be claimed, and colonized, and strip-mined: my future.

And there was a girl, too, someone I met. She was staying with her parents in a cabin not far from my mother's—a recent high school graduate in the midst of her summer-before-college, seventeen years old. I think her name was Michelle. We made love on the beach, on the edge of the Morrisons' watery grave. It was her first time, she said, and afterward I made a hole in the sand with my bare foot and buried my used condom—my seed, my potential sons and daughters sealed in their plastic coffin, earth tapped down gently over them with the palm of my hand. Michelle sat close by, shawled in a beach towel, silent and full of regret.

My mother, in her cabin bedroom, was asleep. She appeared in my mind, but I thrust her away. She was the one thing I didn't want to think about.

To tell the truth, that last summer I spent with my parents was soon forgotten—just as the Morrisons were, moving from the front page of the paper to the back sections, and, finally, drifting out of the range and interest of jounalists forever. I went on: I finished school, I took various jobs, I moved into different cities and apartments and shuffled through girlfriends. All through my twenties I kept thinking, "My life would make a great movie!" It wasn't until I sat down to write it that I realized that it didn't amount to much of anything. It was just a series of disconnected incidents.

Then, almost ten years after the Morrisons, my mother herself disappeared.

My mother vanished sometime in August. I had been trying to telephone her for a few weeks, and then I finally called the police— thinking, naturally, that she would be dead, rotting alone in the hallway between the kitchen and the bedroom, or sitting on the toilet like Elvis, frozen in a heart attack.

But this wasn't the case. The cabin, they said, appeared to be abandoned, and when I drove out a week later this seemed to be true. Most of the furniture was there, but the closets were nothing but bare hangers, and the refrigerator was empty and unplugged. The front door had been left wide open.

In some ways, I suppose I wasn't surprised. My father had died three years earlier, of a sudden stroke, fifty-two years old, buried beside Lori's tiny grave. Since then, I hadn't been able to get any perspective on the things my mother told me. She had been saying strange things lately—the cabin spooked her, she said, she felt like someone was watching her, and then she was sure of it, and finally she began to think that someone was trying to break in. Outside, she claimed to have found thin scrapes around the lock on the door—the new lock she'd put in—and on the windows, scuff marks on the wood, as if someone were trying to jimmy them open. "I get afraid," she said. "Sometimes, I get really scared." That was the last time I remember talking to her.

Her fears had not sounded that serious, I have to admit. They were buried in a long list of complaints and worries—from her health to the new people who had moved next door—which had become the main topic of conversation when I called. I would tell her what I was doing, but I could sense her impatience.

Yet she didn't seem crazy. That's what I told the police when they asked. "Did she seem disoriented in any way?" one officer asked me, and I had to simply shrug my shoulders. "Not really," I said. "Maybe a little." I told them that last Christmas, when I visited, she had given me a bunch of old photo albums and memorabilia. "You might as well have this junk now, as soon as later," she'd said. "Keep what you want and throw the rest away." It was mostly pictures of us when we were a family—me, my father, and her—and old relatives I didn't recognize, and gifts of jewelry and knickknacks my father had given her, and some of my old report cards and childhood drawings that she'd saved.

There was nothing of that sort left in the cabin: the closets, the drawers, the storage spaces were spotlessly empty and smelled of Lysol. I found a nickel in one of the bottom drawers of her dresser. In another, I found an ant trap. The kitchen floor had been waxed. I opened the cabinet under the sink and found that she'd put a fresh garbage bag in the trash can.

I don't know why, but it was at that moment that I was certain that she was dead. A sort of terror slid over me, like a cloud's shadow, and suddenly I was aware that it was night, and I was alone in the silent cabin. Outside the kitchen window, a certain tree looked like a human figure, standing there. The tree was at the very edge of the light from the kitchen, and for a moment it appeared to be a woman in a long robe—a nightgown, maybe. I jumped, and fled the house as quickly as I could.

There are times, lots of times, when I think that maybe she is still alive. They never found her car, or her clothes, and her bank account was nearly empty. I can picture her, driving through various landscapes, her eyes straight ahead, her driving sunglasses reflecting the road. I see her living under an assumed name, in New Orleans, in Fargo, on a beach in Florida. Sometimes, when the phone rings at an odd time, I have the quavering sense that it might be her. When there is silence at the other end of the line, I can't keep from whispering, " . . . Mom?" And yet, I don't think she would call me, even if she were alive.

There are times when I would like to tell this story to my father. What would he make of it, I wonder? Is it the story of a woman who fell out of love with her son? Is it the story of a woman who realized that love wasn't that important, after all? Or is it the story of my failure—my failure to figure things out, my failure to interpret, my failure to need her?

What can you do with a woman like that, my father would say, and I would recall her wading in the lake, one day, about a week before the Morrisons were discovered, knee-deep in the calm gray water, running the tips of her fingers across the surface of the lake, wearing that blue one-piece bathing suit she had. "Water's warm!" she called to me on the shore. And if I would have lifted my head from the book I was reading I would have seen her expression, I would have seen what she thought as she looked at her son—a grown-up man, now—I would have watched more carefully as she walked into the lake, deeper and deeper, until just her head was showing. I know the lake was glowing with the reflection of the sunset. I know she was looking back at me. I know she was thinking something.

"Why do people do anything?" my father would ask, and he would dismiss every moment I thought important. He would ask me if they'd dragged the lake for her body. And I would tell him, yes. And I would tell him that we hadn't found her there, either. Wherever she was, she wasn't there.

Avulsion

Kathleen Halme

And though I grieved, my time in hell
was sure and short. Those gaseous veins
of gorgeous mineral states told me more
than I could know on the sedgy plains of earth.

There was no voice like yours
in hell. The saxophones were verdigris
and cold. There was no voice at all,
not yours, and not my own.

I cannot say whose empty house it was
that burned throughout the wrinkled night.
I can tell you that morning brought intelligent
blue light not seen by anyone on earth.

I don't remember much—just this:
the lid was screwed on tight
and no one cared if heaven fell
to earth or gathered us in light.

Two Poems

Sharon Olds

By Fire

When I pass an abandoned half-wrecked building,
on a waste-lot, in winter, the smell of the cold
rot decides me—I am not going
to rot. I will not lie down in the ground
with the cauliflower and the eggshell mushroom,
and grow a fungus out of my stomach
like a foetus, my face sluicing off me,
my Calvinist lips blooming little
broccolis, my hair growing,
my nails growing into curls of horn, so there is
always movement in my grave. If the worm
were God, let it lope, slowly, through my flesh, if its
loping were music. But I was nearby when ferment
moved, in its curved tunnels, through my father's
body, nightly, I have had it with that,
I am going to burn, I am going to pour my
body out as fire, as fierce
pain not felt I am leaving. The hair
will fizzle around my roasting scalp, with a
head of garlic in my pocket I am going out.
And I know what happens in the fire closet,
when the elbow tendons shrink in the heat, and I
want it to happen—I want, dead, to
pull up my hands in fists, I want
to go out as a pugilist.

By Earth

Or I will lie at the front of a church, in a box,
a kind of low, dirt altar,
I will be inside it, on my back, without
breath, without brain, and my friends
will come by—they will be only the grain
of the wood away, its pouring currents,
one may lay a palm on it, as if
resting a hand on a waterfall.
They will not hate me for being mortal.
They will know I can't help it—the lips, grimace, stroke-
flung-down hands. They'll forgive the blood
congealed, the shit bacterium
passing, at last, through the walls into
the whole body. I used to want to
ask my mother to forgive me for my life,
for my body that stood in the light of her death,
and for my rogue mind—she wanted a boy
obedient to her, I came here without
a penis and judged her. I felt she could not
forgive my two dark eyes, one
the soil-black pansy, one the earth-brown
Mourning Cloak. And later, when hair
poured from my cruxes, like a corpse's in the grave,
I felt as if she did not like it,
she did not want more matter of his matter,
or even of her own. But my friends will forgive
my bark hide, my hard bones,
the gloss of my mound of Venus could be like a
hill grove in their mind while I rot, they will forgive my rot,
the microbes flooding as if between corals
on an ocean floor. Even my nipples
will die, these hard hearts I count on,
I will lie in my coffin easy as a baby
asleep at the center of a family—I love
your life-line, I love your love-line, I love them on the
rosewood roof of my heaven, the balsam cot.

Two Poems

HeidiLynn Nilsson

"We Are Easily Reduced"

—Franny Key

My groom, I fear, has grown
untidy. His litter now anticipates

my fixing—spits
of dinner chicken,

thunder in the coffee pot.
As said, my groom has grown

almost eight miles distant. Bending
toward a parade of vacated

shirt, shorts, warm
towels, I recall my mother

quick as an animal
gathering the touches

of my father—
boxers, breakfast dishes. Marriage

would fit differently
for us. Life would commence

tidily around us and between us
appetite, I thought.

Also I often
thought that to be spirit

which was heat only. Now
this affection reminds me

of Arizona—volcanic landforms,
intractable river

dammed. My mother sweeps
all day in my mind.

Canyons there
that can't be helped.

Talking Processes

Even prayer, anymore. Whatever
else we wonder, whatever else our body
creates, distributes, falls
among the useless, it seems, stars.

If I could tell you the light
infested sky—if I could tell you
I'm dancing here, remember, in the same
weeds where we sent our bodies
spinning—if I could collect
sentiments, sound now,
and tell you—

The choice, once, of what to be, was mine.
Whatever else I am grows
from the indolence. I chose,
you ought to know, to come here and to feel,
among these rows of open space, this
cold joy.

Wouldn't you give anything
to open your conscience wide as this?
Clear as this.
The weeds almost
honéy-colored in this light—
there is enough, here,
of the sky.

My mother, kindly, prays for me—she talks
easily. In school, too,
I've been spoken for. It's true
I keep myself, you would recall,
quiet. So do you and so
if I could tell you, once, our lives

rubbed and I've made
many sounds since—
I've been many women since—
if I could tell you the extent
of pelican wings, the swamp
I know to be nearby—

You have become, I mean to say,
a foreign language. I am surprised,
in this life, when you come to me—
when I can't stop, I mean, your coming
from myself.

Two Poems

Paul Hoover

Final Real Things

At age fifteen, she tasted
like desire, but in

the mouths of children
the river was incessant

as memory and rain.
Reduced to style,

she wore silk and canvas—
a shopworn child

with a smile like
powdered glass.

All beautiful women
are haunted by scars

and the hands of nuns.
But she was simply

the color of winter,
a pair of warm scissors

cutting through water.
On balcony afternoons

they often made love
until they were disfigured—

his pale face twisted
on the tall iron bed

as he placed his hands
on skin and pleasure.

They fell asleep then,
their stone hair spread.

All new pain would
soon be immortal.

Poverty in silk was
stronger than mother.

She had to learn sadness
by seeming transparent,

serene in traffic.
The old gossip spread

like rivers and deserts
as they lay in darkness

brighter than structure.
Extraordinary logic

of piercing songs
spans these decades

so she might sit
on the edge of

comfort bearing such
tongues. All that

is gone inside all
dusk. Now he calls,

several years later,
to speak of damage,

and she can only breathe
rivers and mountains.

Things That Don't Exist

Surrounded by direction and stone fathers sleeping,
things that don't exist shine in the dark,
having little shape but a vague fluorescent aura.
Nobody knows their names. We have to imagine
their thickness—surfaces as thinly painted
as a Lake George window. Eternity blinks
at what isn't. Solemn as pancakes, novel objects
occupy space which itself must be imagined—
a fork, with its three fingers, ancient in the mind.
          An image is the private life of an object.
In an endless house with no back door,
the universe is ready-made. You can have it all,
but only with your tongue in cheek, the rest in plaster.
          Original objects are all in hiding,
for which we must be grateful.
When they emerge, as real as bruised fruit,
we will have to convey their meaning—
as snow falls and moisture rises,
as the streets are wet with sunlight
beside a vivid ocean, as the window
is never transparent, as a knot of glass
within us makes the rule the rule,
as we construct our human wishes
from days of cold sun, vertigos of rice,
and a guttering star.
          Desire longs for imperfection.
It wears it in its hair. But we who turn in darkness
gaze in exaltation at what might have existed—
leafless, rootless, and branchless—
each moment sovereign beyond all habit.

Three Poems

W. S. Di Piero

Girl with Pearl Earring
by Johannes Vermeer

He put the concentrate
the light pip not only
in each eye's albumen
concentrate of starlight
but must have been taught
how to do that by first
finding it in the pearl
he posed then corrected
in dusty studio light
that pounced on the window
behind which sits the cheeky girl
pear and apple blossom cheeks
a fake description naturally
of their plain fleshiness
drably golden and her lips
from Haight Street's darlings
nose studs jacket studs
girls with that kind of eye
one by the ATM machine
casual juicy and so fair
like Vermeer's Netherlandish type
panhandling strangers
pomegranate seed ball
bearings agleam in her nose
pearls not sea-harvested

but imagined seen put there
by a certain need and fancy
because love says it's so
picture that picture this

The 1950s

Trained for it at school,
I ducked for cover, arms
over head, crouching
tight to wall or stoop
when noon sirens blared,
or under my ironhoofed desk,
holding this leaky breath
until an all clear sounded,
or until the light-storm struck
as it did at station break,
Howdie Doodie Time.
The four-piece family,
smiling over supper,
sit in the seedy air
of primitive TV
like a situation
of stars, or a promise
of new planets, routined.
Outside, a siren rings,
all four break from table,
crouching each to a corner
until the all clear sounds
or the new Cold War wind
shreds china, pitchers, drapes,
weightless forks and flowers
creaming the air, and we,
thank God unhurt, tune in
for emergency information.
The same light, that drizzled
seedy atmosphere,
came on again tonight.
Instead of supper (not
to make too much of this)
the video fisheyed down
an L-shaped counter. Shelves.

Then, in flannel shirts
and watchcaps sleeved down
like Hittite helms, "two youths,"
jabbing what seem like guns
at two counter clerks who,
now visible to us,
smear in the nuclear wind
and fall out of the frame.

The Bull-Roarers

Young men in an Australian tribe are seized
by masked men, carried far from their familiar
surroundings, laid on the ground, and covered
with branches. For the first time they face
an absolute darkness made terrifying by the
approach of divinity announced by the bull-roarers.

They come for me when it gets dark.
Large and silent, wearing mummers' masks,
badger claws chinging at their waists,
orange street cones on their heads
like party hats, tied with gut.
They lift and carry me from bed
to a field near our red movie house,
to bury me in the pit they've primed.
The stars rub their great noise on me.
I think: *I have my own things to bury*
before it's too late. Herewith, first,
I bury anger, may its sparky pus
not touch my lips again hardly ever.
Second, into that pit I send greed,
may it choke on its ashen, hairy tongue.
Get down, you too, covetousness,
and lick the earth's dungy scabs.
But for myself I keep the following:
Lust, 0 perfect panic. Charity
for my friends and a few exceptions.
Desire, because what else is there
when warm chestnuts split their skins?
Last, I keep willfulness,
to shoot my mouth off as I please,
even when the roaring buries me
and dirt crawls ear to throat to tongue.

Cat in an Empty Apartment

Wisława Szymborska

Translated from the Polish by Joanna Trzeciak

Dying—you wouldn't do that to a cat.
For what is a cat to do
in an empty apartment?
Climb up the walls?
Brush up against the furniture?
Nothing here seems changed,
and yet something has changed.
Nothing has been moved,
and yet there's more room.
And in the evenings the lamp is not on.

One hears footsteps on the stairs,
but they're not the same.
Neither is the hand
that puts a fish on the plate.

Something here isn't starting
at its usual time.
Something here isn't happening
as it should.
Somebody has been here and has been,
and then has suddenly disappeared
and now is stubbornly absent.

All the closets have been scanned
and all the shelves run through.
Slipping under the carpet and checking came to nothing.
The rule has even been broken and all the papers scattered.

What else is there to do?
Sleep and wait.

Just let him come back,
let him show up.
Then he'll find out
that you don't do that to a cat.
Going toward him
faking reluctance,
slowly,
on very offended paws.
And no jumping, purring at first.

Contributors

Brian Bouldrey is the author of *The Genius of Desire* and *Questions of Travel.* He is also the editor of *Wrestling with an Angel: Faith and Religion in the Lives of Gay Men* and the annual *Best American Gay Fiction.* ★★★ **David Breskin**'s first collection of poetry, *Fresh Kills*, was published by Cleveland State University Press, 1997. His work has also appeared in the *New Yorker, DoubleTake*, and *Denver Quarterly.* ★★★ **Kevin Casey** was born in Kells, County Meath, Ireland, and lives in Dublin with his wife (the poet Eavan Boland) and their two daughters. He is the author of three novels, a number of anthologies, and two plays, and is currently working on a collection of short stories. ★★★ **Dan Chaon** is the author of *Fitting Ends and Other Stories* (TriQuarterly Books, 1995) the title story of which appeared in *Best American Short Stories of 1996.* "Among the Missing" is the title story of a collection in progress. ★★★ **W. S. Di Piero**'s most recent book of poetry is *Shadows Burning* (TriQuarterly Books, 1995). ★★★ **Elliot Figman**'s work has appeared in *Poetry, Pequod,* and *American Voice.* He lives in New York where he serves as executive director of Poets & Writers, Inc. ★★★ **Rachel Hadas**'s book *Halfway Down the Hall: New and Selected Poems* is forthcoming from Wesleyan University Press in November 1998. ★★★ **Kathleen Halme**'s first collection of poetry was *Every Substance Clothed* (University of Georgia Press, 1995). Her new collection, *Equipoise,* is forthcoming from Sarabande Books in the fall of 1998. ★★★ **Paul Hoover** is the author of six poetry collections, including *Viridian* (University of Georgia Press, 1997). He is also editor of the anthology *Postmodern American Poetry* (W.W. Norton, 1994) and the literary magazine *New American Writing.* ★★★ **Kawita Kandpal** received an MFA in poetry from Bowling Green State University in 1997. ★★★ **Rachel Levine** received her MFA in poetry from New York University. She lives in Chicago. ★★★ **David H.**

Lynn is editor of the *Kenyon Review*. He is the author of *The Hero's Tale* (St. Martin's, 1989) and many stories and articles. ★★★ **Blake Maher's** fiction has appeared in *Alaska Quarterly*, the *Greensboro Review*, and *Carolina Quarterly* and has been broadcast on National Public Radio's *The Sound of Writing*. ★★★ **Gabriel Motola** is a frequent contributor to the *Nation*, from which his essays on the Holocaust are being collected into a book. He has published fiction and non-fiction in the *Antioch Review*, the *New York Times*, the *Sewanee Review*, and the *American Scholar*. ★★★ **HeidiLynn Nilsson** is an MFA candidate at Washington University in St. Louis. ★★★ **Joyce Carol Oates** has just published her twenty-eighth novel, *My Heart Laid Bare* (Dutton, 1998). ★★★ **Sharon Olds** has published five books of poetry including *The Wellspring* (Knopf, 1996). She teaches in the Graduate Creative Writing Program at New York University and helps lead a writing program at the Sigismund Goldwater Memorial Hospital, a public facility for the severely disabled. ★★★ **Leslie Pietrzyk's** stories have appeared in a number of journals, including the *Iowa Review*, *Shenandoah*, and the *New England Review*. "No Last Names" is a chapter in her novel *Pears on a Willow Tree*, to be published by Avon Books in the summer of 1998. ★★★ **Mark Rudman's** recent books include a long poem, *Rider*, which received the 1994 National Book Critics Circle Award in Poetry; *Realm of Unknowing: Meditations on Art, Suicide, and Other Transformations*; *The Millennium Hotel* (1996); and the final volume of the trilogy, *Provoked in Venice*, forthcoming in 1999 (all from Wesleyan). His translation of Euripides' *Daughters of Troy* has recently appeared in the University of Pennsylvania Series. He teaches at NYU. ★★★ **Catherine Seto** is a recent graduate of the MFA program at the University of Michigan. Her stories have appeared or are forthcoming in *The Asian/Pacific American Journal*, *Scribner's Best of the Fiction Workshops* (1997), *Nimrod*, and *Glimmer Train*. ★★★ **Wisława Szymborska,** winner of the Nobel Prize for Literature in 1996 and the Goethe Award in 1991, was born in 1923 in Kornik, Poland. She has produced nine volumes of poetry, including, most recently, *Koniec I Poczatek* [*The End and the Beginning*]. ★★★ **Joanna Trzeciak** has been an authorized translator of Szymborska since 1989. Her translations have appeared in the *New Yorker*, *Harper's*, *Poetry*, the *Times Literary Supplement*, and the *Atlantic Monthly*. She is currently at work on a collection of her translations of Szymborska's poetry. Her translation of Tomek Tryna's novel *Panna Nikt* [*Miss Nobody*] is scheduled to be published in 1998 by Doubleday. ★★★ **David Wagoner's** most recent book of poems is *Walt Whitman Bathing* (University of Illinois Press,

1996). He won the Lilly Prize in 1991, the Levinson Prize in 1994, and the Union League Prize in 1997. He edits *Poetry Northwest* for the University of Washington. ★★★ **Tom Wayman**'s most recent collection is *I'll Be Right Back: New and Selected Poems 1980–1996* (Ontario Review Press, 1997). He is co-head of the writing program at the Kootenay School of the Arts in Nelson, B.C. ★★★ **Kathryn Winograd** has recently published poems in the *Denver Quarterly* and the *Journal*. ★★★ **Robert Whittaker** is the co-editor of Russian editions of the American letters to Tolstoy and of the letters of the nineteenth-century poet and critic Apollon Grigoriev, the latter of which will be published in Russia in 1999. He has also completed a biography of Grigoriev entitled *Russia's Last Romantic*.

CHICAGO REVIEW
Contemporary Poetry & Poetics
A Special Issue

Contributors

Amiri Baraka

Anne Carson

Alan Golding

Mark Halliday

Michael Heller

Brenda Hillman

Paul Hoover

Susan Howe

Barbara Jordan

Derek Mahon

Jed Rasula

John Shoptaw

Keith Tuma

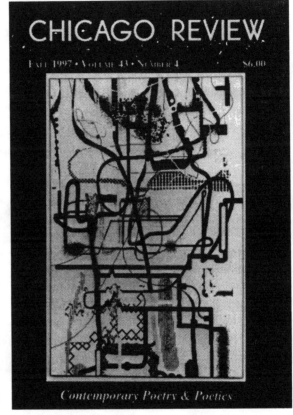

CHICAGO REVIEW

Fall 1997 • Volume 43 • Number 4 $6.00

Contemporary Poetry & Poetics

Vol. 43, no. 4 • $ 6

1998 Subscription Rates:
$18 individual, $42 institution. Overseas subscribers add $5
postage and handling. Send check drawn in U.S. funds to:
Chicago Review, 5801 S. Kenwood Ave., Chicago IL 60637

MICHIGAN QUARTERLY REVIEW

PRESENTS A SPECIAL ISSUE
SPRING 1998 / SUMMER 1998

DISABILITY, ART, AND CULTURE

EDITED BY SUSAN CRUTCHFIELD AND MARCY EPSTEIN

Essays: Ross Chambers, Bell Gale Chevigny, James Ferris, Anne Ruggles Gere, Sandra M. Gilbert, Joseph Grigely, David T. Mitchell and Sharon Snyder, Carol Poore, Robyn Sarah, Tobin Siebers

Reviews: Rachel Adams, G. Thomas Couser, Rosemarie Garland Thomson

Poetry: Karen Alkalay-Gut, Michael Blumenthal, J. Quinn Brisben, Elizabeth Clare, Mark DeFoe, Susan Fernbach, Brooke Horvath, Willa Schneberg, Joan Seliger Sidney, Floyd Skloot, Reginald Shepherd, Jean Stewart, Charles H. Webb

Fiction: Stephen Dixon, Michael Downs, Dallas Wiebe

plus a portfolio of art work with an introduction by Diane Kirkpatrick; artists include Mary Duffy, Bob Flanagan and Sheree Rose, Matuschka, Tony Mendoza, and Jo Spence

This double issue will explore the aesthetic world of disability, the language and imagery by which the condition of disability is represented or misrepresented, the situations of dependence and independence, and the contemporary social and political systems that affect disabled people.

For the two volumes of this special issue send a
check for $14 (includes postage and handling) to:
Michigan Quarterly Review, University of Michigan,
3032 Rackham Bldg., Ann Arbor, MI 48109-1070

Coming in Fall of 1998: A special issue devoted to Arthur Miller, on the occasion of the 50th anniversary of *Death of a Salesman*